RICK PARTLOW
REVELATION RUN

REVELATION RUN

©2019 RICK PARTLOW

Print and eBook formatting, and cover design by Steve Beaulieu.

Published by Aethon Books LLC. 2019

ALSO IN THE SERIES

WHOLESALE SLAUGHTER

TERMINUS CUT

REVELATION RUN

MAELSTROM STRAND

PROLOGUE

Captain Ruth Laurent had never imagined she'd meet Lord Aaron Starkad, Overseer of the Supremacy. She certainly hadn't expected him to be this big of an asshole.

"Let me make sure I understand your story, Captain," Starkad said, legs crossed, fingers clasped over his knee.

The hereditary leader of the Starkad Supremacy, the largest and most powerful of the Five Dominions, was a head taller than her, even seated, and extremely handsome, though the effect was somewhat ameliorated by the sense he knew exactly how good he looked and reveled in it. A curl of blond hair hung down strategically over his piercing blue eyes, and the corner of his mouth was twisted in what seemed to her to be a perpetual sneer. He gave the air of someone who considered the unadorned, sterile-white interrogation chamber beneath him, as if he were wasting his valuable time being there.

"Your former commanding officer, my former Intelligence chief, Colonel Aleksandr Kuryakin, commandeered one of the newest and most *expensive* heavy cruisers in my fleet, the *Valkyrian*, for a mission he authorized without my knowledge or consent, to chase down a Goddamned *mercenary* company?"

"My Lord," she said carefully, very cognizant of the man's reputation, "he was convinced this 'Wholesale Slaughter' mercenary unit was merely a front for an intelligence operation by the Guardianship of Sparta. He saw footage of the unit's commander, a Captain Jonathan Slaughter, and insisted the man was actually Logan Conner, the eldest son of the Guardian himself, Jaimie Brannigan."

"Why the hell," Starkad demanded, gesturing expressively, "would the heir to the Guardian of Sparta not use his father's last name? And why haven't I heard anything about him before if he's this important intelligence operative?"

She was about to answer when Saul Grieg stepped in. She'd already learned not to interrupt Colonel Grieg. He was short and stocky, the corners of his flattop as squared off as the epaulets on the shoulders of his grey dress uniform or the cut of his jaw.

"Lord Starkad," the Intelligence officer explained with a tone that might have sounded sharp and impatient coming from someone else, but was just the way Grieg spoke, "Logan Conner took his mother's last name to honor her after she was killed in what the Spartans call 'the Treason,' that rebellion twenty years ago or so under Duncan Lambert." He shrugged casually. "We had a hand in it as well, if I recall, but nothing they could prove. As for why you haven't heard of him, that's because he *isn't* some sort of intelligence agent, he's a junior platoon leader in an armored battalion."

"He *was* a junior platoon leader," Laurent corrected him, letting impatience and annoyance get the better of her innate caution. "But as of the launch of Colonel Kuryakin's mission, he hadn't been seen in his unit for months. The Colonel believed it was him and he authorized the mission in the hopes of capturing him alive and using him for his strategic value against Sparta."

Starkad barked a cynical laugh.

"You mean the crusty old bastard wanted to use him to buy

himself a seat onto my Privy Council," he corrected her. "Old Alek always had his eye on politics. So, he leads my best and brightest off on this wild goose chase and what? You say he just stumbled onto an old Imperial treasure trove?"

"The Spartan operatives were searching for it, following a transmission we didn't pick up until we were closer. The Colonel figured out Logan and the others had masqueraded as mercenaries in order to pass through Starkad space without alerting us to their presence. My Lord, it was Terminus Cut, the legendary Imperial research station. We were there, we saw the riches it contains…"

"You were there," Grieg cut her off, "with a top-of-the-line heavy cruiser and a company of mecha, and yet Kuryakin let himself get suckered in and defeated in detail. The man wasn't a combat soldier. He should have realized his own limitations." The stocky Marine-turned-Intelligence officer paced around the room behind her, making her shoulders itch with the need to turn around and look at him. "If he had, he could have waited until the *Valkyrian* had destroyed their transport before he launched his attack, then taken his time and starved the enemy out."

"Tell me again, Captain," Starkad urged, the hint of a smile on his smug, too-handsome face, "just how you managed to escape."

He leaned forward, as if he thought it was a marvelous adventure story he could share over drinks with his toadies. She forced herself not to sigh in exasperation, staring down at the glove on her right hand. The centimeter gap between the glove and the end of her uniform sleeve revealed the livid, red burn scars there and she fought the urge to pull the sleeve down to hide it.

I can't hide my face, she thought, bitterness still roiling inside her gut.

"I was badly injured in the explosion of one of their dropships," she reported dispassionately, shutting out the emotional pain the way she'd learned to shut out the lingering pain from the burns. "I was blown clear and buried beneath some wreckage.

None of the enemy noticed me, and I was able to sneak inside the Terminus facility and steal food and medical supplies."

She squeezed her eyes shut tightly for a moment, remembering nights spent gritting her teeth against the pain to keep from crying out, huddled behind supply crates, so damned close to surrendering just to get proper medical treatment.

"When they began loading supplies onto their drop-ship to leave the system, I hid in one of the crates and then managed to find an unoccupied storage bin on their starship. When they made their stop on Guajarat to ship their personnel back to Sparta, I snuck on board their drop ship using a stolen uniform and made my way from the spaceport to a Starkad intelligence agent I knew was running our operations in the capital."

She hissed out a breath through clenched jaws. Her description had been dry, matter-of-fact, leaving out the desperate fear, the sheer panic, the hunger and thirst gnawing at her in the times when she couldn't sneak out to forage. Leaving out the constant, sleepless agony...

"Well, that's an impressive story, Captain Laurent," Aaron Starkad allowed, leaning back, hands behind his neck as he regarded her through hooded eyes. "If it's true, if you're not simply a Spartan plant, a double-agent." He glanced over at Grieg, who was standing at parade rest near the center of the small room, a statue dedicated to the spirit of martial readiness. "You're my *new* Chief of Intelligence, Colonel Grieg. What say you?"

Grieg's eyes were the neutral, flat black of a military service pistol and his stare felt much like a loaded gun being pointed her way.

"Her story checks out," the man made his judgement with the finality of a gavel banging on a courtroom desk. "There's always the possibility she's crazy, but she's not lying."

"In that case," Starkad said, pushing himself up to his feet, palms flat on the flimsy, plastic table, "we shouldn't waste any more time. It's been, what?" He glanced at Laurent. "Months already? We can't let Sparta have access to that sort of weapons technology. Grieg, you're going to lead the mission personally and I don't want any fuck-ups this time." He cocked an eyebrow at the Intelligence chief. "Do you have any idea how much a heavy cruiser costs? You better not lose me another of them." He began to turn back to the door, but paused and waved at Laurent. "Oh, and just in case, you're taking her with you. If she's telling the truth, give her a promotion and a medal. If she was lying, you can shove her out an airlock."

Starkad's nose wrinkled as his eyes went to Laurent's face. "And if you have the time, see if there's anything the medical team can do to make her look less hideous."

Is it treason, Laurent wondered, *to fantasize about punching your king in the face?*

1

Terrin Brannigan tapped the console impatiently, as if the motion would make the upload go faster. The status bar was virtually crawling from one side of the display to the other and he wondered if there was anything else he could be doing.

Record the last of the stardrive field propagation data? *Did that.*

Re-check the calculations for antimatter output from the design specs for the solar-powered orbital factory? *Did that.*

Finish the report on conversion procedures to refit antimatter-powered devices to fusion plant throughput? *Did that.*

No, this was it. All he had left to finish today was uploading the last of the Terminus Cut facility database to data crystals and getting it on the next cargo run to Sparta. He would like to have been able to bring the computer language crew back here to do the work of decoding the more deeply encrypted sections, but the more people who came to Terminus, the greater the danger of being discovered.

"A watched pot never boils."

Terrin didn't jump at the interruption of his thoughts, but only because he'd come to expect it. The voice was perky and upbeat and annoying as all hell. He closed his eyes for a moment, gathered his patience and turned to face Petty Officer Third Class Francesca Hayden, apparently the most cheerful and effervescent computer technician in the whole Spartan Navy. Even when she was standing still, she gave the impression of constantly bouncing on the balls of her feet.

"Pardon?" he said, the actual content of her words lost in his irritation.

"It's just a saying my great grandmother used to tell me," she clarified, still grinning brightly, her teeth almost painfully white in the glare of the temporary lighting they'd set up in the auxiliary control center down on the third level of the Terminus facility. There'd been too much damage to the primary control center from the fight with Starkad, and this one had come with actual, physical input terminals instead of haptic holograms. "If you watch a pot of water on the stove, it seems like it takes forever to boil, you know."

"I don't believe I've ever had the occasion to boil water on a stove," he admitted. He winced, realizing it made him sound like a privileged douchebag, and he amended the statement. "I mean, in college, I made my own meals sometimes, and in the lab at the university, but those were all just ready-made heat-n-eat bowls." He shrugged, trailing off.

Why did she always have this effect on him? She was no different than any other tech. Okay, maybe she was cute, if you were into the whole pixie look, with her bobbed brown hair and upturned nose and the impish grin. She certainly did nice things to a set of blue Navy utility fatigues but that could have been the effect of months away from civilians. He glanced around the control room to see if any of the other technicians had noticed his embarrassment, but the only two he could see looked to be absorbed in their work.

"I love a home-cooked meal," she went on as if he hadn't

tripped all over his tongue. She leaned on the hard plastic of the control console and eyed the two-dimensional display screen fitted there. "It's what I'm most looking forward to when I get back to Sparta, visiting my family and sitting down for dinner with my family. Do you and your family ever eat dinner together?"

"Not generally." He sniffed. "My father usually works through dinner unless it's some sort of formal occasion, and until all this…" He waved a hand around them, indicating the base and the whole mission. "…my brother and I could barely sit in the same room together without yelling at each other."

"Oh, right," she said, nodding as if she'd only now remembered, though he must have told her a half a dozen times already. "I keep forgetting you're Captain Conner's brother." She laughed. "Did you guys really have to call him 'Captain Slaughter' on the mission?"

"Yeah, well, he was undercover. The rest of them could be released from service without too much attention, but he's the Guardian's son. Someone would have noticed that."

Or at least that's what they kept telling me. I wouldn't have any idea.

"Is he coming back to pick you up once the initial study is done?" she wondered. "I really want to see that ship you guys found!"

"I don't know. The last I heard, the ship was being put through its paces on some proving ground system way out at the edge of Spartan space." He shrugged. "But I guess they'd want to send it out to pick up the shipment of Imperial technology. They might be able to smuggle technicians and work crews in and out on commercial ships but we won't be able to sneak mecha and battlesuits and hovertanks out that way. We'll need the stardrive for that. Since it's reactionless, we can sneak past Starkad pickets to the jump-points before they detect us."

"Well, technically," she corrected him with a puckish grin, "it's not a stardrive without an antimatter power source to take it past the lightspeed threshold. And the Starkad picket ships will still be able to detect it, since it has to vent reactor heat. They just won't be able to identify it as a spaceship with the fusion flare." A giggle, surprisingly girly. "And they wouldn't be able to accelerate fast enough to catch up with it anyway."

Terrin scowled at her, annoyed again though not clearly understanding why.

"If you already know all that, Petty Officer Hayden, why did you bother to ask me?"

"Just making conversation!" She touched him on the forearm and he stared at her hand with a look of incomprehension. "And I told you, call me Franny."

He was still trying to formulate a response when the alarm klaxons sounded. They weren't quite as jarring as they might have been had they been built into the structure of the room. Instead, they vibrated out of tinny speakers attached to the walls with adhesive and hooked to the makeshift intercom system through repeaters set at intervals in the corridors. They were as frightening for the message they carried, one drilled into him over the last few weeks by one rehearsal after another. A ship had jumped into this system.

"Attention all personnel, report immediately to the shuttles!" The voice was familiar, serious and brooding. Terrin thought perhaps the Ranger captain was self-consciously trying to live up to the legendary standard his boss, Major Randell had created for officers in the elite Special Operations unit. "Repeat, all personnel report immediately to the shuttles. We have Starkad warships inbound and only thirty-five minutes to take off in time for the escape ship to reach the jump point! This is not a drill!"

Though would Captain Cordova actually tell them if it were?

Terrin swallowed hard and looked at the progress bar of the upload. Seventy percent.

"Get out," he ordered, his voice breaking slightly. He cleared his throat and repeated himself as Franny and the other two technicians stared at him. "All of you, go! I'll be right behind you after this data finishes uploading. We can't leave this for Starkad to find."

And I'll be damned if we did all this for nothing.

If there were really Starkad ships inbound, he knew what the procedure was. Cordova had gone over that often enough, too. He'd seen the thermonuclear charges the Rangers had set, knew the procedures for arming them…and knew the process was irreversible once it had been locked in.

The other two techs hadn't required any more convincing; they'd vacated their posts and taken off out into the corridor. This was technically the night shift, though it meant little in an underground base, but most of the regular crew would have been in their quarters, sleeping, and wouldn't be passing this way to get to the surface and the shuttles there, so he wouldn't have to worry about anyone else. Except Franny, who was still standing there, hands on her hips and a stubborn expression on her face.

"Franny, I said you need to go."

"Just as soon as you do," she insisted, her voice as firm as her stance. "If this is important enough for you to stay and wait for it, it's important enough you shouldn't be doing it alone."

"Damn it, Petty Officer, get to the shuttle!" He tried to make the words sound commanding, the way his brother or Lyta Randell did when they dealt with unruly subordinates, but it came out a lot more pleading and petulant than he'd intended.

"You aren't in my chain of command," she reminded him. "If you stay, I stay." She moved around him and logged into her terminal then tapped in a series of commands with expert, practiced motions.

"What are you doing?" he asked her.

"We can't count on the charges to destroy everything," she explained, her voice less impish, flatter and atonal when she was doing her job. "I'm going to set the system to wipe itself once the upload is over."

He let out a breath somewhere between a sigh and a bellow, fists clenching and unclenching as he tried to think of an argument to convince her when logic clearly wouldn't. Nothing came to mind and he checked the status bar again, the alarms beginning to wear at his nerves.

Seventy-five percent.

Shit. If the data had been uploading at a constant rate, they'd have plenty of time, but it had slowed down and sped up during the process and he had no idea how long the rest would take. At least Cordova had shut up.

"Terrin, what the fuck are you *doing* down here?"

It was the same self-consciously dramatic tone from the speaker, but without the remote tinny effect. Captain John Cordova was somehow in full armor and carrying his rifle, what Lyta would have called "full battle rattle," despite the late hour and what had to have been very little warning. He was even wearing his helmet, though the visor was up, revealing the square-jawed, recruiting-ad face beneath.

"Get your ass to the shuttles right now!" Cordova snapped, pointing back out the door with the muzzle of his rifle.

"I'm uploading the Terminus database," Terrin told him, gesturing at the row of data crystals standing upright in their slots on the console. "I wish we'd scheduled this earlier," he added, slapping a palm against the console in frustration at how slowly the status bar was moving. "There's just been one technical problem after another getting the two systems to synch up. But we can't leave without it, Captain."

Cordova's jaw worked as if he were chewing up the curse

words before he spat them out, but finally he sucked in a deep breath and seemed to calm down.

"Here's what we're gonna do, Dr. Brannigan," he said. Terrin knew Cordova was angry, because the Ranger officer only addressed him as "Doctor" when he was pissed. "I'm going to go finish setting the charges to bring this place down. When I come back through here, which should be no longer than ten to fifteen minutes, you and Petty Officer Hayden *are* coming with me to the shuttle. If the upload isn't finished, take what you've got because…" He glanced over at the readout. "…eighty percent of the Imperial database is better than nothing at all. Do you under-stand me?"

Terrin didn't like it, but he knew he had no choice but to agree. Cordova was the sort who'd put him in restraints and drag him to the shuttle if he had to.

"Right," Terrin said. He reached under the console into one of the plastic storage totes they'd stacked there to hold supplies and came up with a small, shielded lead case for the data crystals. "We'll be ready to go."

Cordova gave him one last, disapproving scowl before he strode purposefully from the room, breaking into a jog once he was through the door.

"He's always so bossy," Franny said off-handedly, not looking up from her keyboard and monitor. "You'd think he was in charge here and not you."

"I'm in charge of the scientific staff, Cordova's the overall commander."

It had been Logan's decision to leave him here along with a couple other technicians after they'd salvaged what they could from the *Shakak* and rigged up a docking collar for the drop-ship onto the Imperial starship. The research and salvage crew had come in later, along with food and equipment, and he'd figured a new mission director would come with them. He'd been surprised to find out he was still in charge of the technical end of things.

But Cordova was the ranking military officer, and this was definitely his decision to make.

And he's right, most of the data is better than none at all.

Still, he was going to give it to the last second. He had nightmare visions about going through the information back on Sparta and finding out he'd cut it off right in the middle of a detailed explanation of how to construct a stardrive. Even examining the working model they had, no one had yet been able to figure out how the thing had been built. It seemed to require some sort of exotic matter no scientist in the Five Dominions had even theorized about. The antimatter it needed for power they knew how to manufacture, it would just take most of the gross planetary product of a large and well-developed world like Sparta or Stavanger to produce, and wouldn't happen anytime soon.

Someday though…

Someday, they wouldn't need the jump-points, wouldn't be restricted to travelling only between systems connected by the gravito-inertial threads, trudging through the real-space between them, taking weeks to get anywhere. Someday, they'd be as advanced as the giants of myth, able to sail the universe on waves of warped spacetime.

"What did you say about giants?"

He started, realizing he must have been thinking out loud and was stuttering through an explanation when Cordova burst back through the door, his usually stalwart face pale and drawn.

"We have to go now!" he shouted, bracing himself against the side of the doorway, panting, sweat pouring down his face. "Enemy drop-ships have already launched."

Terrin didn't take the time to respond, instead he leaned over the control console and shut down the upload. Ninety percent. Ninety percent of the knowledge of all the ages from the time man had climbed out of the cradle of Old Earth and clawed his way to the stars, all the way to the fall of the Empire of Hellas. It would have to be enough.

The indicator flashed green and he carefully yanked each of the half-dozen crystal cards out of their slots and placed them into the cushioned interior of the lead case, then clapped the case shut and twisted the lock in place. A small square lit up red next to the lock and he pressed his right thumb against it until it changed to green. Now it was keyed to his thumbprint and any attempt to open it without that identification would destroy the contents.

He grabbed the case by handle built into the lid and Cordova moved out of the doorway, motioning for the two of them to clear out. Terrin didn't wait for the Ranger. He pushed Franny ahead of him and ran. The dimly-lit corridors seemed to bring the looming threat closer to reality, and he was filled with a sudden desperation he'd been able to hold off before with the focus of finishing his task. Now all he could think of was the Starkad troops heading their way and the timers on the fusion charges counting down and he needed more than anything to get in the shuttle and get out of this damned place.

It wasn't that far to the surface from the auxiliary control room through the back way. When they'd first entered the facility, months ago, they'd come in through the main cargo entrance out to the flats beside one of the finger lakes branching out from the Cut, the huge canyon running kilometers deep on the otherwise lifeless planet. They hadn't found the second entrance until a few days later, up a set of stairs through the living quarters. He'd climbed the same stairs every day for weeks now, yet this time they seemed elongated, a kilometer instead of a couple hundred meters, and by the time they reached the external hatch, he was out of breath and dripping with sweat.

Franny passed him on the stairway and slammed her shoulder into the thick, metal door to stop herself, grabbing at the manual locking wheel and slowly, laboriously turning it to the left. Terrin hesitated for a beat before he abruptly realized he should be helping her and found space for his hands on the wheel, putting his weight into the turn. The door unlocked with a loud clank and the two of them pushed against it at the same time, sending the heavy portal swinging open so violently Terrin almost fell through it.

He caught himself with a hand on the side of the doorframe and scrambled out carefully through the narrow doorway, moving aside to make room for the others. It was dark outside, but then it was never *that* light deep inside the Cut, except at high noon. It was also cold as hell, certainly below freezing, and the light windbreaker he'd been wearing to cut the underground chill seemed entirely inadequate.

Terrin hugged his arms across his chest, already starting to shiver, and tried to let his eyes adjust before he moved. The emergency exit came out much higher up the cliff than the cargo entrance, and the trail down to the landing zone was steep and treacherous and he definitely planned to let Cordova go first. Only the floodlights they'd set up on temporary tripods stood out against the blackness, illuminating the one remaining shuttle and the crew scrambling around to get it ready while the last stragglers from the base filed out of the cargo entrance and boarded.

There had been three aerospacecraft down in the flats, but only charred circles in the rocky surface remained of the other two, the marks of their belly jets from takeoff. He couldn't even see their exhaust in the night sky. He whispered a prayer of thanks to a God he didn't really believe in that they were in time to catch this boat.

"Come on," Cordova urged them, switching on the blindingly bright white light attached to the fore-stock of his rifle and shining it down the path. "Follow me!"

"Wait!" Franny grabbed at the Ranger officer's shoulder as he was about to head downward. "What's that noise?"

Terrin hadn't noticed it until then, mostly because his own pulse beat was louder in his ears than anything from the run up the stairs, but now he heard it. It was a distant rumble, echoing off the walls of the canyon like the thunder of a far-off storm. But this thunder didn't fade as the seconds went by, it kept rolling down the Cut, louder and closer, and Terrin had an awful feeling he knew exactly what it was.

"Get down!" Cordova yelled, yanking Terrin by the arm, pulling him and Franny to the dirt and covering them with his own body.

Terrin wanted to protest, wanted to push him off, but then he saw the glow against the grey of the low-hanging clouds, heard the unmistakable whine of turbojets overhead.

"This is Cordova!" the Ranger was speaking into his helmet's radio pickup but, with the visor up, his voice carried enough for Terrin to make it out. "Get the bird off the ground now!"

The calculations were cold and heartless and automatic; they ran across his mind like chalk on a blackboard and he knew. *Too late.*

The laser was clearly visible, refracted in the low clouds and the particulate haze at the bottom of the canyon, burning a sheath of superheated plasma through the air. The plasma was an illusion, trailing the lightspeed burst by fractions of a second, but brilliant and flashy as a thunderbolt, fooling the eye into thinking it had done the damage rather than the laser. The people in the shuttle didn't care, they were just as dead.

Terrin squeezed his eyes shut instinctively, covered his head with his hands, but the explosion was so bright he could see it through his closed eyelids. The shuttle was a kilometer away and three hundred meters down the hill, but the sound hit him like a solid wall, running microseconds ahead of the concussion, an earthquake trying to toss the three of them off the hillside. By the time he opened his eyes, all that was left was a swiftly-rising mushroom cloud, glowing an angry red from within, and the fiery rain of debris already beginning to make its way back to the ground. And coming down just a few hundred meters away from the conflagration was another aerospacecraft, much larger and uglier, a drop-ship, lowering itself to the ground on white-hot columns of fire.

Terrin couldn't hear, couldn't move, couldn't *think* for long seconds, but he felt something shaking him and finally realized Cordova was trying to pull him to his feet. Franny was already up, running back to the open doorway. It seemed like a damned good idea and he followed her, encouraged by Cordova pushing at his shoulder. By the time they'd made it inside, his hearing had returned enough to hear Cordova cursing in three different languages, and his thinking had recovered enough to understand the why.

"We are so fucked!" Cordova said, finally going back to a language Terrin understood. "Once the escape ship sees the shuttle's been scragged, they're going to be burning at high gees for the jump point." He sucked in a deep breath, obviously trying to get himself back under control. "We can't stay here; the fusion charges will be going off in less than an hour. Maybe we can get to those caves on the other side of the lake and try to wait them out..."

Terrin was barely listening to him. A thought was crystallizing out of memory and desperation, rising to the surface like a piece of driftwood in the ocean, the last hope of a drowning man.

"I think," he said, his voice still sounding muffled in his battered ears, "I might have another way out of here."

2

Saul Grieg had begun his career as a Marine, Ruth Laurent remembered. You could tell, you could still see it in the precision of his movements, the way his eyes scanned carefully for threats with every step. Even the martial riches of the old Empire, the rows upon rows of hulking, impossibly massive mecha, the ranks of three-meter tall suits of powered armor, the huge chamber full of hover tanks couldn't entice Grieg to gawk like a tourist or drool with avarice. He simply stood beside her at the center of the wedge formation of Supremacy Marines and advanced as they did, his service pistol held at the low ready.

He hadn't issued Laurent a weapon, but she hadn't complained too much. If two companies of Marines and the platoon of mecha guarding the outside approaches wasn't enough to keep her safe, it was unlikely a handgun would do it. She was just grateful to be pain-free after months of having to choose between constant agony or mind-numbing drugs. The medical bay on the heavy cruiser *Sleipner* had been able to repair her burns with cloned skin grafts in the three weeks it had taken them to travel from Stavanger to Terminus and her hair was even starting to grow back.

"I believe they must have evacuated everyone, sir," Captain Gerhardt announced, her high-pitched, nasal voice incongruous coming from the external speakers of her menacing black armor and dark-visored helmet. "We haven't been able to find any of them, but there's plenty of evidence they left in a hurry."

Grieg ceased his constant scan for threats long enough to eye the Marine officer balefully.

"I don't believe they managed to get everyone out," he declared. "They were still boarding the last shuttle when we destroyed it. Keep searching."

"Yes, sir," the woman said without hesitation, turning back to her troops. Her voice no longer projected from the helmet's speakers, but Laurent knew she was addressing them over her radio because a squad detached itself from the lead platoon and double-timed their way up the corridor leading out of the chamber where the hovertanks were stored.

"I didn't get to see much of this last time I was here," Laurent murmured, staring at one of the hovertanks.

They were each twenty meters long and fifteen wide, resting on plenums constructed of some sort of honeycomb composite material she couldn't readily identify, the turrets heavily armored and built around the ten-meter long emitter of what might have been a coilgun or perhaps a plasma cannon.

"It's just as you said it was," Grieg admitted, perhaps a bit grudgingly. "I will make sure you're rewarded for your dedication in getting the data back to us." His natural, perpetual scowl deepened. "Though if Kuryakin hadn't gotten himself killed, I'd put a bullet in his head for not reporting all this before he pursued the *Shakak*. Had he arrived with sufficient forces, the Spartans would never have stood a chance."

She nodded, silently acceding the point. It hadn't been her place to tell Colonel Kuryakin how to run Military Intelligence, but he'd put his own advancement above the good of the state, and he'd paid the price.

"Colonel Grieg!" The urgent call caught Laurent's attention a half-second before the motion drew her eye.

Both had come from the far corner of the huge chamber, where shadows swallowed what looked to her to be a storage room of some kind. A Marine fire team was dragging a man between them, his arms secured behind his back with flex cuffs, desperate fear playing over his boyish, chubby face. His work uniform was Spartan Navy issue, the rank on his shoulder a Technician's, one of their common workers.

"We found one of them, sir!" the sergeant who led the fireteam announced redundantly, his rifle trained on the captive. "He was hiding back there in that storage room."

There was a cold pit deep inside Laurent's stomach as she watched them bring the Technician forward, hands at his armpits, his feet limp and scraping against the floor. She should have been exhilarated at the discovery, at the intelligence the prisoner could give them, but instead she was flashing back to her own experience hiding for weeks among the enemy, terrified she might slip up and be captured or killed. He was the enemy, operating illegally in Starkad space, but all she could think was that he was living out her nightmares.

"What's your name?" Grieg asked, stepping nearly nose-to-nose with the man.

She didn't know why he was bothering to ask; the man's name was printed across the tape on his left breast: "Fuentes." Fuentes said nothing, simply staring at Grieg with eyes wide and white.

"It's not a difficult question," Grieg persisted, his voice dangerously quiet. "Tell me your name, Spartan."

"Fuentes, Eduard B.," the soft man stuttered. "Technician Second Class, Sparta Navy. ID number 549811B."

Grieg snorted in amusement. He stroked the man's cheek with a gloved finger and Fuentes flinched away.

"Do you really think we're going to make an official Enemy Prisoner of War report with your service number, Fuentes? Do you imagine this whole business coming to involve ambassadors and ministers and negotiations?" He shook his head. "Because I don't see things unfolding that way. You're a spy, by all agreements between the Five Dominions, subject to the laws of the state in which you're captured. Starkad executes spies. No trial necessary."

Fuentes was shaking now, and Laurent found her own shoulders shuddering in empathy.

"But it doesn't *have* to be so brutal and abrupt, Eduard." Grieg showed his teeth in what might have been called a smile, if you were feeling generous. "As little use as Starkad has for spies, we have great appreciation for intelligence sources. If you tell us everything you know, perhaps a place can be found for you on Stavanger. A new identity, a little money?" The lips closed and the wolf smile disappeared into something even less pleasant. "This offer is temporary, and is entirely dependent on you telling me everything you know about this place in the next ten seconds."

"I don't know anything," Fuentes insisted. "I'm just a tech! I maintain the air conditioning systems! I was asleep when the alarm sounded and I missed my shuttle! They don't give me any classified information!"

"Nine."

"Honestly man!" Fuentes would have thrown himself to his knees, Laurent thought, if the Marines hadn't restrained him. "I don't know nothing! The Rangers run everything! Guy named Cordova!"

"Eight."

"Mithra's Blood, man, I don't know!"

"Oh, the hell with it," Grieg snapped and shot Fuentes in the leg..

Laurent jumped, suppressing a yell. Fuentes didn't try. He was screaming, and now the Marines did let him fall, let him clutch at his left thigh as the blood spurted from the wound. It had hit the femoral artery, she realized with a cold horror. Grieg knelt over the man, prodding at his leg with the barrel of his gun, giving the screams a higher pitch.

"You're dying, Eduard," he told Fuentes. "You have minutes unless I allow my troops to give you medical aid. I will do that when you've told me what I want to know."

"Mithra's Blood, I…" Fuentes trailed off, his face twisted in agony. "The place, it's rigged to blow. Fusion bombs." He paused, sucking in a breath. "I helped install them. Cordova will have set the timers."

"How do I disarm them?" Grieg demanded, his casual façade falling away. He grabbed Fuentes by the collar of his fatigue blouse and jerked his head up. "How do I stop the timer? Is there a code?"

"It can't be stopped," Fuentes told him, shaking his head, eyes already beginning to glaze over in shock. "Not once it's armed. Except by disassembling the whole thing, and that would take hours. The SOP is for the timer to be set for an hour, no more."

"Fuck!" Grieg spat, straightening, shoulders tensed as if he wanted to shoot someone else in his frustration. Laurent shrank away from him, realizing she was a handy target. Finally, Grieg seemed to calm down and he leaned over Fuentes again. "Is there anyone else left here but you?"

"I think…." Fuentes head lolled and Grieg slapped him across the face lightly, bringing the coherence back to his eyes. "I think Terrin might still be here. I didn't see him leave the control room…"

"Terrin who?" Grieg shook his shoulder. "You're going to die in a minute unless we stop the bleeding, you moron! Terrin who?"

"Brannigan." Fuentes gasped the word. "Terrin Brannigan. The Guardian's son."

Now Grieg *did* smile, a real smile. He stood up and casually shot Fuentes through the forehead. Laurent didn't jump this time, but her hands clenched in an automatic defensive gesture.

"Captain Gerhardt!" Grieg called into his 'link. Laurent didn't look around, but she assumed the woman was still involved in organizing the search outside their chamber. "Terrin Brannigan, son of the Guardian of Sparta is in this facility. Find him, no matter if you have to tear this place down to do it! You have less than an hour!"

"Sir," Laurent said, tentative but feeling someone had to ask it. "What about the fusion bombs?"

Grieg sniffed at the question with a dismissive wave of his hand.

"I'm not leaving here empty-handed, Captain Laurent." He speared her with a glare. "And neither are you."

Terrin felt an insistent itch at the back of his neck, as if a mosquito was buzzing around him, landing just long enough to bite before flying away again. It wasn't fear. Not that he was immune to fear, he was simply familiar with it by now, and this was something different. He thought perhaps it was pressure to perform, pressure not to let everyone down, which was something he *wasn't* that familiar with.

"Where the hell are we going?" Cordova asked, probably for the third time.

He hadn't answered yet for several very good reasons. They had very limited time, the hike up these damned stairs was *killing* him and he couldn't spare the breath, but mostly, because he didn't want to admit he really wasn't sure.

"Something I saw going over the plans for this place," he gasped, taking a break for just a moment, leaning on the railing.

The stairwell was narrow and dark, lit only by the occasional chemical striplight. They'd started out the climb in the bare, unfinished area behind the living quarters, a section they hadn't had the time nor personnel to investigate as of yet with so much else to do.

"It's something that might not even be there," Terrin admitted, "but if it is, it's a ship, sort of." He shook his head and waved a hand. "We'll figure it out when we get there!"

"I don't know about the rest of you," Franny said, shocking Terrin with the taut hostility in her tone, "but I'd rather not die here. Can we discuss this while we run?"

Terrin barely remembered the readout he'd seen in the construction reports. It had only been random chance he'd even brought up the record, just a review of the decryption program they'd developed. He wasn't sure at the time if it had been an ongoing project or simply a blue-sky proposal from some overeager engineer, but at some point in the last few minutes, he'd convinced himself it existed. All he had to go on was a single line in Colonel Walken Zeir's personal log regarding real-location of antimatter fuel for the ships the Imperial complement at Terminus had sent out seeking food and supplies, just a single mention of diverting fuel from the *"Courier."* If the *Courier* was someone's pet time-sink that had never materialized, they'd come a long way and spent a lot of energy for nothing.

He nearly ran headlong into the door, bouncing off it with his shoulder instead by the grace of stepping with his right foot instead of his left. He felt for a physical latch but couldn't find one, couldn't see anything else.

"Captain!" he yelled, then turned and realized the Ranger was about ten centimeters behind his right shoulder. "Can you shine a light here?"

Even in the dark, Cordova moved with trained precision, stripping the weapon's light off his rifle and holding it up to shine on the door. Squinting against the glare, Terrin spotted the locking panel fitted flush with the wall beside the dull-grey metal of the door and stabbed at it with a finger to try to activate it. If the damned thing had developed a short, or they hadn't gotten around to wiring the power down here yet…

It flickered fitfully to life and he almost shouted with exhilaration before he remembered where he was. The display settled down into an input screen waiting for a code and he tapped the command override they'd found in Zeir's notes and murmured a reflexive prayer.

Damn. Praying again. This spy business is going to make a believer out of me again.

He'd been raised Reformed Imperial Zoroastrian, like most people in the remains of the old Empire, but he hadn't been observant since he'd been old enough to start blaming Mithra for his mother's death. In the last year, he'd seen enough of what humans were capable of doing to each other with no divine intervention to begin giving his deity the benefit of the doubt.

The other side of the door lay in utter darkness, unbroken by as much as a glimmer, and he froze for a moment, unsure of his next step.

"Let me through," Cordova said, trying to squeeze past with his flashlight, but he needn't have bothered.

Less than a second later, light panels dark for over four centuries began snapping to life, illuminating one section of the room after another in quick, linear succession.

"Yes!" Now Terrin *did* yell, pumping his fist and be damned if anyone heard him.

The *Courier* was just as he'd imagined it…more or less. A

cylinder a hundred meters long by thirty wide, it was smaller than a shuttle and showed no sign of any conventional reaction drive, just a series of vectored thrust nozzles along its belly and matching air intakes on the upper hull. It was bright silver, unadorned by any symbol or alphanumeric designator. He saw only one obvious point of entry, a circular patch on the hull near the bow. It rested on nothing—well, to be more precise, it rested on magnetic fields from electromagnets set in the floor, keeping it a meter off the solid rock just as they had since last humans had darkened the small chamber. Some sort of monitoring equipment surrounded the ship, though he couldn't identify what they measured by the look of them. Maybe things he didn't even have names for yet. He was more interested in what was missing than what was there.

When they'd found the ship Jonathan had insisted on calling the *Shakak II* months ago, it had been stored at an angle, tilted upward to match the section of roof configured to open for its launch. The *Courier* was horizontal, barely fitting in the chamber, which seemed to have been cut to fit the ship, whatever equipment they'd used to construct it and not much else, and it was definitely not meant to egress through the roof. Directly in front of it was a tube, smooth as glass and probably cut by a laser, only centimeters wider than the ship itself, going on into the rock face of the wall further than he could see.

A steep, narrow set of stone-cut steps led down from the doorway to the platform where the *Courier* sat, and Terrin scrambled down them, hands sliding over the railings, suddenly full of energy again.

"What the hell *is* that thing?" Cordova asked him. "Some sort of shuttle?"

"It's a prototype short-range starship they called the *Courier*," Terrin told him, jogging across the platform at the base of the stairs, scanning the hull for a control panel to open the hatch. "It doesn't have a jump drive, just the Alanson-McCleary stardrive and an antimatter reactor to power it."

"*That* thing has a stardrive in it?" Franny asked, eyes narrowed in obvious skepticism. "It barely looks big enough to get us to orbit!"

"I'm just hoping they left some fuel in the damned thing," Terrin said, finally finding the lock panel for the ship's hatch.

No code necessary, it slid silently aside with a slap of his palm on the plate…and he cursed long and loud.

"What's wrong?" Cordova asked, jogging up beside him. Then, "Oh."

The cockpit was sealed off from the rest of the ship, and cramped, stuffed with monitors and displays and two very tiny seats. Only two.

"I'm small," Franny was saying, very little hope in either her statement or the expression on her face. "Maybe I could sit on someone's lap…"

Terrin didn't argue with her because he didn't want to be the one who said it, but it was obvious only two of them could fit into the thing. Hell, it was so cramped he wasn't sure he could squeeze through to the left-hand seat. And maybe, he thought, he shouldn't try.

"Here," Terrin said, forcing himself to do the right thing before he let his fear get the best of him, shoving the storage box of data crystals toward Cordova. "You two go. I'll surrender to Starkad. I'm too valuable to kill and Dad can negotiate for my release. It's the data that's important."

Cordova sneered at the box and pushed it back at him.

"If you think I'm going to be the one to tell the Guardian I left his son behind for the enemy to capture, you're fucking nuts. Get in the damned ship and make sure it can fly." He motioned sharply into the hatch. "Now. That's an order."

Terrin stared back at the man, wondering if he should try to argue, but realized he wasn't going to win. He wasn't sure if he wanted to. He clambered inside, having to eel his way over the right-hand acceleration couch to reach the pilot's chair. He left the storage box in the right seat and fought to free his right boot where it was caught on the center command console.

How the hell am I going to fly this thing?

The ship they'd found a few months ago had come equipped with the equivalent of a neural helmet on a mech, a small halo type device that read the intent of the wearer, but as he settled into the pilot's seat, he didn't see one. A ring of lights had come on when he'd opened the hatch, illuminating the controls, but the main displays were still frustratingly dark. He began touching the controls, hoping a haptic hologram would pop up, or maybe a magic genie to give him three wishes.

Because the first one will be for another damned seat!

"You should go, sir," Franny said, her voice carrying through the hatch, high-pitched and a bit grating. "Seriously, you know secrets and stuff. I'm just a tech, I won't be very much use to them."

She's trying to be brave, but she sounds scared shitless.

"Petty Officer Hayden," Cordova replied, clear and final, "I am the ranking officer here, and I will be the one to decide who gets on this ship. The decision has been made. Your job is to do your duty, follow your orders and get your butt through that hatch."

He wondered if Cordova was scared. The man didn't seem scared of anything, but it could have been an act, a front he put on as a leader, to inspire his troops. He knew Logan got scared sometimes, even though he didn't show it. Maybe even Lyta got scared. *Naw, probably not.*

It was all going to be a waste of time anyway, unless he could figure out how to use these controls.

"Come on, *Courier*," he murmured. "Give me some help here."

The command console display lit up so abruptly and unexpectedly, Terrin nearly jumped out of his seat.

"System initializing," a voice sounded behind him and this time he did jump, craning his neck around until he realized it had come from speakers set in the headrest of his acceleration couch.

Synthesized computer voices weren't unheard of in the Five Dominions, but they weren't very popular. Legends of the AI Wars and the collapse of the old Terran Republic were the fodder for horror stories told around campfires to this day, and no one wanted to make their computers seem too human-like.

"What did you require assistance with?" the computer asked him.

"Fuel storage display," he snapped, disliking the idea of talking to a computer, but lacking the time to worry about it.

The machine complied and a status bar appeared on the main screen, depressingly close to empty. Terrin's gut twisted and he dreaded asking the next question.

"How far will that take us?" He thought about the fact they hadn't brought any food with them and weren't likely to find any on a ship stored in a facility whose original crew had starved to death. "At top speed," he added, lest the computer start quoting Hohmann Transfer orbits to take them out of the star system in a century's time.

"At the maximum sustainable speed for the Courier with the current fuel load, the vehicle can reach 9.3581 light-years, including initial orbital insertion within seventy-four hours and fifteen minutes."

Shit.

Nine and a half light years on what had to be two percent of the maximum fuel load was damned impressive, but this place was quite literally in the middle of nowhere. Was there anything habitable that close? He thought about asking the computer before remembering its records would be over four hundred years out of date. Instead, he fished his 'link off his belt and called up the star charts he'd downloaded from the base's main computer system to help him run alternate courses of approach for hauling out the technology.

Won't have to worry about that.

And there it was. Far from ideal, but something.

"Franny!" he yelled, leaning over toward the hatch. "Get in the ship!"

She'd still been arguing with Cordova and his call seemed to snap her out of whatever logic loop had deceived her into thinking she had a chance of winning. She shut her mouth and climbed through the opening into the right-hand seat, grabbing the storage box and settling it between her feet on the deck.

Cordova leaned inside and fished three ration bars out of the thigh pocket of his fatigues, handing them to Franny.

"You'll need these more than me." The officer frowned. "Are you going to be able to make it? Is there enough fuel?"

"Enough to get us nine light years," Terrin said with a shrug. "There's a system out there with a private asteroid colony I think we can reach."

Terrin caught Cordova's eye as the Ranger was about to pull back out of the hatch.

"Thank you, Captain," he told him. "Is there anyone you want me to contact…?" He trailed off, unsure how to ask a man who was about to die to save them what he wanted his family to be told.

"No one who matters. Just tell Colonel Randell I did my duty."

Terrin didn't have the chance to respond. A burst of gunfire echoed through the chamber, bullets ricocheting off the hull of the ship, punctuated by shouted commands from the entrance to the chamber. The enemy had found them. Terrin swore and flinched away as a round passed through the hatch and smacked into the inner bulkhead, bouncing off and dying on the deck, a tiny, smoking tantalum dart.

Cordova was returning fire one-handed, spraying burst after burst at the doorway as he stepped away from the hatch and slapped his left palm against the control plate. Metal slid into place, sealing them into the tiny cockpit of the starship. Franny was staring at the bare grey inner surface of the hatch, pale and disbelieving.

"Courier," Terrin said clearly, "take us out of here at maximum survivable boost and get this ship into orbit."

"Initializing atmospheric thrusters," the *Courier* replied, and Franny's eyes widened even further.

"Is the *ship* talking to us?" she asked, almost as if the concept offended her more than the idea of being shot at.

"Heading required before takeoff," the ship's computer reminded him, not paying attention to Franny's question.

"Do you have a system in your navigational files called Beta Tauranis?" Terrin asked, double-checking the name on his 'link as he spoke, trying to force his mind to keep working, not to give into the panic.

"I do. It is 8.943 light years distant, a red giant with no habitable planets."

"Our destination is at the inner edge of the system's asteroid belt. There'll be a nav signal once we get close enough. We're looking for a place called Trinity."

"Prepare for launch." The *Courier*'s computer seemed cheerful about the whole thing, as if unaware of the gun battle going on just outside its hull.

Terrin checked the restraint straps on his seat and saw Franny do the same, then checking to make sure the storage box was wedged in tight at her feet. She was still leaning over, pushing experimentally at the sides of the lead container when the ship began to vibrate and a distant roar filled the cockpit, the growl of a big cat about to spring. Ten gravities slammed Terrin back into his acceleration couch with the abrupt brutality of a traffic accident and everything went black.

3

Ruth Laurent had never been in a gunfight. She'd narrowly missed out on one here at Terminus when she'd first arrived, but she'd been unconscious for most of it. This one seemed fairly boring; she was stuck in a dark stairwell, unable to see as Grieg's Marines streamed past her. The spiteful crack of rifle fire took a deeper tone as it echoed off the narrow walls of the tunnel, growing in intensity as the seconds slipped by.

"Move!" Grieg screamed at the Marine troops who seemed to hesitate at the mouth of the stairwell exit, backlit by brilliant lights from inside the chamber. "Get in there now!"

The Marines pushed ahead and Grieg lunged forward with them. Laurent advanced behind the Colonel hesitantly, suddenly very conscious of the fact she wasn't wearing armor. But the bulk of the fire seemed to be outgoing, so she just tried to keep Grieg's substantial form between her and danger as she stepped down onto the stone staircase leading down into the yawning, oblong expanse of the chamber.

At first, distracted by the raucous stutter of automatic weapons and trying to pick out where the Spartan troops were while still ducking behind her superior officer, she almost didn't notice the massive, silvery shape at the center of the room. When it did finally register, she dismissed it as a storage tank, something the enemy shooter or shooters were hiding behind. Until the screaming whine of turbines drowned out the gunfire, drowned out Grieg's bellowed orders and she saw the gaping hole in the wall across from the cylinder and suddenly she began to understand.

It was a ship, and it was taking off.

"Sir!" she yelled into Grieg's ear, grabbing at his shoulder. He tried to shrug her hand off but she just yanked harder. "Brannigan has to be on that ship!"

She saw realization in the man's face and he tried to shout instructions to the Marine Captain, but the sound of the jets was just too loud. Laurent ducked down on the steps and covered her ears, knowing what was coming. The blast of superheated air wasn't enough to kill any of the Marines, not encased from head to toe in armor, and she and Grieg were too far away and too high up for it to do more than batter their ears and take their breath away with the sudden flash of heat. But bodies went flying, at least three Grieg's Marines tumbling off the side of the staircase and slamming into the smooth, polished stone of the floor three or four meters below.

The rush of hot wind thrashed at Laurent, threatening to break her death-grip hold on the metal railing of the stairs, bringing PTSD flashbacks to the drop-ship explosion and the months of living with the horrific burns, yet still she held fast. She squeezed her eyes shut, opened her mouth and screamed to relieve the pressure, but ran out of breath before the roaring stopped and nearly passed out. The roaring in her ears was so loud she nearly didn't realize when the roaring of the jets faded.

When she opened her eyes, the ship was gone and all it had left behind was a roiling cloud of steam and dust, gradually being sucked upward into the ventilation system. A line of Marines, toppled like dominoes down the staircase and onto the platform, some blown a dozen meters by the blast of the engines, scrambled to their feet, some searching around them for their rifles. Grieg was still just in front of her, laid flat out on his back, a thin trickle of blood running from a cut on his cheek. His eyes blinked fitfully, his jaw working as if he was trying to pop his ears. He clawed at the stone with his fingers, looking for his weapon.

Laurent saw the handgun laying on the steps between them and grabbed it out of reflex, putting it back into his hand. He gave her an odd look, and she wasn't sure if it was surprise at her action or mistrust of her having the weapon. Either way, he nodded his thanks and pushed himself to his feet.

"Where's the shooter?" Grieg demanded, yelling loudly and atonally, as if he couldn't hear himself talk.

He didn't wait for an answer, just sprinted down the stairs, weaving through a few of the Marines still trying to recover from the blast of the jets. No gunfire greeted him and Laurent wondered if the enemy soldier had somehow managed to get on the ship before it took off.

"Over here!"

Laurent didn't know if Grieg could hear the Marine calling from across the chamber, the other side of where the ship had been, but he definitely saw him because he sprinted over to where the man had his rifle trained on a prone figure, sprawled out and insensate, black-toned armor still smoking. A rifle lay on the ground beside him, but the Starkad trooper kicked it away and it clattered noisily across the polished stone.

"The blast of the takeoff laid him out, sir!" the Marine reported as Grieg skidded to a halt beside him. Grieg glared at the man.

"Then get his hands and feet secured and check him for weapons before he comes to."

More of the Starkad Marines rushed in to help him and Grieg

turned away, staring at the gaping circle of blackness the ship had launched through. As Laurent stepped down the stairs, closer to the hole, she saw it was a tunnel through the rock, heading upward at about a twenty-five-degree angle.

"Captain Gerhardt." Grieg stepped over to the officer and grabbed her by the tactical vest with his left hand, his right and the pistol in it pointing at the hole. "Get that prisoner secure and get all your Marines up through this tunnel immediately. We need to get this intelligence resource…" He nodded at the unconscious Spartan, dressed in the armor their Rangers wore into combat, the visor still up on his helmet. "…out of here before the self-destruct mechanism detonates."

"Yes, sir!" There was awe in the response, Laurent thought, either at the naked menace Grieg projected or perhaps in Gerhardt's newfound knowledge that there *was* a self-destruct mechanism.

One was probably as useful a motivation as the other, and the Marines were moving in seconds. The scouts moved up the tunnel cautiously, then the others following at a quicker pace as reports were radioed back, presumedly of a lack of threats inside. Grieg waited until the fire-team charged with carrying the bound and disarmed prisoner entered before he took a step up into the laser-cut tunnel through the mountain. Laurent stayed where she was, eyeing the blackness doubtfully, and Grieg glanced back over his shoulder at her, grinned and cocked an eyebrow.

"Would you rather deal with unknown salvation or a known death, Captain Laurent?"

The question reminded her of Colonel Kuryakin. A surprise, as it was the *only* thing about the man that reminded her of her old superior. She wished she had more time to consider her answer to his question, but time was a luxury, survival a necessity. She followed him into the darkness.

Terrin Brannigan was having one of those nightmares where you felt as if you were falling and you woke up as you seemed to land in bed. Except when he woke up, he was still falling.

He jerked against his restraints, sucking in an agonized breath and opening his eyes. There was no gravity, no acceleration anymore, and he was surrounded by darkness. The cockpit's holographic display projection swallowed up everything in a star-filled black emptiness, vast and unfathomable. Yet when he focused on a single patch of the heavens, it was as if he rushed abruptly forward and bits of emptiness were suddenly full, asteroids passing by dizzyingly close, ice giants rotating with gelid languor deep in the isolation of the outer system.

"This is amazing, isn't it?" Franny's voice pierced the haze around his thoughts and snapped him back to reality. She pointed to a readout floating in the projection beyond the sea of stars. "If I'm reading that right, we're already travelling at relativistic speeds."

He felt there were something he was forgetting, something important. It nagged at the back of his mind, but eluded him.

"*Courier*," he said, his mouth dry. *Is there water on board? There has to be, right? Shit, I hope there's water on board...* "Do you have any data about other ships in this system?"

"I do," the computer responded. There was an odd timbre to the thing's voice, now that he had the time to consider it. Self-satisfied, almost, a child who has learned something new and is damned proud of it. "There are two, both heading for the antisolar jump nodes."

A computer simulation snapped into existence in front of his face, the holographic projection showing not just colored icons but the general shapes of the respective ships. The Starkad ship was a wedge-shaped monolith a kilometer long, burning across the system on the miniature sun of a hugely-outsized fusion drive, a weapon looking for a target. That target was halfway across the simulation's field of view, running with everything it had.

He knew the lines of the escape ship, the *Acrotiri*, from when it had brought in Franny and the rest of the technical crew. It was a standard cargo ship, unarmed and unflagged, not registered as a Spartan government vessel but rather as a private interest. Lacking the streamlining and armor of a military ship, it was bulbous and utilitarian, but damned fast; the drive was military class even if nothing else about the ship was. It had a head start on the Starkad heavy cruiser and was boosting at somewhere around six gravities according to the sensor reading.

"How long before the ships reach the jump point?" he asked the computer.

"The smaller vessel will achieve jump capability in fifty-five minutes and thirteen seconds if it continues at its present acceleration. The larger one will arrive at the jump node nine minutes and three seconds after that, also assuming its current acceleration."

"Thank Mithra," Franny sighed, closing her eyes as if in prayer. They popped open abruptly and she leaned forward against her seat restraints. "Is there any way we could catch them, dock with them before they jump?"

There was no response, and Terrin repeated the question, wondering if the computer had imprinted on him like a baby chick when he'd been the first human to address it.

"No, that would not be possible," the *Courier* answered. "This vessel wouldn't be able to dock with another ship without first deactivating the drive field due to the tidal effects of the warp field. The instant the drive field is deactivated, this vessel would lose all its momentum except for the momentum gained before we achieved orbit."

"Shit," Terrin hissed. He nodded to Franny. "It was a good idea, anyway." Good enough to give his brain a kickstart and remind him what he'd been trying to think of before the acceleration of launch had made him pass out. "Courier, can you get a message to the smaller ship via tightbeam transmission before it jumps?"

"This ship can transmit tightbeam using the Alanson-McCreary field as a focusing lens. If we broadcast it within the next twenty-two second, it is possible."

Twenty-two seconds?

He tried not to stammer, tried to organize everything he should say into a sentence or two and blurted it out.

"Transmit this immediately: This is Terrin. I'm on an experimental ship with limited fuel and I have the downloaded database from Terminus on data crystals with me. I'm heading to Trinity. Will be waiting there. End transmission and send."

He felt out of breath, as if he'd just run a forty-meter dash back for his track team in college.

"Transmission sent," the Courier reported dutifully. "Transit time is fifty-one minutes. Probability of successful reception is sixty-three percent."

"What?" Franny blurted before Terrin had the chance to ask the same question. Then he had to ask it anyway, because the ship kept ignoring Franny.

"We transmitted at fifty-one light minutes from the target using a tightly focused microwave signal," the Courier explained. "At time of transmission, there were no intervening physical bodies or magnetic fields which could interrupt the signal, but my database lacks up-to-date navigational charts for the system."

"He means if an asteroid or a moon or even a particulate cloud gets in the way," Terrin explained to Franny, "it would block the signal." *And we'd be fucked*, he added to himself, reticent about cursing in front of a woman.

"I know what it meant," Franny fired back, her normally pale face flush with anger. "I'm not an idiot, even if I don't have three PhD's yet."

"I never said you were an idiot!" he protested. "You're a computer systems tech, how would I know what you do and don't understand about high-energy physics?"

"Maybe if you'd listened when I was telling you about my mother working in the particle accelerator research facility in the Outer System Lab, you'd know!" She was almost shouting now, so much louder inside the tiny cockpit, and he thought he could almost feel the heat of her anger.

"I'm…" he tripped over his words. "I mean, I'm…sorry."

He had to drag the word out of his gut kicking and screaming, but he doubted anything else would do and he didn't want to have to deal with her flying off the handle in a space barely big enough for the both of them. It seemed to mollify her, and the red left her cheeks, retreating back to her ears, beneath the protection of her short-cut red-brown hair.

"It's my fault," she demurred, waving a hand. If she hadn't been strapped in, he thought, she would have gone floating away with every word. For someone in the Navy, she hadn't had a lot of time in zero gravity.

Neither did you until a few months ago, he reminded himself.

"I'm just…" she went on, gesturing again helplessly. "I'm just still upset. I mean, what Captain Cordova did for us and…well, I knew a lot of the people on that shuttle."

She wiped at her eye and Terrin suddenly felt like an ass. He'd been so wrapped up with their own situation, he'd barely given a thought to all the people who'd died when Starkad had destroyed their lander. And as for Cordova…

"I hope for his sake he went down fighting."

Franny's head snapped up at the words and he shrugged.

"I mean," he clarified, "I don't want to think about what they'd do to him if they got him alive."

The cold was a living thing, relentless and malevolent, moving through the surface of the smooth rock and through her hands and feet where she touched it, leeching through to her core despite the best efforts of her jacket's electric heating coils. Ruth Laurent wanted to stuff her hands into her jacket pockets to warm them, but it was pitch black inside the tunnel and she needed to feel the wall to avoid walking into the back of someone else, and *by the horns of Mithra, when was this damned tunnel going to end?*

It hadn't actually been so long. She knew on an intellectual level that they couldn't have been climbing more than ten minutes. But the cold and the dark and the slickness of the floor demanding her complete concentration dragged every minute into subjective hours.

That, and the fusion bombs on a timer that could go off at any second.

When Laurent first began to see hints of movement in the blackness, she thought for just a second her eyes were adjusting before realizing how stupid the idea was. There was no light in the tunnel for them to adjust to. Unless they were nearing the surface. She moved faster, nearly colliding with the back of one of the Marines. She wanted to push him out of the way and run, wanted more than anything to be outside again, no matter how cold it was, no matter how thin the air.

And then, almost as if someone had flipped a switch, there was the exit, the sky not so bright as she might have thought, still very early morning on a world with constant cloud cover, but a clearly delineated circle of grey against the black. Marines began clambering downward from the sharp, unnatural lip of the exit, handing down weapons to those already over the side before dropping down themselves; an efficient assembly line but it stopped abruptly when the fire team carrying the Spartan soldier between them approached.

There was an awkward process of lowering the enemy soldier from three Marines standing on the edge to four more below. The Ranger began to struggle and they nearly dropped him and the whole delay was making her want to scream. She danced from foot to foot like a child waiting to pee, and in the grey and muted light of pre-dawn, she made out the disdain on Colonel Grieg's face.

"A little composure, Captain," he chided her, edging forward as the Marines regained control over the enemy soldier and lowered him head first to the crew below. "This isn't the first time you've faced death, after all."

"No, sir," she agreed, gritting her teeth to keep them from chattering. "That's how I'm so sure I don't want to die."

"All humans die. We can only hope to die an honorable death in service to the Supremacy." He nodded toward the edge, where a Marine waited with an extended hand. "But by all means, you go first."

The tunnel had emerged high on the opposite side of the cliff face, where the lip of the Cut sank backwards at a gentle angle until it levelled off, and the wind lashed over the featureless rock, driving temperatures already below freezing down lower still. Laurent cursed vociferously, as if the heated language would warm her up, having to squint her eyes against the dirt particles carried by the wind.

But they were out, thank Mithra, and being clear of the place gave her a surge of adrenalin, though she couldn't know how far away would be far away enough. She shielded her eyes against airborne dust with a bladed palm and tried to see which direction would be the quickest descent back down into the canyon. She looked over to Grieg to see if he had a better idea of where exactly they were.

"Which way should we…"

The world shifted beneath her and suddenly she was flat on her stomach, the vibration coursing up through her body and into the air, her teeth clattering so hard she bit her tongue and tasted blood. She wanted to close her eyes but she had to see, had to know if death was coming this time, if she'd finally used up all of her luck. Fissures opened up further down the gentle slope, gaping black wounds in the rock, spewing geysers of dirt and sand and steam.

Below them, she knew, the treasures of the Empire, weapons and technology worth more than a planet, were being vaporized in nuclear fire or buried under mountains of rock. She felt the loss even as she still feared for her life, felt the opportunity slipping away. Sparta had slipped in under their noses, a thief in the night; and now, caught in the act, they were throwing it all on the fire rather than let their enemies have it.

She should have felt rage. It would have been the proper reaction as a loyal officer of the Supremacy. But a sense of loss weighed her down instead, at the waste of it all, of yet another remnant of the Empire slipping from their hands and leaving them all the less for it.

The quaking died away to a few tremulous aftershocks, fading in intensity with each second, and she carefully pushed herself back to her feet. Grieg was dusting off his uniform, all the anger and frustration she hadn't succumbed to apparently drifting over to wash against his shores.

"Sir," Captain Gerhardt said, coming up to a knee, a hand against the side of her helmet as if she could shut out the external sound and hear the radio more clearly, "it's Lt. Gustaf. He reports there was a major landslide down in the Cut." She hesitated. "He says the drop-ship is intact and flyable, but six of our mecha are damaged, two of them buried. We have two KIA and three wounded who should make it if we get them back to the *Sleipner* quickly."

A longer pause and even though Lautner couldn't see Gerhardt's face, she was fairly certain the woman was scared to relay the next pronouncement.

"Gustaf also says he heard from the *Sleipner* and they weren't able to intercept the enemy starship before she jumped. Captain Dennison is decelerating at maximum gees and should be heading back to Terminus orbit soon."

Grieg didn't answer the Marine officer, didn't even look at her. With long, determined strides, he stepped over to the prisoner, still prone in the dirt while the Marines who'd been carrying him regained their footing and secured their weapons. Leaning down, Colonel Grieg grabbed the Spartan by the front of his tactical vest and yanked him to his feet, a hiss of expelled breath the only hint it had taken any effort at all.

"You think this is funny, Spartan?" he yelled into the soldier's face. The Spartan was grinning tautly, through a mask of pain from the bruise already forming on his cheek where one of the Marines had slugged him during the struggle. "You think you outsmarted us?"

Grieg's right fist flashed in a short, brutal jab, catching the enemy soldier square in the face with a flat, sickening smack. The Spartan toppled backwards, blood pouring from his nose, eyes glazed over, and Grieg let him fall then followed the punch with two vicious kicks to the ribs. Laurent jerked backwards with each kick, almost as if Grieg were striking her instead. The prisoner wheezed and coughed, features screwed up in agony, a river of red flowing across his cheeks from his smashed nose, but said nothing.

"Get him up," Grieg snapped at the Marines. "Captain Gerhardt, tell Gustaf to have the mecha that are still mobile load immediately, then have him land here and pick us up. We're a good forty-five-minute hike down the cliff from the landing zone and I don't trust this one…" He indicated the prisoner by spitting in his general direction. "…not to try killing himself on the way down."

Two of Gerhardt's troops grabbed the enemy soldier and hauled him back to his feet. Grieg tensed as if he wanted to hit the man again and Laurent flinched in anticipation. Her superior controlled himself this time, visibly and with apparent difficulty.

"When I get you in the interrogation room on my ship," Grieg told the prisoner, the words each filled with more violence than any kick to the ribs, "you're going to wish you'd saved a bullet for yourself."

4

"I wish every day could be like this," Logan Conner mused, fingers tracing a line down Katy Margolis' bare shoulder.

Nearly two weeks of sunshine had turned her skin to a soft brown and brought out the highlights in her hair. She'd let it grow longer and between the tan and the hair and the swimsuit, she might have passed as a native of these islands, the heir to the fortune of some interstellar shipping firm who passed her days sipping tropical drinks on a sailboat.

It was a fair assumption, given they *were* lying on the foredeck of a sailboat, sipping tropical drinks. But the truth was, Katy had been born on one of the rougher colony worlds to a doctor and a priest of the Old Religion and had wound up as an assault shuttle pilot in the Spartan Navy. How she'd wound up with Logan was a much more convoluted story.

"If every day were like this," she countered, draining the dregs of her drink from among the ice cubes, "we'd both get bored pretty damn quick."

He shrugged, resting his head back against the towel and staring out at the sea stacks off Golden Beach, backlit by the setting sun, a ball of fire sinking into the sea. Two other sailboats were visible in the distance, rocking in the waves at the mouth of the inlet, sails down, anchored like them. Maybe diving for lobsters, or maybe just enjoying the sunset as the two of them were.

"I'd be willing to give it a shot," he allowed.

"What?" She chuckled and the rich throatiness of the sound tickled at his stomach. "You're going to give up being a mech-jock, give up being the son of a Guardian, groomed to be the next ruler of Sparta, to become a beach bum?"

"There's no law that says the Council has to choose from among the family of the Guardian," he reminded her. "They could just as easily pick one of their own to follow my father."

"No rule," she agreed, rolling over off the towel onto his chest and looking him in the eyes over the top of her sunglasses, "but a shitload of tradition." The warmth and the slick softness of her skin pressed against his own threatened to break his concentration on what she was saying and he had to force himself to stay focussed.

"Let's say you gave up on being Guardian," she proposed, "what then? Could you sit back and watch someone else take over from your father after he retires or, God forbid, passes away?"

She crossed herself reflexively as she said it and he tried not to frown. He knew she'd been raised the Old Religion, what had been called Christianity back before the Empire had instituted Zoroastrianism as the state religion, but she'd been trying to convert when he met her. Since their experiences hunting for Terminus, though, she seemed to have begun falling back to the path of her youth. He didn't know why it bothered him, but it did.

"What if it's someone who's unqualified?" she kept prodding. "What if you think you'd do better? Could you just stand by and watch them run all of the Guardianship of Sparta aground just so you could stay out of politics?"

"I don't know." He was honest with her because he was

always honest with her. "All I ever wanted to be was a soldier, but sometimes I feel like I've done enough fighting for two lifetimes."

"I heard someone say once that the average person only sees like fifteen seconds of real danger in their whole life," Katy said. Her fingers teased at his chest hairs, a playful gesture but belied by the troubled expression passing over her face. "I think the two of us are making up for a planet-full of cloistered librarians and priests."

"So, let's give it all up," he said, raising his head off the towel.

The boat tossed back and forth fitfully on the gentle bobbing of the waves, but their eyes remained locked on each other. She pulled her sunglasses off and dropped them to the deck with a clatter of plastic, peering at him carefully, as if she were trying to make sure she wasn't misunderstanding him.

"Let's give it all up," he repeated. The words fell off him like a weight, one he'd been carrying around for weeks. "I can ask for a training position here on Sparta." He sucked in a deep breath, swallowed hard. "We could get married, start a family."

"I love you, Logan," she assured him, punctuating it with a quick kiss, leaning into him in time with the motion of the waves, then darting back out again, "but I don't know if I'm ready for a family yet. I'm definitely not ready to give up being a pilot."

"I wouldn't ask you to," he insisted, hands going to her shoulders, sliding down to her upper arms. "Maybe not go on any secret missions where you get shot down and almost killed..." He shrugged.

"So, you'd play stay-at-home Dad, working as a training officer here," Katy summarized, cocking a skeptical eyebrow. "while I go gallivanting around on maneuvers as an assault shuttle pilot?"

"Sure!" He laughed. "I know my dad would spoil the hell out of any grandchildren he had."

"Oh, God, Logan," she sighed, resting her chin on his chest. Her hair tickled at his neck. "You *would* spring this on me after we've been spending most of the last two weeks out here in paradise, after you've plied me with strong drink and first-class food."

"And great sex," he reminded her, grinning with a bit of smugness he was happy to acknowledge.

"That goes without saying." She made a "pshaw" sound. "*I* was here."

"Ooh," Logan made a checkmark in the air, acknowledging the damage. "That's a low blow. Are you saying I wouldn't be able to perform satisfactorily without your help? Do I need to provide references now?"

Katy glared at him, though the half-upturn at the corner of her mouth told him it wasn't entirely serious. "Perhaps the moment when you're trying to convince me to marry you and have children isn't the right time to be mentioning all the other women you've slept with."

"Hey!" He put his hands up, palm-out, defensively. "I never said there were *that* many."

"I'm sure," she said, skepticism rich in her voice. "Handsome, dashing, son of a king, mech-jock…you probably had all sorts of problems getting girls."

"He's not technically a king…" He trailed off, frowning at the far-off rumble of jet engines. "What's that?" He sat up, bringing her up with him and scanned the sky, the blues already turning purple as the primary star sank deeper below the horizon.

"There." Katy spotted it first, used to looking for aircraft.

It was a glint of reflected light coming in opposite the sunset, from the mainland, only a few hundred meters off the water.

"Well, that's illegal as all hell," Logan grumbled.

Of the many things he loved about Golden Beach, one was the lengths the island and the surrounding shoreline communities had gone to in order to preserve the isolation and beauty of the place. And chief among those was outlawing aircraft overflights. If you wanted to get to Golden Beach, you came by sea, either in your own boat or the hovercraft ferry from the mainland. No exceptions, other than emergencies...

A chill went down his back, and he was fairly sure it wasn't from the onset of night.

"That's a government bird," Katy declared as it came even lower and slower, a silvery dart with military markings on the side.

Logan grabbed a t-shirt off the deck and slipped it on before getting to his feet to watch the approach. In a moment, Katy was beside him, wrapped in a terrycloth robe, slipping an arm around his waist and leaning into him. A light shudder ran through her shoulders and into his side and he knew she was feeling the same sense of dread he was.

The VTOL aircraft lowered itself on vectored-thrust nozzles, throwing up a spray of water as it skimmed the flat water of the inlet only a hundred meters away, settling down onto pontoons extending from struts on the lower fuselage. The jets sputtered again, slowly pushing the bird across the waves until it came to a gliding stop off the starboard bow of their sailboat. The hatch cracked open two meters to the rear of the cockpit, lowering a set of steps downward, and onto them emerged a short, dark-complexioned, round-faced man in the dress blacks of Spartan Military Intelligence.

"Acosta!" Katy exclaimed as if he were the last person on Earth she expected to see.

And perhaps he was. She—and Logan—had known the man as Lt. Francis Acosta, assigned as her co-pilot on the mission to find Terminus. They hadn't discovered until they'd arrived on the lost Imperial base that he wasn't actually Francis Acosta and he wasn't even in the Navy. He was with Military Intelligence under General Nicolai Constantine, and…

"My name is Patrick Bray," the man reminded Katy a bit truculently. "*Major* Bray, if you're of a mind to observe military courtesies, Commander Margolis." He shook his head as if realizing the pettiness of what he was saying. "Forget it. You two need to come with me immediately."

"What's wrong, Bray?" Logan demanded. He'd been promoted to Lt. Colonel himself—though secretly—so he didn't feel bad about not being particularly deferential. "Why are you here?"

"Your father sent me. I'm afraid your vacation's over. Wholesale Slaughter has another job."

"Show me," Logan said curtly. Katy's eyes grew wide at his tone, but she didn't say a word, shrinking into her chair. At least it was a comfortable chair, as well as antique and probably worth more than the whole house where she'd been born and raised. But what else would she expect from the Palace of the Guardian?

If General Nicolai Constantine noticed the insubordination in Logan's voice, he gave no indication. He tapped a command into the control panel built into the hand-polished oak of the Situation Room's ornate central table. Constantine was everything she'd imagined from the legends floating around him and the stories Logan had told her, a razor-sharp sword sheathed in an elegantly-tailored dress uniform, probably the most dangerous man in the whole Guardianship of Sparta if you counted up the men and women who'd died by his hand or at his command. And yet he was not nearly as intimidating as Logan's father, the Guardian himself, Jaimie Brannigan.

He towered above her, above Logan, even above the slender

height of General Constantine, and yet he still seemed stocky and massive across the chest and shoulders. He could have been a barbarian of ancient days, with a flowing mane of hair and a wild beard to go with it, but his red-blond hair was cut to nearly regulation length and his mustache and beard were neatly trimmed as befitted a former military officer and mech pilot. And if his uniform wasn't exactly what he'd worn in the Spartan Guard, it was close enough to seem a natural fit.

Jaimie Brannigan stood at the rear of the room, arms folded, eyes fixed in a glare at General Constantine. She knew from what Logan had told her that the Guardian blamed Constantine for not aborting the mission to Terminus once he'd found out Terrin was on board the *Shakak*, and apparently, that anger had resurfaced once the news of the Starkad attack on the base had come in.

A star map appeared in the holographic display projected into a tank nearly the size of the far wall, an extravagance she hadn't seen outside the theaters and museums in downtown Argos. Holo-tanks were damned expensive. The three-dimensional map rotated as Constantine traced a finger along a touch-pad and the view zoomed into a single system highlighted in red, down to the rocky, nearly-lifeless world orbiting the star. The word "Terminus" floated in space beside it, glowing green.

"This is what we know now. It was passed along to us by a system of undercover Military Intelligence relay ships set up in every system between here and Starkad. A ship receives the coded transmission, moves immediately to the jump-point, crosses through and transmits to the next ship, etc.... It still took days to get back to us, so bear in mind we are dealing with old intelligence here."

"Just get on with it, Nicolai," Jaimie Brannigan growled.

"The attack came without warning from any of our sources in Starkad, so we aren't sure how they found out about Terminus, but they came with one of their newer heavy cruisers, possibly the

Sleipner or the *Tyr*. Two of our three landers were able to make it to the escape ship in time, but the third was caught by one of their assault shuttles and destroyed on the ground…and Terrin was trapped."

Katy could have cut the tension in the air with a butter knife and while she knew Logan's father blamed Constantine, she also knew Logan was blaming himself for leaving Terrin on Terminus in the first place. She brushed the edge of his hand with hers, a reminder she was still there, and she thought she saw him let out part of the breath he'd been holding.

"We don't know the details of what happened next. The *Acrotiri* received a single transmission, lasting just a few seconds, from a ship their sensors clocked at over half light-speed."

"It's a stardrive-powered ship," Katy murmured, then blanched when Constantine glanced her way. Maybe Logan was used to dealing with the movers and shakers of the Guardianship, but she didn't like being around this much polished brass.

"Indeed," Constantine said with a nod. He touched another control and Terrin's voice came over the room's hidden speakers, as loud and clear as if he were standing beside her.

"This is Terrin. I'm on an experimental ship with limited fuel and I have the downloaded database from Terminus on data crystals with me. I'm heading to Trinity. Will be waiting there."

"The *Acrotiri* received this less than ten seconds before they jumped," Constantine added as a postscript.

"Where's Trinity?" Logan wanted to know. "Hell, *what* is Trinity?"

By way of an answer, Constantine slid his finger across the touch screen control and the view on the star map zoomed out and scrolled to their right so quickly she couldn't follow the distance in the digital ruler at the bottom of the display. It finally settled on a K-class star with two terrestrial-sized planets further in, colored black which meant they were lifeless, and glowing yellow, which meant they were also dangerously irradiated. Further out in the system, a single, massive gas giant loomed over all the rest of the worlds, but its larger moons were also black tinged with yellow.

"This used to be the Volturnus system, back when it was an Imperial outpost. It's smack in the middle of the Shadow Zone, the systems ravaged in the fall of the Empire and the civil wars that followed. According to the most complete records we could find, it used to have four habitables, two planets and two of the moons of the gas giant. Now, they're too highly irradiated to even land without heavy shielding." He shrugged and indicated the gas giant with a nod. "The atmosphere still works fine for mining helium and heavy hydrogen, though, and there are several wildcat platforms with crews scraping by a living selling to pirates and bandits and smugglers, and anyone else who'd rather stay away from legitimate sources of fuel. And this..." He scrolled again over to the system's asteroid belt, to one of the largest rocks. "... is Trinity. It's a fairly large asteroid turned into an operations station, business negotiation hub and recreational center for the gas miners."

"Is it like Gateway, then?" Logan wondered.

Katy knew what he was talking about, even if she hadn't had the chance to go aboard the pleasure station herself. Gateway was a quasi-legal space habitat in the fringes between the Dominions. It was where Logan and Lyta Randell had gone to recruit Captain Donner Osceola and his ship, the *Shakak*, to be part of the operation to find Terminus.

"Not at all," Constantine disagreed, shaking his head firmly, "other than that they both began life as a rock. Gateway is a product of the Empire, with its typical raw-power-solves-everything approach. They drilled the core of an asteroid, spun it and heated it up to create an oblong, hollow cylinder. This is just a rock." He jerked a thumb toward the representation of Trinity on the map. "Drilled into a bit at a time, until it has levels going all the way around in some places, but it's still a maze. Spun for gravity by the expedient of hitting it with successive rocks until it started spinning fast enough. It's crude and confusing and run by whichever criminal gang is on top at the moment."

"Good Lord," Katy murmured, an open pit forming in her stomach at the General's words. She leaned forward as if she could reach into the image. "We have to get him out of there!"

"But we can't afford to send a Spartan military force through other Dominions without permission," Constantine reminded her. "Not openly. Things are already tense enough right now with the Starkad forces seizing the contested systems on the border with Clan Modi. We could spark a war here, and not just with the Supremacy."

"Wholesale Slaughter has to go," Logan said.

Katy saw his eyes flicker her way with what might have been a bit of guilt in the look, and she knew he had to be thinking of what they'd said on the boat.

"It's your brother," she said, covering his hand with hers, and be damned what General Constantine or the Guardian himself thought. "We'll get him back."

And the rest of it can wait.

Logan nodded, either agreeing with her conviction they would get Terrin back or her judgement of their future plans, or perhaps both.

"We're going to need the crew gathered together within the day," he said, addressing the statement both to his father and the general. "And we're going to need the ship, if we're going to get there in time."

Jaimie Brannigan stepped forward, one hand going to his son's shoulder and the other to Katy's. She tried not to flinch away at the touch, even though it was from a man whose presence intimidated the hell out of her. It felt...familial. Accepting.

"You'll have whatever you need," he assured them. He glared at Constantine meaningfully. "Won't they, Nicolai?"

"Major Bray is arranging for equipment and troops to be on the drop-ships by the end of the day," Constantine said, not acknowledging his ruler's anger any more than he had Logan's curtness. "As for the ship…Colonel Randell is handling it."

"Bring Terrin back to me, son," Jaimie said, so softly Katy almost missed it right next to him. "And bring yourself back, too."

5

Lyta Randell wouldn't have admitted it, but she hated free-fall. Everything tilted and twisted and she was never sure which way to align herself, which threw off her inner ear even more than the microgravity. Her head was constantly stuffed up, she had no sense of smell or taste, and no matter how much anti-nausea medication she took, she was perpetually on the verge of puking.

Which was all just one more reason she hated Commander Larrabee. Besides being an officious, self-important prick, he seemed to be one of those rare people who were totally at home in microgravity and took every opportunity to show it. The ship-yard's control station was necessarily a zero-gee environment, built into the framework of the construction cradles, but it was aligned with a natural up and down for convenience and it was considered good manners to align yourself with the person you were talking to. Yet every time he approached, he was off at some angle relative to her and would always apologize in that patron-izing way of his and spin around like a damned ballerina and stop himself exactly in place with that smug smile plastered over his face.

"The modifications are complete?" she asked him, refusing to watch his acrobatic maneuvers this time, keeping her eyes locked on the ship.

The last time she'd seen it this way, able to look down the whole length of it, had been when they'd discovered it in the underground hangar on Terminus. It had changed considerably in its time at the shipyard orbiting Hecate, the larger of Sparta's moons, its sleek, slender lines kludged and muddied in an attempt at maskirovka. A fusion drive bell had been added to the stern for use when under observation to conceal the secret of the ship's reactionless stardrive, and dummy fuel tanks were clustered around the aft to add to the illusion. It was a shame; the ship had been beautiful, deadly and graceful, but now it looked like a freighter, which was the idea.

"Oh, certainly, Colonel," Larrabee replied. "I mean," he equivocated, "there may be a few minor cosmetic issues to clean up, but the changes were mostly external to begin with, except for the addition of the point defense system and the new control suite. And, of course, we kept the whole thing compartmentalized, as you and General Constantine ordered."

So compartmentalized, you throw Constantine's name around at the drop of a hat, she thought, checking out of the corner of her eye whether any of the duty crew had been listening.

"Would you care to see footage of the tests we ran her through at the proving grounds before we began the modifications? It's quite impressive."

"I've seen it," she said flatly. "And even if I hadn't, no one in the crew here is cleared to be present for it."

It *had* been impressive. Even lacking the antimatter power plant the Imperial vessel had been designed around, it could till accelerate at the equivalent of nearly thirty gravities and, more importantly, lose its forward momentum immediately upon deactivation of the drive field and immediately boost off on another heading. The drive field also acted as a defense shield, more effective than the deflectors Dominion military vessels were equipped with, able to shunt aside lasers as well as projectile weapons. It had seemed surreal watching the lasers—well, the computer simulations of the lasers, since the actual beams were invisible in a vacuum—*bending* away from the ship, following the line of warped space around it.

And that wasn't even considering the weaponry, which was some sort of particle beam. They still couldn't figure out exactly what *sort* of particle it accelerated, and it wasn't nearly as powerful as when it had been fed by an antimatter reactor, but it could still overload the deflector screens on all but the largest of military ships with one or two shots.

If we had a fleet of these, we could take down Starkad in a single battle.

But they only had the one, and its mission wasn't quite so dramatic, though nearly as important.

"If I may say, Colonel," Larrabee droned on as if he hadn't noticed the rebuke she'd couched in her answer, "I don't know how you can rationalize putting such a powerful weapon into the hands of these…well, *criminals* isn't too strong a word. This ship should be crewed by the best Sparta has to offer! Why, I'd be honored to be considered for a position on her!"

"Commander, the people crewing the *Shakak II* have proven themselves in battle. You have not. They've shown themselves capable of maintaining operational security under some very dark circumstances. You can't keep your mouth shut just slapping a new paint job on the *fucking* ship."

Lyta's words were as hard as a naked nuclear core, but her glare was even harder, and finally a bit of green made its way onto Larrabee's face. She bit down on what she wanted to say next, realizing her elevated rank wasn't a license to tell every rear-echelon wannabe what she thought of them, even one who thought he could jump from a drydock babysitter to a spot on a ship he probably considered invulnerable. She sucked in a breath, held it for a moment, let it out.

"If you want to serve in a combat command, I suggest you put in for a transfer to the active fleet and do your time on a line vessel. Once you've laid your life on the line in the face of the same long odds these people have, then you can apply for a place among them."

Larrabee's face fell in on itself and she thought just maybe he finally understood what he'd said.

"Ma'am, I didn't—"

"Just have this ship put together and ready to sail in six hours, Commander. That's your mission, and I won't accept failure."

She pushed away from the bulkhead and headed out of the control room, leaving him to consider what, exactly, she'd meant.

"This is what that bastard calls 'cosmetic issues?' I'm going to have his ass cleaning the shitters on that fancy drydock of his!" Lyta Randell's face was turning a very interesting shade of red. Kamehameha-Nui Johansen couldn't make up his mind if it would best be described as coral or salmon, but he was thinking about buying a shirt in the color.

"It's not as bad as it looks, *ho'onani*," he insisted. The word meant "beautiful" in his great-grandmother's tongue, a language called Polynesian. "It's just kind of how things ended up."

He waved at the nightmare of cables, bypasses, and splices all kludged together with insulated tape and all running out of the rear of the center command console and then out to the rest of the bridge's stations. The command console's displays were haptic holograms, as sophisticated and beyond their technological level as anything else they'd found on Terminus; but the stations slaved to it were conventional, with two-dimensional touch-screens and even the acceleration couches at the terminals seemed jury-rigged and half-assed.

"I mean, this is an operating system based on a fucking neural halo like in a mech, but not just for things like balance and fine motor skills; this thing read the pilot's mind. It wasn't easy patching conventional controls into it, and the only access point was the emergency manual control terminal." He gestured at the source of the spider-web of cables. "We had to run everything out of one point, and that means no redundant systems, which means everything has to be out in the open in case we get a break or an overload." The big man laughed. "I guess we could have just counted on Katy to be the pilot for every trip, since the damned system wouldn't work for anyone else after she turned it on, but I think she likes shuttles a bit more than starships."

"I suppose," Lyta sighed, fingers wrapped in the loop of a handhold affixed to the bulkhead to keep her from floating away with the exhale of breath. "But it doesn't seem very military."

"I like it," he told her, grinning broadly. It was the only way he knew how to grin. "It reminds me of the old boat..." He shrugged, the motion of his broad shoulders trying to carry him away from the acceleration couch and control station at the center of the ship's bridge. It seemed even more out of place and rigged together than the others, perhaps because of who wasn't there to sit in it. "It reminds me of the Captain."

He felt guilty for bringing up Donner Osceola. Sure, he'd loved the Captain like a brother, but Lyta had *loved* him. Pain sailed across the familiar seas of Lyta Randell's eyes, but she forced it back as she always did. He'd begun calling her *ho'onani* as a pet name when he'd first met her, when she'd been running an undercover operation for Spartan Intelligence and needed to hire a smuggler. But he should have called her *ikaika*, strong.

"Don would be proud to see you as Captain, Kammy," she told him. "He always thought you deserved your own ship."

He nodded, but couldn't speak. He'd seen the life drain out of the Captain's eyes after the battle with the Starkad cruiser *Valkyrian*, seen him slip away just as salvation was at hand, just as Katy had destroyed the enemy vessel with this very ship. He couldn't get the image out of his head, and unlike the Captain, he didn't have the temperament to drink away bad memories.

"What are you two doing on my bridge?" Tara Gerard demanded, coming up behind Lyta and wrapping an arm around her shoulder. "Isn't it a big enough mess already?"

Tara was all that was left of the *Shakak's* original bridge crew besides Kammy, a fixture at the Tactical station. She looked for all the world like she'd just come off a three-week bender, her gaunt face perpetually drawn and flushed, her eyes showing the slightly blurry haze of the recently buzzed, her dark brown hair short and yet still somehow frizzy and uncontrolled.

The only thing organized about the older woman was her uniform, the same utility fatigues Kammy was wearing, with the logo of Wholesale Slaughter on the arm and the breast. Kammy knew Tara wouldn't have consented to wear the uniform of the Spartan Navy for all the money in the Five Dominions; but the blood they'd shed, the friends they'd lost had cemented them together under the banner of the mercenary company, fiction though it was.

"You heard the news?" Kammy asked her.

"About Terry? Yeah." They both knew his real name was Terrin Brannigan, younger son of the Guardian, but they'd come to know him as Terry Conner on the mission to find Terminus and it was hard to think of him any other way. "What are we waiting for? Let's go get him."

"That's why I'm here," Lyta told her. "It's more than just Terrin, though. He has the data files from Terminus, and since they probably had to blow the charges when Starkad raided the place, it's all we have left. We can't let anyone else get ahold of it."

"That shit's all well and good, *Colonel* Randell," Tara said with a dismissive snort, "but this is Terry we're talking about, and we're going to pull his ass out of the fire."

Kammy nodded enthusiastically. "What she said."

Lyta grinned, and Kammy knew she couldn't stay mad at Tara because no one could, not even the Captain.

"All right, then. The drop-ships will be arriving in four hours. If there's anything you need to do to get this boat ready to go, do it now."

Valentine Kurtz held his head and wished among all the technological treasures of the Empire they'd discovered on Terminus, they'd been able to find a cure for a hangover. The motion of the bus didn't help any, nor the close proximity of the other mech-jocks and their duffle-bags and backpacks. Half of them had been at the same bar in downtown Argos when the MPs had arrived, and the smell of stale beer and staler body odor was enough to make him want to puke.

"You know," Gerald Paskowski said, leaning in next to his ear to be heard over the rumble of the bus tires on the old, cobble-stone road, "maybe if you'd listen to me about mixing beer and liquor, you wouldn't be in this bad of a shape."

Kurtz looked up, feeling several days' worth of beard scraping against his hands as he met the taller, older man's eyes. Paskowski was obscenely fresh for a man who'd been on the same bender as the rest of them…well, the officers anyway. You didn't do this sort of thing with the enlisted, or even the Warrants.

"I thought the whole idea of this was to get in bad shape,"

he protested, his own words echoing inside his aching head. "We were supposed to be getting shitfaced in memory of Marc."

Marc Langella had been First Platoon leader, Logan Conner's second in command during the Terminus mission, but he hadn't made it to their objective; he'd died fighting a splinter group of Jeuta pirates along the way. Kurtz couldn't remember whose idea it had been to have this memorial, but it had seemed like a good time for it, with Colonel Conner away on leave with his girlfriend.

"There's shitfaced and then there's shitfaced," Paskowski said unhelpfully. Kurtz couldn't tell if he was being so cryptic because he was still buzzing or if it was just the way he was. Probably the latter. It had taken a good two hours to stop by the Bachelor Officers' Quarters and grab everyone's go-bags and personal items and they'd all pretty much dropped whatever buzz they'd been carrying.

"I drank enough to feel good," Paskowski went on. "I don't think Marc would have wanted me to punish myself. We only get one go-around and I don't see the point in making myself miserable."

"Dude," Mandy Ford moaned from behind Paskowski, putting a hand on his shoulder, "you're way too fucking philosophical lately. Can't we just get drunk for once without turning it into a church service?"

She was one to talk. She looked as if she'd just shown up for a parade formation, despite the fact she'd been hitting it as hard as any of them. Aliyah Hernandez shared a seat with her fellow platoon leader and had the decency to at least share in Kurtz's disheveled appearance if not his obvious pain.

"Just face it, Val," Hernandez said, not slurring her words but savoring each one, "you're a lightweight backwoods colony world hick who can't handle city life and can't hold your liquor.

It's probably just as well you're going into combat, where it's safer for you."

"You think that's where we're headed?" Summer Prevatt asked. She hadn't been along on the pub crawl; the bus had grabbed her at the BOQ. Kurtz thought she hadn't felt comfortable coming along because she was the newest of them and still just a newly-minted Sub-Lieutenant, field promoted from Warrant to take over Langella's platoon after his death.

"No," Kurtz drawled, eyeing her balefully, "I think they sent MPs after us at two in the morning because Colonel Conner got bored out there on his beach vacation and decided he needed us to really make it a good time."

Prevatt reddened in obvious embarrassment and Kurtz sighed, blaming the sarcasm on his hangover.

"Sorry, yeah, I'm pretty sure there's a fire burning someplace they'll be wanting us to put out."

"I hope they got my new Arbalest set up the way I asked." Ford sniffed impatiently. "I don't trust these dirtside crews. Wish they'd just let Chief McKee work on our mecha down here like he does on board the ship."

She was, he noticed, rubbing at her left shoulder unconsciously as she spoke, and he wondered if it was actual pain or just the memory of the injuries she'd received when her missile platform mech had been disabled by an enemy machine. She'd nearly been killed, but it didn't seem to have bothered her. Not that she'd let on, anyway.

"You can get the Chief to go over it en route," he suggested instead of asking her if she was okay, which was his first instinct. Some things you just didn't talk about. "Quick as they shanghaied us on this little trip, I just hope they have our damned mecha loaded on the drop-ship."

"You're about to find out." That was the driver, an enlisted man who'd said not a word to them the whole trip until this point.

They might as well have been riding an automated city vehicle, except the military didn't use automated vehicles. Got all those enlisted troops sitting around, might as well use them to drive the trucks. "We're here."

Kurtz blinked and peered out the side window, realizing the Private was right. He'd been so wrapped up in his headache, he hadn't noticed they'd reached the main gate of the military space-port outside Argos. It was sliding aside on motorized rollers, the automatic sensors reading the clearance codes in the vehicle's transponder, and the driver edged forward through before it had fully opened, tires bumping roughly over the couched security spikes.

"There it is," Paskowski decided, gesturing at the massive, hundred-meter-long lifting body shape of a drop-ship resting on a landing pad a half a kilometer down the service road.

A train of power-loaders cycled in and out of its cargo bay, each carrying a heavy pallet of parts or ammo or raw materials. Unlike every other aerospacecraft at the port, it lacked the seal of the Spartan military on the fuselage, carrying no markings other than a temporary clearance number. Once they were on board, the techs would affix the Wholesale Slaughter badge to the side.

Op-sec, the same reason they were wearing their Spartan Guard uniforms rather than their Wholesale Slaughter fatigues. Those too would be donned once they were on board the *Shakak II*, just in case Starkad spies were watching.

Ain't no "just in case" about it. The bastards have spies everywhere.

"This is where you officer types get out," the driver announced, pulling the bus up behind a cargo truck being drained by power-loaders and taken pallet by pallet up the belly ramp. "Don't leave any of your shit on my bus."

"I'd chew that fucker out," Kurtz assured Paskowski, grabbing his bags, "but I can't yell with this headache."

Paskowski snorted a laugh, throwing his duffel bag across his back.

"I've never heard you yell at anyone, Val. I'm not sure you've got the constitution for it."

"I yelled at my dog once," Kurtz assured him. He frowned. "I don't think he ever forgave me."

Logan Conner was waiting for them at the foot of the ramp. Kurt didn't salute despite an almost overwhelming urge to; they'd been instructed to avoid it on the flightline, again for operational security.

"Good morning, sir," Kurtz said, nodding to the man instead. "I think you got yourself a tan still."

Logan Conner lacked his father's intimidating height and mass, but there was something resolute in his grey eyes, in the squared-offset of his jaw that gave a hint of the determination he brought in a fight. If the man wasn't fearless, he at least hadn't shown even a moment's hesitation in battle. He knew Logan was worried people would think he'd been given his Colonel's rank because of his father, but in Kurtz's opinion, he'd earned it.

"Glad they were able to scrape you guys off the bar, Val," Logan told him. His expression sobered and he regarded each of them as they lined up at the ramp. "I can't tell you all the details until we're in the ship, but Terrin's in trouble. He's on the run and we have to go get him."

Kurtz swallowed hard, his headache forgotten. He shared a look with the others, a hollow opening up in the pit of his stomach. Terrin had been on Terminus, and if was in trouble, that could only mean one thing. Starkad had found them. Terminus had fallen.

"Let's not stand around jawin' then, sir," Kurtz said. "Let's get this bird in the air and go find your brother."

6

"I wish we had a gun," Terrin fretted, tapping his fingers on the control console while he waited for traffic control to reply.

"You think we'll need one?" Franny asked, her voice telling the strain of the last three days.

The ship had water, and while they were getting pretty hungry, the ration bars Cordova had given them had kept them going. But the confined quarters had been maddening. Three full days trapped in a space barely large enough for the two of them to fit, unable to move, unable to stretch…it had felt like being buried alive. Not to mention the smell, and the embarrassment of having to use the weird zero-gee vacuum device to go to the bathroom while sitting right next to each other.

"In this place?" Terrin nodded toward the image projected on the front display, the slowly-rotating surface of Trinity, glinting and glimmering with solar collectors. "Hell yes,"

There were two docking hubs, one at each pole, and he was waiting to access what they'd dubbed the north polar dock behind a pair of orbital transfer vehicles, standing out like a whore in church. If you looked carefully enough, you could see the weapons batteries wedged between the solar panels and around the docking hubs of the dwarf planet, targeting anyone who threatened the station or its clientele…and probably anyone who tried to leave without paying docking fees.

"What kind of space station lets you bring a gun inside?" Franny wondered. "Even way out here, isn't that nuts?"

He tried not to sigh. He knew she found it annoying. After three days cooped up with each other, he was pretty much an expert on what she found annoying.

"It's only nuts if you assume the ownership and management are trying to cater to the sort of clientele who would think it's nuts to bring a gun onto a space station." He also tried hard not to roll his eyes; she didn't care for that, either. "It's right there in the files on my datalink. This place was built for outlaws and pirates and mercenaries to do business with each other."

"And there's nowhere else we could go?" The question was a whisper, Franny's eyes fixed on the docking hub, yawning wide and dark and hungry ahead of them.

"We're down to minutes of fuel," Terrin said, shaking his head. "Once we dock, I doubt this ship is moving again unless someone tows it away."

"Unknown spacecraft, please identify yourself for docking records." The female voice coming over the cockpit speakers was professional sounding for a place like this, he thought, but maybe doing the same thing every day made you seem more businesslike about it.

"We don't have an official registration," Franny said, tension written on her face as if she'd just realized it.

"Neither do most of the other ships here," he reminded her. "They just want a name to put next to our identification profile for convenience." He scratched at his arm where the sleeve of his Wholesale Slaughter work fatigues was rolled up, feeling dirt under his fingernails. It felt as if he'd never get clean again.

His first thought was to name the ship for his mother, but he rejected it immediately, because there was a good chance he'd never see the thing again and he'd already lost his mother once.

"This is the orbital transfer vehicle *Francesca*," he told traffic control, just blurting out the next name that came to him. "We're a tender for the freighter *Margaret*."

The woman working traffic control snorted laughter. "If you're an orbital transfer vehicle, I'm the Imperator of M'beki. But I don't give a shit as long as you pay the 300 credit docking fee in tradenotes or Dominion scrip upon debarking. Proceed to polar docking collar A3."

"Right," Terrin answered, his stomach twisting into a Gordian knot. "No problem."

"Umm…" Franny stuttered, a strange look on her face, which he was sure had something to do with him naming the ship after her. "Do we have any money?"

"*Courier*, take us into the docking bay," he told the computer before turning to her and shrugging helplessly. "Not a single credit," he admitted. "All I have is my family account, if I can even access it here."

"Even if you can, should you?"

Maneuvering thrusters banged impatiently against the hull as the ship's computer guided them into the hollow cylinder of the docking bay, interrupting his answer and giving him another few seconds to think about it.

Shit. Why couldn't it be Logan dealing with this instead of me? I'm a scientist, not a soldier.

"No. But this isn't the kind of place where you can blow off the fees, and we don't have any other options."

The computer slid them into their berth as slickly and smoothly as any pilot who'd ever flown him. Better than Katy even.

Guess it's a good thing we can't build Artificial Intelligence that sophisticated anymore or she'd be out of a job.

The docking collar tightened around the courier's universal airlock with a resounding clunk he could feel in his sinuses and they had arrived. He yanked the quick-release on his restraints and pushed the control to open the hatch. It hissed aside as if the ship was sharing in his sigh of agitation.

"Courier," he instructed, "after we leave, seal the hatch and don't open for anyone except for the two us. If someone breaks or burns or blows through the hatch, I want you to wipe system memory. Do you understand?"

"I understand and will comply, Mr. Brannigan." If the computer was disturbed at the thought of suicide, it gave no indication.

"Franny," Terrin said, the pieces of a plan coming together in his mind even as he spoke, "when we get into the station, I'm going to see about using my family account to get some Trade-notes. We're going to need them, and it will be better if I only do the one transaction anyone can trace. Maybe we can buy transportation off this place before anyone can track it down," he said with more optimism than he felt. "While I do that, I need you to take the data crystals with you and go find someone."

"Find who?" she asked, her voice going a bit shrill. She'd released her own harness but was clinging to it like a life preserver. She was, he thought, close to panic and he didn't blame her.

"Something Lyta told me about," he explained, trying not to give into the gibbering building up inside him. "Someone you go to in places like this when you need things taken care of. They call them a broker."

"You'd trust someone *here?*" She looked between him and the opening hatch, the harsh light of the docking bay beyond it.

"No," he said, squeezing past her to lead the way out of the ship. "But I think we're going to have to."

I was not trained for this, Francesca Hayden screamed inside her head, wishing she had the luxury of screaming on the outside as well. *I'm a computer technician!*

She huddled in the corner of the lift car, clutching the case with the data crystals against her side, striving not to make eye contact with the ten other people squeezed into the elevator, and trying to make sure she was aligned correctly for when the rotation of the asteroid turned one of the walls into a floor.

She'd never felt more alone in her life. Not when her father had died and she'd hidden under the table where the bowls of sandalwood strips were kept to be tossed into the sacred fire, refusing to come out and talk to her friends or family. Not when she'd left home against her mother's wishes to follow in his footsteps and enlist in the Sparta Guard, not even on that horrible first day of military recruit training when they'd taken her civilian clothes, shaved her head, poked and prodded her, inoculated her, and shoved her into a grey jumpsuit. Not when the training sergeants had screamed at her and made her do push-ups until her arms wanted to fall off.

It had taken them nearly an hour to get through security, most of it due to Terrin haggling with the customs official about letting him pay for the docking berth before departure instead of leaving a deposit now. He'd finally had to agree to take one of the customs workers along with him to the currency exchange to get the deposit—and a healthy bribe—with the rest to be paid upon departure.

"You go, Franny," he'd told her, the broad-bodied, menacing bulk of his escort hanging impatiently over his shoulder. "Our 'links will work on the system here, so just message me and let me know where to meet you after you find what we're looking for."

And then he was gone and she'd been left staring at the thick-jowled little weasel who ran Customs for the station. He rested in a net running across the open, three-walled booth he inhabited to keep him stationary in free-fall, a bearded, sweating spider in his web. But the armored, helmeted guards anchored to the deck with magnetic boots beside him kept the customers respectful, or at least the backpack-fed lasers they carried did.

"Where can I find a broker?" she'd asked him, trying not to stutter the words out.

The man sniffed in derision, as if he didn't think much of the profession; but he waved a hand down the corridor, where a small crowd of inbound travelers were heading for a lift station.

"Those termites are in the walls almost everywhere," he grumbled. "But I suppose the most reliable is probably that bitch Kane in G-42."

She'd wanted to ask him where G-42 was, but she'd felt as if it would have been pushing her luck. Fortunately, the elevator came with a sort of map, although it was as complicated as a circuit diagram. Her eyes wanted to cross just staring at it and the car was already moving before she'd found the corner of the rock labelled "G."

Did anyone actually plan this place out, she wondered, *or did it grow organically like a crystal in a solution?*

"What the fuck's a 'Wholesale Slaughter,' anyway?"

Her eyes were furtive, like a bird's, and she realized she must look like prey to these people and made an effort to move calmly as she turned to see who had asked the question. It was a woman, probably from either a low-gravity world or a Belter since she had to be nearly two meters tall and was painfully thin. Her face was stretched out like a waxworks figure caught in a fire and the image made Franny's skin crawl. She wore a shoulder holster openly over her quilted vest, and the handgun nestled in it seemed oversized, its handle no doubt custom made for her long, slender fingers.

"Mercenary company," she said, trying to sound confident.

Apparently, it didn't work. The woman guffawed far too loudly for the packed elevator, drawing stares from the other passengers.

"You're a mercenary? What? A fuckin' mercenary accountant?"

"I'm a computer technician," she confessed.

The woman shrugged it off and looked away, probably thinking it was a reasonable answer.

"I've heard of Wholesale Slaughter," someone else spoke up, a man this time, normal sized at least, even if it was the only normal thing about him. His hair was hardened into orange spikes and tattoos of winged snakes crisscrossed his face, running downward onto his neck before disappearing under his shirt. "You're the ones who took out the Red Brotherhood."

"Yeah, and those Jeuta assholes out in the Dagda system," someone she couldn't see put in from behind the Belter woman.

"Umm, yes," she agreed readily, then gulped as the car began to descend outward toward the rim of the asteroid, and centripetal force began to pull them all to the deck. "But I wasn't with them for those; I just signed up a couple months ago." Hopefully, they wouldn't ask her a lot of questions she couldn't answer if they believed she was a new recruit.

"They pay good?" the spike-haired man asked, sounding sincerely interested. "I'd love to get off this fucking rock and back to Revelation."

Oh, shoot, she thought with a surge of panic. *I don't know what they're supposed to pay!*

"We, umm..." she fumbled for something likely-sounding. "We each get a share of the profits and salvage. How much depends on the job. There's a signing bonus," she added in a flare of creativity, "but it depends on your specialty, experience and former military rank."

"What the fuck do you care, Larry," asked a short, dumpy woman who looked eighty to Franny but was probably forty given the medical technology out here. "You won't be able to pay off your debt to Salvaggio for another ten years! She'll have your balls if you try to duck out on it, and where would you go anyway?"

A confusing, rapid-fire cross-talk ensued and she wasn't able to follow all if it, though she got the general idea Salvaggio was the one who controlled Trinity, or was allied with the ones who did, and a lot of the people who lived and worked there were from a place called Revelation and owed Salvaggio money. The conversation petered out as the lift began making stops, and she thought the people who'd been interested in her had left for one level or another, but then Larry appeared next to her, squeezing past the new entries and leaning in conspiratorially to speak in her ear.

"Do you think you could sneak me out of here?" he asked her, voice so soft she could barely hear him. "I mean, if they want to hire me? Or I could pay you a little and maybe work the rest off?"

The man, she realized, was desperate; she could smell his fear and it was contagious, infecting her by osmosis. Her breath was coming quicker, oncoming panic pressing down on her like the faux gravity, increasing the further the lift descended.

"I'll ask," she blurted, perhaps a bit too loud. "I'll ask my team leader and see what he says."

"My name's Larry," he told her urgently as the lift stopped again and his eyes darted toward the door. "Larry Tirado! I'm a tech in operations in level M-63…don't forget!"

And then he was gone, sliding out the door and merging with the crowd beyond, and she tried to breathe again. She barely had herself back under control when she saw the indicator flip to G level and she joined the press of bodies heading out the door, the storage box cradled in her arms. The corridor outside the lift was broad but low-ceilinged, barely tall enough for the Belters who frequented the station to avoid scuffing their heads against the cheap light panels or the air recycling vents sealed into tunnels burned through the rock. Water dripped from the vents into catch basins and was vacuumed up, presumably to be recycled as well.

The place was nothing like the orbital stations or military bases she'd been aboard back in Spartan space. Those had been metal boxes, antiseptic and ruthlessly efficient. This was a cave, albeit one dug by humans rather than water erosion. The people wandered through the tunnels like blind mole-rats who would never see the sun, never feel it on their skin. They bustled from one task to another, from one meal to another, from one vacuous entertainment to another and barely lifted their hopeless eyes.

She shivered at the image, but steeled herself, clutched the data crystals to her chest and stepped out into the maze of rats.

7

The bald man squinted at Terrin over the screen of his terminal and smirked, the glow of the display lighting up his face green in the low light of the little cubicle.

"You know there's a pretty big fee for this, right?" he asked. "I mean, like, there's a 300-credit fee and also a twenty percent charge on top of that. And if you ain't in the latest updates, you're gonna have to wait until the next relay ship comes through the jump-gate with new data. Sure you ain't got nothing you can sell?"

Terrin was very conscious of the oversized thug from Customs standing over his shoulder, but he considered, for just a moment, whether he might be able to sell the *Courier*. It was useless to him and anyone else without processed antimatter fuel, and he was sure no one would be able to reverse engineer the thing without destroying it, but it felt wrong. Besides, it would probably get him into trouble even quicker than the funds transfer.

"No, let's just do it."

"It's your money, kid." The bald, doughy-faced clerk tapped at the surface of the touch screen with the desultory crawl of someone who was going to be working all day whether they helped you or not. He spun the screen around and pointed to a pad on the corner. "Put your thumb there for DNA ID and stare into the red dot for a retinal scan."

It won't tell them my real identity, he assured himself, following the clerk's instructions without enthusiasm. *Not yet.*

No, it wouldn't tell the clerk, but if anyone was smart enough to back-trace the routing codes, they'd be able to tell it went pretty far up the Spartan government ladder. And what was that saying Lyta had kept trying to drum into him? "Just because they're bad doesn't mean they're stupid."

"Okay," the clerk said, tilting his head back and forth like a metronome as he waited for the system. "…and there we go."

He opened a drawer of his desk, pushed a button and then nodded to an armored guard propped up on a stool in the corner. The man had been motionless and Terrin had thought he might be asleep behind the closed and darkened visor of his helmet, but he pushed up to his feet almost immediately and stepped over to a safe set in the wall. He raised his flechette gun across his chest, barrel at about a forty-five-degree angle, what he'd heard Lyta refer to as high port, and watched as the clerk entered a code into the lock panel, making sure to put his back between Terrin and the display so he couldn't read it over his shoulder.

When the clerk turned back around, he held a stack of paper-thin plastic chips, each infused with a pattern of nano-circuits programmed with a non-counterfeitable code. Terrin took them gingerly; he'd never actually used them before, though he'd seen them in action and mystery shows he'd streamed. Their texture was rough, bumpy, like the skin of a fruit except so thin he could fold them in two and fit them in a pocket. Sweat trickled down the back of his neck as he counted out the amount he owed Customs and handed it back to the agent. The big man counted them again before nodding, his greasy dreadlocks waggling in the lower gravity, and turning away to head for the lift station.

"Be careful with those, kid," the clerk advised him. "You got a big enough stack there, some people might kill for it."

Terrin shoved the bills in his pocket quickly, getting them out of sight before he stepped out of the tiny office. Tradenotes were the life-blood of the black market, the only currency everyone took wherever they went without any sort of identification or authentication or an established account required. He felt eyes on him, as if he wore a sign around his neck advertising fresh meat, and he hurried away from the area, hoping if he got far enough, no one would know he'd been there.

He heard the chime of his 'link and fished around in his jacket pocket until he found it and raised it to eye level. It was a message from Franny and he sighed with relief just to be getting it. He'd been worried about her going off alone. He read the text scrolling across the display of the 'link and allowed himself a smile. She'd found them a broker. He fashioned a quick reply and headed for the lift banks.

It was time to get rid of all this money.

The place was dark and intimate without seeming stifling or claustrophobic, the soft grey of the curtains separating the room from the stark reality of bare rock. It reminded Francesca of a blanket fort she'd made with her cousins during a sleepover when they were six.

"Your friend here tells me you're the money man," the woman said in a strange, outland accent, leaning back on her thick cushion as she regarded Terrin. "I am Lana Kane, and I make arrangements. What would you like to arrange?"

The room suited Kane. Her robes were the same soft grey as the curtains, perhaps made from the same materials, and cheaply fabricated bits of jewelry shone red and blue and green where it was braided into her thick, auburn hair. She had the mannerisms of one of the actors who performed on the street corners outside the temples for the glory of Mithra…and contributions from the faithful.

It had taken Franny almost an hour to find the woman. G-level was a fractal pattern of blind curves and dead ends and she'd been terrified to ask anyone, but she'd finally worked up the courage to speak to one of the custodial workers. Then she'd had to find someone else to ask because the directions the custodial worker had given had deposited her at the door of a kiosk selling some sort of fried soy on a stick. The soy *had* been delicious, even if it had cost her the golden anklet her last boyfriend had given her as a birthday gift.

Even when she'd found the broker, she hadn't wanted to risk approaching her alone, not carrying the data crystals. She'd wound up waiting another half an hour for Terrin to find his way to her. It hadn't taken him as long because he'd been able to trace her 'link's location and follow her path.

"How do I know we can trust you?" Terrin asked.

"You can ask around, if you have the time," she invited him, her voice lilting, almost musical. "Or I can give you some sob story about how I worked my way up from mopping floors to brokering deals for the big boys and girls in the five years I've been stuck on this Mithra-forsaken rock trying to pay off my debt to Momma Salvaggio. Or you can just get down to business."

Terrin's eyes flickered from Kane to her assistant, a stooped-over old man pushing a broom across the floor.

"Gustavo," Kane said sharply. "Leave us for now."

When the other man had gone, Terrin gestured for Franny to hand him the storage box with the data crystals. He set it gently down on the low table in front of Kane and let his fingers slide off it with obvious reluctance.

"I need this kept safe," he told Kane, gesturing at the box.

"There are going to be people coming, I think, who want to take it, and we can't have it with us when they do."

Kane ran the tip of her forefinger across the lid, but didn't ask what was in it.

"And if you don't return for it?" she wanted to know.

"Someone is going to come looking for me. My brother, a man named Jonathan Slaughter." From the slight hesitation in his voice, Franny could tell he'd almost used his brother's real name, Logan Conner. "He's the only one you can give it to. I'll pay you everything I have right now, ten thousand credits, and he'll give you that much again if you keep your eyes open and contact him when he boards this station."

Kane's eyes went wide, though Franny thought she saw some skepticism amidst the awe at the price he was offering. Terrin pulled the Tradenotes out of his jacket pocket and handed them over to the woman and her hazel eyes grew wider still, her mouth nearly falling open. Then her expression narrowed in what might have been caution, or perhaps fear.

"Who's going to be looking for this?" she demanded.

"The Supremacy," Terrin answered with an honesty that surprised Franny. "And if you're thinking you could sell it to them and get a better deal, I don't think they're in a bargaining mood." He made a face, as if he were remembering what had happened on Terminus. "They're more in a 'let's take this and kill everyone who ever saw it' kind of mood."

Kane seemed to consider it for a moment, eyes travelling between the box and the money until greed won out over caution like a switch being flipped, visible in her expression.

"All right," she said, tucking the money away somewhere under her robes. "It's a bargain." She spat into her palm and offered him her hand.

Terrin regarded the hand for a beat, clearly disturbed by the gesture but just as clearly not wanting to give offense. He raised his palm up to his mouth and copied her gesture before shaking her hand. Kane unfolded smoothly, with the grace of a gymnast or a dancer, picking up the box as she rose. She half-turned as if she were going to take the thing away with her, but paused and gave Terrin a significant glance.

"This is a lot of money," Kane said, frowning. Franny had the impression the other woman was unhappy more about the pang of conscience she was feeling than she was about how badly she was ripping them off. "It's enough to pay for this, as well." Kane reached under her voluminous robes and pulled out a compact handgun, offering it butt-first to Terrin.

The young man took it gingerly, as if he were reluctant to touch it, but he kept the barrel pointed at the floor and checked the chamber and the safety with moves exhibiting some training, if not a great deal of practice.

"Thanks," he said with a nod, then tucked the weapon into his right jacket pocket. "Remember," he told her, "no one but Jonathan Slaughter."

"You paid your money," she said, ducking through a gap in the curtains to one of the back rooms, "and I'll do my job."

Franny waited until she was sure the woman was gone before she turned to Terrin, unable to contain the anger burning in her chest.

"You gave her *all* the money?" she exploded with righteous indignation. "We could have bought passage on a ship back into the Dominions with that much money!"

Terrin furiously shushed her and motioned towards the door. She followed him, grinding her teeth at the effort of keeping silent. When they were outside and down the corridor, in the sanctuary of the anonymous crowd, she cut loose again.

"She could just toss the box out an airlock or fucking *give* it to Starkad just to avoid getting into trouble," she hissed at him, shocking herself with her own language—she almost never cussed. "Why give her all our money and the box instead of trying to make a run for it?"

"Because no one here is going to give us a ride anywhere they could get spotted by the military or police of any of the Dominions," he shot back tautly, his voice low but intense. "They'd take our money then dump us and the data crystals out an airlock."

They were still walking, but Franny had no idea where they were headed, just an aimless weaving through the crowd to keep moving.

"Then why not just hold onto them until your brother gets here?"

"Because we're not going to last that long," he said. The anger had fallen away from his voice, the intensity gone from his eyes. His words had the tone of a terminal prognosis from a weary physician. "Someone's going to trace the money transfer. They won't know exactly who I am, but they'll know I'm Spartan government and that's enough to put a big, damned target on our backs."

His right hand was still stuffed in his jacket pocket, probably wrapped around the pistol. Cold realization settled into her core. He expected them to be attacked, taken prisoner, and he was going to use the gun to make sure they were killed instead. She wanted to scream at him, wanted to take the gun away, make him run back to Kane and get their money and the crystals back. This was insane…

"Terrin," she said, "there has to be something else, something we can do. Maybe that Kane woman could help us hide."

She knew the answer, knew the utter hopelessness of the words even as she said them, but they had to be said, a ritual she had to perform before she let herself give up hope.

"She can't hide us *and* the data crystals, Franny," he told her. He didn't seem annoyed with her, which was good because she probably would have hit him, commander's brother or not.

"Believe me, I don't like this at all." He whooshed out a breath as if he'd just run a mile. "I am not a soldier."

"Do you know how to use that gun?" she wondered.

"Yeah," he said, shrugging. "I've never used one on a person, though." He glanced over hopefully. "Do you want me to give it to you?"

"I've shot a pistol twice," she confessed, "and the last time was when I qualified during my promotion testing two years ago."

"Great."

They kept walking and she began to look around, trying to distract herself from the oppressive paranoia. No one seemed to be watching them, no one even glanced up from their own business, whether it be workers trudging from one task to another or travelers seeking their next deal. She began to notice the food kiosks; the fried soy hadn't quite filled in the gap left from three days at a ration of a quarter of a protein bar a day.

I'm hungry, she realized. *Maybe I'm not dead yet.*

"Did you at least save enough money to get us a room somewhere?" she asked. "Maybe some real food?" She nudged him with her shoulder, and the simple touch made the darkness lighten. "I mean, there's no point in being miserable while we wait around for someone to hunt us down."

He eyed her sidelong, snorting a disbelieving laugh.

"Yeah, I got a few credits left. Not enough for the Executive Suite, but maybe somewhere we could shower." He pulled at his collar with a finger and made a face. "And maybe we could buy some new clothes..."

He didn't finish the sentence. Between one step and the next, he stiffened and convulsed; there was the space of a heartbeat when she believed he was having some sort of attack and raised a hand to catch him. Then she saw the dart in his neck, sleek and metallic and still discharging an electric stun charge. He was collapsing, his eyes rolling up in his head, too stunned to even cry out, and she wanted to help him, to grab the gun from his pocket, wanted more than anything to run.

She was turning, spinning in place trying to find out where the attack had come from. She saw them, two men in dark clothing, nondescript, identical to the workers she'd let her gaze pass over. One of them had the dart launcher raised, pointed straight at her chest.

She never saw the round that hit her, just felt the instant surge of pain and then blackness.

8

"Great Mithra, how do people live in this place?" Saul Grieg murmured, shaking his head. He'd worn his combat armor, but left the helmet behind and Laurent wondered if it was for comfort or simply to assert his authority.

He seemed to be big on asserting his authority, so she guessed the latter. He certainly hadn't shied away from throwing his weight around here on Trinity, starting with the head-on approach in the *Sleipner,* guns trained on the station's polar docking ring, broadcasting a warning for all ships in dock to remain there or face destruction. She supposed after that, it had been wise to board the station in force to avoid hurt feelings leading to a confrontation, and a full company of Marines was enough to ensure no confrontations.

"They don't have much choice in the matter," she told him, speaking softly from her spot walking at his left shoulder, both of them clomping along the floor of the docking bay in magnetic boots.

Dull, soulless eyes stared back at her in silent resentment from the crowd of station employees held at bay by the guns of the Marine squad surrounding the Customs office.

"Most of the workers are little more than indentured servants forced to take jobs here to pay off their debt, or their family's, and the crews who come here for rest and recreation, or to make deals, are selling to outlaws or are outlaws themselves."

He eyed her sidelong, without turning his head.

"How are you such an expert on this damned hole in the wall, Laurent?"

"Intelligence analysis of the Periphery was my specialty, sir," she explained. Once, a lifetime ago, she would have said it enthusiastically. Now, her voice was as lifeless and listless as the faces of the workers. "It's how I spotted Wholesale Slaughter to begin with."

"Sir, I checked the security logs," Lt. Poretti reported stepping out of the Customs office, the jowly little man who ran it floating after him, a Marine's fist wrapped in the collar of his jacket to guide him.

Poretti's face was a dark blur inside his visor, but he had come to Laurent's acquaintance shipboard along the way. He looked as harmless as the delivery boy who'd brought raw food for their kitchen processors when she was a kid, but he was a computer network wizard who could break into anything but government and the very highest end corporate systems.

"It confirms what this one…" He jerked a thumb at the weaselly little man. "…told us before." He held up a field tablet and showed Grieg and Laurent an image taken here in the docking bay, showing a young man and an even younger woman, both wearing grey utility fatigues she recognized as the field uniform of Wholesale Slaughter, both appearing disheveled and weary. "The male identified himself as Terrin, no last name given; the female gave no name. They obtained Tradenotes to pay the Customs fee at the exchange, using a secure code I already traced back to a Spartan government account."

"I want to speak to the clerk who issued the funds," Grieg

declared. "And I want to know who they spoke to while they were here."

"What did they say to you?" Poretti asked the Customs agent, jabbing a gloved finger into the little man's chest. The Marine had purchase with his magnetic soles anchoring him, but the Customs man had none, and he would have floated backward if the trooper holding him hadn't tightened his grip. "What did these two tell you?"

"I don't know, man!" the local insisted, raising his hands palms out, defensively. "It was like four fucking days ago! Do you know how many people we have come through here?"

"Perhaps," Grieg suggested, "his memory would improve in the interrogation chamber on board ship." He sneered. "It certainly did wonders for the Ranger Captain, that Cordova fellow. May he rest in peace."

Laurent winced. She'd been forced to watch what they'd done to Cordova. Intelligence would never be a clean job, but there were lines she'd thought even someone like Grieg wouldn't cross. She was wrong.

"Wait!" the Customs agent cried out in desperation as the Marine behind him started to hustle him away toward their shuttle. "They…they asked about a broker!"

"What, in this context, is a broker?" Grieg asked him, the footsteps of his magnetic boots echoing through the passageway as he approached the little man. Laurent was impressed how menacing the Intelligence officer made those innocuous sounding words. He hadn't been asking her and she knew she was risking his wrath for speaking out of turn, but she answered anyway.

"They're go-betweens. Deal-makers. They arrange meetings, hold sensitive data, facilitate funds transfers." She shrugged. "The Spartans might have given the data crystals to a broker to safeguard or even try to smuggle them out of here."

"Who was this broker?" Grieg asked the Customs agent. "Who did you recommend them to?"

"Lana Kane," the man answered immediately. "She's small-time, but they seemed like small-time customers so I figured she'd be in their price range. She's got a storefront down in G-42."

"We're going down there," Grieg decided. "Poretti, bring this man with us so we don't get lost. Captain Gerhardt!"

The woman appeared at Grieg's elbow as if she'd materialized from thin air, an armored homunculus awaiting his command.

"First platoon is coming with us to search for this broker," he told Gerhardt. "You stay here with Second and keep trying to get into that damned ship." He indicated which damned ship with a jab of his finger back toward the docking umbilical leading out to the courier, the experimental Imperial ship the Spartans had arrived in. "If you can't access it without destroying it, then I want you to appropriate whatever equipment you need to from the station's dock-workers and get it loaded into the hangar bay on the *Sleipner*."

"Immediately, sir," Gerhardt assured him.

"No, *not* immediately, Captain," Grieg snapped at her, the downward curl at the corner of his mouth giving away his impatience with her fawning. "Keep trying to cut through the airlock with the torch. If we can get into it now, we may be able to get into its computer systems. And while you're supervising that effort, have Third platoon begin a search starting at the outermost level and working its way back here to the hub. If those Spartans are on this station, your people will find them. And if they aren't, you'll find *someone* who knows where they went."

"Of course, sir, I'll get on it."

Grieg sniffed doubtfully, but let her step away and get to work.

"Come along then, Mister…" Grieg trailed off. "What was your name again?" he asked the Customs official.

"Maduro," the man told him, licking his lips nervously as if he thought Grieg was some sort of wizard who could use his true name to control him. "Alfonse Maduro."

"Come along then, Mr. Maduro." Colonel Grieg motioned impatiently. "Take me to this broker. And don't dawdle."

"This is it, I swear!" Maduro insisted, trying in vain to pull away from the Marine who'd been escorting him for the last forty minutes, the same hand still twisted into the man's collar.

That has to be getting uncomfortable, Laurent mused. *Don't his fingers ever cramp up?*

She tried to focus on the details of the chamber, tried to look for clues of where this woman Lana Kane had gone from the spilled coffee staining one of the throw rugs lining the stone floor, or the short-legged, padded stool over on its side. The Marine squad flooded into the room, pushing aside the curtain partitions, hunting for the missing broker or any sign of the data crystals. A Private grabbed one of the partition walls and tried to rip it down off the rod set into the rock wall with bolts, but it was thick and tough and resisted his attempts.

"Leave it, for God's sake," she told the man, rolling her eyes.

The Marine hesitated, looking between her and Grieg uncertainly.

"Captain Laurent is your superior officer, is she not?" Grieg asked, an eyebrow going up.

"Yes, sir," the enlisted man acknowledged. "Sorry, ma'am," to her.

"She left in a hurry," Grieg deduced, ignoring the apology and

Maduro's protestations of innocence. "She must have received word we were on our way."

"It's not as if we tried to keep it quiet," Laurent pointed out. She'd advised a more circumspect approach, but Grieg didn't seem to understand the meaning of subtlety. She shrugged. "There's no way she's getting off the station without us noticing."

"Unless she left before the *Sleipner* made it within firing range. There were a few outbound shuttles the long-range sensors picked up leaving immediately after we jumped in." The Colonel paced across the chamber, sweeping curtain partitions out of his way and making a full circuit of the subdivided room, hands clasped behind his back.

"Maduro," Grieg said, snapping his fingers, then pointing the forefinger between the eyes of the Customs official. "Who are her friends, her allies? Who would help hide her?"

"I ain't friends with her, sir," Maduro insisted, spreading his hands in a gesture of helpless ignorance. "I know she has business relationships with a bunch of ships." Grieg's lip twisted in a snarl, and his right hand tightened into a fist, and Maduro saw it as clearly as Laurent did, and started talking faster. "I know those shuttles you're talking about, though! They was off the fuel refinery *Mirahz* and the cargo ship *Liahua*. I don't know if she was connected to either of the ships or anyone on them, but you could look at the security logs for their shuttles leaving and see if she was on one of them!"

"Lt. Poretti," Grieg called the man over from where he was trying to access a data terminal. "Go with Mr. Maduro here back to the Customs offices and check the security logs for twenty-four hours before we arrived, concentrating on anyone who entered either docking bay." He shot a baleful glance at Maduro. "I assume you know what this Kane looks like? Would you have a still photo of her?"

"There's a file on her," Maduro told Grieg. "Just like there is on all the workers from Revelation. But those'd be in Momma Salvaggio's office and you'd have to get them from her people."

"Who or what is a 'Momma Salvaggio?' It sounds like the sort of restaurant chain I try to avoid."

"She's sort of in business with the station's owners. Well," he amended, "the current owners. It's a bit complicated. You see, there's kind of a shifting ownership based on who can invest the most…"

"I don't give a shit," Grieg assured him, taking a step forward, his nose only centimeters from Maduro's. "Get to the fucking point."

Laurent smelled the fear coming off Maduro in glints of perspiration on his forehead.

"Well, Momma Salvaggio, she's like into the strong-arm side of the business," the weaselly man explained quickly. "She runs security here. Like if anyone causes too much trouble, or gets too hot with the Dominions and is gonna' cause trouble, she sells them out for the bounty. She got started with a mercenary unit that she used to hire out to Periphery worlds and crime bosses who needed the leverage a few mecha can give you in a fight, but she hasn't been doing that much since she took over Revelation."

"She took over what?" Laurent interrupted.

"Revelation. It's a world just a couple jumps from here. Just a backwater no one cares about. She brought in most of the workers here from Revelation; she has some sort of deal with them where they owe her money and they work it off here."

"Including Lana Kane?"

"Yeah, I suppose." Maduro shook his head. "I never asked her, but she talks the same way most of them do. She's been here a long time, though."

Grieg gave Poretti a curt nod, then waited for him to escort Maduro out of the room before he turned his attention back to Laurent.

"All right, Laurent, you've clearly got something on your mind. What is it?"

She was a bit surprised he'd noticed and even more surprised he cared.

"This is her turf, sir," she said. "We're not going to find her here, not unless we bring in another company and spend weeks looking. It's a maze down here. But this Salvaggio's a business-woman...." She shrugged. "Maybe we can do business."

⊕

"I don't know what you're talking about," Breckenridge said flatly, elbows braced on his metal desk as if they'd come into his office to ask about having their taxes done.

He had the face, dress and mannerisms of an accountant, which was exactly what he claimed to be. Not yet middle-aged, he nonetheless had the eyes for it, dull and listless and lacking the fire of the youth he otherwise exhibited. He wasn't Momma Salvaggio, didn't know where Momma Salvaggio was or when she'd be returning, they'd established that much immediately, and things had gone downhill from there.

"Your boss runs security for this station," Laurent insisted, casting a subtle glance aside at Grieg, who was seated next to her across the desk from Milo Breckenridge. She expected Grieg to erupt at any moment, but so far, he'd let her do the talking. "Surely you keep tabs on the comings and goings of people who arrive, particularly in a vessel as singular as this one."

"My security chief, Mr. Brown, has taken a temporary leave of absence," the accountant said, with the sort of expression that screamed "I know you won't believe this, but I'm going to say it anyway." "Without him to access the records, I can't answer your questions."

"How fucking convenient," Grieg murmured, not so much in

an angry tone as perhaps an…admiring one? The Colonel pushed himself up in his chair and made sure Breckenridge was meeting his eyes. "Let's cut through this bullshit, Mr. Breckenridge. I know Momma Salvaggio has the fugitives. They were young, inexperienced, obvious. I can't imagine they lasted more than a day. Here's the bottom line: they have something I want, something I'm willing to kill as many people as necessary to retrieve…or pay as much as necessary." He shrugged. "Either way works for me and, honestly, there's less reports to file for the killing. I'll leave it to you to decide which you'd rather I do."

For the first time since they'd entered the spacious if sparely decorated office, Breckenridge seemed uncomfortable. Just subtle hints, a tightening of the muscles in his face, a shifting of his shoulders. He took Grieg seriously, which was a good decision. He *might* think the Colonel was bluffing about his preference for killing over negotiating, but he still took him seriously.

"I still can't give you the data from the security files without approval from Ms. Salvaggio," Breckenridge said, "but maybe we could arrange something. Perhaps an employment contract between you and our firm?"

"I'm nothing if not reasonable," Grieg lied. "What did you have in mind?"

Lana Kane couldn't breathe. There wasn't enough room to inhale, wasn't enough space to expand her chest, to spread her shoulders, to take in a full breath. She could feel the wall just in front of her in the utter darkness, could feel her exhalations reflected back at her, and each time she exhaled, it was as if the walls closed in another millimeter.

It's your imagination, she reassured herself, trying to

remember the breathing exercises her great aunt had tried to teach her as a teenager. *Just take in air, let it out. Take in air, let it out…*

It didn't help. This particular hidey-hole was concealed beneath the floor of her office on Trinity, but she kept seeing herself in another, one dug into soft dirt instead of asteroid rock, covered with a sheet of plywood and a throw-rug. She hadn't been alone in that hole; her mother had pushed her baby brother in with her, told her not to make a sound and not to come out, no matter what she heard. He hadn't been old enough to understand what "pirates" meant, but she'd known and she'd promised.

When the screaming had started, Alec had tried to shout for their mother, and Lana had been forced to hold her hand over his mouth. She'd whispered lies in his ear, told him everything would be all right if he just stopped yelling. They hadn't left the hole until she'd smelled the smoke and figured out the house was on fire. She hadn't been able to keep Alec from seeing what was left of Mother's body.

She shuddered, sucking in air and panicking anew when her shoulders wedged tighter into the space. She wouldn't be able to smell smoke this time, wouldn't be able to hear the Starkad Marines when they left—if they left. The trapdoor was sound-proofed so their sensors couldn't pick up her heartbeat, insulated to prevent her body heat from being detected by thermal imaging equipment.

Airtight, her mind screamed at her. *It's airtight and you're running out of oxygen…*

She'd just black out. Painless. Not a bad way to go. *No. Can't leave Alec alone.*

The trapdoor swung open with a startlingly loud creak of ancient hinges and light flooded the little spider-hole, blinding her. She threw up her arms instinctively, as if she'd be able to fight off a squad of Supremacy Marines bare-handed.

"Lana, it's me."

The blur of light solidified into the image of a woman, perhaps ten years her junior with a wide-eyed, child-like expression that made her seem even younger. She was dressed in the clothes of a station worker, faded with use and discolored with old stains that would never come clean.

"Mira." She hissed the word in relief, letting the woman pull her up to her feet. "Thanks be to Lord Mithra." Her eyes flickered from one curtain partition to another, the furtive glance of a hunted animal. "Are they gone?"

"They're leaving," Mira assured her, "but word is, they've made a deal with Momma Salvaggio, and her people are going to be coming after you. You need to get out of here."

"Damn it," she murmured. Still, it wasn't more than she'd expected. It just pushed things forward. She leaned back down into the spider-hole and grabbed the box.

The damned box. It was going to get her killed. Or perhaps it would be their salvation. She reached into an interior pocket of her robes and retrieved the money the boy had given her. Counting out half, she handed it to Mira. The younger woman stared at the wad of Tradenotes, uncomprehending.

"Give that to Captain Fujimori. He'll be staying in the Vista Suites, but if he's not there, he'll be at the cargo shuttle for the freighter *Ultra* in the antipolar docking bay. Tell him it's time to pay back the favor he owes me and he'll get the other half once I'm on board."

Mira nodded, tucking the money away.

"Where will you go, Lana?" she wondered.

"Where else could I go? Home."

9

"This is a long damned flight for an orbital transfer shuttle," Valentine Kurtz complained, squirming in his acceleration couch.

"Stop being a whiner," Commander Kathren Margolis said, craning her head around against the one-gravity boost pushing them back toward the tail of the shuttle. "You spend hours and hours sitting inside a mech cockpit! How is this any worse?"

"I don't know," Kurtz admitted. "Maybe because I'm driving my mech and all I'm doin' in this bird is sittin' here with my thumb up my…" He hesitated. "…nose."

Lyta Randell snorted a laugh from the seat ahead of him and to the left, not looking back but he still saw the mocking grin on her face.

"I find it hard to believe someone who works with Mandy Ford and Aliyah Hernandez could be watching his language because Katy and I are females," she said, still chuckling.

"It's just old habit," he allowed, shrugging it away.

"Val's from Buckskin Holler," Logan put in, laughing softly. "They do things differently out on the fringes." *No, I should call him Jonathan again now that we're under cover. Or Colonel Slaughter. Don't fuck up and forget while we're on the station.*

"It's Buckland Vale," he corrected his commanding officer, grinning at the old dig. Marc Langella had first used it and it had caught on. He didn't mind too much. "And yeah, we're a bit more reserved with our language in front of females out there. And children, and older people. It's called bein' respectful. Though I know you fancy city folks on Sparta or Nike wouldn't understand that."

Plus, though he never would have admitted it to any of them, he respected the hell out of Logan Conner, or Logan Brannigan, or Jonathan Slaughter, or whatever he wanted to call himself; and where he was from, you didn't use bad language in front of the loved ones of people you respected. Even if those loved ones could blow you out of the sky without breaking a sweat.

"Anyway," Logan —*Jonathan, dammit*—went on, "we launched this far away because we didn't want them to get too close a look at the *Shakak II.* We had to keep that rock between us and them, and asteroids aren't nearly as close as they look in those adventure stories you like to watch at the Tri-D shows."

"I thought the whole idea of putting all that ugly shit on top of the girl was to make her look normal so we could hang out around civilians without being noticed."

"Theoretically," Katy answered, still turned partway. *Not as if there's anything for her to hit if she takes her hands off the stick. And we're pointed backwards anyway, since we started the deceleration burn.* "But it's her first time out and we didn't want to take any chances."

Since she'd been promoted and they'd headed off on this rescue mission, Katy had become more involved in the operational decisions for the ship as well as the auxiliary craft. He'd noticed the change in her; she'd always been competent and confident within her own area, but it seemed like the area was growing, and her confidence with it.

She might captain her own ship someday. If we all live long enough.

"We're coming up on their Traffic Control net," Katy announced after a few minutes more. "Time to cut braking boost and cruise on in."

Damn. If there was anything he liked less than being stuck in a tiny lander for six hours, it was being stuck in a tiny lander in free-fall.

"Hey boss," he said to Jonathan, mostly to avoid saying his name so he wouldn't screw it up. "I know the plan, but why'd you bring me along instead of one of Colonel Randell's leg-breakers?"

"You ever been in a bar fight, Captain Kurtz?" Lyta asked him, stepping in to answer his question with a question. "Maybe a go-round with one of the boys back home when you were on leave?"

"Sure," he said with a shrug. "Who hasn't?"

"None of my Rangers get into bar fights," Lyta declared. "You know why? Because I don't teach them how to win a fist-fight, I teach them how to disable and kill as quickly and efficiently as possible. Trinity..." She nodded toward the image projected on the front display. "...is a rough place, but if we go into every confrontation leaving bodies piled behind us, we're going to attract attention and get ourselves a bullet in the head pretty damn quick."

"We wanted someone who could take a punch without ripping someone's throat out as their first response," Jonathan summarized.

"Glad I'm good for something," Kurtz murmured.

"Holy shit, glad we're working on a government expense account," the copilot said and whistled softly. Kurtz didn't know him too well, but he thought his name was Acosta. Acosta tapped his headphones, indicating the transmission he was getting over the comms channel. "Damned station is charging us 300 credits just to dock, and Mithra only knows what they'll ask per day."

"Don't haggle," Lyta warned him. "They won't appreciate it."

Kurtz had imagined the place would be so primitive, they'd have to exit the shuttle in vacuum suits, but docking turned out to be fairly routine. Katy made every docking seem smooth, of course. The woman could fly a shuttle like nobody's business.

He waited his turn at the airlock while Lyta Randell retrieved her sidearm from the utility locker and strapped it on, then handed holstered weapons back to him and the others, letting the gunbelts float across the ship like angels of the *Spenta Mainyu* were guiding them to each of them. Everyone got one; they'd decided earlier they wouldn't be leaving anyone behind with the shuttle, and he wondered if that was because they needed everyone along or because Katy had objected to being left to drive the getaway car.

Kurtz strapped the belt around his waist, cinching it tight. He liked the feel of the solid weight of a reliable weapon at his hip, but he wasn't feeling it now; he had to strap the damn thing down to his thigh to keep it from flapping around in the microgravity.

"Ain't never been on a space station before where they let you go heeled," he commented, pulling the service pistol from his holster and quickly checking its load. "Not even military stations."

"Well, this place isn't like any other station you've been to," Lyta warned him. "But like I said, try not to use that thing unless there's no other choice. The less attention we attract, the better."

She pulled open the outer airlock and they all filed out through the docking umbilical…and into the yawning muzzles of half a dozen ugly, practical-looking flechette guns, held in the hands of ugly, practical-looking armored security.

"Don't fucking move!" someone was yelling, but he hadn't planned on it.

"I think we attracted some attention," he commented drily, keeping his hands away from his sides.

"You're mercenaries, huh?" The woman asked, pacing back and forth through the gap between their chairs.

She wore leather, real leather he thought rather than the expensive, vat-grown kind you bought in the big cities. Out in the Periphery, the cheapest way to get leather was to kill a damned cow and skin it. The smell of the black leather was thick and pleasant, nearly offsetting the overpowering scent of whatever perfume she'd sprayed over it.

Logan—he'd been working hard on making the mental transition from Logan Conner, officer in the Sparta Guard, to Jonathan Slaughter, mercenary commander, on the trip from Sparta, and it hadn't quite taken hold yet—waved a hand across his face when he thought she wasn't looking, trying to clear the air in front of his nose for a clean breath. Maybe water was rationed on Trinity, or maybe it was a personal thing, because Security Chief Chica Lopes didn't seem to take too many baths. Instead, she tried to cover her body odor with thick leather and thicker fragrance. The combination was more intimidating than her size, her muscles, or even the nearly featureless, grey holding cell where he and Kurtz had spent the last three hours.

Most of it had been just stewing, making them wait in a locked room to show how little control they had over the situation. Security had taken their weapons and put them under guard in separate rooms, he and Kurtz together while Katy, Acosta and Lyta were in a neighboring compartment. He was grateful he'd used the head on the shuttle ride, because the Security guards had not been polite enough to offer trips to the bathroom.

"Is that a question?" he wondered, finally responding to Lopes after she stopped her pacing and fixed him with a hard stare. "Because you know what we are, and you know who I am. It's all in my registration documents and I sent those over before we docked. So, what's the problem?"

He wanted to swear more. Lopes looked like someone who appreciated a good foul-mouthed rant. But she also looked like someone who'd have him handcuffed and then slap him around a little just to show who was in charge, and he didn't have time for the games.

"The problem is," she said, leaning down to put her scarred, hard-edged face into his, "we don't need hired guns in here trying to push their way into our arrangement. Momma Salvaggio runs this place and you and your fucking Wholesale Slaughter better not forget that."

"*That's* what this is about?" Logan's eyes went wide and he began laughing. He hadn't meant to, knew it was probably a bad idea, but he couldn't hold it back. "You think we're coming in here to take this place over and cut you out?" He shook his head in disbelief. "You think we *want* this fucking place? It's a cave, lady! We're here to do business, just like everyone else who comes here." He scowled. "At least, that's what I had *heard* about Trinity, that people came here to do business. Maybe you should ask your boss if that's how she wants to keep it, because if we spread the word around that this is how you treat your visitors, maybe everyone'll find somewhere else to take their money."

He leaned forward in his chair, not getting up but bringing his face even closer to hers, defiant and not the least bit afraid of her attempts at badassery.

"Is that what she wants? Because if you know who I am, then

you know our reputation. Wholesale Slaughter doesn't need your station to get work."

Kurtz eyed him doubtfully, and he knew why. He was talking out of his ass; he had no idea whether they'd heard of Wholesale Slaughter and their grand total of two successful jobs way out here. But he knew General Constantine had done his best to spread the word about them in an effort to improve the depth of their cover, and if it hadn't spread this far…well, as Lyta always said, attitude was everything.

Lopes drew in a breath, silent, jaw clenching, and he knew he had her. She straightened, tugging her jacket down and smoothing it, a nervous tic to buy time.

"You have to understand," she said, her tone shifting gradually from hostile and in command to slightly more conciliatory, "we've had some trouble here lately. Starkad bully boys coming in here with their Marines and trying to push everyone around a few days ago, thinking they're back in the Core." The hackles stood on the back of Logan's neck. They were too late…Starkad had already been here. But he couldn't let the shock show on his face, couldn't let her see it mattered to him.

Lopes made a face, probably much braver than she'd considered when she'd been nose to nose with the Supremacy Marines. "That shit's bad for business and we had to make sure it wasn't happening again, you know?"

"I understand that," Logan assured her. Damn it, he was still having trouble thinking of himself as "Jonathan," having trouble getting his game face on. Maybe it was the fear for his brother twisting inside his guts, or maybe so much time away from this life had left him too far away from Jonathan Slaughter to come back to him. "What the hell did Starkad want all the way out here? I didn't think they gave a shit about what happened in the Periphery."

She looked as if she wanted to tell him, but reconsidered before she could blurt it out.

"That's between them and Momma Salvaggio," Lopes grumbled. "What's your business here?" she asked him.

He thought about telling her that his business was none of hers but the question had the sound of a prelude to it, of her searching for a way to save face and still let them go on their way. What story to give her, though? The cover they'd come up with was a scheduled meeting with one of their agents who'd come to scope out a client; but if Starkad had already come searching for Terrin, it might not be a good idea to be associated with him.

"We were supposed to meet a potential customer here," he said, improvising quickly. "Though I don't even know if they're going to show with all the shit happening. They were squirrelly to begin with, and this might have scared them out of even coming here."

"This client have a name?"

"They sure do," he replied, deciding he'd been forthcoming enough. "And an interest in not sharing it."

She grunted at the answer, as if she'd expected it. Then she jerked her head toward the door.

"All right, you're free to go. My people will return your weapons once you're outside the secure area."

The guards moved aside at her words, their flechette guns dangling loosely on their slings as they relaxed. He had a passing thought they were letting their guard down too early, of how easily he could take them down, grab their guns and shoot his way out, but he shook it off, shook off the disdain he felt when he heard Kurtz sigh a breath of relief on the way to the door. He'd been hanging around with Lyta too much; he was starting to think like a Ranger.

The gravity here was slightly heavier than standard. Security was located far out on the rim likely for just that reason, to put confined miscreants at a disadvantage, as well as to keep them isolated from the more heavily populated levels, and Logan felt his joints creaking from being seated for so long. He shook them out as he walked, stepping into the corridor just behind Valentine Kurtz. The others were filing out of the next door down, and Katy looked as if she wanted to ask him a million questions, but Lyta restrained her with a glance.

"It's just a misunderstanding," he assured them. "Everything's fine and we can get back to business."

They took the hint and lined up a few steps behind the guards leading them out toward the lift bank, Katy keeping pace beside him. The walls were white and antiseptic here, a plastic lining over bare rock, cheap and ugly. The doors were sturdier, thick metal mounted deeper into the asteroid's nickel-iron, impossible to break down, unlikely to be taken out even with high explosives. You didn't want to get on these people's bad side without a company of Supremacy Marines behind you...or maybe a company of Spartan Rangers.

At the lift station, one of the guards began returning their gun belts and the flechette gun muzzles tracked back to them, the other Security troops alert again as they fastened them on.

"Leave 'em in their holsters until the lift doors close," one of the guards instructed. "I see a gun in anyone's hand before that, I unload on them."

"No problem," Logan assured him, but didn't stop buckling on the holster. He didn't want to provoke the guards, but he also didn't want to seem like a pushover. Reputation might sound like a stupid reason to risk a confrontation, but he was playing the part of a merc; and for a merc, reputation was everything.

The elevator arrived after almost a minute of the tense, paranoid, utterly ridiculous stare-down and Logan hesitated at the control panel, eyeing the guards just outside the doors, their fingers still on the triggers of their weapons.

"Where do you go to find someone to broker a deal in this place?"

He thought they might not answer, as worried about losing face as he was, but one of them surprised him. A woman, naturally. Women were as concerned about image as men, but they expressed it differently.

"Most of them," she told him, "are on G level."

"G level it is, then," he said, smiling in gratitude and hitting the control.

"What the fuck was that all about?" Acosta—he still couldn't think of the man as Bray, which he supposed, was the point of having a cover—exploded the instant the car went into motion.

"Aren't you worried the car is bugged?" Lyta asked, cocking a wry eyebrow at the Intelligence officer.

"Well, I fucking would be," he snapped back at her, "if I didn't have a jammer field sewn into the lining of my jacket."

"Why the hell do you have a jammer sewn into your jacket?" Kurtz demanded. He stared at Acosta as if the other man had grown an extra head.

"He's Military Intelligence," Logan told him. Acosta glared at him and he rolled his eyes. "Sorry. Valentine, don't tell anyone."

"Oh yeah," Kurtz said, nodding dumbfounded agreement. "Who would I tell?"

Acosta still didn't seem happy about it, but he sighed and turned back to Logan. "Now, what happened and do they know who we are?"

"As far as I know," Logan said, "our cover is still intact." He was calm, mostly as a reaction to Acosta's lack of it. "The bad news is, Starkad was already here and gone."

"Oh, shit," Katy spat the words out. "Did they get him?"

"I don't know," he admitted. "I'm fairly sure they got the ship he came in on." When they hadn't seen it coming into the bay, he'd just thought it was in the antipolar docking hub; but if Starkad had already been here, they'd have grabbed it.

"That's why you asked about a broker," Lyta guessed, eyes narrowing with a penetrating discernment that had made so many of her enemies uncomfortable over the years. The others were staring at her and Logan in confusion and Logan wondered if he'd have to explain, but Lyta took pity on them. "Brokers are just what they sound like. They make deals, exchange favors. If Terrin was thinking straight when he got here, he might have gone to one to try to get passage off the station."

"If they didn't sell him out," Logan added, hand going involuntarily to the butt of his holstered handgun.

"We'll get him back," Katy said softly beside his ear.

He nodded gratefully, but wasn't comforted. He'd made the call to leave Terrin behind on Terminus. If he'd gotten him killed, he wasn't sure if their father would ever forgive him.

"I want him back, too," Lyta said into the silence that had fallen over the car. "But there's something else to consider."

"The data he was carrying," Acosta added, a little heat behind his words telling Logan he was annoyed at how quickly they'd forgotten what he considered the crux of their mission. "If he was captured, did he have it on him?"

"That's why you're along, Major Bray," Logan told him, his voice going cold. "General Constantine sent you to find and secure the data. Me, I have a mission directly from the Guardian." His eyes bored into the Intelligence agent's. "I'm here to save my brother."

10

Kathren Margolis wondered sometimes if she was ready to be a Commander. The promotion had come with success, and with success and promotion, more responsibility and expectations. How long could it be before she rose to the level of her own incompetence?

Take this mission, she thought, trying not to let her hand move toward her gun with every possible threat that passed in the packed corridors of G-level. *What the hell am I doing in here anyway? I'm a pilot, not a spy or a commando. Why do I keep insisting on putting myself into these situations?*

Mostly because she didn't like being told what she was and was not qualified to do. She knew the answer, but that didn't make it any less ridiculous.

Stop whining, she adjured herself. *It's not like Logan was trained for this any more than I was.*

Or Kurtz, for that matter. If anything, he looked more lost and out of place than she did, head swiveling around like an owl on the hunt. They were spread out in a tight wedge moving through the crowd, with Logan at the point of the arrow, Acosta and Kurtz spread out to the right and left and her and Lyta at the rear. It was a Ranger thing, she assumed, and she wondered what was wrong with just walking in a straight line.

It must not be tactical enough.

She knew Lyta was always concerned about proper tactics and formations, but honestly, she was more concerned about how the hell they were going to find anything in this rat-maze of a station. Maybe it had started out neatly organized, but now there was a business or a kiosk squeezed into every nook and cranny, and half the time, the people who ran the business lived next door to it or in the back room.

What she didn't see were any children. Maybe they were kept in schools or daycares on different levels, but she couldn't recall seeing anyone younger than a teenager the whole time she'd been on the station.

Curious. Of course, the criminal low-lives who came here to do business with other criminal low-lives wouldn't bring kids along, but if people moved here to run businesses, you'd think at least some of them would take their families with them. She shrugged it off; it wasn't pertinent to their situation.

Logan had stopped again, speaking in low tones to a frumpy, tired-looking woman who was sitting behind a table stacked high with counterfeit datalinks probably fabricated off black-market patterns stolen from the Shang Directorate. He held out the screen of his own 'link—a Spartan model, much more reliable in her opinion—with an image of Terrin on it, and she shook her head, waving negation. Logan sighed and his shoulders seemed to sag just a fraction. They'd been at this for hours with no luck, and Katy was getting discouraged, too. At this rate, they could be here for days and never find a clue about what had happened to Terrin.

"Excuse me, miss?"

Katy nearly jumped right out of her skin, did pull her gun halfway from its holster until she saw the young woman wasn't armed.

"Jesus lady," she breathed, pushing her pistol back down into the hard-plastic sheath of the holster and trying to slow her heart rate back down. "You scared the shit out of me."

The woman was young, her clothing simple and hand-made, too roughly-sewn to be the product of a fabricator. Dark robes hid all but her hands and face, but the face seemed unlined and far too innocent for one who lived in such a place.

"Are you with the ones they call Wholesale Slaughter?" she asked, her voice tiny and tentative.

A cold, electric shock went up her back and she waved at Lyta without looking away from the woman.

"We are. Who are you and what do you want with us?"

The young woman checked aside each way, as if making sure no one was watching.

"Meet me in G-42 in ten minutes," she said quietly, then was gone, merging into the crowd before Katy could get another word out.

"Who was that?" Lyta asked, coming up on Katy's right shoulder, staring after the young woman. "Does she know something?"

"Maybe." She caught Logan's eye from across the corridor, where he was about to accost a worker sweeping up the floor, motioned to him to come back to her. "Let's find out."

"Are you sure this is the right place?" Logan wondered.

The room designated G-42 was empty, picked clean to the bare walls, even the door stripped off its hinges. Lyta and Acosta were searching every corner for any trace left of whoever had once occupied the space, but the effort seemed wasted. All that was left were the light fixtures embedded in the ceiling, and those probably would have been taken as well, if anyone had the time and tools for it.

"It's the address she gave me," Katy told him, shrugging. "I can't say whether she was wasting our time or not."

Kurtz was leaning in the frame of the vacant doorway, gun in his hand but held down low by his leg, watching their backs. He craned his head back around inside, snorting ruefully.

"I think everyone in this damned place is wasting our time. Seems t'be their hobby."

"We need a fallback plan if this doesn't pan out," Lyta said quietly, crouched over what seemed to be a trapdoor in the floor. She pulled it open, but the spider-hole beneath it was as empty as the rest of the room. "Maybe we could try to penetrate their security systems and see if anything was recorded."

"Bribes are always popular," Acosta commented drily from the opposite wall, feeling at a section of it as if he was about to find a hidden chamber. "It sounds as if Salvaggio already has a deal with Starkad though, so we might be pitting greed up against fear, and Mithra alone knows what wins that battle."

"Boss," Kurtz said, the tone of his voice changing, tense and expectant. "Someone's coming. I think it's that girl."

Lyta and Acosta came to their feet, the Ranger officer edging to the side of the room, putting her back to the outer wall.

"Back off and put the gun away," Logan told Kurtz, motioning the man away from the door. "We don't want to scare her off."

"Ain't nobody been worried about scaring me," Kurtz murmured, but did as he was told.

Logan hadn't seen the woman who'd spoken to Katy, but the one who stepped through the door matched the description: same clothing, same age and appearance. Her eyes narrowed at the sight of them gathered inside, staring at her, and she jerked away and nearly bolted when she spotted Lyta against the wall, but Katy stopped her with an upraised hand.

"You wanted to talk to us?" Katy prompted.

"Which of you is Jonathan Slaughter?" the woman asked, stuttering the words, furtive and frightened.

Logan bit back a sigh, wishing he could say "None of us." Despite what his father and General Constantine wanted, he was fairly sure he'd never be Jonathan Slaughter again.

"I am," he said instead. "I'm Jonathan. Who are you and what can we do for you?"

"My name is Mira." The woman's spine seemed to stiffen with the pronouncement, as if her name were a magic spell to regain her courage. "I worked for Ms. Kane, the broker whose shop this is…." She winced. "…used to be, I mean. She left a message for me to give to you."

"Did she record it?" Acosta asked her.

"Lana—Ms. Kane—told it to me." Mira shook her head. "She doesn't like to record things. She says anyone can hear a recording. She told me she has the thing your brother, Terrin brought with him. He left it for her to give to you in case something happened to him, but it was too dangerous for her to stay, even after the Starkad soldiers had left." She grimaced and added, "Colonel Grieg, the man who led the soldiers, made a deal with Momma Salvaggio's people to find her and what she carried, so she had to run."

"Run where?" Logan asked her. "Where did she take the…" He paused, unwilling to give away information the woman didn't have. "…the thing my brother brought with him?"

"She said she was going home, to Revelation."

"Is that a planet?" Katy wondered. Logan noticed Acosta frowning, as if he was trying to remember something; finally, he pulled out his datalink and began tapping on the control screen, but Mira was already answering.

"It's only two jumps from here. It's the closest living world to this place, and most of us who work on Trinity live there." Her expression went harder. "Or, we used to, before Momma forced us here, to work off our debt."

He wanted to ask her what debt they were working off, but now wasn't the time.

"A planet's a big place. How do we find her?"

"There's only one real city on the planet. It's called Revelation City."

"Of course it is," Acosta mumbled.

"Maybe people out here are more interested in surviving than coming up with imaginative city names, Lt. Whatever-Your-Name-Is," Kurtz chided him. A grin tugged at the corner of Logan's mouth as he remembered the man's home planet and its capitol city shared the same name, as well.

"It's actually 'Major Whatever-My-Name-Is,' Captain," Acosta corrected him, then fell silent.

Mira's expression pinched with annoyance at the interruption, and there was a reproving tone in her voice when she continued.

"She told me you should try to find the house where her family used to live. If you go there, she would see you."

"Well, that sounds so damned easy," Kurtz commented. "I'm sure a bunch of insular colonists out here on the Periphery are going to be *really* trusting of strangers coming into their town and asking about a local."

"I only know what she told me to tell you," Mira insisted.

"What about my brother?" Logan wanted to know. He'd restrained himself, waiting for the girl to relay her message, but he couldn't contain it anymore. "Where is he? Did the Supremacy take him?"

"I didn't meet your brother," Mira said, but her eyes glanced away as she spoke, and General Constantine had taught him long ago the motion was a sure sign of deception.

"But you know what happened to him, don't you?" Lyta asked, undoubtedly picking up the same signals since she'd been trained by the same man.

Mira wouldn't meet Lyta's eyes either; she began edging back toward the door, but Lyta stepped to block her way. The younger woman fell into a deeper stance, a motion inside her loose clothing that seemed to transform the very shape of her body. Her head swiveled as she tried to watch them all, as if expecting an attack from any side.

"We won't hurt you," Logan promised, holding his hands up. "But this is my brother. I need to find him. If you can help us, we'll repay you however you want. I swear."

The girl seemed to relax, or at least she relaxed in her stance, straightening back to a normal posture. Her dark eyes finally met his, searching for the truth of his words. Finally, she seemed to cave in on herself just slightly in what might have been a surrender to her circumstances.

"If I tell you," she said, her voice so low Logan could barely hear her, "I can't stay here. It wouldn't be safe for me anymore. I'd need you to take me back home to Revelation with you, and I'd need enough money to pay off my family's debt." She eyed him with obvious doubt. "It's a lot of money."

"It won't be a problem," he assured her. "We'll take you wherever you need to go and give you as much as you need." Logan took a step closer, hands pressed together almost in prayer. "What happened to my brother?"

"He was taken," she said slowly, the words seeming as if they had to drag themselves out of her, "but not by Starkad. It was Salvaggio's bounty hunters. And he could be anywhere."

Morning light filtered in hesitantly, reluctantly through the thick glass of the narrow window, as if it didn't want to be in the dingy cell any more than Terrin Brannigan did. He moaned and covered his eyes, rolling over on the cot and setting off a cacophony of protesting creaks and groans from the ancient bed. Dull pain flared behind his eyes at the intrusion of the light and it seemed to pierce through the haze over his thoughts. He opened his eyes wide and pushed himself up.

Sunlight?

"Where the hell are we?"

He'd meant for the words to be a loud exclamation, but they came out a dry rasp and he coughed fitfully, trying to clear the cotton from his mouth. Wait…*we?*

Francesca was lying on an identically old and beat-up cot across the room, eyelids fluttering, hands moving to her face, touching it almost experimentally like she wasn't sure what she'd find there. She looked as bad as he felt, squinting from a face scrunched up in pain, hair matted and sticking up at angles away from her head, her clothes wrinkled and—he judged after a careful whiff—smelling of days of body odor. But at least she seemed unharmed and, he decided after a careful assessment, so did he.

"How did we get here?" Franny mumbled, rolling over and trying to find the floor with a boot before she committed to sitting up. "Weren't we on the station?"

"Here" was a cell. He'd never been in a cell before, but he knew one when he saw it. The walls were a rust-colored brick, sandstone maybe, the offensive windows too narrow to squeeze through even if he could have broken the centimeter-thick glass. And it looked like real glass, not polymer, which wasn't rare on Periphery worlds. Plastics required petrochemicals, refineries, plants to manufacture the plastic, machinery to shape it…which all could be had, but not without a prohibitive monetary invest-ment. Glass was much simpler and cheaper to produce.

The door was not glass, nor plastic, nor yet local brick. It was metal, dull and thick and featureless except for the lines of a rectangle at about eye level, a viewing slit that could only be opened from the other side.

"We *were* on the station," Terrin answered her question after realizing he'd let himself drift off into a haze again for a few seconds. "Someone stunned us."

"Shock darts," she agreed, nodding, still holding fingers to her temples, massaging slowly. "I saw them get you and I tried to help but…"

"There was nothing you could have done," he assured her, trying to be comforting but then noticing a hint of a scowl on her face and realizing that might have sounded condescending. "I mean, I had the gun, right?" He leaned back against the wall, the air going out of him as he realized what had happened. "Which did me not one damn bit of good. Just knowing how to shoot isn't good enough if you aren't smart enough to see the threat coming up behind you. I was useless."

"Neither of us is a Ranger, Terrin," she reminded him, pushing herself up off her cot and stepping across the small, four-meter-square cell to sit down beside him. Her hand was warm on his arm even through the sleeve of his fatigues. "I think you kept your head pretty good, getting rid of the…"

He hurriedly shushed her with a finger across her lips, flicking his eyes around them to signal the room might be bugged. She nodded…and then he realized he was still holding his finger against her lips and pulled it away quickly, embarrassed. He suddenly wondered if he smelled as bad as she did.

"You did fine," she said. "I think your dad and brother would be proud."

He looked away, embarrassed again, and his eyes fell on the blue sky outside the high windows. He stood on top of the cot, steadying himself against the wall to get a look out through the glass. There were buildings at the edge of his vision, not tall or imposing, just one-story brick. Most of what he could see was a dirt road running into low scrub, then on into twisted, stunted trees growing impossibly from sandy soil.

"What do you see?" Franny asked him.

"Not much," he admitted. He stepped down off the cot and fell back to sit beside her, his legs still feeling weak and shaky. "We're on a planet, though, and the nearest world to Trinity was at least two jumps away. They must have kept us drugged up for days. Maybe as much as a week."

Probably catheterized us, too, he realized, horrified. He didn't want to think about what else they might have done.

"Mithra's Flaming Horns, I need a bath," Franny sighed, pulling at her collar. "And some water…"

Terrin forced his legs to work, stumbling over to the door and slamming his fist against it. Three times, a pause to listen, then three more times.

"Come on!" he yelled. "Someone's got to be there."

The view-slit slid open so abruptly it almost made him jump. Through it he saw bloodshot brown eyes, the brows over them bushy and shot with grey. He decided he was just as well not seeing the rest of that face.

"What the fuck do you want?" The gravelly voice went well with the eyes, a perfect match.

"Could we get some water?" he asked the man. He wanted a lot more than that, but he had a hunch he should start small.

Red-eyes grunted and slammed the slit shut. Terrin sighed, leaning against the door, trying to catch his breath. Lying around sedated for days took it out of you, and it wasn't as if he'd been able to do much exercising on Terminus.

"Back away from the door." It was the same, gruff voice, muffled now by the intervening centimeters of metal. "Get up against the wall."

He scrambled backwards, falling back onto the cot beside Franny. Her hand slipped into his and he gave it a squeeze, mostly to comfort himself. He heard a bolt being thrown, loud and scraping, telling tales of rust and neglect, before the door squeaked open just enough to admit a small tray made of cheap, orange plastic. It looked just like the ones you could find on shipboard, and he imagined that's where they'd acquired it, but the pitcher and cups sitting atop it were locally-blown glass, as was the small plate piled with what looked like sandwiches.

The tray scraped across the stone floor, pushed by a thick and calloused hand until it was in far enough for the door to close again. Terrin scrambled over and grabbed it, then had a sudden thought.

"Can you tell me where we are?" he called. "I mean, what planet?"

It was a forlorn hope; he didn't expect the man to reply and was shocked when he did.

"If nowhere has an ass end," the jailer growled, "then you're in it."

A pause and Terrin thought that might be as good an answer as he was going to get, but the man apparently wasn't as bad as his eyes and voice made him seem.

"Revelation," he said. "You're on Revelation. And Mithra help you both."

11

The Palladium was a grand name for a seedy nightclub patronized by the scum of the Dominions. Lyta Randell was sure she'd seen worse in a career spent slicing through the dark underbelly of society with a bayonet, but she couldn't think where. The driving beat of music ten years out of date, the bass vibration she felt in her sinuses, the raucous undertone of people yelling at the top of their lungs just to be heard, the disorganized thrashing that passed for dancing, all that would have been bad enough. The borderline pornographic videos running on a loop on multiple flat screens at the perimeter of the dance floor were the capper, though, the straw that broke the camel's back of bad taste.

"Places like this," Kurtz confided in her at the top of his lungs, "are why I don't like the city."

"We're inside an outlaw space station as remote as your Coonskin Holler," she yelled back into his ear. "This is not 'the city,' at least by any definition of the word I ever heard."

He shrugged, apparently confident he'd made his point anyway, and kept scanning the crowd with eyes a bit too wide to be inconspicuous. She almost kept at it—giving the country boy shit was more fun than she'd imagined it would be—but she was too busy trying to track Logan and Mira on the other side of the dance floor. The girl wasn't happy to be here at all. When Logan had sent Katy and Acosta back to the shuttle to keep it ready for a quick getaway, Mira had begged to go with them; but Logan had insisted she personally identify the bounty hunters.

She understood the girl's fear, but Logan had made the right call in bringing her along. In a situation like this, you didn't want to be guessing whether you had the right targets. Of course, Lyta wasn't happy to be here either, but for different reasons. She and Acosta had taken the unpopular position that they should have headed to Revelation immediately to secure the data crystals. Not that she didn't love Terrin like a little brother, but the mission always came first. She'd almost been relieved when Logan had overruled her, not because she thought she was wrong, but simply because she *wanted* to rescue Terrin first and following orders was as good an excuse as any to take what she knew was the less responsible course of action.

She also wasn't happy they couldn't bring their guns into the club. She'd tried to convince Mira to wait for the men outside one of the exits so they could do this while they were armed, but the young woman was insanely paranoid about being conspicuous. She was convinced Salvaggio's people could get to her family back on Revelation if they knew what she'd done, and she might have been right.

Mira was staring intently at someone Lyta couldn't see, at a group of tables behind a section of the club walled off from the dance floor. She tried to raise her hand to point, but Logan intercepted it by her side and shook his head. Lyta grinned in spite of the situation. The boy wasn't bad at this, for all that he made a living driving a mech. If he lived through all this and eventually wound up as Guardian after his father, at least the head of the Spartan government would be someone who could keep his head under pressure.

Logan had pulled out his datalink and punched something into it before tucking it back on his belt, so she wasn't surprised when her own 'link vibrated for her attention. The message was brief and to the point: TARGETS ACQUIRED.

"Come on, Country Boy," she nudged Kurtz. "Showtime."

Making their way across the dance floor was worse than trying to traverse a mine field, because at least the mines stayed in one place. More than anything, the gyrating, out of control swarm of intoxicated bodies reminded Lyta of martial arts training; halfway across, she began treating it like a session in the dojo, blocking and ducking and weaving. Poor Kurtz wasn't as experienced and she saw the man take an elbow to the neck and nearly go down. The "dancer" barely noticed, despite Kurtz's snarled warning, and Lyta had to yank on Country Boy's arm to keep him from taking a swing at the one who'd hit him.

"They're over there," Logan told her when they made it across to his position. He nodded surreptitiously over to the tables and she tried to glance in that direction out of the corner of her eye. "And guess who's with them?"

She didn't have to guess. She remembered the Security officer, Chica Lopes very well from their short acquaintance, most of it from over the barrel of a gun. Lopes wasn't in uniform at the moment; instead, she wore a surprisingly feminine outfit of soft colors and trailing ribbons totally unsuited to her personal demeanor.

Well, sometimes a gal just wants to let her hair down, I suppose.

The two men with her weren't potential suitors or dance partners, though. They were dressed for business, if your business was busting heads. Their matching black leather jackets weren't a uniform, but she could tell they were reinforced with armor, probably bullet-resistant and definitely protection against blades and stunners. The jackets and the general air of thuggish badassery were the only things the two men had in common; otherwise, they could have been opposite ends of the genetic spectrum. The one on the right was tall and thin, with a face like the head of an axe, so narrow his eyes seemed in danger of meeting in the middle. Everyone called him Ham, according to Mira, though she had no idea why.

His partner was at least a head shorter and twice as wide, with arms as big around as the taller man's legs and so long that his knuckles almost dragged on the ground when he walked. Mira had told them he was known as Monk, and Lyta could at least see the reference for that one, having encountered monkeys on the various worlds where the climate had been appropriate to introduce them after terraforming. Though she thought this guy was more akin to a mountain gorilla than a monkey.

According to Mira, they were Momma Salvaggio's bully boys, both a side hustle and a means of keeping the riff-raff in line. Nearly everyone who did business on Trinity was wanted by one Dominion or another, and those who stayed long-term, or used the station as a place to do business were urged to pay protection to Salvaggio's security force. The ones who chose not to take advantage of the service were scooped up by the bounty hunters and turned in for the reward.

The woman had an eye for making a profit, Lyta had to give her that.

"Lyta," Logan said right next to her ear, "circle around the other side." He motioned at the short set of stairs on the other side of the dance floor, leading up to the next level where the tables were located near the restrooms and the rear exits. "Kurtz and I will talk to them at the table. Mira," he told the younger woman, "you wait by the exit, okay? If anything goes wrong, just head straight for our shuttle and Katy will take you back to the ship."

The girl took off immediately, apparently happy to be as far away from them as possible, and Lyta snorted in amusement. Life was so much simpler when you stopped expecting to live through it.

Moving back across the dance floor was simpler without trying to drag Kurtz along. She danced herself, whirling and eeling through the crowd, hugging the edges, her right shoulder scraping along the stone and plastic there. She was grateful the sleeve of her utility fatigues was thick because the wall was damp with something, probably a lot of different somethings. She held her breath, determined not to figure out what they were, and finally she reached the steps, squeezing by a tall, statuesque young woman wobbling precariously on ten-centimeter heels, each hand holding a colorful cocktail.

She'd been worried Lopes would notice her approach and recognize her, but the security officer seemed absorbed in whatever conversation she was having with Monk and Ham, gesticulating broadly like she was telling them a war story.

Probably bragging about how badly she intimidated us.

In fact, the woman barely noticed when Logan and Kurtz stepped right up to the table beside her. Monk and Ham spotted them immediately, their hands leaving the sweating glass of their drinks and reaching automatically under their jackets. Her nerves buzzed an alert up and down her spine, a suspicion they'd bribed guns past the club security—or maybe simply bullied their way through on the strength of their position with Salvaggio's organization. She glanced around quickly, searching for makeshift weapons, found a quartet of pool tables squashed too close together in an alcove just beside the bathroom. People were playing on them—badly, drunken—despite the close quarters, but none noticed when she slipped a cue from the rack on the wall.

"Slaughter," Lopes said, surprise heavy in her voice as she finally looked up and saw the two men. "What are you doing here?"

"That's 'Colonel Slaughter,' Officer Lopes," he admonished

her with a stern brashness she knew was affected. He was most likely mimicking his father, she thought. "And I'm here because I wanted to speak to your friends here."

"Do we know you?" Ham demanded, obviously the more talkative of the pair. His hand hadn't quite made it beneath his jacket, but it was close enough to get there quickly if need be.

"You don't. But we were here to meet a potential client, a potentially lucrative client, and I've been told you were the last ones to see him."

Monk snorted but said nothing. Ham grinned broadly.

"We've been the last thing a lot of people have seen, you know what I mean?" He turned his neck to the side, cracking the vertebrae loud enough to be heard over the bass beat. "You'll have to be more specific."

His accent was Starkad, she thought, somewhere urban, maybe Stavanger itself; and from his bearing and attitude, she was sure he was former military. An asshole, but a dangerous asshole.

"His name is Terry Conner," Logan told him, acting as if he really expected an answer. "He was here just over a week ago."

They tried, she'd give them that. They did their best to pretend the name meant nothing to them, but Ham had a tell, a muscle twitching next to his right eye.

"Never heard of him," Ham grunted, then shut himself up by taking a swallow of his drink. Monk said nothing, and Lyta was beginning to wonder if he was actually capable of human speech.

Finally, Chica Lopes spoke up, and Lyta got the feeling it was because the bounty hunters had stopped talking and the security officer's instinct was to fill the gap.

"The gentlemen have said they don't know your friend, *Colonel* Slaughter," she told Logan, clearly trying to assert some authority, though her voice sounded distinctly buzzed and not conducive to the effort. "So, why don't you just move along?"

"I think I know the kind of people you're used to dealing with," Logan said, ignoring Lopes, directing his words at the bounty hunters.

His tone had drifted away from the emulation of his father's imperiousness and towards a different voice, one uniquely his own. She'd initially thought of it as his "Jonathan Slaughter" voice, but she'd changed her mind. This *was* Logan Conner now.

"Outlaws, men and women with a price on their heads, no backup, no support. People you can make disappear and no one will notice." Logan moved a step closer, hands flat on the table, leaning over Ham with an expression as deadly as the one the bounty hunter had affected. "I am *not* one of those people. I don't kill people retail, one at a time for spare change. Like it says right here…" He nodded toward the unit patch on his shoulder. "…we deal in *wholesale* slaughter. It's not just my name, it's a job description. Believe me when I say, if the two of you get between me and a deal that could make me money, keep my mecha repaired and my people fed, I will leave your bodies bleeding in these tunnels and no one will ever remember they used to be scared of you."

Lyta was impressed. Putting together a credible threat was an art form, and his was as good as any she'd used in a long and colorful career. She was even more impressed by the lack of fear behind it. Not that Logan wasn't afraid; he wasn't a psychopath, and facing down stone killers in a nest of outlaws was enough to give anyone pause. But he hadn't shown a micron of it, and she saw the worry in Ham's eyes, maybe even a bit in Monk's stolid expression. Neither of their hands continued the slow traverse under their jackets.

It might have ended peacefully with the two bounty hunters giving them the information they needed, except for the one thing guaranteed to screw up the smoothest of transactions: a self-important drunk who believes they've been disrespected.

"You listen to *me*, fucking Colonel gun-for-hire," Chica Lopes spat the words, pushing herself up to her feet and getting into Logan's face. "You may be used to pushing people around, but not on *my* fucking station!"

Lyta saw it before Logan or Kurtz, saw the woman's hand reaching back under her frilled, mauve jacket, grasping the handle of the concealed pistol, and she was in motion, swinging the pool cue in an arc she'd learned with a *katana* as a young teenager. The end of the cue smacked into the security officer's wrist with a double-crack of faux-wood snapping at the hinge point and the wrist breaking a microsecond later. The gun went flying and Lyta made the rookie mistake of trying to follow its flight, desperate for a real weapon in the face of the guns she assumed the bounty hunters had.

She'd taken her eyes off of them for the briefest of moments, but it was long enough for them to make their move, prodded into action by the sudden violence, the breaking bone, the piercing scream as the agony burned through Lopes' alcohol haze. She rushed in to take them out before they had the chance to try to run, but it was too late. Lopes stumbled into her way, swinging at her one-handed with admirable spunk and a natural brawling abil-ity, and she had to waste the second it took to plant what was left of the cue across the woman's jaw and the side of her neck.

Lopes went down like a felled tree, collapsing backwards and getting in her way just long enough. Ham had bolted, running straight into Logan and trying to bowl him over, but the kid had a low center of gravity and enough training from her to take the rush and redistribute it into a hip toss. The tall bounty hunter flopped through the air and tumbled right over the dividing wall onto the dance floor, flailing legs and arms catching everything around him and took three of the club's patrons down with him in a tangle of limbs. Shouts, screams, breaking glass all sent ripples of disruption through the crowd like a rock thrown into a pond, sent people stumbling out of the way, bumping into other dancers, spreading the chaos.

Logan followed him over the wall, leaving her and Kurtz to deal with Monk, who didn't seem in the mood to run. The big man roared like a wounded elephant, tossing the table on its side in a fountain of cheap liquor and broken glass, and charging directly into the unlucky Valentine Kurtz. To his credit, Kurtz didn't turn and beat feet in the opposite direction, despite the fact the big man had a good ten or fifteen kilograms on him. Lyta was still a good three steps away and there weren't too many *good* strategies for dealing with someone that much stronger and heavier, but Kurtz, at least, didn't choose the worst of them.

He went low, diving for Monk's knees, risking taking one of them right to the face in an effort to get beneath the big man's center of gravity. Lyta didn't wait to see if the strategy worked; she threw herself over the upturned table and slammed the jagged end of the broken pool cue into Monk's right shoulder blade with as much force as two solid decades of training could impart to it. She had no illusions the improvised weapon could penetrate the armored jacket, but it didn't have to—it just had to keep the muscle-head from drawing his gun. The scapula was too large and too deep for her to hear it break, but his right arm went limp and the breath went out of him in an agonized *whoosh*. She resisted the urge to put the next blow behind his right ear, since they needed him alive. Instead, she jumped onto his back and wedged the half of a pool cue under his chin, yanking him backwards.

"Get his gun!" she yelled at Kurtz just before Monk collapsed back onto her.

Lyta tucked her head in close beside his and tried to turn him, tried to force his body to the side to let his weight land on his shoulder instead of her back, but she was only partially successful. A dull, concussive pain exploded in her back and up through her ribs as her shoulders slammed into the floor, then rebounded with the weight of the bounty hunter on her chest. Monk thrashed to the left, trying to work himself free with his good arm, trying to throw her off, and he nearly succeeded.

She couldn't breathe, couldn't think, couldn't see through the flashes of stars in her vision. Her ribs felt cracked, but she held on, ignoring the agony in her side and pulling back on the pool cue with everything she had. More weight piled on to the already-substantial bulk of the bounty hunter and she thought it had to be Kurtz, but she couldn't see anything past the wild tangle of Monk's blond hair.

Her vision cleared in time to see Kurtz yanking the gun from Monk's shoulder holster. It wasn't a conventional pistol, though, it was a dart launcher, maybe loaded with drugged hypodermics, maybe with stun capacitors. Just the sort of thing a bounty hunter would find useful for capturing wanted men and women. He tried to aim it at Monk and Lyta clenched her teeth reflexively, about to scream at him not to do it—a stun capacitor would conduct right through him and into her—when he visibly changed his mind and crashed the butt of the gun down into the bounty hunter's jaw.

It didn't knock the man out, but it took the fight out of him and she was able to sink the choke hold in, pressing the pool cue home into his carotid until he went slack. She held it a few seconds after that, knowing he wouldn't be under long, and when she let go she had to wave at Kurtz to come help her move the big man off her.

"He'll have restraints," she said, her voice still a croak as breath rushed back into her lungs. She squirmed out from beneath Monk while Kurtz held him up, heard the mech-jock grunting with the effort. "Get them on him."

"This guy stinks like a whorehouse at high noon," Kurtz complained, keeping the gun trained on the unconscious man while he patted him down.

Lyta, finally able to catch a full breath, had to agree: what

Monk lacked in oratory skills, he made up for in the sheer amount of cologne he'd managed to dump over himself. She managed to stand, trying to keep one eye on Kurtz and his hunt for the elusive handcuffs as she kept a watch around them and tried to see if she could spot Logan.

Lopes was still on the floor, moaning softly now, holding her bruised jaw with her unbroken hand, but she wouldn't be a threat injured, drunk and unarmed. Other customers were staring at them, but none who wanted to get involved, if she was any judge. But anyone, a bartender, a customer, a janitor could have already called security and they needed to get out of here while there was still a chance.

She spotted Logan almost immediately. The dancers and wait-staff had cleared a large spot on the floor around him and the bounty hunter they called Ham, as if the two of them were going to compete in a freestyle dance-off. To her, it looked more like a secondary school wrestling competition set to a bad music track. Logan had trapped Ham's right hand against his body under his left arm, trying to keep the man from drawing his weapon, and was holding the left fist away from his face as they circled, each trying to hook the other's leg. It could have been amusing if things weren't so close to going to utter shit.

She was about to vault over the wall herself and help him, but he made his move while her hand was grabbing the edge. It was subtle, a shifting of his stance, pushing inward and forward instead of out and back, at just the right time, something you couldn't learn drills and training, something you had to spar and spar and spar to get a feel for. A blink at the wrong time and she would have missed it—one second, they were in the middle of their high-stepping dance and the next, Ham was sprawled out on the floor with Logan's knee in his chest.

Then the boy broke the cardinal rule she'd taught him in a

thousand different sessions in the dojo: he punched Ham square in the face.

Don't hit someone in the face with your bare knuckles, damn it, she chided him mentally.

She understood the action even as she mentally condemned it. Her lessons had always stressed hitting soft targets with hard, and when you were sitting on someone's chest, the only soft target readily available was the throat, which could have killed one of the men they were trying to take alive. Two punches, three, two in the nose to blind the man with pain, a sharp jab to the point of the jaw to stun him, then he was stripping the gun out from beneath the man's jacket.

Lyta tore her eyes away from the scene on the dance floor and checked on Kurtz, who had found two pairs of flex-cuffs in Monk's pockets and was using them to secure the big man's wrists and ankles. Monk was shaking his head, about to come to, but Kurtz aimed the dart launcher and fired into the bound man's neck. It was a shock capacitor, she could tell by the way the muscular bounty hunter spasmed and thrashed as the stun charge coursed through his body.

It's going to work, she dared to let herself think. *We're going to make it out of here.*

Then she saw the first station security troops tromp through the front entrance, three of them in full armor, helmets on but faceplates up, hands filled with what looked like sonic stunners. The woman in the lead was panting and sweating under the brow of her helmet, having sprinted to the scene as fast as she could bearing the load. She glanced back and forth, unsure of where the emergency was with the lights still dimmed and half-naked bodies glowing on the video screens.

"Well, damn," Lyta said mildly.

Logan already had Ham thrown over his shoulder, and she could see Kurtz struggling to get Monk up off the ground. She rushed over and helped him, getting the bulk of the heavy bounty-hunter up onto a fireman's carry, then pushing the man toward the exit. The music had stopped. Her ears had grown so accustomed to the onslaught, it took her a moment to notice.

"Go!" she said in a harsh bellow, loud enough to make Logan turn in his tracks. "Go!" she repeated, motioning at the rear exit. "I'll hold them off!"

She could see the battle raging inside him played out across his face, but he knew the situation as well as she did. This was the mission, and he'd chosen it. He lumbered toward the door, the lanky man hanging over him like a cape, Kurtz struggling to follow.

Lyta smiled as she hefted the half of a pool cue, spinning it around artfully in her right hand like the escrima sticks she'd learned to use as a teenager. She grabbed the edge of the dividing wall and bounded over it, taking the landing in a crouch. The video screens had gone dark and the lights came up as her feet touched the floor, bathing her and the security troops in a harsh, white glare.

One of the braver, or perhaps more intoxicated club patrons, a man tall enough to have been raised on a lighter-gravity world, lunged at Lyta with arms wide. Maybe he was trying to impress his date, or maybe he thought she was just your normal, brawling miscreant. Either way, she didn't want to hurt him too badly, so she didn't use the stick. Her elbow impacted his solar plexus and he pitched forward, suddenly unable to breathe.

As if his fall was a cue, the bouncers, two men with more testosterone flowing through their bloodstream than their tiny brains could handle, decided they'd be the heroes of the day and hand the crazy woman over to the security troops. Lyta sneered, deciding they didn't deserve the restraint she'd shown with the first attacker; they'd had ample warning. Her stick flashed out, breaking an arm just below the elbow, then lashed backwards and dislocated a knee. For big men, they screamed like babies, one writhing on the floor while the other stumbled away holding his arm. The people who'd been crowding the dance floor watched her with wide eyes, frozen in position, as if they were more afraid of what she'd do if they tried to run away than they were of what she'd do to them if they stayed.

There was no missing her now. The armored woman was looking straight at her. The security troops aimed her way and advanced through the foyer, ignoring the alarms from the weapons detectors as they passed. The bouncers weren't there to berate them, anyway. Lyta edged a step closer to the nearest cluster of dancers, and indecision narrowed the eyes of the woman in the lead, the muzzle of her sonic stunner wavering as she glanced back and forth at the civilians surrounding Lyta. She was thinking of pissed off customers, Lyta figured, and how much trouble she'd be in if she wound up knocking out a dozen of them to get one trouble-maker.

Lyta didn't intend to give her the time to sort it out.

With a rising, ululating yell, she charged into the security troops, her stick raised...

12

"Not that way!" Logan yelled to Valentine Kurtz, waving him away from the control panel for the lift station.

Kurtz frowned in confusion until he saw his commander lugging the semi-conscious, bound Ham toward the emergency stairwell.

"You've *gotta* be fucking kidding me, Boss!" he exclaimed, already puffing from the effort of lugging Monk around. "There's no way…"

But Logan had already pulled open the door and there was no option but to follow him. Kurtz took a sideways step, wondering if anyone was watching them. There were plenty of people milling about the lift station, heading up or down, back to the docking hubs or out to the various night spots on this level, but no one gave the two of them more than an idle glance. Apparently, this wasn't the sort of place where it paid to be too curious.

"There's no way I can carry this heavy-assed lunkhead all the way down to the docking bay!" Kurtz reiterated, letting the stairwell door slam shut behind him.

The stairs were narrow, spiral, and little-used, added early in the construction of the place because they'd a way to get out of the cave if the power failed. Chemical light-strips lined the upper edge of the walls, giving just enough illumination to navigate the steps without falling and breaking his neck but not nearly enough to feel comfortable. He'd seen them in the mission brief and almost immediately dismissed them, thinking they'd be too slow and too confining to be of any use.

"Spin gravity gets lower the closer we get to the hub," Logan reminded him, his voice echoing off the walls, tinny and hollow. "He'll get lighter. Plus, Mira is taking the elevators down to the docking bay, and I don't want her caught up in this."

Kurtz glanced around instinctively, realizing he'd forgotten all about the girl in the confusion.

"Aren't we going to wait for Colonel Randell?" he asked. The words cost him breath he couldn't spare and he was fairly certain he'd strained something already, but he had to know.

"No." Logan's voice was harder to make out this time, lacking the projection and enthusiasm of his previous answer. "She knows what she's doing. She'll do better on her own without us slowing her down."

There was a lot more Kurtz wanted to say, but he clenched his teeth and concentrated on keeping his balance, on anything other than the pain in his neck and shoulder, and core muscles, and the increasingly intolerable stench of the man. There was a reason he drove a mech instead of hauling a gun and a ruck across Hell's creation like the Rangers, and this whole thing was giving him a nice, painful reminder of it. The stairway twisted downwards, the DNA strands of the station stretched out in a never-ending spiral through every level from the rim to the hub. He didn't even want to think about how close they'd been to the rim. Not *all* the way out, of course, but far enough.

Logan was right though. As each landing passed, carrying the bounty hunter seemed to get easier. He would have chalked it up to his own rugged, hard-bitten nature if he hadn't known it was the pull of the centripetal force decreasing, and he resented science for the disillusionment even as he appreciated the relief. As grateful he was for the decreased pull of spin-gravity, he was even more grateful for the lack of company. The stairwell might not have been deserted—it was impossible to see more than a dozen meters or so in either direction due to the curvature—but no one had happened to be in the same isolated section they were or happened to be wandering out onto one of the landings as they tromped through. Which was a damned good thing, because Ham had come to after a few minutes, and wasn't happy at all.

"You won't get away with this!" the tall man bellowed, the echo of the shouting off the laser-cut stone walls almost more annoying than the inanity of the declaration. "You don't know who we are, asshole! You don't know who we work for!"

Logan didn't pause in his pace down the stairs, just pivoted his upper body and whacked Ham's head against the nearest wall. The bounty hunter squawked and groaned, his head lolling and a bruise already starting to form under the small pressure cut.

"I know exactly who you are," Logan told him, strain in his voice. Kurtz wondered if it was the physical stress of the quick descent or maybe the emotional toll of leaving Lyta behind. "You're the piece of shit who kidnapped *my brother* a week ago, and you're the same piece of shit who's going to tell me exactly where you took him if you ever wanted to walk on your own two feet again. Until then, you can shut the hell up."

Kurtz snorted under his breath. The Boss had a way with words. Ham did as he was told, either from fear of getting smacked again or maybe an incipient concussion, and it was only two more landings before the gravity was light enough they were taking the steps three and four at a time. Then their luck ran out.

They were only three levels up from the hub and the apparent gravity was somewhere around a tenth of a gee in Kurtz's estimation, based solely on what he remembered from brief training visits to smaller moons during his military career. Not low enough to float like a feather on the wind just yet, but Kurtz felt as if he weighed about as much as a good-sized salmon from the Chilkat River back home.

Logan was just a few steps down from the landing for level four when the stairwell door popped open right between them, nearly slamming Kurtz in the face before he could bring himself to a stop.

"What the hell?" the man who stepped through exclaimed, staring down at the receding back of Logan Conner and the bruised and bleeding face of Ham the bounty hunter. "What do you think you're doing?"

Kurtz could only see part of the back of his head, and all he could tell was the guy's head was shaved and he was wearing some sort of a uniform, though he had no idea if it was Security or janitorial. But he already had his 'link in his hand, getting ready to make a call, and Kurtz was willing to bet it wasn't to his girlfriend to tell her about the odd thing he had seen today at work.

He shrugged Monk off his shoulder as easily as tossing away a jacket, able to handle him so easily both because of the light gravity and because he didn't care if the big man fell flat on his face. He'd stuck the dart gun in his belt back at the club, hesitant to leave the weapon laying around for someone else to pick up and use on him, and he clawed at it now, struggling to free the front sight from the material of his fatigue pants before the intruder noticed him.

"I said stop!" the bald man called again at Logan's back. "I'm calling Security!"

Another second to find the safety and Kurtz fired from nearly point-blank, putting the dart in the man's right shoulder and leaving him spasming in the throes of an electric stun charge. The gun had barely made a sound when it fired, not much louder than a balloon popping as the magnetic launcher shot the capacitor out at over a hundred meters a second. Kurtz didn't bother to put the gun away this time, just flicked the safety back on. Baldy was stuck half-in and half-out of the stairwell entrance and he took the time to pull the man out and kick the door shut before he went back for Monk.

By the time he caught up with Logan at the next landing, the stairs were more useful for their railings that let him guide himself with the edge of his hand, and the spin gravity was barely enough to remind him which way used to be down.

"We're getting close," Kurtz called. "Maybe we should be thinking how we're going to get these assholes past the security checkpoint."

Logan nodded, dragging a foot across the wall to slow himself down, then pulling his 'link out of his pocket and raising it to his mouth.

"Acosta," he said tersely. "Whatever you're going to do, do it now."

Patrick Bray had been masquerading as Francis Acosta for so long, he was beginning to forget which was the real him. It was disturbing, and his lack of any family ties on Sparta only made things worse. He really needed to take a trip home to Nike soon, visit his parents and his sisters, get a feel for who Patrick Bray really was.

First though, he had to blow something up. Nothing big, he didn't have enough explosives for a big bang, and it would have been counterproductive anyway. He wanted to distract the security guards at the customs station, not force them to lock down the whole docking bay.

He'd known what was expected when they'd gone over the

plan, and he'd had hours to think about it, had even bounced it off Commander Margolis. She'd thought it was too wimpy, which meant it was probably just this side of reckless, given her predilections. He wasn't entirely satisfied with it, but he had a bad habit of paralysis by analysis. His superiors had said so on his last personnel evaluation, and he'd signed it, so it must be true.

Acosta drifted down from the shuttle's docking collar, leaving the girl Mira with a disgruntled Katy Margolis back in the umbilical tunnel. Katy wanted to be involved, but she was a pilot, not a field agent or a soldier, and he wished Colonel Slaughter or Colonel Conner or whatever the hell he was calling himself this trip would have the balls to remind her of it. Just because someone was brave enough to face down the enemy with a gun didn't mean they were the best qualified for the job. At least he'd assigned her to the shuttle for this mission, though he'd had to stress they were going to need a quick getaway to get her to agree with it. He wanted to blame it on their relationship, but he was sure she'd be just as much of a wildcard if they hadn't been together. Acosta had managed to convince her he needed her to keep an eye on Mira and make sure she didn't warn the guards or steal their shuttle while he created the distraction.

The explosive was compact and easily disguised, so he'd slipped it into the hollow shell of a cased datalink. It looked incredibly normal to be meandering along in the broad, multi-tracked docking cylinder carrying a datalink, nothing that would attract any attention. It even gave him an excuse not to make eye contact with the customs agent. The weaselly little man gave him the creeps and it had taken nearly an hour to convince him they'd straightened things out with station security after Lopes had cut them loose. Acosta flashed the pass the little man had given him after much hemming and hawing and protest and was waved through.

The station security guards anchored behind the customs

booth regarded him dully, probably only noticing at him at all simply because of the earlier ruckus. Acosta waited until he was sure they'd turned back to check the next newcomer in the customs line before he peeled the backing off the adhesive strip on the back of the dummy 'link and affixed it to the raised frame of a staff-only restroom behind the customs office, then pushed quickly away.

If they had camera monitors, he might have been seen, but it would look like nothing more than an attempt to maneuver in free-fall, to get a boost toward the lift station. Now that it was set, the nerves began to eat at him, sweat beginning to gather at the small of his back despite the inherent chill of the docking bay environmental systems. He had his gun. While it was a comfort, it was also a temptation he couldn't give into. They'd agreed they didn't want to kill anyone and, more importantly to him in particular, these guys were wearing armor and he wasn't. The odds were, if any shooting started, he'd be one of the first to die.

He touched his earpiece, connected to the real 'link on his belt.

"Go," he transmitted.

The door to the emergency stairwell wasn't locked because it would have defeated its purpose. Even a bunch of money-hungry outlaws wanted to make sure people could get out if something went wrong. Mass death was bad for business. And since it was such a pain in the ass to actually get anywhere via the narrow, twisting stairs, almost no one used them; which meant no one was paying attention to the door when it opened and Logan and Kurtz came out, dragging the two bounty hunters with them.

Both the captives were bound hand and foot and seemed to be unconscious, which wasn't as conspicuous in microgravity as it might have been otherwise, but wasn't going to completely escape notice either. Acosta muttered a curse. This was all last-minute, on-the-fly planning, but couldn't they have at least *tried* to be a bit subtler?

There were murmurs now, just a few newcomers. Acosta wondered if the people who'd visited before were so used to seeing shit like this that they didn't even think twice about it. But some heads turned as the two Spartan mech-jocks passed. Acosta watched the eyes and read the thoughts, the progression from "Gosh, there's something weird about those guys," to "I wonder how drunk they have to be…" to "are those two guys tied up and unconscious?" and finally, inevitably, "should we tell someone about this?"

The process was nearly universal and it usually took a predictable amount of time, maybe ten seconds from start to finish. Fingers raised, pointing, the shouted words "Hey!" and "Wait!" rising above the general hubbub of the docking cylinder but almost lost in the twisted acoustics of a cylindrical compartment three hundred meters across and nearly as deep. But the reaction spread like dominoes falling, following the Spartans and their captives in a chain of hands braking on the guiderails and fingers pointing and raised cries. It was only a matter of seconds before the guards became aware of the racket and connected it to Logan and Kurtz.

Acosta touched a control on his 'link, then covered his ears, closed his eyes and brought his knees up to his chest.

For such a small lump of explosives, it made quite a bang.

Even fifty meters away, the heat was the warm glow of a fire in the hearth on a cold winter's night, the concussion a palm slapping him in the chest like a friend's greeting, then the thump of the wall fetching up against his shoulder. It wasn't a painful impact—there wasn't enough of a charge for that—but he knew it would be worse for the security troops closer to the wall. He'd taken the chance their armor would keep them from getting seriously hurt, and maybe it had, but they'd still lost their magnetic anchor to the floor and were floating free, arms windmilling wildly.

"Move your asses!" he yelled into the audio pickup of his earpiece, pushing away from the wall.

A woman was crouched beside him, curled into a ball, still holding her hands over her ears, eyes squeezed shut and mouth open in a silent scream, as if she expected another explosion on the heels of the first. Something about the terror in her expression bothered him, sticking with him as she faded from view behind.

Other screams hadn't been so silent, and they were easy to hear now, cutting through the background noise and the wailing alarms, through the haze of smoke and the confused shouting. They were screams of alarm rather than pain, he judged, though he couldn't be sure. The blast had been close enough to the customs kiosk to cause injuries in the staff working the table, but he'd done the best he could and he wasn't going to agonize about it.

Instead, he grabbed the nearest guiderail and propelled himself back toward the shuttle, building up reckless speed in the midst of the herd of panicked human sheep. He knew how to maneuver in zero-gee, had aced at least that much of the tactical course mandated for field agents by General Constantine, and he used every bit of that training now. You had to know the physics, of course, but you had to know it on an instinctive level, not thinking about which motions would send you spinning one way or another, just *doing* it.

He twisted and spun and clutched at the bar to brake himself when he needed to, leaving a bit of skin behind, and ducked into a ball when impacts were inevitable. A tall, gangly Belter dressed in tight, dark elastic grunted and spun away in a tangle of long limbs as Acosta ricocheted downward and barely pushed himself back up in time to avoid plowing into the floor.

Stopping was the hard part. The shuttle's docking collar was only ten meters away and if he just grabbed tight on the railing, it would probably dislocate his wrist. Instead, he twisted around and scraped the sides of his boots against the rubber padding, tightening gradually until he'd bled off enough momentum to kick off sideways and glide into the umbilical.

Katy clapped in appreciation.

"You may be a shitty copilot," she said, "but you sure as hell know how to run away."

"Go get this thing ready to blast out of here," he told her, making it an order even though he wasn't a hundred percent sure he outranked her anymore. "And get the *Shakak* moving!"

Katy, surprisingly, didn't argue with him, just nodded and headed back through the shuttle's lock, pushing off toward the cockpit.

"What should I do?" Mira wondered. Her hand was wrapped around a safety strap, gripping it white-knuckled like she'd be sucked into space if she let go. She was young, he thought, not for the first time. Too young to be caught up in a place like this.

"Go belt yourself in," Acosta instructed. *And stop distracting me*, he added silently.

The Intelligence officer leaned back out of the docking collar, wondering exactly how long they had before someone added two and two together and came up with "let's go shoot the mercenaries," and whether Logan and Kurtz would make it to the shuttle before or after the realization. They were close now, though they couldn't hope to move as fast as Acosta had, lacking both the training and the freedom of motion since they were dragging along the bounty hunters. Less than fifty meters, which still seemed way too far, but at least the path was clear and there didn't seem to be anyone…

"Stop right there!"

The call was amplified, perhaps by the external speakers on the security guard's helmet or perhaps via a connection with the public address system, or maybe both, but the reverberation made it harder for him to pinpoint the source.

There. Twenty-five meters or so behind Logan and Kurtz, two armored station security troopers were jetting toward them using some sort of hand-held, compressed-gas propulsion guns. Damn. He hadn't noticed those. They complicated things. They were going to catch up, and when they did, they weren't going to bother trying to stun the two of them or trap them. The full-auto, drum-fed flechette guns they both carried would rip the two mech-jocks apart and if the bounty hunters got hit in the process…well, collateral damage was always a danger.

Kurtz glanced back over his shoulder at the pursuing troops, but Logan was fixed on his goal, pumping his arm along the guiderail in dogged determination.

Which leaves it up to me.

He pulled his sidearm from the cross-draw holster on his left hip. Colonel Randell always made fun of the cross carry, saying he was trying to look like a gunfighter, but it just felt right to him. He stretched his arm out, bracing it against the rim of the docking collar and wedging his feet on the inner ring to absorb the recoil. The handgun was standard military issue for Sparta and Modi and available commercially everywhere else, as common as dirt, each of them with a pop-up electronic sight. His trainers at the field agent course had criticized it, saying it wasn't practical for shooting on the run, but propped against a rest, it was almost ideal. He *could* have aimed for the troopers' faceplates from a rest this still, taken them out even at fifty meters, but there was that whole damned thing about not killing them…

He shifted his point of aim to the left hand of the lead trooper, where he was holding the compressed gas gun and fired off three shots as quickly as he could. The gun bucked, the roar of the 10mm slugs screaming out of the barrel subdued by the built-in suppressor but still enough to pop his ears. Sparks and a jet of flame shot out the side of the propulsion unit and the lead trooper rocketed off at an angle to his original course until he let loose of the gas gun and wound up tumbling backwards helplessly.

By then, Acosta was shifting his aim but the second guard in line had realized they were being shot at and was trying to adjust his course laterally and bring up his flechette gun at the same time. There was no choice, no time for a carefully-guided shot at the gas gun. Acosta fired off the rest of the magazine at center of mass, counting on the man's armor to do its job.

A 10mm slug travelling over 600 meters per second wouldn't penetrate the thick chest armor the man wore, but it would still hurt like a son of a bitch, and probably scare the shit out of him. At least that's what Acosta was hoping. The station security guard jerked wildly at the impact of the volley, and more significant than whatever momentum the slugs imparted to him was his haphazard waving around of the gas gun. The hand-held compressed-gas propulsion unit twisted him in an out-of-control spiral that abruptly ended in a collision with the opposite wall between two docking collars.

Acosta reloaded automatically, dumping the spent magazine and switching out to a fresh one. The empty mag spun slowly away, ricocheting off the opposite side of the docking umbilical in a distracting spiral arc, but before he could think to try to retrieve it, Logan barreled through the opening, nearly taking Acosta with him.

"You're welcome!" Acosta called after him, squeezing against the side to let Kurtz in along with the broad-bodied great ape he was carrying with him.

Once they were inside, Acosta shut the outer lock then retreated back to the inner one and slammed it closed before he bothered to holster his gun.

"We're in, Margolis," he called up to the cockpit. "Cut us

loose before someone with two brain cells to rub together figures who's behind this!"

"Wait!" Logan exclaimed, head snapping around from where he was strapping the lanky, long-faced goon into one of the acceleration couches. Now that the bounty hunter was still, Acosta finally noticed they'd gagged him with a strip of cloth, the same color as the shirt beneath the tall man's leather jacket. "Lyta could still be trying to reach us! We can't leave dock until she gets here!"

"You're in command, *sir*," Acosta assured him, putting a bit of the cynicism he was feeling into the "sir." "But if we stay here, they're going to block us in with one of their tugs or just start ventilating us with one of their antimissile Vulcan cannons. We *have* to get out of the bay and under the cover of the *Shakak's* guns."

"He's right," Katy put in before Logan could protest again. She was twisted around in the pilot's seat, her face taut with anguish, but she was smart enough to understand the situation and Acosta appreciated the support. "We'll come back for Lyta…but we can't do that if were dead."

Logan's face twisted into a snarl, and, for a moment, Acosta was sure he was going to do something stupid like grab a gun and go blasting back out into the docking bay. But whatever he thought of Logan Conner's lack of leadership experience, the man was Jaimie Brannigan's son, and was no one's fool.

"Right," Logan grunted, tightening the strap across the bounty hunter's chest tight enough to squeeze the breath out of the man, making his eyes go wide. "Get us out of here, Katy."

Acosta stifled the sigh of relief building in his chest, not wanting to antagonize his commanding officer any more than he probably already had. Besides, it would have been disrespectful. He valued Colonel Randell's level-headed leadership probably more than anyone else. She served as a counter-weight to the younger, more impetuous bent of the too-quickly-promoted Colonel Conner and Commander Margolis. If she'd been here, if the situation was reversed and he or Logan or Katy were the one trapped inside, Acosta was sure she'd be making the same decision.

At least telling himself that made it easier to live with the sweet feeling of impending safety washing over him when the shuttle broke away from the docking collar and began maneuvering out of the bay. The bang-bang vibration of the steering jets startled him more than it should have, all too reminiscent of projectiles hitting the fuselage.

Someone was screaming over the radio from up in the cockpit until Katy reached out and shut off the speakers.

"Well, Traffic Control isn't happy with us," she announced. "They say they have an emergency in the docking bay and want everything locked down, but I told them to piss off, that we paid our fees like everyone else and don't want to sit around and get shot at while they try to figure out how to do their job."

"They won't fire at you yet," Mira said out of nowhere. Acosta shot her a curious glance as he passed by on the way to the cockpit.

"How the hell would you know?" he asked her, buckling on the restraints in the copilot's position. He'd barely tightened the strap across his chest when Katy hit the steering jets again and sent them boosting forward out of the docking cylinder, the glaring yellow of the work lights of the inner ring fading to the gentler glow of the stars against the infinite black.

"It's what I do for Ms. Kane." Mira flinched at the ringing thump of the maneuvering thrusters. "I get to know people, tell her what I find. Customs and Traffic Control are very blustery, but they can't afford to bully too much or the customers would go elsewhere." She sniffed a reserved laugh. "People do not come to Trinity because of the luxury."

"Well, thank Mithra for small favors," Acosta mumbled. He pulled up the sensor display for his station and began hunting through a forest of lidar, radar and thermal signatures, the footprints of all the various starships gathered around Trinity. "Where's the *Shakak*?"

"She's coming in using the stardrive," Katy told him, her voice a bit distracted as she plotted a burn on her station's navigation system. "Trying to keep her signature quiet until she has us in the hangar."

"If anyone sees her boosting in without any visible fusion drive," Acosta warned, "we're blown. The whole operation is blown."

"Starkad found Terminus," Logan reminded him, voice so grim Acosta felt the need to turn in his seat and look back at him. "They have the stardrive ship Terrin brought out here. The operation is *already* blown, *Agent Bray*." He bared his teeth. "If Starkad knows, who the hell are we hiding it from?"

"Brace yourselves," Katy Margolis said, and for a moment, Acosta wasn't sure if she was warning them for the upcoming boost or the future of the Dominions until she clarified. "Two-gee acceleration in five."

She would have been right either way.

13

"Play it for them, Nance," Kammy ordered, a sigh hissing off the end of the Communications Officer's name.

If there'd been gravity, Logan expected the big man would have been stooped over, shoulders dragged down by the sorrow and weariness he was obviously feeling. Instead, he was hanging from the safety rail at the edge of the bridge, every muscle relaxed except for the hand anchoring him. Kammy had seemed more animated when he'd asked them to come straight from the ship's hangar bay to the bridge on arrival, but maybe whatever it was had more time to sink in by now.

Nance was one of the few members of the original *Shakak*'s crew who'd survived the battle with the Starkad heavy cruiser *Valkyrian* back at Terminus, and though she'd received a promotion and a few medals for her actions, she still occupied the same position as Comm officer. She hadn't wanted to give up her assignment to the new *Shakak II* to take a position commensurate with her new rank on some other, lesser ship.

The same was true of everyone from the Spartan Navy and Rangers who'd served on the first Wholesale Slaughter mission: not one had elected to leave their position even though every single one had been offered more authority in another assignment. As for Captain Donner Osceola's original crew, well…he wanted to think, cynically, that the pay was better working for Sparta than going freelance, but he shook the idea away as unworthy. They'd been faithful to Osceola and they'd transferred that loyalty to Kammy when he'd taken over as Captain.

Nance seemed as fretful and depressed as Kammy, almost reluctant to touch the control to play back the message. When she did, the image came up on the two-D auxiliary screens rather than the main holographic display, the screens they'd installed during the refit. The face on the screen was unremarkable, unthreatening, an accountant's face, the suit beneath it an accountant's clothing. The expression on his face didn't match his appearance. His anger radiated off him like the heat waves from an optical illusion on a desert road.

"We know it was you, Slaughter. We've seen the security videos from the club, we know you were there personally. We want Grieves and Jackson back and we want them now."

"Grieves and Jackson?" Katy repeated.

"Monk and Ham," Mira supplied. "Those are their real names. That man is Milo Breckenridge, Momma Salvaggio's operations manager. He handles things when she's away from the station."

"In case you think you can just scoot out of here in your ship, bear in mind this station has the weaponry to disable any civilian ship."

"Not this ship, Mister," Katy muttered.

"If that isn't enough reason for you," Breckenridge went on, "perhaps this will be."

The camera view shifted, jerky and halting, evidence that the video pickup was held in someone's unsupported hand. Logan caught a brief glimpse of what looked like the detention cell in the security offices where they'd been held earlier before the image settled on Lyta Randell and his breath caught in his throat.

She was seated in one of the same metal chairs they'd occupied before, except her hands were cuffed behind her, her head slumped against her shoulder. The left side of her face was bruised, her left eye swollen shut, and blood trickled down her cheek from a cut above her brow. Logan thought for a terrifying second she was dead, but then she moaned and her swollen and split lips parted, gasping in a breath.

"She looks pretty bad," Breckenridge judged, his voice half a lament and half a taunt. "The injuries occurred while she was being apprehended, I assure you." He ducked back into the image, almost playful. "So far. But I can't promise how long I can keep it that way, because the head of security, Officer Lopes, is having her broken arm treated right now in the clinic, and I understand she's *quite* upset and has promised to, and I quote, 'break every bone in that fucking bitch's body.' Now I am not a violent man." Breckenridge motioned down at himself as if his suit proved it. "I don't believe I could stop a determined woman such as Officer Lopes, even if I wanted to."

Logan's pulse was pounding so loudly in his ears he barely heard the man finish with: "You have one hour to return Ms. Salvaggio's employees to the docking bay, unharmed, or your woman here dies unpleasantly."

The video froze on the harmless-looking man's pleasant features and Nance scowled, slapping the control to cut the feed to the screen.

"We could rip right through their fucking docking hub and core them like an apple with our main gun," Tara Gerard snapped, pounding a frustrated fist into her control panel. She bared her teeth and looked back to Kammy. "Just say the word, Cap, and I'll rip them a new one and show them who they're fucking dealing with!"

"There are innocent people being forced to work on that station!" Mira exclaimed, eyes going wide. She pulled herself along the safety rail, planting herself in front of Logan. "You can't just kill them!"

Logan regarded her silently, knowing she was right but still filled with rage and wanting to strike out. He felt Katy's hand on his arm and his breathing slowed, the pulse-beat beginning to fade along with the red haze over his vision.

"What's the word, Boss?" Kammy asked him.

"Mira's right," he declared firmly. "We can't take the chance of just blowing the shit out of them, as satisfying as it might be. But Tara's right, too."

"Of course I am," the Tactical Officer agreed. "About what?"

"They don't know what they're dealing with," Logan explained. "And they don't know we give a damn about the innocent civilians inside the station. They think we care about Lyta," he went on, beginning to feel a plan of action coming together even as the words spun out of him like a spider's web. "They think we care about her enough to give these guys up without a guarantee they'll even return her to us."

"You noticed that too, huh?" Kammy wondered.

Logan nodded. Breckenridge very carefully had *not* said they'd exchange Lyta for the bounty hunters; he'd just said she'd be killed if they weren't turned over.

"He thinks he has all the cards," he went on, wishing he could pace. He thought better when he walked. "We have to show him he has next to nothing…" He trailed off, remembering why they were here. "And we have to get what we need out of Monk and Ham, Grieves and Jackson, whatever you call them." He pointed to Nance, snapping his fingers and making a rolling gesture. "Get me Acosta. He's down in Security with the prisoners." He pointed to the flat-screen displays. "On video."

The Security section was just a generic compartment, but the Spartan engineers had managed to bolt in a few holding cells, just clear, polymer, soundproof boxes with a cot built into the side. In the video pickup from the comm screen, Monk and Ham were visible in adjoining cells, floating listlessly. Acosta turned to the call of the screen with what might have been annoyance on his face.

"What is it?" he demanded, adding "sir," after he saw it was Logan.

"They have Lyta," Logan told him. "You may have as little as an hour, and we *are* going to find out where they took Terrin before we turn those two back over to them."

"Oh, great," Acosta sighed. "Get back to me in an hour, then." He reached out toward the screen and the feed went dark.

"What now?" Kammy asked him.

"Nance," he said, "get me this Breckenridge on the horn. I want to talk to him. And Tara...." He nodded to the woman. "Find me a target."

Milo Breckenridge wiped a thin sheen of sweat away from his high forehead, then tugged at the tight collar of his dress suit.

"Why's the gravity so damned high down here, anyway?" he complained to no one in particular, leaning against an ugly, utilitarian metal desk. He didn't know who it belonged to, but he was sure they were lower in the pecking order than he was.

"It's 'cause we're closer to the rim, Mr. Breckenridge," one of the guards, an affable fellow with a much larger concentration of muscles in his arms and chest than brain cells in his head, replied. Breckenridge glared at him, but the man seemed pleased with his scientific insight.

"It's to make prisoners feel less comfortable."

The real answer came from an unexpected source: their captive. She seemed more awake and aware now that the effects of the sonic stunner had worn off, though her words were slurred somewhat from her swollen lip. Even with the bruised face, she gave him the distinct impression she could kill him in a second if someone was unwise enough to loosen her restraints.

"It's not that easy on the guards, either," the big, dumb one grumbled, his back resting against the stone wall, arms crossed.

"No one cares about prison guards," the woman remarked with a hint of a sneer on the half of her face that wasn't bruised. "And I imagine no one else wants to live out here."

"Since you're feeling so talkative," Breckenridge said, stepping closer to her, leaning over but not too close, "why don't you tell me your name?"

She regarded him coolly with a single green eye, the other refusing to open.

"Why? Are we going to have long conversations deep into the night regarding the nature of humanity and become life-long friends?"

Breckenridge laughed, forgetting the drag of the extra gravity for a moment.

"Oh, I like you already," he told her. "You probably clean up pretty nice. But you also managed to put half a dozen of my people in the clinic, even though they were wearing armor and you weren't. So, why don't you avoid getting any more damage done to that face and tell me your name?" He smiled with all the insincerity he could work up in one expression. "I'll start. I'm Milo Breckenridge, and I run things here at Trinity when Ms. Salvaggio is away."

"Is she away a lot?" the mercenary asked, seeming as innocent as a newborn babe. Breckenridge was sure if she could have batted her eyes, she would have.

"Enough that I get to make the important decisions," Breckenridge confided. He hauled off and kicked the leg of her chair and smiled when he saw her flinch just slightly. "Like whether to use enhanced interrogation techniques against prisoners."

She nodded just slightly, like she was giving him his due.

"My name is Lyta Randell," she told him. "I command Wholesale Slaughter's infantry company."

"There, that wasn't so hard, was it?" Breckenridge clapped his hands together as if he'd just completed a difficult task. "So, tell me something, Lyta, why did you and your boss kidnap two of Ms. Salvaggio's most valuable employees right out of a busy nightclub and then set off a damned *bomb* in the Customs kiosk to smuggle them out of this station?" He cocked an eyebrow. "Why would you do such a thing on our peaceful place of business?"

"Your men had information we needed," Lyta said easily enough he knew she'd been rehearsing the answer. "We tried to ask them nicely, and I think they might have been willing to help us, but your dumbass drunk of a Security Chief got her feelings hurt and pulled a gun, so we went with Plan B."

"That sounds exactly like something Officer Lopes would do," he admitted readily. In fact, he'd already seen her do it on the video feed from the club. "And honestly, I respect your willingness to do whatever you needed to close the deal. I operate by the same principle. Which means I will do whatever I need to do in order to get Mr. Grieves and Mr. Jackson back."

"That's up to Colonel Slaughter," Lyta said. "The mission comes before the troops."

Breckenridge frowned. Her tone was more troubling than her words. He wasn't necessarily sure he believed she was disposable, but he definitely believed she was *willing* to die for the mission. It was an uncommon attitude among mercenaries, and unless she was the exception in this Wholesale Slaughter company rather than the rule, he might have to rethink how he was going to deal with this situation.

"Mr. Breckenridge?"

He turned at the call, curious because it wasn't the big, dumb guard the Security officer in charge had assigned to watch Lyta.

This was one of the clerks manning the data terminals, watching the input from the internal and external security cameras and the communications center. The woman wasn't wearing a Security uniform, just the normal work coveralls of the station staff, but she looked a great deal more intelligent than the self-appointed expert on spin gravity.

"What is it?"

"There's a transmission from the mercenary ship, sir," the woman told him, "the *Shakak*. It's a Colonel Slaughter and he wants to speak to you personally."

Breckenridge grinned.

Excellent. Now they'd find out just how much this woman was worth to them.

"Bring it up," he encouraged the woman, losing patience and shoving her out of the seat, hunting for the control until he found it himself.

A woman in a grey uniform appeared on the screen, her face thin and dark and angular, her expression businesslike.

"This is Milo Breckenridge," he said. "Where's Colonel Slaughter?"

"Wait one for the Colonel," the woman told him curtly, reaching past the video pickup to hit a control.

Impatience and irritation surged through Breckenridge's bloodstream like adrenalin. It was a cheap trick, an old trick, but one that worked every time: asserting your dominance by making the other person wait. The video feed went dark for just a moment, and when it returned, it brought with it a face he'd seen before in the security feeds. The man was young, younger than Milo by at least five years, though with some of the stress lines of hard experience aging him at the corners of his eyes and his mouth. His hair was blond and short for a mercenary's, though certainly longer than the regulation for most of the militaries Breckenridge knew about.

"I'm Jonathan Slaughter," the officer said. "You have Lyta Randell, my infantry commander. I want her back."

"Unless you want her back in pieces," Breckenridge replied in a low growl, letting the anger from the disrespect get the better of him, "you'll send back Mr. Grieves and Mr. Jackson immediately."

Slaughter didn't reply for a moment, glancing off to the side of the video pickup, one of his eyebrows cocking upward in what might have been a questioning gesture. When he turned back, it was with a confidence which could only mean he'd received the answer he wanted.

"You have an unmanned supply barge decelerating to match velocities, Mr. Breckenridge," he said. "It's ten thousand kilometers out. You may want your external cameras to take a good look at it."

Breckenridge scowled at the screen, but went ahead and switched the call over to the Operations Center.

"Sensors," he snapped, "do we have an incoming barge?"

The screen had split; he still had Slaughter's image on the left side, while the right displayed a pasty-faced, overweight younger man who'd obviously neglected to take advantage of the complimentary sun lamp time every employee was afforded. Breckenridge reminded himself to send out a memo about that.

"Yes, sir, Mr. Breckenridge," Pale-face stuttered. "It's in its final braking boost right now, coming in around..." The man's eyes hunted off-screen as he checked a reading. "Just over nine thousand kilometers. Should be prepping for off-loading soon."

"Do we have a drone feed of it?" Breckenridge asked him. "Optical?" At the man's hesitant nod, Breckenridge clucked impatiently. "Then put it up on my damn screen instead of your white, lumpy face!"

The drones weren't much, just free-floating cameras attached to transmitters and a set of maneuvering thrusters to keep them in the correct orbit around Trinity, but they extended the range of the station's sensors in a cheap and ready way. The military didn't use them much because their signals were easily jammed or hacked, but his customers weren't usually so technologically sophisticated.

The view from the drone feed was unremarkable, just a shot of the ugly, utilitarian lines of the cargo barge. It was little more than a framework for rounded cargo capsules, with a fusion drive and a ring of fuel tanks at each end. The automated flight systems were primitive and the ship was unarmed, mostly because it wasn't worth stealing. Iron-ore powder from the asteroid mines for the fabricators and soy paste and spirulina from the system's orbital farms for the food processors were necessary for the day-to-day life of the station, but they were easily replaced. And the ship itself was as cheap as you could make a spaceship, one of dozens making their way back and forth across the system, useless except for the fusion drives, which were cheap and readily available.

"I see the barge," Breckenridge told Slaughter. "What the hell's so important about it?"

"Sir?" That was Pale-face again. His image didn't interrupt the feed, but Breckenridge recognized the voice. "The mercenary's ship, the *Shakak*, it's moving toward the barge." A pause. "Our sensors say it's accelerating at twenty gravities sir, but that's not possible if there are humans in it, and sir...I don't see any drive flare."

"What the hell are you talking about?" he exploded. Was the man trying to be a smartass? "Get me visual on them now!"

Now the screen was split into thirds, with Slaughter, the barge and...their ship. Breckenridge's mouth dropped open. There was nothing extraordinary about the lines of their ship; it could have been any one of hundreds of private cargo ships he'd seen pass through the system over the last few years, small enough he wouldn't have figured it could carry enough fuel to even maintain five or six gravities of acceleration for more than a few minutes.

And yet the sensor readings projected into the corner of the display said it was boosting at twenty-three gees, and not even glimmer of light shown from the fusion drive bell. It was absolutely…

"Impossible," he murmured, unable to keep himself from finishing the thought aloud.

"They're three thousand kilometers from the barge, sir," Paleface reported, still a disembodied voice. "And…oh, my God!"

He didn't have to ask what had brought on the exclamation. He could see it just as clearly as the sensor tech could, see the readings on the screen. The *Shakak* had simply stopped. She hadn't decelerated, hadn't done a skew flip and a lengthy, painful braking burn, she'd simply *stopped*. Which was just as impossible.

She was close enough to the barge for them to both be in the same shot from a different drone feed, and the image switched to that view, replacing the separate feeds. The *Shakak* hung in the blackness like a lion crouched in the high grass, awaiting the approaching wildebeest as they galloped across the savanna. Something glowed a spectral blue, a shimmering oscillation in the space separating the two ships, connecting the nose of the *Shakak* with the still-firing bow fusion drive of the barge.

There shouldn't have been any visible beam from any sort of energy weapon he'd ever heard of, not in a vacuum, but given the three impossible things he'd seen in just the last minute, the blue glow seemed almost insignificant. One of a few things should have happened when the energy beam struck the barge. The likeliest was nothing. The barge may have been unarmored, but it was also big and had a lot of empty space. Even a military laser might not do much to it unless it hit just right. The second was, if it did get that million-credit hit, the fusion drive would shut down.

Damage to the fuel feed or the reaction chamber would have caused an immediate, automatic shut-down. And the last was if the beam had hit the fuel storage tanks. That could have caused damage, could have sent the metallic hydrogen fuel pellets scattering across empty space.

Instead, the barge seemed to ignite at the point of the hit, a singularity of glimmering light expanding instantaneously into a nova, a second star in the system, nearly as bright as the primary star.

It was the fuel stores, it had to be. Nothing could cause a blast that size but a fusion explosion. Whatever they'd fired had penetrated the storage tanks and fused the metallic hydrogen. Breckenridge let out a breath he hadn't realized he was holding, reaching out with trembling fingers to switch off the feed from the drone.

Jonathan Slaughter stared back at him with the eyes of the Sphinx.

"Your station's walls are very thick," he said. "We probably couldn't burn through very far. But we could certainly destroy both docking hubs and put you out of business for months, if not years."

"Sir!" A call from Operations split the screen again. Not Paleface, but Koji, a Salvaggio employee and one of the weapons crew. "Do you want me to target their ship with the lasers?"

"Don't be a moron," Breckenridge told him. "Are you not watching this?"

He switched off the call from Koji impatiently.

"We still want our people back," he told Slaughter. "I assume you want to work out some sort of exchange."

"One hour," Slaughter told him. "My shuttle will bring your men in and leave with Lyta Randell. Anyone targets the shuttle, we take appropriate actions."

"Right." The word came out as a grunt, as if he'd been body-punched. Mithra alone knew what Momma Salvaggio would do to him when she found out about this. "She'll be ready."

The screen went dark.

Lyta Randell was laughing softly. He wanted to put his fist into her face, or better yet, have Big Dumb Muscle guy do it, but the part of him that made a living assessing risks and rewards decided it would be a stupid impulse to indulge.

"Who the hell *are* you people?" he asked her instead.

"We're Wholesale Slaughter," she said, pride dripping off the words. "And don't you ever fucking forget it."

"Is she going to be all right?" Logan asked, hanging off a handhold just inside the med bay's hatch.

He'd tried to keep his voice low enough for only Dr. Coldwell to hear him, but across the small clinic, Lyta Randell turned in the webbing of her bed to focus her good eye on him. She looked a lot better now than when she'd been brought aboard an hour ago, but one eye was still just a slit and would be until the swelling went down.

"This is nothing." She snorted a laugh and he thought she was probably already medicated. "You shoulda' seen me after the bar fight I got into as a buck sergeant on Nike!"

"She may have a slight concussion," Coldwell said, clucking like a mother hen. The paunchy, slack-jowled older man, looked like some country doctor pulled off a backwoods colony rather than a twenty-year Ranger medic who'd gone in for formal medical training in his forties. "Definitely a cracked orbital socket, cracked ribs and a sprained wrist. But she'll make a full recovery."

Logan nodded his gratitude to the older man and moved into the ward, squeezing past or sometimes over the treatment equipment attached to rails in the deck till he could secure himself at the edge of Lyta's bed.

"Forget about the bumps and bruises," the Ranger officer urged him, smacking him in the arm hard enough to nearly send him floating away. "Did we get what we needed?"

"We did." He shrugged. "Or should I say Acosta did." He blew out a breath. He hadn't been comfortable using the interrogation drugs on the bounty hunters. They could have dangerous and unpredictable side-effects, but there hadn't been time for anything else. "Starkad doesn't have Terrin yet. This Momma Salvaggio made a deal with the Starkad commander, Colonel Grieg, to recover the data Terrin downloaded and left with Lana Kane, but she's playing fast and loose with him. She knows Terrin is Sparta, and she's keeping him and the tech who came with him secret from Grieg as a hole card."

"Colonel Saul Grieg?" Lyta's eye narrowed. "I've heard of that asshole. Used to be a Marine company commander…he was the one who slaughtered those Mbeki POWs on Connaught. Got a commendation for it, the son of a bitch. Now he's in charge of Starkad Intelligence."

"Then we need to get Terrin away from Salvaggio before Grieg gets his hands on him."

"You know where he is, then?" she asked him.

"He's the same place Starkad is heading. The same place this Lana Kane is taking the data files. Revelation."

14

The mech was so old that Terrin couldn't recognize the model other than it was vaguely humanoid and, at only ten meters tall and probably twenty tons, most likely a scout. It shuffled down the dirt road behind the jail like an old man doggedly moving from one task to another, raising a cloud of dust as it walked. A woman and her son walked by along the main road right at the corner of Terrin's view, and he saw her shoot a glare at the machine.

Not happy about the current administration, I guess.

He stepped down from the cot and looked around the cell.

Neither am I.

Franny was sitting on the floor, back against the wall, face buried in her hands. She'd been that way since coming back from the post-breakfast bathroom break. They were allowed three a day, the only time they left the cell, and he'd tried to be keenly observant, hoping he could spot some weakness, some way out. But it was just a short, block hallway with two doors, one leading to the windowless bathroom, the other thick metal and obviously leading to life outside this stinking jail.

They'd even been given time to wash up and after the second

day, offered a change of clothes. Though Terrin didn't think much of the dull, brown work coveralls, he accepted them just the same. Their Wholesale Slaughter duty fatigues had been ripe enough to stand up by themselves. Neither the change of clothes nor the bathroom breaks seemed to have done anything to improve Franny's mood. He considered trying to cheer her up, but decided he wasn't qualified for it and settled on drawing her out instead.

"What do you think they're going to do with us?"

She finally looked up, her eyes red but no trace of tears surviving the scrubbing of her palms against her face.

"They must know who we are," she declared, voice wavering even if her expression was firm. "If they're smart, they're trying to sell us to Starkad." She shrugged. "I mean, sell you." Bitterness creeped into her words, growing more pronounced with each one. "They're probably just keeping me around to use as leverage, someone to kill in front of you to show they mean business."

"Don't say that!" Terrin exclaimed, crouching down beside her. He hesitantly put a hand on hers, squeezing in what he hoped was a comforting gesture. "We're both going to be okay." He winced, realizing he sounded pretty unconvincing even to himself. He tried a new tack, determined to get her mind off their situation. "Hey, you know all about me and who my family is, but you haven't told me anything about yours. Where are you from?"

"Sparta," she said, shrugging as if it wasn't important. "I'm from Elysium," she added, "across the mountains from Argos. I don't get to the city very much."

"What about your mom and dad?" he prompted, trying to keep her talking.

"They work in civil engineering, city planning," she told him. She shrugged, as if she was surrendering to his efforts despite her mood. "They met there thirty years ago when they were entry level techs, and now they run the district office. My sister works for them, but I decided I want to travel." She snorted humorlessly and the sound morphed into a sob she wasn't quite able to stifle. "Great life choice, huh? Now, I'll probably never see them again."

Her shoulders shook and Terrin patted her hand, feeling utterly helpless. He awkwardly slipped an arm around her, letting her lean against his shoulder.

"I'm sorry," she told him, wiping her face off against his sleeve. The intimacy of the gesture felt good, even on the darkness of their circumstances. "I'm being selfish. You have to be scared, too, and I'm sitting here whining about myself."

"I'm worried," he admitted, "but I don't know that I'm scared, if I'm being honest. After everything that happened on the mission to Terminus…"

He closed his eyes, trying to squeeze out the images of the Jeuta Wihtgar , who Donner Osceola had sheltered and given a home on the *Shakak* despite the enmity between humans and the genetically-engineered race the Empire had used as slaves. Wihtgar had betrayed them and tried to kill them all, would have strangled him if Kammy hadn't shown up to take the traitor down. The moment had haunted his dreams for weeks, but now he felt nothing.

"It scares me that I'm not scared," he said. "If that makes any sense."

"Do you have anyone back home, waiting for you?" she wondered.

He stared at her, uncomprehending for a moment, ready to answer with something inane about his father worrying about him, when he realized what she meant.

"No. I haven't really had time for a relationship for a while."

"I decided I didn't want to leave anything hanging at home as long as I was going to be in the service," she said. "There really hasn't been anyone since then. I've just been too caught up in the job."

She was leaning closer to him as she spoke, and despite the

lingering smell of sweat the sponge baths couldn't quite banish, despite the frizzy, out of control mess of her hair and the knowledge he was just as big of a mess, he wanted very badly to kiss her. The idea scared him worse than the thought of Starkad getting their hands on him, but he leaned into her and closed his eyes.

The door to their cell slammed open and he jerked away from Franny, forgetting about the kiss and hopping up to his feet. The woman who stepped into the cell was shorter than Franny, much shorter than him, and probably weighing less than fifty kilograms. The brown uniform jacket she wore seemed like a tent on her, as if she were a child playing soldier, and the unit patch on the shoulder did nothing to change the impression.

"Salvaggio's Savages," it read in stylized text, over the image of a kilted warrior with skin painted blue and a two-handed sword held over his head. It was the crest of a mercenary unit, over the top and cheesy as most were. He remembered thinking how ridiculous "Wholesale Slaughter" was as a name until he'd seen some of the names of actual mercenary companies.

Yet for all her girlish stature and the extravagance of her uniform, there was something in the woman's startlingly blue eyes, in the wild mane of red hair, in the hard line of her mouth that was a clear warning not to underestimate her. Or maybe it was the heavy, stamped-metal handgun hanging in a skeleton holster at her right hip that did it. It was tied down to her thigh and the way her hips swayed with its weight spoke of a deadly familiarity with the weapon.

"Your girlfriend's right, boy," she said, her voice a clear, pleasant contralto. "I'm going to sell you to Starkad, and Mithra knows what they'll do to you." She laughed, mouth twisting into a cruel smile. "I'm sure it won't be anything pleasant."

Franny grabbed Terrin's hand and he helped her to her feet. She shrank against him for a moment, but then pushed away and stood facing the woman, arms crossed over her chest, a study in forced determination. An odd surge of pride went through Terrin's chest, though he wasn't sure how he had the right to be proud of her.

"There's another option, though," the red-headed woman told them.

She took a step further into the cell and two armed guards moved up behind her, tall and massive and carrying drum-fed flechette guns. They didn't come inside, just reinforced her authority with their presence.

"I'm Captain Josephine Salvaggio." She grinned at Terrin's look of disbelief. She couldn't have been older than thirty. "Yes, I'm the 'Momma Salvaggio' you've heard so much about. My people run things here and at Trinity. We don't have much time, so I'm going to lay this out for you simple. Starkad wants something you have. Their head honcho, Colonel Grieg, told me to be on the lookout for some data crystals, but I know you didn't have them on you when you were taken on Trinity, so I have to assume you passed them off to that broker you went to see, Lana Kane."

Panic roiled in Terrin's gut at how quickly his plans had unraveled and his eyes darted around, searching for any route of escape. There was none except through the two hulking guards and the yawning muzzles of their shotguns. Salvaggio regarded him with cool amusement, as if she could smell his fear.

"Unfortunately, Ms. Kane absconded with the goods before we could locate her, which complicated everything, including my agreement with Colonel Grieg. But I think our dear Lana has taken herself and your data crystals to the only place outside of Trinity where she'd be able to find sanctuary." A demonstrative wave of her hand. "Right here on Revelation. You see, most of the workers on Trinity are from Revelation. I took care of a problem they had some time back and unfortunately for them, they were unable to pay the price we'd agreed upon, so I'm taking it out in trade for a portion of their wages."

"How enlightened of you," Terrin murmured.

It was an old story, one he'd heard of many times during his time on the *Shakak*. Mercenaries were notorious for upping their price in the middle of a job—they were hardly better than the bandits they'd been hired to fight, most of the time.

"You've got once chance to get out of this with your skin intact, boy," she said, her affected good mood vanishing in a flash of irritation. "You work with me to find Ms. Kane, get her to give you the data crystals back, then you give them to me." She inclined her head toward him. "The minute I have them, you and Little Miss Pixie here get a free ride to the nearest non-aligned settlement and we never have to see each other again."

Terrin's jaws ached from keeping his mouth shut. He'd wanted very badly to blurt out his insistence they weren't going to be handing over the data crystals to Starkad no matter what she or this Colonel Grieg did to them. He almost felt the smack on the back of his head Lyta Randell would have given him for saying something so stupid.

"Grand gestures and noble words are for politicians, boy," was how she'd put it if she were here.

"How do I know you won't just kill us after we get the data crystals for you?" he asked instead. "How do I know you won't just lean on Starkad for more money, then turn over us *and* the data?"

Franny's mouth dropped open, her eyes wide with disbelief as she stared back at him over her shoulder. He tried not to meet her stinging glare of betrayal, instead focusing on Salvaggio's reply.

"Well, you *can't*, sugar," the mercenary commander admitted with a low chuckle. "But you can know it's much safer for me to just turn you over. And you can also know your girlfriend was right about her role in all this."

Salvaggio struck out with rattlesnake speed, grabbing Franny's wrist and pulling her back against her chest, one arm wrapping around her neck and the other drawing her pistol. Terrin took an instinctive step forward, but the mercenary warned him off with a tap of her pistol barrel against Franny's right temple.

"You see," Salvaggio went on, her thumb playfully flicking the safety of the handgun off and then back on again, "Starkad doesn't give a shit about her, so I could put a bullet through her brain, toss her body in a ditch and never even have to tell them. Or, you could cooperate and everybody wins. Which is it going to be, sugar?"

"Don't tell her anything," Franny ground out through clenched teeth, eyes squeezed shut. "I'm not afraid to die."

"You're lying, girl," Salvaggio said into her ear, running the barrel of the weapon playfully through her hair. "I can feel you trembling."

Terrin's mind was working furiously, trying to find the right thing to say, the right move to make. He couldn't let Franny die because he was too slow, too clumsy to do the right thing. Logan *always* did the right thing, always managed to accomplish the mission.

Logan's best friend died accomplishing the mission, his memory taunted him.

"All right, I'll do it," he said, hands raised, palms out in surrender. "I'll help you find her, but you got to get me out of this cell. I can't take it in here any longer." He shook his head, trying to sound desperate, which wasn't difficult. "I was trapped underground on Terminus for months, and I've been in here for days and I can't take it anymore! Take me wherever you need to, just get me out of here."

"Now there, you see?" Salvaggio smiled broadly, relaxing her hold on Franny. "I knew we could all be reasonable and come out of this as friends." She turned back toward the two guards outside the cell door. "Johnny, Drake, go pull a car around back. We're all going for a ride to spread the word to Ms. Kane's friends in Riverton Farms that her friends from Trinity are looking for their property."

One of the two turned immediately and went to pull open the door to the outside, but the other seemed reluctant.

"You sure you don't want me to stay with you, Cap?" he asked. His accent spoke of an origin somewhere deep in Clan Modi territory, drawling and drawn out.

"I think I can handle these two trained killers," the woman replied, imitating his accent in mockery of both him and the two of them. She jerked her head toward the door. "Go make sure Johnny doesn't run into anything. You know the poor boy can't drive worth a damn."

"Yes, ma'am," Drake grumbled, shaking his head and slinging his weapon.

"Good help is so hard to find in this business," Salvaggio lamented. "I'm sure I don't have to tell *you* that. Wholesale Slaughter has a pretty good rep, you must get mobs of recruits everywhere you go."

"I had someone try to join when I was on your station," Terrin said, putting more rancor into the words than he meant to. "He seemed pretty eager to get anywhere else as quick as possible."

"You can't keep everyone happy," Salvaggio mused. "Business is business…"

She was gesturing carelessly with her gun, holding it loosely in her hand, and she'd kept the other resting on Franny's arm, keeping her simultaneously too close and not well secured. Terrin saw it and wished he could say something, wished he could tell Franny now was the time, but he didn't have to. Franny struck in an overhand blow, forearm to wrist and the handgun went flying. Terrin dove for the weapon, feeling awkward and clumsy and far too slow.

He caught it before it hit the floor, twisting to land on his back, hands wrapped around the dull grey slide of the heavy, metal handgun. It was an old design, blocky and primitive and unfamiliar in his hands, but he managed to get it pointed in the right direction just as Salvaggio braced to make a lunge at Franny.

"Don't move!" he barked, trying to keep the gun pointed at her as he scrambled to his feet. "Stay right where you are!"

He remembered the manual safety and flicked it off with his right thumb. At least he hoped he'd switched it off; she'd been playing with it so much, he couldn't be sure.

"Take it easy, boy," Salvaggio urged him, hands raising in front of her. "That's my favorite gun, and I'd hate to get killed with it."

She didn't seem worried enough for his comfort, but then she was a professional mercenary and had likely been on the business end of a lot of guns. He had not been on either end of very many guns and was a good deal less comfortable with it.

"Move out of the cell slowly," he said, gesturing with his left hand, keeping the gun still in his right. One of the many things his father and Lyta Randell had taught him when he was younger, and they had still hoped he might be a soldier, was that guns were for shooting, not to use as pointers, back-scratchers or clubs. "Toward the door. Franny, get behind us."

The grips of the handgun were a red-brown wood inset with some sort of circular, metallic emblem. He hadn't bothered to read it, but he could feel it pressing into his hand; he was gripping the gun so tightly, the pattern would probably be etched into the skin of his palm.

"I'm going, kid, I'm going," Salvaggio said. "But I don't think you've considered what you're going to do when Johnny and Drake see you coming out behind me with a gun in your hand. Those boys aren't that bright, and without guidance from higher authority, they're apt to do something fatal for all of us."

She was edging out of the cell and toward the door, still a meter away from it. He'd told her to move slowly, but he felt as if she was stalling, waiting for help.

"You better make sure they don't do anything stupid then," Franny told her, nearly yelling the words. Terrin wanted to shush her, but she looked manic and keyed up and he was afraid she'd just start yelling at him, instead. "Because you'll be the first one to get shot!"

"All right, calm down." Salvaggio pushed the door open and was about to take a step out when Terrin put a hand on her shoulder, making sure he had control so she couldn't just bolt.

"Small steps," he reminded her. "Don't run or I'll shoot, because we'll be dead anyway."

He felt an instant's doubt, wondering if he could do it, if he could shoot her down in cold blood. He'd killed before. He'd cycled the airlock and executed Wihtgar when Captain Osceola had given him the choice. He'd shot Starkad Marines in the battle for Terminus Cut. This felt different, though he couldn't have explained why. He hoped he wouldn't have to find out.

It was late morning and he squinted at the glare of the primary star, trying not to give in to the natural instinct to hold his hand up over his eyes. Instead, he maneuvered Salvaggio ahead of him and ducked into her shadow, maintaining a clear view up and down the back of the building. It was sandstone block, just as plain and primitive on the outside as the inside, with a wood overhang sheltering the concrete walkway leading a few meters out from the back door.

The mech he'd spotted earlier was sauntering through the main street of the town, visible over the slate rooftops off to his left, while on the right the dirt road headed away from the low-slung block and wood buildings and out into rolling, red hills. There was no one else in sight and he was giving serious consideration to tying Salvaggio up and making a run for it, but before he could put the notion into words, he heard the rumble of the car pulling around the back of the building.

It was a generic all-terrain rover, dented, faded, and blasted by years of dirt, sand, and sun, its knobbed tires cracked and caked with dust. The cab of the rover was covered by a take-down canvas roof, but the back was an open bed, and the guard called Johnny was standing in it, flechette gun resting against his shoulder while one hand anchored him to the roll bar. He seemed to be happy to be basking in the sun and totally oblivious to Salvaggio and her "prisoners." The one she'd called Drake was driving the vehicle, shading his eyes from the glare with a hand across the windshield, not even looking over at them until the vehicle came to a stop right in front of the rear door.

Terrin swallowed the lump in his throat and pulled Salvaggio closer to him, jamming the muzzle of her pistol into the small of her back.

"Hey, ma'am," Johnny frowned, one hand reaching around for his shotgun. "Why are you…"

He trailed off, eyes widening as he finally noticed what was happening. Inside the cab, Drake swore, the sound of the words lost to the rumble of the old, internal-combustion engine, and threw open the driver's door, trying to jump out and grab his gun at the same time.

"Tell them to drop their guns and get out of the truck," he said, his voice a dry rasp. "Tell them if they don't do it now, I'll shoot."

"Boys, just settle down," Salvaggio said, voice raised in a commanding tone that could have come from Lyta Randell or Captain Cordova. "I want you both to do *exactly* as I say, do you understand? Do exactly what I say and not a damn thing else. I want you both to tell me you understand me."

"I understand, ma'am," Johnny replied immediately, freezing in mid-step, one foot halfway off the back of the truck.

"Yes, Captain," Drake added, standing in the open driver's door, glaring at Terrin and Franny with murder in his beady, piggish eyes.

"Set your guns down, boys. Do it now."

"In the truck," Terrin amended. "Put your guns in the front seat of the truck."

"Do it," Salvaggio urged them. "Then move away from the vehicle." She turned her head back toward Terrin, scowling. "You gonna shoot me with that gun or drill into my spine with it, boy?"

He pulled the barrel back a bit, realizing he'd been digging it into her back a bit too hard. He nearly mumbled an apology but stopped himself. It would show weakness.

"You shoot it with it pushed that hard into me," the mercenary pointed out, "you'll jam it up and it won't feed the next round, you know that, right?"

He didn't answer her, but his ears burned with embarrassment. Salvaggio's men had stepped back from the rover, up against the back wall of the jail; he was about to tell Franny to check the vehicle, but she was already jogging around the front end, as far from the reach of the mercenaries as she could get. She slid into the driver's seat, shoving over the flechette gun Drake had left behind and checking the controls to make sure the vehicle had been left drivable. It took her only about ten seconds, but it seemed to drag out into an eternity before she leaned over and threw the passenger door open.

"Get in!" she urged him, her elfin features distorted into something desperate and furious. "Hurry, before someone else comes!"

He backed toward the open door, fighting to keep his balance and maintain a hold on Salvaggio and keep an eye on Johnny and Drake. He hunted blindly with his left foot for the floorboard of the rover's cab

"You go through with this, boy," Salvaggio warned him, her

tone almost matronly in its concern, "you'd best be prepared to go all the way. I don't have anything in particular against you, but I'll be obliged to hunt you down. You know that, right?"

For some reason, the threat steadied him and he settled back into the seat, letting loose his hold on the woman but keeping the gun pointed her way. Salvaggio regarded him with eyes of blue crystal.

"I've been hunted by worse, ma'am," he told her. Then, aside to Franny, "Go!"

His door swung shut as the truck pulled away down the dirt road, leaving a cloud of red dust behind them.

15

To say Revelation City was the prime real estate on the planet was to pay it too high of a compliment, Ruth Laurent decided. The entire southern hemisphere was a wasteland, desert and bare, arid rock surrounded by oceans choked with matts of algae, and the north was attractive only by comparison. Low desert gave way to high, and a few mountain-cradled valleys where the annual rainfall was enough to support the transplanted, genetically-engineered trees, brush, and wildlife.

They'd flown over the coastal algae farms during their approach in the drop-ship and she'd wondered what sort of life the workers there must have. Much of it was automated, but not nearly enough. Out here, when something broke down, the parts to repair it had to be something you could fabricate locally or you might as well throw it in the recycler. Sometimes, it came down to men and women and even children in wooden boats scooping algae matts off the surface of the water.

The train tracks ran right up the coast, where tankers waited to be loaded then picked up by fusion-powered engines and hauled inland to the processing plants. Along the way, they'd pass the soy farms and pick up barrels of protein paste and between the two staples, the colony could survive…if you could call a diet of processed spirulina powder and soy paste living. Larger colonies with more arable land and a better climate might manage to grow enough fodder to support herds of aurochs or bison, might husband citrus groves or greenhouses, but not Revelation. If anyone down there raised anything larger than goats, she'd be shocked.

It was a world with nothing worth having except its people, and people who only stayed because they were too poor to migrate someplace better, marooned by the decay of the Empire which had once made planets such as these desirable places to live. Upper-class Imperial citizens had traveled here simply to climb the sandstone cliffs or drive all-terrain vehicles up their sandy tracks, and the tourist trade had made the world a place for the ambitious to build a life. Until it had all fallen apart.

There probably hadn't been any Jeuta raids or wars for succession out here, no bloodshed or destruction. The ships had just stopped coming, stopped bringing the tourists and their money, the spare parts, and the new technology. What was left was stripped away and taken toward the core, and the people had been abandoned to fend for themselves with what little remained.

Their history had played out on one world after another all across what the Dominions now referred to as the Periphery, the playgrounds of the rich turning into wasteland, detritus, prey for the vultures picking over the corpse of a galaxy spanning civilization.

And what are we, if not simply the fattest vultures?

She said nothing during the descent, having learned better than to try to make small talk with Colonel Grieg. He sat in the acceleration couch beside her and endured the braking boost in obdurate silence, dark eyes hiding an even darker heart. It would have been easier if the man were stupid, a simple brute; but he was intelligent, or at least clever. Anyone who underestimated him did so at their peril, and if she'd learned anything from the failure of her former commander, it was not to underestimate your opponent.

The touchdown was rough. The Revelation City "spaceport" was a rock-strewn plain cleared half-heartedly by a tractor whenever they got around to it. Two other landing craft squatted with heads bowed against the afternoon sun, one a passenger shuttle and the other a cargo hauler modified for use as a drop-ship, the standard craft for mercenaries and bandits alike.

Not that there's much of a difference between them.

She stood off to the side with Grieg and his command staff and waited while Captain Egeland walked his Mobile Armor company down the massive belly ramp. The machines fanned out and spread into a perimeter, guarding the drop-ship while the rovers disembarked in their wake, knobbed tires shifting up and down on the off-road suspensions as they passed over the ruts and ridges of dirt and sand left by the mecha footpads.

"Officially, we're working with this Salvaggio woman," Grieg told Captain Gerhardt, pacing back and forth between the tire tracks. The Marine commander listened attentively, unmoving, her rifle at low ready as if she were one of the sentinel statues on Stavanger. "But that means nothing. She's mercenary trash and the people here have no loyalty to her and less to us. When we go in, we go in to occupy a hostile city. Take no chances, assume no allies. None of the damned mercenaries touches a weapon or pilots a mech while we're in the city. Am I clear?"

"Clear, sir!" Gerhardt barked, and Laurent heard an echo from Egeland on the general net on her 'link. Grieg had been speaking not just to the two of them but to all the Marines and mech-jocks…and possibly to her, as well.

She had a gun this time. She hadn't asked for it, but Grieg had insisted.

"If you're a Supremacy officer," he'd said, "then you're one of my troops, and my troops always go armed."

The compact pistol seemed to drag at her shoulders, a tumor growing beside her breast. She'd have to use it this time. She felt it. This would be the mission where she'd get her first kill, lose whatever innocence she had left.

The thought wouldn't leave her, wouldn't be scoured away by the high desert wind, the sand blasting against the armor plating of their rovers, wouldn't be shaken off by the rhythmic thumping of the tires on the sandstone as they drove into the town. The ride was blissfully short, mostly because there wasn't that much to the place. The town was built around the train depot, the processing facilities, and the storehouses surrounding it, simple, aluminum sheeting buildings three or four stories tall. The fusion reactor powering all of it lay outside of town, built on the banks of a nearby river, diverting some of its flow to cooling stacks. From the air it had seemed ancient, and had probably been left behind when the Empire pulled out because it was too large to loot. She wondered how they managed to keep it running.

Further out from the food processing and storage units were smaller factories. She hadn't seen a planning schematic for the place, but she imagined it held whatever industrial fabricators they'd been able to scrounge up, along with the raw materials to feed them. Those were harder to come by and she didn't recall anything in the mission reports about surface mining facilities or anything at all in the asteroid fields or on the moon. That meant they were totally dependent on interstellar shipments for fusion fuel pellets, iron ore, plastics, superconductor fiber, precious metals…pretty much everything except food.

And this Salvaggio controls all traffic in and out of the system, I'd wager.

Past the industrial areas, there were a few restaurants, no doubt catering to the workers at the factories. Well, *diners* more than restaurants. Two different bars, and she'd have been willing to bet one served as the watering hole for Salvaggio and her people while the other was for the locals, whether it had started out that way or not. All the structures had a crumbling, degenerate air to them, their facades faded and peeling under the dry, warm wind. It made them seem neglected, almost abandoned, for all she could see locals moving past on the sidewalks.

The children stared at their vehicles in open curiosity, but the adults averted their eyes and quickened their step, as if afraid being caught staring would attract unwanted attention. They reminded Laurent of the buildings, beat up and neglected, falling apart with each passing day.

"This is it," the driver announced, pulling their rover up to the curb of a one-story block building caked in crumbling stucco.

A sign mounted above the front entrance, once bronze but long since green with corrosion, advertised "Revelation City Hall."

"How optimistic," Grieg murmured.

She and the Colonel had been sitting wedged between two armored Marines and when the vehicle bounced to a halt, the two troopers piled out, weapons going to their shoulders as they watched for threats. Across the street, a man in faded blue coveralls broke into a trot to get out of the line of fire, one hand holding a floppy, brimmed hat tight to his head. She wanted to chuckle at the sight, but the laugh died in her chest, killed by the thought of how that man viewed them, as invaders brought in by other invaders, just one more nail in the coffin of the life he'd grown up with.

"You must be Colonel Grieg."

The woman was petite, unimposing…*cute*, even, with a heart-shaped face framed with curly red hair and adorned with the bluest eyes Laurent had ever seen. They were currently aimed like a sighting laser at Saul Grieg, who returned the stare unabashedly.

Behind her, three men lined up like an honor guard, two of them large and probably considered intimidating, dressed in armored vests over their brown fatigues but with no weapons evident. The third was a mech-jock, she guessed from the one-piece coverall and the set of his stance. Mech-jocks seemed to instinctively hunch their shoulders inward all the time, as if they were squeezed into a cockpit.

"How did you know it wasn't me?" Laurent asked the woman, the corner of her mouth quirking up at someone who clearly must have been underestimated over and over in her career judging her so quickly.

Salvaggio regarded her with what might have been amusement or perhaps disdain.

"The message I received from Breckenridge sounded scared. You don't look like you've ever scared anyone in your whole life."

"If you believe me to be so frightening, Captain," Grieg said, climbing the rough, stone steps up to the front porch of the city hall, towering over the woman, "why do you not seem intimidated?"

"I said Breckenridge was scared," she corrected him, head tilted back to look him in the eye. "I didn't say I was."

"Yet you should be."

Grieg slammed a fist into the wall beside her head, the armored knuckles of his gloves cracking the plaster and sending fragments flying. Salvaggio tried not to flinch and did a fair job of faking it, but the tightening of the muscles in her cheek told the story of her surprise and the brief flash of fear. The men behind her weren't as practiced at hiding their reaction and the two big foot-soldiers started to push away from the wall, halfway into a step toward the Intelligence chief before they stopped at the levelled muzzles of the Marine auto-rifles.

"I reviewed your message on our way down from the ship,"

Grieg went on, his voice even, mouth a hard line. "You had the fugitives here, in this very building…" He sneered at the huge crack in the stucco his fist had left. "…in this very *old* and shitty building, and you let them escape!"

The volume had gone up on the last three words until he was yelling almost into Salvaggio's face, but she was prepared this time and didn't lean back from it.

"I *allowed* them to escape, Colonel," she corrected him, arms at her side, stance strengthening as if preparing to meet a charge. "And you should be thanking me."

Grieg ceased to loom over her, more a shifting of his stance than any discernable motion, but a concession nonetheless. He waved a hand in invitation, though his sneer made it a mocking one.

"Enlighten me."

"If we'd left those kids on Trinity for you to stumble on, what would you have done with them?"

"Our interrogation procedures are very thorough," Grieg assured her, a bit smugly Laurent thought. Her stomach twisted. She was very aware of how thorough they were. And how final.

"And they'd have told you what?" she prompted, her tone dangerously condescending. Salvaggio might have not noticed the sudden, threatening shift in Grieg's expression, but Laurent certainly did. "That they'd turned over the data crystals to Lana Kane, the broker, correct?" She shrugged. "Which you already knew. And then you'd come here and be no closer to finding what you were really looking for. This Kane woman is a local, from one of the small farm communities outside the city. She's got no living relatives we know of, but she knows everyone and has used her connections to help most of them at one time or another."

Grieg said nothing for a moment, still seeming as if he might be about to order the mercenary commander summarily executed, but finally he nodded.

"You set them up as a Judas goat," he deduced. "How are you tracking them?"

"Come inside," Salvaggio invited him with a sweep of her hand toward the door. "I'll show you."

Dusk fell over the ruins of the house in a cloak of ruddy gold, adding some beauty to the charred and scattered wreckage. Whatever had laid waste to the homestead had been fairly recent, at least within the last few years. Grass grew tall over the cobblestone walk, but Terrin could still make out the steps. Brush had overtaken the interior of the house, but it still held its original boundaries at the corners. Dirt had begun to bury the collapsed sections of roof, but what had survived the destruction still held in place, giving shade to whatever animals called it home.

Terrin paced through the tall grass, Salvaggio's pistol hanging heavy in his right hand, trying to see further into the shadows of the house's interior, wondering if it was safe to go inside or if the floor would collapse under him. Something flew out of the open section of roof right over his head, screeching like a damned soul and he nearly shot it before he realized what it was. It flew in impossible silence, wings not making a sound, and disappeared into a nearby thicket.

"Barn owl," he told Franny, after he'd recovered his breath. She had one of the flechette guns to her shoulder, but she lowered it and let out a whooshing sigh. "We used to have them on our ranch back home," he added.

This place made him miss their old house, made him wish he'd spent more time there before he'd left on the mission with Logan.

"What the hell are we hoping to get out of this?" he murmured, shaking his head.

"The people at the farm down the road said this was the last place Lana Kane lived," Franny reminded him. He squinted at her, wondering if he still detected resentment in her voice.

"They had no reason to trust us. We're strangers in a stolen car." He jerked his head toward the rover. "A stolen car with about a quarter of a tank of whatever it runs on left."

"Alcohol, I think. I could smell it. And it would be easy to distill out here. Probably a lot easier to fabricate an internal combustion engine out here than it is to replace worn out fuel cells or capacitors."

He sniffed, accepting her explanation because he had no idea.

"Look, you don't think I was actually going to give Salvaggio the data crystals, do you?" He'd been meaning to ask her for over an hour, since they'd gotten away from the town and were sure they weren't being followed, but it had been hard for him to come up with a natural way to broach the subject. He still hadn't, and he winced at how awkward it came out. "I was just trying to string her along," he went on. "Trying to give us a chance to get out of there somehow."

"Well, it worked," she judged curtly, not sounding convinced. "Congratulations."

She turned back to the rover and he took a step after her, ready to keep arguing despite a little voice whispering in his ear he should shut up. When he spotted the blur out of the corner of his eye, he thought at first it was another owl, or maybe a deer—he'd seen a deer along the way, so he knew they had them here, introduced at the same time as the rest of the Earth-based wildlife, after the world had been terraformed.

Something about the cadence of the crashing steps didn't sound right for anything four-legged and he spun around in time to see a flash of brown hair and blue shirt streaking away from the back of the house and into the field of sagebrush, heading out toward a stand of gnarled trees and the cover they offered. It was a boy, a young teenager at the oldest.

"Hey, wait!" Terrin yelled, bolting after him..

He wasn't sure why he was chasing the boy, he just felt the imperative to do it, as if they were drowning and this kid was the only lifeline they'd been thrown. The boy was fast and Terrin hadn't had the chance to run in months, and despite having starred on the track team in college, he thought the kid was going to outrun him and disappear into the trees, leaving Terrin panting and embarrassed, but fate intervened and the boy tripped. He was young and agile and he didn't fall flat on his face the way Terrin might have, but the misstep cost him time enough for Terrin to make a lunging grab at his shoulder.

He caught the inside of the kid's collar and the full weight of the boy jerked at Terrin's shoulder, but he kept his hold and the teenager went down, legs flying out in front of him. The boy struggled to scramble back up, but Terrin put an arm across his chest, leaning into him. The kid didn't say a word, didn't make a sound, just snarled at Terrin with feral rage, teeth snapping.

"Just wait a second," Terrin insisted, panting with exertion. "We don't want to hurt you! We're just looking for…"

"Put the gun down and let my brother go."

Lana Kane was just *there*. One second there'd been nothing but dirt, rocks, and sagebrush and the next, the woman was standing there, standing a meter in front of him, a compact pistol stretched out in her left hand, pointed between his eyes. She looked different than she had on board Trinity, less the fortune-teller con artist and more the wilderness scout in rough, home-spun pants and jacket, a floppy, brimmed hat pulled down over her hair.

"Oh, thank the Lord," he breathed, coming to his feet and releasing the boy. "I didn't think we'd find you…"

"Put the gun down," she repeated, voice harsh, eyes dark and cold, "or I'll shoot you in the head."

"Put yours down, Ms. Kane," Franny insisted. Terrin risked a glance over at her and saw the flechette gun at her shoulder, aimed at Kane. Her stance was wide and she was leaning into the stock, evidencing a training he was surprised to learn she had. "Neither of us want to hurt you or your brother, but we need those data crystals."

"You shouldn't be here," Kane said, not lowering her weapon, apparently not as impressed with Franny's firearms prowess as Terrin was. "Did Salvaggio bring you here?"

"She brought us to Revelation from Trinity," Terrin confirmed. "We were in her jail, but we escaped and came to try to find you."

"You escaped," Kane repeated, straightening, her pistol going to her side, her face twisted into obvious skepticism. "How the hell did *you* escape her jail?"

"She was trying to get us to go along with helping to find you and get you to give back the data crystals so she could sell them to Starkad," Terrin explained. He grinned, feeling a bit self-satisfied now that he'd actually found Kane. "I went along with it until she was getting ready to take us out of the cell, then Franny grabbed her gun and we used her to get the vehicle."

Kane appraised them both, mouth dropping open.

"Mithra's swinging cod, please tell me the two of you aren't that stupid. Momma Salvaggio screwed up and let a couple of eggheads like you grab her gun? And I bet there was a unicorn with cotton-candy wings outside, ready to fly you away." Her voice dripped with scorn as she pulled her brother to her side, draping an arm over his shoulder. Standing side-to-side, it was easy to see the family resemblance in the set of his dark eyes, the narrow jaw and flowing brown hair. He still hadn't said a word.

"She let you go, you morons. She wanted you to lead her to

me, and now you've gone and done it." She used her pistol as a pointer, indicating the stolen rover. "You two get in that damned truck and get out of here before you get the both of us killed. She's probably tracking it right now."

"Oh, shit," Franny hissed, her eyes going wide.

Terrin's stomach twisted inside out and he rocked back on his heels, filled with a sudden paranoia. Kane was right and he was an idiot. The realization smacked him upside the head and his mouth worked as he tried to formulate an answer and couldn't.

"Just give us the data crystals and we'll leave, then," Franny said. Her voice was harsh and grating, as if she was paving over fear with stubborn anger.

"Those crystals go nowhere until I get what I want for them," Kane shot back. She shook her head. "Besides, handing them to you would be the same as giving them over to Starkad."

"Then we're going with you," Terrin insisted. "We stay with you until we get those data crystals back, like it or not. Your only other alternative is to shoot us, and you'll have to be fast to get us both."

"I think I could manage it," Kane growled, taking a half-step in front of her brother. Terrin's breath caught and he thought she might actually go through with it, but a noise from back down the dirt road brought all their heads spinning around.

Terrin felt the jolt of alarm before he even recognized the sound for what it was: truck tires. Something was coming.

Kane bit off a heated curse and motioned for them to follow. "All right, damn it," she acceded. "But we have to go now! Alec!" she called to the boy. "Come on, we're going!"

She and her brother took off at a jog and Terrin rushed after them, back into the stand of twisted and gnarled trees, adapted from whatever they'd originally been to survive in the arid conditions here on Revelation. They twisted together as if bonding for added protection against the harsh realities of the world, clustered in groups of three or four, their branches so interwoven he could barely tell where one ended and the other began. He nearly tripped half a dozen times over winding roots and half-expected to hear Franny go tumbling over somewhere behind him, but she was somehow able to avoid the arboreal minefield.

Beyond the forest ran another road…well, more of a hiking trail, but parked on it was a vehicle. Smaller than the one they'd stolen, it lacked an open bed for cargo, with just two rows of passenger seats.

"Get in," Kane barked at them. "But leave behind the guns and everything she gave you. There's bound to be a tracking device somewhere you wouldn't even think of."

Terrin's face fell. He gestured at himself, then at Franny.

"We…umm…we kind of got these clothes from Salvaggio, too," he admitted.

Kane rubbed at her face and showed her teeth in a frustrated snarl.

"Lose them, then."

Terrin's eyes went wide and Franny's expression reflected pure horror.

"We'll get more where we're headed," Kane assured them. "Just strip to your skivvies and get in, or I'm leaving you here."

Terrin opened his mouth to say something, closed it again, looked helplessly over at Franny. She threw her flechette gun to the ground and shrugged out of her borrowed shirt. Luckily, she'd kept her own underwear.

"Don't just stand there," she told him. "Get your damn clothes off."

"Have I mentioned how much I love this damn ship?" Kammy murmured, speaking softly, as if the ships orbiting the planet on the main viewscreen could overhear their conversation.

Revelation was a world with a lot of red and brown to go with its blues and whites and greens, not hospitable even if it was habitable. The color combination made the starships floating in geosynchronous orbit over the northern hemisphere stand out plainly in the magnified view from the optical telescopes. A monolithic, silvery wedge sliced across the ruddy mountain ranges separating east from west, the streamlined, overpowered lines of the Starkad heavy cruiser *Sleipner*, the most dangerous ship in their fleet. Beside it, recklessly close in astronomic terms at only a couple of thousand kilometers away, was the mercenary starship, a bulk freighter converted with welded-on armor and shoehorned weapons systems. She was vaingloriously named the privateer *Fortune*, though it wasn't clear if she had, as of yet, earned one for Momma Salvaggio.

"It feels unnatural, somehow," Katy Margolis declared, scowling at the holographic image from where she and Logan hung off the bridge safety railing. "How can they not see us?" She shrugged, the motion bringing her down toward the deck rather than raising her shoulders. "I mean, even without a fusion drive, we have to be running hotter than the background."

"We are," Tara Gerard confirmed, sounding awfully smug about it, Katy thought. Well, maybe she ought to be. She'd worked as hard as anyone to get this ship ready for action while Katy and Logan had been canoodling on the coast. "If we shut down the field, we'd be visible on thermal if they were looking. But the field distorts our thermal signature along the spacetime that propagates it. So even if they happened to turn their scanners this way just to check the jump-point, they'd see a spread out, wonky reading that wouldn't look anything like a starship."

"Of course," Kammy interrupted good-naturedly, "that only works until we get close enough for the distortion to be really noticeable against the background. Then they're gonna figure out something's messed up. But it's better than sending up a signal flare every time we wanna move in any direction, like before." He grinned, what was usually a very amiable smile, but this time seemed more wolfish than usual. "We could still be on top of them before they ever realized what was happening, blast right through their reactor and send them tumbling right out of orbit. Make a great light show for the locals when they re-enter."

"Whoa, Kammy," Lyta Randell spoke up for the first time since they'd jumped into the system. Katy wondered if it still hurt her to talk—the bruising on the side of her face and jaw hadn't faded yet. Katy felt a twinge of empathy followed by one of remembered pain and trauma from her captivity on Ramman, what seemed a lifetime ago now. "It might be satisfying to blow the shit out of a Starkad cruiser, but it's also an act of war."

"We blew the shit out of the *Valkyrian*," Tara pointed out, reasonably Katy thought. "Well, *she* did, anyway," the Tactical officer corrected herself, nodding over toward Katy. "How's this any different?"

"The stakes, Lt. Gerard," Acosta put in, emphasizing her newly-minted rank, probably to remind her she was officially, if secretly, in the Spartan Navy now. Acosta had been hanging back near the hatchway to the bridge, but as he spoke, he pushed forward closer to the holographic display. "At Terminus, we were securing a vital asset that could have turned the course of the history for all five of the Dominions, and there was no other choice than to prevent knowledge of its location from getting out. This is different."

"It *is* different," Logan agreed. Katy noticed he'd let the rest of them debate it while he sat back and listened to the merits of each argument before commenting and she tried to hide a proud grin. He was picking up the little tricks of being a commander. "For one thing, there are a planet full of witnesses here who know that ship is in orbit. If we come in and knock it out of orbit, Starkad *will* find out. And then, my father will have to either offer up Wholesale Slaughter—and us—as a sacrificial lamb, or we'll be looking at open war with Starkad." He shook his head. "And right now, I don't know who'd win."

An idea was forming in her head and she launched into it, hoping the threads would come together as she spoke—something she was much readier to do when it was just them than when she was in front of the top brass.

"We could come in off the ecliptic," she mused, "where they wouldn't expect to see a ship approaching. With our reduced and distorted thermal signature, they probably wouldn't even see us. Then we could insert into orbit on the opposite side of the planet from their ships." She shrugged. "We could launch a drop-ship from there, let it go in nap-of-the-earth under their sensor nets."

"That's not bad," Logan said, eyes on the screen as he nodded slowly.

"They'll have satellite coverage," Acosta warned.

"They *do* have satellite coverage," Tara confirmed, pointing at her sensor display. "Two in polar orbits, one in a geosynchronous orbit over Revelation City and another in a low planetary orbit."

"I can temporarily blind the birds that could spot us," Tara offered. "Just using the lasers. By the time they get their image back, the drop-ship will be under the cloud level and we'll be out of orbit."

"We can go into orbit around their moon," Kammy suggested, indicating the craggy, captured asteroid on the computer simulated display of the system. "Keep it between us and the Starkad cruiser." He shook his head. His short dreads waggled back and forth in the microgravity. "Even if we can sneak you in, though, sneaking back out's going to be the hard part."

"We'll deal with that when the time comes," Logan decided, and she heard the finality in his words. He shot her a glance, grinning playfully. "You up to flying the drop-ship?"

She snorted, returning the smile.

"Try and stop me."

Terrin scratched at his chest through the rough, homespun material of his new shirt, eyeing the ragged hand-me-downs ruefully. The clothes Salvaggio had given them at the jail hadn't been much, but the ones the people they'd met in the canyon had found for them were a definite step down. Franny didn't seem any happier with the clothes than he was, and a good deal less comfortable with the company they were keeping.

Given the suspicious glares and dirty looks the people gathered under the lean-to were giving the two them, that went both ways. He couldn't have told anyone where they were if they'd threatened him at gunpoint, so circuitous had been the route Kane had taken to the isolated canyon, just one winding dirt road after another, some of them through clefts in the rock he could have sworn were too small for her beat-up little rover to squeeze through, and half of them in darkness with no headlights. Yet when they'd arrived, there had already been a welcoming committee waiting for them, upwards of thirty people, most of them either old or young. It was hard to judge on a backwards Periphery colony with not much in the way of modern medical treatment, but he was fairly certain no one he'd met in the camouflaged lean-to was between eighteen and fifty. And not a one was glad to meet them.

"Why did you bring them here, Lana?" The man was at least sixty, though the shadows the portable lanterns threw didn't do him any favors, with grey creeping into his short-cut blond hair, skin tanned to leather, weathered and cracked with decades of exposure to the dry wind of Revelation. "This is a huge risk. What if you were followed? What if they have drones up? Or the satellites Salvaggio has used against us before?"

"No one followed me," Kane insisted. She still had the boy with her, holding onto him as if she were afraid he'd run off if she let go. He hadn't said a word the whole time and Terrin was beginning to get the idea he couldn't speak. "How many times have I been to our old house? I know the routes to take by now."

"You take too many chances," the woman standing beside the older man declared harshly, hands on her hips as if scolding. "These two found you there! Who else might have?"

She was of an age with the man and stood close enough to him that Terrin thought she might be his wife. They were dressed in similar fashion, work clothes of local fabrics, wool and cotton, hers with a long, hooded cloak but both a neutral, natural gray.

"I know it's a risk," Kane admitted, surprising Terrin with the contrition in her tone. "But it's where our parents are buried and Alec needs to see them." Her arm tightened around her brother's shoulder when she said the name. "I appreciate you looking after him while I've been gone, but you won't take him there."

"Because it's not safe…" the woman said, but Kane interrupted her with a raised palm.

"Right now, there are more important things for us to consider."

She squeezed Alec's shoulders and gave him a comforting look as if she were trying to anchor him in place, then paced over to where Terrin and Franny stood apart from the cluster of locals. The lean-to was colored to blend with the rock of the canyon and concealed well under the spreading shade of the twisted trees with their short, hardy tufts of needles, and large enough Kane had been able to pull her rover all the way beneath it. He and Franny were leaning against the side of the car while the council of elders and some youngers sat on boxes of supplies or sandstone boulders or just leaned back against the canyon walls.

"This one," Kane waved at Terrin, "has a brother who is the commander of a mercenary company called Wholesale Slaughter. His brother will be coming for him and I have…" She hesitated. "…certain leverage I can use to influence this Jonathan Slaughter." She smiled broadly. "This could be exactly what we've been looking for, a way out of all this."

"A way out of what?" Terrin demanded, a sinking feeling in his gut. "What do you want from Wholesale Slaughter?"

"Lana," the old man began, stepping on the woman as she began to remonstrate with Kane as well, "you can't make this sort of decision unilaterally…"

"No one's made any decisions yet, David" Kane held up a hand to forestall the objection. "I'm just giving us options… which is more than we've had in a long time."

"Options to do *what*?" Terrin demanded. "You need to tell me what this is all about, lady. We had a deal."

"And the deal was for me to turn over what you gave me to

your brother, wasn't it?" She cocked her head. "He's not here, yet. If you'd like to survive till he gets here, maybe we should amend the agreement, because I don't recall saving your asses being part of it."

"Like I said," Terrin repeated, trying not to let his impatience cost him his temper, "what do you want?"

"This place has always been rough," Kane said, waving a hand around demonstratively. "We don't make much anyone else wants, but the upside of that has always been that no one messed with us. Until the Red Brotherhood popped up a few years ago, that kind of loose alliance between a bunch of bandits and pirates. Then all of them started getting this idea they were like a government and wanted someplace to call home, a base where they could set up on a habitable planet and fortify against attack from the Dominions."

"They won't be doing that anymore," Terrin assured her, feeling a visceral sense of satisfaction for his part in the mission. "We knocked the head right off that snake."

"Not in time for us." Kane clutched her arms to herself, eyes closing as if she were reliving a memory. "He called himself Captain Fowler and when he and his people landed with a few platoons of half-assed foot-soldiers and six or seven slapped-together Hopper scout mecha, there wasn't a damned thing we could do to stop him…though some people tried."

"Is that what happened to your parents?" Franny's question was quiet, hesitant. Terrin understood. He wouldn't have had the nerve to ask it.

Kane's eyes opened to narrow slits regarding Franny from just beneath the brim of her cap.

"It's what happened to a lot of people. So, when we were able to get the word out, we asked for help on the Merc-Work net, anyone who'd come and work on spec. And who we got was Momma Salvaggio and her Savages. They weren't much more than Fowler had, weren't equipped much better, but she had actual combat experience and all he'd ever done was terrorize civilians who didn't have much more than you can fabricate from local materials. She kicked his ass and hung him from a pole out in front of the city hall. Everyone cheered…"

"And then she wanted to get paid," Terrin presumed.

"And we had nothing left to pay her with…except our labor."

David cut in then, his voice sad but somehow resigned.

"Trinity was having problems getting enough workers," he explained, "because no one in their right mind wants to get paid poverty-level wages for the privilege of living in a damned cave. Salvaggio cut a deal with them and received a hefty piece of their action in return. But she didn't count her new percentage toward our repayment. That has to come out of the wages of the workers."

"And since our pay is so low," Kane added, "it's going to take forever. Which is fine with her, since she's made Revelation her own little fiefdom until the debt is paid off."

"Shit," Terrin murmured. It was about what he'd expected.

"It's not as if she's been cruel or harsh," the older woman beside David admitted, obviously reluctant to give Salvaggio her due. "Not like Fowler. She hasn't killed anyone or tried to take our food or businesses. But her word is law, and she controls all shipments in and out of the system. If we wanted to live under the rule of a tyrant, we could volunteer as cannon fodder for Starkad."

"Especially considering they're here," David said grimly.

"What?" Kane exclaimed, head snapping around toward him. "When?"

"A few hours ago. They're all over the city, an invading force…looking for *them*, I assume." He pointed at Terrin and Franny.

"Looking for what we gave you," Terrin corrected. He cursed

under his breath, then gave up and slammed a palm into the side of the rover and just shouted it out loud instead. "Shit!" Kane stared at him and he waved his hands at her in frustration. "When they come, they'll walk right into it."

"They'll be okay," Franny assured him, putting a comforting hand on his shoulder. "We're talking about your brother, and Colonel Randell and the *Shakak.*"

He wanted to laugh at how confident she sounded, as if there were no odds Logan and the others couldn't overcome. He didn't, because he knew she still hadn't completely forgiven him for going along with Salvaggio at the jail. Pissing her off again wouldn't help any.

"What do you guys have?" he asked Kane and David and the woman. None of the others gathered around had said a word and didn't seem likely to without encouragement. There were lots of wide eyes and frightened expressions and their lack of confidence didn't inspire any in him. "I mean, do you have any weapons at all? Any armor?"

David and the woman shared a look, but it was Kane who answered.

"We have a couple old armored personnel carriers we salvaged from Fowler and repaired," she said, shrugging. "They have missile launchers but we don't have any more missiles for them. We were able to fabricate ammo for their heavy machine guns. Plus, we have some cargo trucks we've welded armor onto and we have machine guns we put onto turrets we made for them. We couldn't do anything against their mecha, but we can help against their infantry."

"Maybe Salvaggio's infantry," Terrin scoffed. "Not Starkad Marines. I know you guys are in a bad situation here, but if we go up against Starkad *and* Salvaggio, they'll burn the whole city down around your ears. The Supremacy doesn't mess around."

He turned away from them and rested his hands on the hood

of the rover, trying to think. Logan would know what to do. Lyta would know what to do. Hell, even Katy would know and she was a pilot. He was an astrophysicist, and this didn't seem like a problem he could solve with hyperdimensional math.

"How will we even know when our people get here?" he wondered. "It's not like they're going to announce it on the public net." He snorted humorlessly. "If you even *have* a public net here."

He thought Kane was about to answer back, probably with something angry, but the sound of an engine brought everyone's head around and some of the teenagers who'd been taking shelter under the lean-to grabbed rifles or shotguns and disappeared into the darkness. Terrin looked around for somewhere to take cover, some direction to run, but everything outside the circle of light beneath the lean-to was utter blackness—his eyes had adjusted to the lamps and the canyon was a dark mystery to him.

He'd just about decided to steal the rover and drive out the way they'd come in when someone called out of the black.

"It's okay," a young, male voice said. "It's Chloe!"

Chloe turned out to be another of the teenagers, no older than sixteen or seventeen, with ratty, brown hair tied into a ponytail and a long, narrow face. Riding goggles rode atop her head and she was pushing a dirt bike up the rock-and-sand floor of the canyon toward the lean-to, flanked by two of the boys who'd run to investigate.

"What is it, girl?" David asked her. "You were supposed to be keeping an eye on the city hall. If they send out a patrol while we're all bunched up here…"

"Something's happened, Dad," she interrupted him, making an impatient slashing motion. "Julia was bringing food in for Momma Salvaggio's night shift, like she always does, but they weren't on duty. She said those Starkad assholes…"

"Honey," the older woman with David admonished. Terrin still hadn't gotten her name. "Language."

"Sorry, Mom," Chloe said, rolling her eyes just slightly. "Anyway, the Starkad Marines had taken over the office and they were on all the monitors and everything. Julia heard them complaining about how shi…sorry, *crappy* all the equipment was. They took the food, though, even though they said it was crappy, too."

"Starkad didn't waste any time," Kane murmured. "I suppose they don't trust Momma any more than we do, which shows uncommon good sense."

"Isn't this something you could have told us when we returned to town, honey?" Chloe's mother asked, gently reproving. "Riding all the way out here at night without lights…"

"That's not it!" Chloe insisted, fingers clenching as if she were about to tear her hair out. Instead, she pulled off her goggles and gestured with them. "Julia was there when the alarms went off. The Marine dude brought in one of Salvaggio's people and they told them the two satellites in polar orbit had been…" She trailed off, frowning in concentration as she tried to remember. "…flashed? I think the guy said flashed. They were all worked up, thought something was happening, but they called their ships and they couldn't detect anything so they figured it was some sort of malfunction, but I thought I should come tell you."

"Well, there you go," Franny said. All eyes turned toward her, including Terrin's, and she reddened slightly at the attention. "You wanted to know how we'd know when your brother arrived," she clarified to Terrin. "Two satellites don't get blinded at the same time by accident."

She pointed upward, at the stars they couldn't see for the overhang of the lean-to.

"They're here."

"Are you sure they didn't see us land?" Acosta whined, peering upward through the canopy of the drop-ship's cockpit.

Katy closed her eyes, counted to ten, and prayed, then yanked the quick-release for her seat restraints before she answered him. When he was in his element, the Intelligence agent turned copilot was self-assured and in control. But put him out in the field during a combat operation and he sounded like a scared twelve-year-old.

"I'm sure if they'd been looking, they might have seen us, Francis." She was never going to call the man Patrick, no matter how many times he asked. He just looked like a Francis. "But this isn't Stavanger, or Sparta or even one of the busier Periphery worlds. This is the ass-end of nowhere and they neither have the money nor the need to put out drones or remote sensors on every stretch of God-forsaken wasteland." She hopped up, yanking a pair of levers to open the external compartments where the camouflage netting was stored. "Of course, once those satellites are back up, they'll be able to spot the drop-ship, so we'd better go on out and make sure the camouflage is in place before that happens, right?"

In other words, why don't you *go make sure they're in place and get out of my damn way?* she thought but didn't say. Even though they were the same rank now thanks to her promotion to Lt. Commander at the end of the Terminus mission, she was still his junior in time and grade. Of course, he was posing as her subordinate for his cover, which made things even more complicated. *What the hell* isn't *complicated about my life?*

The cockpit steps led her down into the hold of the lander, where a dozen mecha were already being lowered to the ground on freight elevators, jagged and menacing silhouettes backlit by the work-lamps along the belly of the craft. She wondered what it would be like to pilot one of the things, to have all that destruction at her fingertips.

Naw, not fast enough, she decided.

"I'm still not comfortable that signal we got was actually from Terrin," Acosta continued, coming down the steps behind her. "It was text-only, not even a voice pattern. If he's been captured by Starkad, they could have forced him into sending the message."

"They could have," Lyta Randell agreed, waiting for them at the bottom of the skeletonized metal steps, dressed in combat black, her balaclava in one hand, carbine secured in the other. "But we won't find out sitting in this bucket of bolts."

Behind her, the rest of the two Ranger platoons she'd brought down in the drop-ship were slipping into backpacks, strapping gear to each other and checking the placement of their spare magazines. They were, Katy thought with some envy, a finely-tuned machine, and she hoped someday she could command an outfit as squared away.

"Your people ready, Lyta?" Logan's voice came over the cockpit speakers and, Katy assumed, in the ear bud for Lyta Randell's 'link as well. Logan was in his Sentinel strike mech, already on the ground outside. "I want to move out before Starkad gets their eyes back."

"My drivers are pulling the trucks out now," Lyta told him. "Give me five."

"Come on, Francis," Katy nudged her copilot. "Let's get the netting in place before we miss our ride."

Logan felt obscenely exposed stomping along in the track of the dry riverbed under the pale light of the planet's pockmarked moon. He knew on an intellectual level the enemy couldn't have seen their landing and, even if their satellites were back up now, the odds they'd be scanning this exact area were incredibly low. It didn't help. Every instinct he'd developed over his short but highly active career kept bringing his eyes back to the passive sensors, waiting for an assault shuttle to come screaming over the horizon and end them.

The darkness provided no comfort, not even a psychological one, not when the mech's night vision and thermal scanners and sonic analysis systems were synthesized into an image in his helmet's visor as clear as noontime in the blazing sun. Ahead was the only shelter that would make him feel less vulnerable, down the wadi and into the rising walls of the canyon. The map coordinates Terrin had sent them had specified this entrance to the maze of dried up waterways.

Well, he *hoped* Terrin had sent the message. It had contained the correct code-words for the last time his brother had been on the *Shakak*, but he had no illusions Starkad couldn't have wrung those out of Terrin's broken body if they'd gotten their hands on him. His stomach lurched at the idea, bad enough he thought for a moment the Sentinel had stepped into a chuck-hole.

He still wasn't completely used to the massive machine,

despite the hours he'd put in the simulator since his Vindicator had been destroyed fighting the Jeuta raiders. He missed the lighter, more agile assault mech, missed its jump-jets and the way it could out-maneuver larger, heavier machines. Even the improvements in armaments he'd been given back on Argos didn't make up for it, but he had to get used to it. The Sentinel was the mech of a commander, which was what he'd become.

He checked the formation in the IFF—Identification Friend or Foe—transponder display at the right side of his vision, saw the rest of the two heavy platoons he'd brought down with him from the ship spread out in a single-file line down the broad swathe of the riverbed. Ideally, they'd be in a wedge formation, but geography dictated their route. He was in the center behind Kurtz's First Platoon and their mobile, agile assault mecha, ahead of Paskowski's strike mecha. Ford and Hernandez hadn't been happy about being stuck on the ship, but he hadn't wanted to chance landing *two* drop-ships in the limited window they'd been afforded.

At the rear of the formation were the two APCs carrying Lyta's force as well as Katy and Acosta. He'd thought about leaving the pilots with the lander, but if it was found, they wouldn't be able to get it back into orbit before Starkad assault shuttles blew them out of the sky. Anyway, Acosta was an Intelligence officer, the only one they had along—as far as he knew— and Katy had always been good to have around in a fight.

"Val," he called up to Kurtz, in the lead of the file, "you see anything yet?"

"Nothin' but a great place for an ambush," Kurtz returned, the skepticism strong in his tone even over the radio.

He wasn't wrong. The canyon had narrowed as they marched into it, going from nearly sixty meters across at the mouth down to barely wide enough for his Sentinel to pass through without scraping paint off its shoulders. The footing was getting worse as well, the path littered with slabs of the cliff face peeled off by winter freezes and jagged boulders half-buried in sand. The gyros and the sense of balance his neural halo gave the machine helped, but if a strike mech toppled over in a space this narrow, it would be damned hard to get it back up.

"Boss." It was Valentine Kurtz, and Logan could see in the IFF display he'd stopped. "You need to get up here. We got company. Dismounts at a hundred meters."

"Are you sure they're friendlies?"

"Well, they haven't tried to kill me so far," Kurtz ventured, the shrug audible. "You want to come up or you want me to try to talk to them?"

Logan eyed the narrow walls of the canyon suspiciously.

"Should I come on foot?" he asked. "Because I don't think I'm going to make it past your platoon."

"The canyon widens out three hundred meters ahead of you. I'll pull everyone up to give you space to get through."

It was still a tight fit to that next three hundred meters, and Logan winced as he banged his left hand pauldron into a granite outcropping, sending the torso twisting back and to the left. Kurtz had been right, though: after threading the needle, the walls began to grow apart and by the time he passed through First platoon, there was room for three mecha abreast.

There'd been water here once, had to have been to carve this canyon. It was gone now, retreated underground or simply dried up like most everything else on this world. Some planets had been completely terraformed by the Empire, while others were half-done, undercooked meat. You could live off of it, but it wasn't pleasant. This one needed more attention, more time in the oven.

How long would it be habitable without more engineering? A hundred years? Two hundred? Would the people here have enough warning to leave the place? Had they even thought of it, or were they so wrapped up in day-to-day survival it hadn't even occurred to them?

Like everyone else in the Dominion, only thinking about now, about what they can grab and hold instead of how their grandchildren are going to live.

There. Kurtz's Golem sulked in the lee of a rocky outcropping, his canopy cracked open so he could shout down to the huddle of dismounted civilians standing just outside a camouflaged lean-to, staring up at the assault mecha with awe plain on their faces. And in the midst of them, grinning broadly, was his brother.

It was difficult to stop a machine as massive as the Sentinel. It took him three full steps to bleed off his speed and dig the footpads into the ground and the frame of the strike mech still shuddered with the violence of the sudden halt. He kicked the canopy latch and the night vision display faded, flooding the cockpit with the darkness from outside. He shouldered the canopy open, then swung out onto the rungs of the emergency access ladder, scrambling down the side of the twenty-meter-tall machine.

He skipped half the rungs, sliding down the last two meters and absorbing the impact on the hard-packed sand with bent knees, spurred on by an urgency he couldn't explain, as if Terrin would disappear if he didn't reach him in the next few seconds. He didn't run, but it took conscious effort not to. Instead, he strode purposefully, still able to see from the glow of lamps hidden under the overhang, heading straight for his brother.

Terrin ran. He ran, he jumped, he whooped and he slammed into Logan nearly hard enough to knock him over, then wrapped him up into a fierce hug. Someone was crying and Logan wasn't sure which of them it was.

"I'm so glad you're here, bro," Terrin said, voice muffled against Logan's shoulder. "I can't even tell you…"

"I know, Terrin." He clapped his brother on the back, holding him for just one more, long second before he pulled free and wiped his sleeve over his face. He looked Terrin up and down, raising an eyebrow at the borrowed clothes. "Are you okay?"

"I'm about five minutes from a nervous breakdown," Terrin admitted, voice still shaky but starting to firm up, "and I have been for about a month. But I haven't had anyone try to kill me in days, so there's that." He waved at one of the others, a skinny, elfin young woman with short, brown hair and an infectious grin. "This is Franny—Francesca Hayden, Petty Officer Third Class. She's been cool as a cucumber the whole time and you need to promote her."

"Consider it done," Logan told her, shaking her hand. She looked mortified and mumbled something about how it was a pleasure to meet him. Before she'd managed to pull herself together enough to say something coherent, the sound of tires scraping on stone and hard ground brought his head around.

The lead truck pulled up behind them and Rangers poured out of it like ants from a hive, setting up a quick defensive perimeter but not specifically pointing their weapons at the civilians. Behind it, further from the light, he couldn't quite make out the movement, but he expected the second platoon of Lyta's troopers to be spreading out in a watch formation facing back the other way up the canyon.

Lyta Randell hopped down from the cab of the lead truck with Katy and Acosta immediately behind her. Katy blew past her to wrap Terrin in a warm embrace, but Acosta seemed agitated, eyes darting back and forth.

"Where's Kane?" he demanded, his voice echoing off the canyon walls. "Is Lana Kane here?"

"That would be me."

The woman wasn't what Logan had expected, wasn't the exotic underworld spy he'd envisioned after listening to Mira. Kane seemed at home in the rough-spun farming clothes, with the solid stance of someone used to working for a living. Her voice and her accent were odd, but Mithra knew what the usual accent was on a place this remote. The teenager tucked in beside her wasn't what he'd expected either, though he should have figured she'd have family ties here, given what Mira had told them.

"Ms. Kane," Acosta said, "I've come to understand you have something of ours, something entrusted to you by Terrin on Trinity. We'd very much like to get it back, and we're prepared to pay handsomely for it."

"I'm afraid it's not that simple," Terrin interjected, sighing heavily, as if this was a battle he'd been fighting for a while. He threw up his hands and let them drop down to his sides again helplessly. "Ms. Kane has certain conditions."

"Like what?" Lyta Randell asked. Unlike her Rangers, she wasn't wearing a balaclava or night vision gear, and the lingering bruises only served to make her look more intimidating.

"This is my home," Kane said, eyeing Lyta carefully, the way you might keep a wary watch on a dangerous animal. "I want it back, from Salvaggio, from Starkad. You have the weapons, the training, the people." She nodded towards the mecha towering over them. "If you want what your man Terrin gave me, you'll get rid of them, get them out of my city and off my planet. That's the deal."

"Are you out of your mind, lady?" Acosta exploded, taking a step toward her. She didn't shrink back, falling into a defensive stance and pushing the boy behind her. Logan had tagged him as her brother; she didn't seem old enough to have a teenaged child. "You expect us to risk an open war with Starkad so…"

Acosta shut his mouth, turning away as if in a conscious effort to control himself, and Logan knew why. He'd very nearly just admitted they were Spartan military rather than a mercenary unit. Lyta Randell shot him a smirk as she stepped past him and came to a halt a meter from Lana Kane. Her suppressed carbine was slung around her shoulder, one arm resting on it casually, making no aggressive moves, yet something about her screamed of potential violence.

"We do indeed have the weapons," Lyta acknowledged, one eyebrow arching upward, "and the training, and the people. So, why would we risk all those things fighting two of your enemies when we could just use it to take what's ours from you?"

Kane's mouth worked soundlessly for a moment, and Logan thought she might have finally been intimidated. But she recovered quickly and set her jaw in determination.

"Because I'm good at reading people," she said. "And I can read you like a book, lady. You're a naked blade, a weapon with no conscience beyond the one wielding it, and if you were in charge, you might do just what you say." She stabbed a finger at Logan. "But *he* won't." Her gaze focused on him and Logan felt a tickling at the hair on the back of his neck. "He's your conscience, I think, and I know he's in command. He knows this is the right thing to do, and I can feel he *wants* to do it."

Logan blinked, feeling as if she'd been reading his mind. It was true, every word of it, but he said nothing, tried to reveal nothing with his eyes. Should he lie, try to bluff her into giving him the data crystals? Or would she be able to read that just as easily?

This was one of those moments his instructors at the Academy had warned him about, one of those command decisions that defined careers and lost battles.

"All right."

Acosta's head whipped around at the words, mouth dropping open, and Lyta stared at him, giving him that old expression he'd seen as a youth, the one with the unspoken question: "do you really know what you're doing?" Katy, though…she was smiling. If Kane had read him through some voodoo sixth sense, Katy had done it the old-fashioned way.

"You're exactly right, Ms. Kane," he admitted, deciding not to hide anything from her. "I *do* want to take down Salvaggio and Starkad, for reasons you don't need to know. But I can't just go off half-cocked here, not when it could get my people killed. We're going to need intelligence, and we're going to need your help."

"We'll do whatever we can," Kane assured him, the optimistic light in her eyes seeming almost out of place, as if she hadn't had anything to be happy about for quite some time. "We don't have much, but whatever we can do, we'll do it."

"Wait a moment," an older man spoke up, pushing forward through the crowd. He shared Kane's sing-song accent if not her optimism. "I'm David Carpenter, the leader of…" He snorted. "Well, of whatever this is. The group who's willing to fight. I'm glad for the opportunity to finally do something to free our city, but you Wholesale Slaughter people are mercenaries just like Salvaggio. How do we know you won't just move in and take over like she did?"

Logan laughed softly, remembering when he'd been asked nearly the same question by the colonists hiring him to fight the Red Brotherhood on Arachne. The answer he'd given her had been mostly truth coated with a few disguising fictions. This time, there was a simpler one.

"Mr. Carpenter," he said, "I want you to take a good look at my troops here." He nodded toward Lyta, her Rangers, and the camo-painted, precisely-maintained mecha. "Then I want you to think about what sort of people and equipment Momma Salvaggio can field, and I want you to tell me if you really think I need to trick a bunch of down-and-out Periphery colonists in order to take over a world of my own."

The older man nodded acknowledgement, but didn't seem totally convinced.

"You're going to have to take the risk or not," Logan told him.

"If we do it without your help, we're more likely to fail, and you'll be worse off than you were before."

"And if we help you and you fail," David countered, hands clasped in front of him as if he couldn't keep them still, "then we're all dead."

"I'll need to go into town," Lyta announced. Kane and David stared at her but she ignored the disbelief in their looks. "To get the intelligence we need," she clarified. "I'll need to go into town myself, to get an idea of the disposition of the Starkad forces."

"Don't you have sergeants for this sort of thing, Lyta?" Logan asked her, suppressing a grin. As if she could resist a penetration mission.

"I do," she admitted, "but we won't have the right equipment to record everything without being spotted, and I need to see it myself." She nodded toward David. "I'm going to need clothes, and a vehicle that won't attract attention. And a guide. Someone who won't be suspected."

"I suppose we could ask for a volunteer," David said, glancing back at the group of teenagers.

A girl dressed in a goatskin vest, riding goggles hanging around her neck, stepped forward, hands defiantly on her hips.

"I'll do it, Dad," she told David. She sounded confident, even cocky. Logan liked her already. "Shouldn't be a big thing."

"Chloe, are you sure…" David trailed off, licking dry lips.

Dad, she'd said. He felt for the man, then thought what his own father must be feeling.

"I'm sure," Chloe insisted. She grinned at Lyta. "This is the coolest thing to happen here in years."

"Girl," Lyta told her, extending a hand, "I think you and I are going to get along just fine."

18

Somewhere, a woman was screaming. Ruth Laurent tried to shut the sound out, tried to lose it amidst the cacophony and chaos that had descended over Revelation City. Plaintive cries and strident shouts amplified by Marine helmet speakers and the bang of doors being kicked in, all up and down the main street of the town. It had started before dawn and the primary star was about a quarter of the way up the sky and it hadn't stopped for more than a few minutes.

Grieg hadn't bothered to wake her. She'd commandeered a cot in the back of the city hall, not wanting to bunk in the warehouse where the Marines had set up shop three buildings down. The mech-jocks had claimed their own quarters, the ones not on duty patrolling the streets. She'd watched as they tossed a family with three young children out of their apartment above a small clothing shop and bedded down in their rooms.

She'd expected Grieg to object to it as a breach of discipline, but he'd shrugged it off when she'd mentioned it, muttering about more important things to worry about. When the Marines had begun to drag in civilians to the jail a few at a time for interrogation, she'd stayed as long as she could, hoping her presence would restrain them. At least they hadn't killed anyone. Yet.

She'd begged off some time after midnight and tried to close her ears to the sounds, squeezed her hands over them and tried to sleep. It hadn't worked and, eventually, she'd strapped on her gun belt and began walking the streets of the town. She'd taken the gun, worrying the locals might blame her for what was going on, might attack her or swarm her begging for mercy. Instead, they ignored her entirely, as if she were a ghost wandering the world of the living, hurrying from one place to another as if one home or business were more secure from the roving Marine squads than the last.

The Marines ignored their movements, their strategies, and their attempts to hide. They had a list of town residents compiled from Salvaggio's records and they were going down the list by name and photograph, and no amount of running or hiding would stop them. There'd been no shots, no fights, no organized resistance. Grieg had seen to that.

The first thing he'd done when Salvaggio had admitted she'd lost track of the Spartan prisoners, when the Marines had come across the vehicle, the guns, the abandoned clothes, and the two of them long gone, was to toss the woman into a cell in her own jail and have her mercenaries penned into the stockade beside their pitiful collection of mecha. Salvaggio hadn't allowed the citizens to keep any small arms during her occupation, which had made theirs easier.

Laurent shuffled across the street, cutting through the narrow alley between two businesses. One advertised fabricator repair service on a hand-lettered wooden slab while the other was a mystery, its windows boarded up and any signs that might have revealed its purpose pulled down.

Had it simply gone out of business, she mused, or had the owners closed it down and retreated out of town to avoid Grieg's inquisition? He'd find them eventually. He'd already announced his intention to start at the population center and fan out through the settlements until he found Lana Kane and the Spartan agents. She knew he'd do it. Someone would break, someone would talk. Someone always did.

Another block over from the city hall and she was into the town's factory district, industrial fabrication centers, warehouses, the terminal for the rail service from the coast. Out near the edge was the stockade for livestock, goats and sheep brought into town for slaughter from farms out in the settlements. None were there now, but she saw the lines of a Reaper assault mech rising above the wire fences. It was the largest machine Salvaggio had in her arsenal—the rest were Hoppers and other scout mecha, slapped together by shade-tree mechanics from black-market fabricators.

A Marine APC stood guard on the street outside the stockade, daring anyone to come close to the collection of outdated and under-gunned mecha. She wondered if they'd shoo her away if she came near, or if they'd respect her rank and ask her politely. At least there weren't any of the locals out here, so she didn't have to hear their shouts and screams. She could pretend it wasn't happening…

No, damn it, there *was* someone. Two women, walking quickly side-by-side. One was younger, perhaps a teenager, dressed in rough, home-spun trousers and a vest, her tanned arms bared to the sky. The other was older, covered up in a dark-hued cloak, a floppy hat half concealing her face until she turned and met Laurent's eye for just the briefest of moments.

Ruth Laurent froze in her tracks, mouth halfway to a shout until she realized there was no one close enough to hear it. Lack of ingrained combat training made her reach for her gun a second too late, after the two women had already turned off onto the nearest side street, disappearing as if they'd dropped down a hole.

She knew that face; she'd seen it when she'd studied the intelligence report on Wholesale Slaughter and cross-referenced it to Spartan military records. Major Lyta Randell. Decorated, twenty-year veteran of the Spartan Ranger Corps. Her file said she'd been disciplined for irregularities in her supply chain, suspicions of dealing with the black market for weapons and military equipment. She'd resigned her commission and signed on with Wholesale Slaughter almost immediately.

Of course, given what she knew about Wholesale Slaughter, the whole thing was probably a fiction and she'd simply been assigned to the mission by the Spartan Intelligence Command.

"Shit," she hissed the word aloud. Wholesale Slaughter was *here*. Sparta was *here*. How the hell did they get here before the *Sleipner?*

She started walking back the way she'd come, a stride at first, then a jog, and finally an outright sprint, arms flailing, breath chuffing like an ancient steam engine. She kept whipping her head around, searching one way then the other for Lyta Randell, convinced the Ranger was going to spring at her from some shadowy corner and slit her throat. There was nothing. Some civilians finally noticed her as she came out onto the main street, watching her with wary suspicion, convinced she was the precursor to yet another swooping raid, another family pulled from their house.

She began to slow, out of breath, out of shape after so many months with no real exercise. Her stomach heaved and she thought she might throw up, but she kept moving, jogging then walking, then jogging again until she reached the raised sidewalk to the city hall/jail/police station. The Marine guards posted outside the front door stared at her from beneath the rims of their helmets, their visors raised to let in air on the dry, hot day, but neither said a word.

She threw open the front door and lurched inside, limping now, through the waiting room and into the government offices.

Captain Gerhardt was sitting at a table they'd turned into a makeshift command post, surrounded by monitors with the feeds from the helmet cameras of her platoon and squad leaders, snapping orders and listening to reports as she micromanaged their movements.

"Where's the Colonel?" Laurent gasped, still trying to get her breathing under control.

"Back in the holding cells," Gerhardt snapped, barely looking at her. "Supervising interrogations."

In one corner of the office, a pair of locals sat face to face in chairs pulled out of the waiting room, their hands flex-cuffed behind their back. They were a man and his wife, she was sure just by the way they looked at each other, older like most of the couples she'd seen here. Everyone above their teens and below their sixties was on Trinity, forced labor. The man was balding, his forehead perpetually sunburned, while the woman had grey streaks through her hair. They both looked deathly afraid.

A scream filtered back from the jail, a woman's voice she thought, and the old couple flinched, sheer terror on their faces. The man was sweating, great, salty drops falling off his brows and into his face and he couldn't wipe them away. Laurent felt an absurd urge to go wipe his face for him but she shook it off and moved slowly, hesitantly toward the heavy, metal door to the city constable's office and the holding cells beyond.

A single Marine guard blocked her way, but relented and opened the door for her at Gerhardt's impatient nod. Sweltering, oppressive heat met her as she crossed the threshold. The government offices were air conditioned, comfortably cool, but the constable's offices and the cells beyond had been left to simmer as a psychological measure.

The Constabulary's front desk was left empty, not even a Marine stationed there much less a local cop. The problems Revelation City had now weren't going to be solved by a citizen's complaint. The screaming again, louder this time, echoing down the hallway to the holding cells. She passed by the first pair, their access slots left open—probably so the occupants would be able to hear the screams even more clearly.

She paused at the first of them, peering through. Josephine Salvaggio squatted in a corner, seeming more annoyed than forlorn and not at all disturbed by the racket. If Grieg thought he could rattle this woman, Laurent had a feeling he was mistaken.

The next cell, though, held locals, another older couple, their clothes slightly more ornate and expensive than the ones in the waiting area had been. City government officials, she remembered from the briefing. The former Constable, pushed out when Salvaggio had arrived, a man named Kraft. He was borderline obese, with heavy jowls and sunken eyes and she wasn't sure how he could ever have policed anything since he sure as hell couldn't police his weight. His wife was his polar opposite, physically, a beanpole with a face narrow enough to cut cheese. What they had in common at the moment was fear. It wafted off of them like the smell of death.

There were more civilians in the cells across from them, but she stopped looking. She didn't want to see them. At the end of the hall, on her right, the door was open. Grieg stood outside the threshold and watched, arms crossed, face impassive, a spectator at a chess tournament. She stepped up behind his right shoulder, wishing she didn't have to look.

She started at the floor and worked her way up, trying to steel herself for what she'd see. The woman's wrists and ankles were flex-cuffed to the legs of the metal-framed office chair and rivulets of blood ran down the backs of her hands from yanking against the bonds. Her clothes were well-made, perhaps fabricated instead of homespun, which put them a step up from most of the people who lived here. Her jacket was stained with vomitus and her face was so wracked with agony Laurent could barely discern her age at first. She was old, older than any of the civilians she'd encountered on the street, and Ruth Laurent vaguely recalled her as one of the major business owners in the town, one who'd done well under Salvaggio.

"Please," she rasped at the woman standing before her. "I've told you everything I know…"

The Marine had stripped away her armor because of the heat, the sleeves of her fatigue top rolled up, but she still wore insulated gloves to handle the stun prod. The prongs at the end of the weapon sizzled with electricity at the touch of her thumb to the activation switch, and her square, hard face twisted into a leering grin when the captive flinched away from the crackling discharge. There was a stench in the air, something noxious, a mixture of fear and sweat and urine. The woman's clothes were dark-colored, but Laurent figured she must have soiled herself during the interrogation.

Laurent realized she was breathing hard again, as if she were still sprinting across the street, but this time with empathy for the old woman rather than exertion. Surely, this woman must have done something, must be dangerous or valuable.

"Is she not talking?" she asked Grieg quietly, nearly forgetting why she'd run here in the first place.

"It doesn't matter," he said with a dismissive snort. "She screams nicely, and it's working on the nerves of the others." He motioned for the attention of the Marine with the stun wand, nodding curtly.

The Marine NCO jabbed viciously into the captive's side and thumbed the trigger. Laurent glanced quickly away, but was unable to spare herself the image of the woman's face spasming in uncontrolled agony, her body shuddering with the surge of an electric shock. She didn't scream until the Marine let off the trigger and her muscles could work again, but when she did it was loud and painful and piercing.

Grieg glanced back at Laurent, mild curiosity in his eyes.

"Was there something you needed to tell me, Captain?" he wondered.

She shook her head, an unnatural, jerky motion, and turned to leave.

"No, sir," she replied, heading back down the hallway, desperate to get back to the cool, fresh air of the main office. "Nothing important. It can wait."

"You're sure she's in there?" Lyta asked, pulling her borrowed hat lower to hide her eyes as she scanned the city hall structure carefully. The three of them, her and two teenage girls, were tucked in behind the water tank beside the shut-down bar across the street, but she didn't want to attract any attention. Yet.

"Of course I'm sure," the girl Chloe had introduced to her as Julia snapped in return, not at all intimidated by Lyta, which the older woman found refreshing. "She's only been the boss of this town for the last three years, I know what she freaking looks like."

"Lunch is in how long?" She was repeating that question as well, and she saw Julia tug at her long, dark hair and roll her eyes in frustration, but she answered anyway.

"About a half an hour."

"I'm going in with you," she declared. "Chloe, you said you could get ahold of a car?"

"It's just an open-frame runabout," the girl qualified. "But it'll seat four people." She chuckled. "Five if they *really* like each other."

"I want you to pull it around behind the jail in exactly forty minutes."

"What if the Starkad assholes see me?" Chloe demanded. "They're not like Salvaggio's idiots, they're *real* soldiers."

"Don't worry. If they give you a hard time, take off and try circling back around. But I think they'll be too distracted." She waved in a dismissive gesture. "Go, now."

Chloe made a face at her, but did as she was told. Julia eyed Lyta sidelong.

"You're awfully bossy."

"I get that a lot," Lyta admitted. "Let's go grab the food."

The front entrance to the diner was boarded up, but Julia led her to a back door, knocking on it in a coded pattern. The man who opened the thin, whitewashed wooden door looked as haggard and weather-worn as the outside of the old building and he glared at Lyta with suspicion in his beady, black eyes.

"Who the hell are you?" he asked, barring the door with his body.

"This is Lyta, Uncle Geoffrey," Julia said quickly. "She was brought in by the Starkad people from Riverton Farms along with her family, and they're stuck here until the questioning is over." She shrugged. "They told her to help me bring the food."

"Sweet Mithra, they're pulling folk from all the way out at Riverton now?" Geoffrey murmured, shaking his head. He stepped out of the way and gestured for them to come inside.

"They won't stop till they've found who they're looking for," Lyta said, playing the part Julia and Chloe had come up with for her only a few minutes ago. "I'm just hoping they'll believe my husband when he says we don't know anything about it."

"Well, here's their damned food," Geoffrey said, handing each of them a heavy tray full of covered dishes. All metal. Not much plastic on this world. "I spat in it," he added, scowling deeply, "and I'd have pissed on it if they wouldn't have tasted the difference."

"It's the thought that counts, Unc," Julia said, laughing and giving him a kiss on the cheek before they left.

"He's not going to get into trouble, is he?" Julia asked her in a whisper halfway across the street to the city hall facility. "For what you're going to do?"

"I don't think so. But you will. That's why you're coming in the car with us."

Julia said nothing, but Lyta sensed nervousness from the girl for the first time. She and Chloe were full of a teenager's conviction of their own immortality, but they lacked the overdose of testosterone males of their age were blessed with, so she was frightened. Sensibly so. Which was why teenaged boys historically made wonderful soldiers and lousy spies.

The tray of food was heavy, but not quite as heavy as the items weighing down the pockets of Lyta's borrowed cloak. Would they be searched? If they were patted down or scanned, this could all fall apart. She was taking the risk because she knew this Grieg, by reputation if not personally, and knew he tended toward heavy-handed sloppiness. He had a Supremacy Marine's disdain for civilians, particularly backwoods civilians.

It'll work.

She repeated it like a mantra, the only prayer she was willing to make. Mithra might be on their side or He might not, but He worked in mysterious ways, and she'd been in the game too long to count on Him tipping the scales.

The guards at the front entrance checked the trays, went so far as to sniff at the food beneath the sheet metal covers, but barely spared the two of them a glance. Well, the male did, not a glance but a predictable leer at Julia. Starkad Marines had a reputation of their own when it came to civilians, particularly female ones. He let them through unmolested this time, though, and Lyta allowed herself the luxury of a relieved sigh when they were out of earshot of the guards.

Julia shot her a look, just a slight widening of her eyes, apparently alarmed that Lyta had been worried. Lyta nodded forward, giving her a stern frown in reply.

Get your head in the game, girl.

"We got your lunch," Julia announced to the woman seated at a desk in the office.

The Marine captain didn't look up, absorbed in directing troops via a multiscreen video display, just waved toward the door to the Constabulary. Lyta stifled the snort of disdain she felt for an officer who sat back in the headquarters building and micromanaged by remote control. Any company commander who tried that shit on her watch would be relieved in a hot minute.

The two Marines at the door laughed as they slung their rifles over their shoulders and took two of the plates from Julia's tray, setting them down on one of the desks and pulling off their helmets, ready to dig into the eggs and chicken sandwiches.

"We gotta get in there," Julia told them, nodding toward the door to the Constabulary. "We got food for the guards in there, too, and the prisoners."

The girl's voice was firm and steady and Lyta was impressed by her composure. The two Marines looked at each other and shrugged. The ones closest to the door, a man barely out of his teens with barely a stubble of dark hair left on his freshly-shaven head, sighed heavily with the bother of it all and slid off the edge of the desk.

"I don't know if the Colonel is going to let them prisoners have any food," he said, an undertone of malice in his laugh. "If you got any left, you bring it back out to us, okay sweet thing?"

He unlocked the heavy door with a magnetic key and pulled it open, waving invitingly before he hurried back to his breakfast plate. Lyta bit down on the feral grin fighting to make its way across her face, forcing her expression carefully neutral despite the wide-open door and the opportunities beyond. She slipped a hand into the left pocket of her cloak and wrapped her fingers around the lump of malleable putty, finding the one hard, plastic square in the center of the mass and mashing down the single button there. There was an unoccupied desk just inside the connecting door to the Constabulary, and she brushed by it casually, pushing the self-adhering mass up under the edge of it.

She would like to have been able to pretend this sort of thing didn't wind her up as much as it had when she'd been a young soldier, but the trip-hammer beat of her heart put the lie to the conceit. The truth was, it wasn't the risk to life and limb that quickened her pulse anymore as much as the risk to the mission from the choices she made. She was a *Colonel* now, and Mithra knew, when she'd enlisted as a teenager, she'd never envisioned having so much responsibility. The freedom of action it awarded her was tempered by the knowledge every single choice she made could kill her whole command or scuttle a mission and cost thousands or even tens of thousands of innocent people their lives.

Like now. She'd made this decision in the spur of the moment, trusting a gut instinct she'd relied on from private to colonel, not knowing if Logan would have made the same call but confident he'd trust her judgement. If she was wrong, the consequences would be horrific.

"Food for the guards and prisoners," Julia announced just ahead of her.

Saul Grieg stood at the end of the hallway, speaking in low tones with a female Marine dressed in sweat-stained fatigues and black, insulated gloves. He was just as harshly ugly in real life as he was in the file photos and videos she'd seen of him, though more intimidating in person with a certain massive physical presence live that he'd lacked in two dimensions.

Grieg looked away from the Marine, frowning impatiently, and nodded to the armored trooper posted at their end of the hall. The guard shifted his weapon down on its sling, getting the barrel out of the way as he pulled the magnetic key cards off his belt and began sorting through them, stepping over to the first cell on their left.

Julia caught her eye and nodded with the barest of motions, confirming this was Salvaggio's cell. Neither she nor Chloe had understood the why of this, the reason getting her hands on Salvaggio was so important, and Lyta hadn't taken the time to explain it, but they'd both accepted it was important. Lyta hoped they were right to trust her.

The 'link was in her hand, concealed under the tray, pressed against it with her fingers, the forefinger hovering over the control. The second the key met the lock, she pushed the button and the charge blew.

She hadn't been able to cover her ears—they would have seen it, and it was crucial they not suspect her. She'd had her mouth halfway open, but her ears still rang and the concussion threw her and Julia against the wall, the heat washing over her, making her skin prickle and the hairs on her arm disappear in tiny curls of smoke. She went with it, sliding down to the floor, covering her face, screaming in feigned terror and real pain. The food was splattered across the floor in smears of yellow and brown and bits of soggy biscuit, and the trays were bouncing soundlessly, their clanging drowned out by the hollow whistling that was all she could hear.

Grieg's mouth was open and she presumed he was shouting, but no sound came out. He pointed, pulled a pistol from his belt and shoved the guard ahead of him, racing forward out into the main office of the Constabulary. He motioned back at the unarmored Marine with the gloves to stay where she was and she nodded her understanding. Then he was out the door to the cell block, pushing it closed behind him, and Lyta Randell was in motion.

The female Marine blinked, perhaps not believing her eyes or perhaps still stunned by the blast. Lyta felt a slight haze of concussion across her own thoughts, but her actions were automatic, a product of instinct built from thousands of hours of training and more experience than she cared to remember. The Marine swung the stun wand at her sidearm, clumsy and ineffective; she'd clearly never used it as a weapon, only as a torture device. Just as clearly, she didn't take Lyta seriously as a threat. Both were mistakes.

Lyta didn't block the stun wand, she attacked the arm, slamming her forearm into the muscle and nerve just behind the Marine's wrist. The younger woman's mouth shaped an "O" of pain and surprise and the stunner went flying down the hallway. Lyta ignored it. The prod was a terror weapon; she was more lethal with her bare hands.

The transition from the disarming strike to the follow-up across the throat was flowing, natural, sinking home with an affirmation of the hard weapons-soft targets philosophy of unarmed combat she'd taught for so long. The Marine gagged, eyes going wide, hands coming back to her throat automatically, without volition, leaving everything else wide open. A straight punch to the solar plexus blew the wind out of the younger woman's lungs, then a leg-sweep put her down flat on her back, unable to breathe.

Lyta stomped downward. Once. Twice. A last time and there was no movement. She bent down to grab the magnetic key at the dead Marine's belt and, as she did, she risked a glimpse into the open cell where the Starkad guard had been standing. Inside was an old woman strapped to a chair at the center of the cell, head hanging limply, eyes open, skin already beginning to turn blue.

The stun wand and the woman's age added two and two together and the sum was a heart attack. Lyta didn't feel anger so much as disgust, but she had no time for either. Julia was still sitting stunned in the hallway, staring first at the dead Marine and then at Lyta, then back again. Lyta ignored her, pushing past into the open cell and finding the woman she presumed was Momma Salvaggio crouched just inside. Salvaggio pounced toward her as if she expected her to be one of the Starkad Marines, but Lyta had anticipated the reaction and caught the smaller woman behind the arm, slamming her into the wall.

"I'm here to break you out, you dumb bitch," she shouted in Salvaggio's ear. "Now come along or I'll leave you for Grieg to torture you to death the way he did that poor civilian at the end of the hall."

That seemed to get through to her. The diminutive mercenary nodded and said something Lyta couldn't make out. She ignored it and pushed Salvaggio out the cell door ahead of her, pausing to grab Julia by the arm and haul her to her feet. The door back into the Constabulary office was still closed, but it would only be a matter of seconds before Grieg figured out there was no threat from the outside and came back through to investigate. And a locked door would just send him out to the back even faster.

She figured out her hearing was returning when the rasp of her breathing finally overcame the tinny whine in her ears as she was pulling the key card she'd taken from the dead Marine out of her cloak pocket.

"Hurry, damn it," Salvaggio urged, her voice muffled despite the other woman being right next to her. It only made her easier to ignore.

Lyta touched the card to the lock of the rear exit and yanked it open. If Chloe hadn't come through…

The rumble of the alcohol-fueled engine vibrating through the door let her know the girl *had* delivered on her promise even before she saw the open-topped frame and the broad, knobby tires of the runabout. Its rear-mounted engine oscillated violently, as if it were about to shake itself apart every second, but it was what they had, and Chloe was already waving urgently for them to get in. She didn't need to tell Salvaggio twice—the woman practically threw herself into the front passenger seat without even the decency to call "shotgun."

Lyta guided Julia into the back seat, grabbing the roll bar and yelling, "go!" before she even had a foot into the car. The rumble of the engine turned into the fierce, feral bellow of a wild horse and the tires ripped up chunks of earth and spat them out the back as it accelerated away from the jail. The roll bar yanked brutally at Lyta's hands and shoulders, but she kicked her legs over the edge of the frame and fell into the hard, bare-metal seat.

Lyta twisted around in the seat, watching behind them as the little runabout raced down the dirt road. A cluster of dark figures was running out the back door, over a hundred meters away now. She saw Grieg snatch a rifle from the hands of one of his Marines and bring it to his shoulder and she yelled a warning to Chloe just before the first bullets began whizzing by the side of the car. The stutter of the automatic rifle fire followed on the heels of the actual rounds and it seemed to spur Chloe more than Lyta's warning.

The runabout swerved wildly and Lyta grabbed desperately at the roll bar, the rough, unpolished metal gouging into her hands. She dropped back into her seat, giving up on any attempt to look behind them in favor of staying inside the car. Seconds later, Chloe veered three meters off the dirt track, slamming the fat tires over a cluster of granite sticking up through the dirt and pack sand. The impact nearly threw Lyta out of the vehicle and she grabbed at Julia's goatskin leather belt to keep her from tumbling over the other side.

There were no seat restraints in the back, though Salvaggio was quickly and desperately strapping herself into the front passenger seat. Lyta opened her mouth to caution Chloe about her driving, but a burst of cannon fire sent a gout of dirt and smoke exploding up from their left changed her mind. She risked a quick glimpse back and saw a scout mech loping out from the edge of town, long strides taking it between the city hall and the next building over, barely squeezing through the space.

"Oh, shit," she muttered. That was a Peregrine, with a top speed of fifty kilometers an hour. "Chloe!" she yelled at the young woman, leaning forward close to her ear. "I don't know how fast this damned thing goes, but it needs to go faster!"

Chloe grinned broadly and pushed the accelerator down to the floor. Lyta grabbed at the edge of the seat and cursed into the wind.

This is, she decided, *so not going to be fun.*

19

F rancesca Hayden, Petty Officer Third Class—*Or is it Second Class now?* she wondered—rolled over in her sleeping bag, threw an arm over her eyes and tried to go back to sleep. No one had slept much last night. There'd been work to do, camouflage netting to set up, covered fighting positions to dig and everyone had taken a turn at the labor, even the mech-jocks. Even Colonel Conner. She wasn't even bothering to think of him as Colonel Slaughter, though she knew she should be. The importance of the cover seemed to have faded for everyone with the loss of Terminus.

Shoot. She couldn't shut her brain off. She didn't want to check the time, but she figured she hadn't got more than four hours of sleep since polishing off a late breakfast. She still felt absolutely exhausted, but she could already tell she wasn't going to be able to get back to sleep, not without asking one of the Ranger medics for a pill.

She sighed and sat up, putting her back against the rock wall. She'd tried to bury herself back behind the supplies the refugees from Revelation had brought with them, but right now it was just making it too stuffy and close in the heat of the day. The rock felt cooler, made her breath come easier. She closed her eyes again, wondering if she could sleep sitting up.

"You doing okay?"

She blinked and rubbed a hand over her face, stifling a yawn. Had she actually fallen asleep? The light looked different now, coming in lower over the canyon walls. People were beginning to move around, their troops and the civilians. She tried to sit up and face whoever had spoken to her and the stiffness in her neck and back confirmed she'd done it. It felt like a triumph…

Slowly, the face came into focus, the strong chin, the light brown hair cut short to frame her face. She still wore her flight suit, but she had an armored tactical vest over it, a handgun tucked in a holster across her chest.

"Lieutenant Margolis," Franny stammered, scrambling to her feet and going to attention. "I mean, yes, ma'am, I'm fine."

"Relax, Hayden," Katy said with a chuckle, waving a hand dismissively. "Have a seat. Plenty of time before we all have to be looking busy. And it's Commander now, not that it matters out here."

Franny looked around, hesitant to squat back down on the ground. Instead, she found a pile of wooden crates someone had stacked up and sat down on top of them, cautiously at first to make sure they wouldn't collapse beneath her. Katy leaned against the rock face beside her, squinting out of the overhanging lean-to and watching one of the mech-jocks climbing down from his machine under the cover of a stretched-out camo net. Franny realized after a moment the machine was a Sentinel and the mech-jock was Logan Conner.

"Do you worry about him, ma'am?" she asked, feeling daring all of a sudden. "I mean, when he gets inside that thing and goes into combat?"

Katy shot her a sidelong look, canny and knowing.

"I do. And I know he worries about me when I'm flying overwatch in my assault shuttle. But it's who we are. I wouldn't have fallen for him so quickly if he'd been anyone else."

"So, you knew right away?" It was a stupid question, a childish question and she kicked herself for it. It was something her little sister would have asked. She tried not to let the other woman see her wincing. Katy Margolis wasn't much older than her, but she *seemed* decades her senior simply for all the life she'd lived.

"I did," the pilot admitted. "I think when it's right, you always know. When it's not, you try to convince yourself, but that never works. And ignoring it when it's right never works, either."

Katy smiled broadly, as if she'd been playing a game, pretending not to know what Franny was talking about, but couldn't keep it up any longer.

"Terry's a great guy," she said flatly. "He's smart as all hell, of course, but he's also brave and loyal and he's always trying to do the right thing, not just the easy thing. And I'm not just saying that because I'm in love with his brother. But I'll be square with you, Francesca..."

"Franny," she corrected Katy automatically.

"Franny. I'll be square with you, he's been wrapped up in his career for a long time and I think he may have forgotten the rules of the game."

"The game?" Franny asked, frowning in confusion.

"Oh, girl," Katy said, laughing softly. "The two of you may be perfect for each other." She shook her head and went on. "He's dense about relationships, like most men, but he's also been on his own for a long time now. You're going to have to be direct and you're probably going to have to be patient with him, too."

"I thought I was being patient," she moaned, burying her face in her hands.

"Here," Katy said, fishing something out of her thigh pocket and handing it to the younger woman. Franny took it; it was a fresh-strip, still in the wrapper. "Clean your teeth and go talk to him before he decides stars are more interesting than people again."

Franny obeyed numbly, feeling the tingle in her mouth as the strip killed the bacteria as it dissolved. She took a deep breath, stood up and headed out across the canyon with a purposeful stride. Terrin was sitting half-in the front passenger's seat of one of the Ranger APCs, with David Carpenter and his wife, who she'd come to know was named Anya, locked into an argument with Captain Lee, Lyta's second in command.

"We have the long-range transmitter," Terrin said, gesticulating as he emphasized each word. "We used it to contact you. Why not try to see if Lyta's 'link could pick up the signal?"

"We need to make sure our daughter is safe," Anya Carpenter insisted, leaning in toward the open door.

Lee rubbed at his temples with his fingers as if the whole conversation were giving him a headache.

"Because if she can pick the signal up with her 'link," he pointed out, his patience obviously strained, "so can Starkad with their detectors. The only reason they didn't when you sent it originally was because their satellites weren't in the right position. And if she tried to answer, she'd just be revealing her own position. I know you're worried about your daughter," he said to the Carpenters, "but we can't do anything right now without putting her at more risk."

"I'm sorry," Terrin told the couple. The air seemed to have gone out of him.

The two of them said something so quietly she couldn't hear, but the woman grasped Terrin's arm before she moved off. Lee waited until they were both out of earshot before shooting Terrin an annoyed glare.

"You know better than that," he chided the younger man. "Hell, you actually know how this shit works…" Lee tapped the side of the vehicle's communications console. "…which is more than I do."

"I do," Terrin admitted. "But they needed someone to listen to them, and I figured if you told them no, it would at least seem like someone important had. Sorry, Captain."

Lee nodded, waving off the apology.

"It's okay, that's part of being an officer I guess."

Terrin shook the Ranger's hand and got out of the vehicle, stopping abruptly when he saw Franny walking up to him.

"Oh, hey, Franny," he said. He had the look she'd only seen from deer crossing the road at night on the back-roads outside Argos, caught in the headlights of a car. "How are you doing?"

"Did you get any sleep, Terrin?" she asked him, already suspecting the answer from the dark circles under his eyes.

He shrugged.

"There was stuff to talk about with…" He stumbled over the words, probably trying to decide which name to use. "…with my brother. I had to let him know everything that had happened." He squinted up at the afternoon sun. "I wish I could let Dad know I'm okay."

"Walk with me a second," she urged him, extending a hand.

He took it, perhaps a bit hesitantly, his grasp cool and dry in the desert heat. She led him back down the canyon, past the fighting positions the Rangers had set up, around a curve where the river had once wound, to where the walls closed in again, and finally to a spot shaded from the sun by an overhanging lip of rock. She pulled him beneath the overhang, blinking and letting her eyes go wider without the sun in them.

"I just wanted to tell you," she said once they were nestled in the shade, so close she could feel his breath tease at her hair, "that I know you weren't really going to cut a deal with Salvaggio, that you were just playing for time."

"That's good," he sighed, sagging back against the rock wall, glancing at it first before he leaned on it. She knew why—they had red, stinging ants here that liked to sneak inside your collar or sleeve or pant leg and announce their presence with a nasty bite. "With everything else going on, I didn't want to think we weren't friends anymore."

"Are we friends, Terrin?" she asked him. She wasn't sure where the words were coming from because they scared the crap out of her, but she was channeling Katy and trying to be brave and open. "Is that what you want?"

She could feel the warmth coming off his skin and could hear his breath quicken.

"I mean," he stammered, meeting her eyes almost as if he was scared to look away "I, you know I like you."

"Do I know that?" she asked, forcing herself to stay close, not to run away like she wanted desperately to. "How would I know if you don't tell me?"

"I…uh, I *did* tell you." He was leaning closer now and she screwed up her courage and leaned forward to kiss him, remembering what Katy said.

"Hey, you wanna help a girl out here?"

"Lyta!" Terrin exclaimed, and then he was running past her so quickly Franny nearly lost her balance.

She couldn't blame him, though, because it *was* Colonel Randell. She was walking slowly and painfully up the path, half carrying the girl, Chloe Carpenter. Chloe's left arm was in a makeshift splint and dried blood plastered the hair to the left side of her head from a cut in her scalp. Lyta had a few rips in her borrowed clothes and scrapes and bruises visible through them, but otherwise looked healthy, if exhausted. Franny felt a brief surge of relief that the two of them were alive and safe…until she saw who was following them.

She didn't recognize the other teenage girl, though she seemed to be cut from the same cloth as Chloe and she assumed the girl was one of her friends from town. The older woman the girl was helping limp up the trail, though, her Franny recognized very well.

It was Momma Salvaggio.

"What the hell is she doing here?" Franny blurted, forgetting for a moment she was speaking to a Colonel.

Lyta didn't seem to notice the insubordination. "That, Petty Officer Hayden," she said, sighing as Terrin took some of the weight of the barely-conscious Chloe off her shoulder, "is a long story."

"Why the hell shouldn't we just kill her?" David Carpenter demanded. A murmuring grumble of agreement rose up from the rest of the crowd.

There were more of them now, called in from farmsteads and settlements outside Revelation City for the meeting, sneaking in under cover of the newly-fallen night and bringing with them a few more vehicles and a few more personal weapons hidden during Salvaggio's term ruling the colony.

She was, Logan Conner mused, quite the popular lady among the locals, though her infamy had, perhaps, been recently eclipsed by Colonel Grieg and his Starkad Marines. Still, there was a case to be made and he was going to have to be the one to make it. Lyta had wanted to do it, but while she was better at infantry tactics, infiltration and extraction than he would ever be, trying to convince civilians of anything was not in her skill set. She was more likely to start cracking skulls together, which wouldn't do them any good.

Logan squeezed Katy's hand for a last bit of emotional support, then stepped into the light at the folding table set up under the lean-to. Most of the fifty or sixty locals gathered around were outside the cover, their faces barely visible in the shadows, but they were all of a type. Farmers, shepherds, mechanics, carpenters, builders…men and women and boys and girls who worked with their hands, who weren't afraid of a fight. His problem was that, until recently, their fight had been with Salvaggio.

She sat behind him, wisely silent if not exactly repentant or submissive. Her left leg was swaddled in a bandage from a shrapnel wound and, from what Lyta had told them, she'd been damned lucky to survive. They'd *all* been lucky to escape the car before the Peregrine's missile took it out, lucky they'd made it to the edge of a forest thick enough to keep the scout mech from finding them.

Julia, the friend of Chloe who'd helped them break Salvaggio out, had come through basically unscathed, and Lyta just had a few scrapes and a bruised shoulder. Chloe had a concussion and a broken left ulna, but the Ranger docs said she'd be okay. The Carpenters were still pissed off she'd been used to help Salvaggio escape custody and were out for blood.

Logan sighed, wondering how his father did it.

"Captain Salvaggio has certainly abused her power and taken advantage of your situation," Logan admitted, pitching his voice to carry across the crowd. The rumbling died down to a low murmur. The people were ready to listen, mostly because of the military force he brought with him.

"Things are different now, though," he went on, looking around, not so much to see them as to let them see him. "You're not dealing with a strong-arm mercenary trying to squeeze you for money and run your imports, you're dealing with the Starkad Marines, and they won't rest until they get what they want."

"Then why don't we just give it to them?" someone in the crowd asked plaintively. The man looked to be one of the younger of the adults Logan had seen, maybe forty or forty-five.

"Because I made a deal," Lana Kane spoke up, stepping up to the table beside Logan.

Her little brother was not clinging to her for once, but only because she'd given him the job of taking care of Chloe. Not that the Ranger medics needed the help, but it kept him out of the way while the adults argued.

"I made a deal to get us out from under her thumb," Kane went on, stabbing a finger toward Salvaggio. "Maybe you think I was reckless to do this, maybe you think I should have consulted with everyone, but there wasn't time to put this through a committee. I had to make a decision on my own, sitting on Trinity, with basically a gun to my head." She eyed them all defiantly, fists on her hips. "Would any of you have done differently? Do you want to give Starkad what they came for and then go back to the way things were?"

"At any rate, part of what Starkad wants is my brother's life, so that's a hard no," Logan declared, cutting through the buzz and cross-talk. "We need Salvaggio's Savages to get rid of Starkad. We might or might not be able to take them on by ourselves, but it would get a lot of us killed and I'm not willing to go that route."

You don't need to know I'm willing to go that route if I have to, he corrected himself silently.

"The commander of our infantry units, Colonel Randell, is going to tell you what she saw on her recon of the city, and the plan she came up with."

And thank God they'll have someone else to be mad at for a few minutes. It wouldn't last. After she'd told them what she wanted to do, he'd still have to go back and sell it.

Lyta was back in her combat gear, black utility fatigues and body armor, a disembodied head floating in the shadows until she stepped up into the light by the central table. A model of the town had been set up there with food containers.

"Starkad Marines have Captain Salvaggio's mercenary troops

locked up in a warehouse here in the industrial district," Lyta said, launching into the presentation without preamble or pleasantries. "They're guarded, but not heavily, for one thing because they've been disarmed and for another, because Starkad has a fairly low opinion of civilians and an even lower one of mercenaries. They'll probably wind up executing them before they leave, if we let them."

She'd said it so casually, so off-handedly, yet Salvaggio blanched, visibly affected by it, the first hint of vulnerability she'd allowed herself to show since she'd arrived.

"Their mecha are secured in the stockyard not too terribly far away," Lyta went on, pointing to a dented metal container surrounded by crackers. She'd wanted to construct a sand table, but Logan had convinced her most of the people wouldn't have been able to see it. "What I propose is my Rangers and I, with Captain Salvaggio and whatever forces you locals can provide, will break the Savages out of their holding cells and lead them in an attack on the Marines at the stockyard. They'll get in their mecha and head out of town, straight for the canyon."

"The Run," one of the teenage boys near the head of the crowd corrected her.

Lyta gave him a glare that had made hardened NCOs wither away and the kid shrugged an apology.

"That's we call it," he stuttered an explanation. "This canyon…it's called the Run."

"Yes, well," she continued, her tone dry and brittle enough to serve as tinder, "Salvaggio's Savages will head straight for the Run, hopefully drawing the majority of Starkad's mecha right behind them to here." The Run had been simulated by a few wooden slats they'd found, and she pointed to where the canyon first narrowed down and began curving. "It's a natural choke-point, and we'll be waiting for them here with our Mobile Armor forces." She shrugged.

"It's a classical ambush, but hopefully one they won't be expecting since they still shouldn't know we've landed. The Rangers, Captain Salvaggio's infantry and those of you who join us will band together to take out whatever Marine forces are left in the town."

"Seems complicated," Logan told her quietly. "I thought you always said the best battle plans were the simplest."

"This situation is so fucked up," she shot back at him, *sotto voce*, "this is the simplest plan I could think of short of orbital bombardment."

"I still want to know why we have to bring *her* along?" Kane demanded, pointing at Salvaggio. "Why not leave her here where she can't betray us all?"

"Because her troops have no reason to follow me or anyone else in Wholesale Slaughter," Lyta pointed out. "If she's not there to hold them together, they'll just scatter and the whole thing falls apart."

"If you leave her with her troops and their weapons," Kane argued, leaning over the table, knocking over half the simulated town as she got into Lyta's face, "after you go, she'll just turn it all back into her own little fiefdom again!" She bared her teeth and Logan tensed, thinking for a moment she was about to go after Lyta or Salvaggio. "She's the reason Starkad is here to begin with!"

"You yokels were lucky to have me!" Salvaggio shot back, hopping up on one leg and putting her nose right into Kane's face. "A world like this is ripe for the picking for mercenaries, raiders, pirates, Jeuta bandits and anyone else with a ship and a few guns! You think any of them would be satisfied with making you do some honest work for your defense? You think they'd treat you as nice as I have?"

"You," Lyta said, pushing Salvaggio backwards, "sit down and shut up."

The mercenary captain lost her balance and plopped back down into the chair, snarling at Lyta.

"And *you*," Lyta leaned across the table and jabbed Kane with a finger to her shoulder, "don't knock over my Goddamned map!"

"Listen," Logan said, raising his voice over the din and arguing starting to rise up in the wake of Salvaggio's response. "I said listen! Captain Salvaggio is right about one thing. Even if we pull this off, even if we get rid of Starkad, you're still going to need protection and it's not going to come cheap or easy." He pointed a finger at his chest. "We're not staying. We'll do this job to get back what's ours, but then we have places to be. Are you going to somehow get together the money to buy your own mecha and guns and people to train you how to use them?"

Salvaggio looked as if she were about to make some smartass remark at the question, but Lyta detected it before he could and raised a cautioning finger to silence the woman.

"What I'd suggest," Logan went on, "is that you formally incorporate Salvaggio's Savages as your planetary defense force and allocate a permanent, but sustainable portion of your gross domestic product to paying them to stay here." He shrugged. "Maybe arrange something like a cut of the import fees, something you can both live with. Everyone who's been forced to work on Trinity would obviously be brought back unless they want to stay."

Some would, he was sure. Or would get work on outbound ships rather than return to a place like Revelation.

"It's not...impossible," Kane admitted, though the look on her face was still unhappy. "I just don't know if we can trust her."

"Then trust *me*," Logan suggested.

This was where things could get really tricky. He hadn't run this part by anyone, not Lyta, not Acosta, and not Salvaggio, but he had to hope he had enough power in this situation to make it stick. These people had latched onto him as their one safety line in the rising waters and that had a lot of cache.

"What if," he suggested, "I make Salvaggio's Savages an official subsidiary of Wholesale Slaughter LLC?"

He might, someday, get used to so many eyes being fixed on him, following his every word. Someday, but certainly not today.

"An official *what*?" Salvaggio repeated, disbelief and skepticism warring for position in her expression.

"You'd work for me," he told her. "And before you shitcan the idea, consider your alternatives. I have bigger guns, bigger mecha, and *much* better people than you. I sure as hell have better funding and I can pay quite a bit more than you're making right now."

"Wait," Acosta interrupted, stepping up out of the shadows where he'd been standing beside Katy. "What? We're *funding* them now?"

"Just an annual stipend," Logan suggested. "Something for upkeep and recruiting, you know?" He'd addressed the last to Salvaggio, but now he turned back to the crowd. "And, of course, since my name is on the product and my reputation is on the line, I'd feel obliged to become personally involved if any word reached me of Captain Salvaggio and her subsidiary operation abusing their authority here."

That got them thinking. The buzz in the crowd this time was quieter and he saw quite a few nods. It was David Carpenter who finally spoke up.

"I think we could live with that," he judged, and Logan fought the urge to blow out a breath with relief.

"All right," he said in an even, professional tone instead. "The satellite and ship coverage is thinnest right after sunrise. Whoever's going along with us on this, get yourself ready. We attack at dawn."

They drifted apart with the decision, small groups getting their jury-rigged technicals ready for the morning, but he managed to track down Lana Kane. She was sitting on the dirt in the ruddy glow of a small lantern at the edge of the lean-to, field-stripping a shop-made automatic rifle while her brother sat crouched beside her, watching with rapt attention.

"Before you ask," he told her, "you're not going."

"What?" she blurted, leaping to her feet quickly enough to send the pieces of the firearm flying. Her brother ignored their conversation and went chasing after an errant spring. "What the hell do you mean I'm not going?"

"In case you've forgotten, you're the only one who knows where the data crystals are." He waved a hand in invitation. "Now, if you want to give them to me tonight, you feel free to risk your life to your heart's content."

The glow of the lantern didn't travel far over the broad hood sheltering it and he could barely see her face, not that he expected someone in her line of work to give away her thoughts anyway.

"All right," she acquiesced. He wondered if it was too easy and if he should be worried. "I'll stay here. But you better hold up your end of the bargain, Colonel."

"We're Wholesale Slaughter," he said, grinning with more confidence than he felt. "It's what we do."

20

"Get them in there!" Saul Grieg bellowed, motioning with his drawn sidearm. "Every last one of them, damn it!"

The civilians being chivvied into the temple were clearly terrified, some of them still bearing the bruises and stun-gun burns of interrogations, others rousted from their beds well before dawn, and they nearly stampeded to squeeze through the narrow doorway simply to get away from the prodding butt-stocks of the Marines' rifles. Even the Marines looked a bit cowed by Grieg, shoving the steady line of residents ahead of them with renewed vigor.

The Intelligence officer seemed manic to Ruth Laurent, and she couldn't be sure if it was the lack of sleep, the paranoia, or simply the fact he was clinically psychotic. To be sure, he hadn't closed his eyes once in the last eighty-four hours, which couldn't have helped, but she thought it was the jailbreak that had done it. He'd been so sure the culprits were locals working in concert with Salvaggio...

She'd thought about telling him of her suspicions that Sparta already had agents here, but abandoned the idea quickly, certain it would have only spurred him to greater madness. His reaction to the escape and the killing of Sgt. Taylor had been to send out every Marine and every mech to round up all the civilians and put them under guard in the city's central temple to Mithra, the only building large enough to hold them all that wasn't already being used for something else.

They must be packed in there like cartridges in an ammo box, she thought with a sort of perverse curiosity, watching one after another traverse the purposefully narrow entrance. It was a statement on how narrow the way to Heaven was. *And a safety violation if it had been on Stavanger.*

Then it happened. She'd been praying it wouldn't, and standing outside a temple seemed a great place to pray, but Mithra, apparently, wasn't listening. Someone panicked. It was a teenager, a boy, probably looking younger than he was, and younger still with the childlike fear on his baby face. He'd been near the door, close enough to see the people squeezing through it, and he bolted. Maybe claustrophobic, maybe just afraid he'd die packed into the building with all those other people, but he broke from the line and ran.

The shouted commands, the cries of alarm, and the screams of the elders all merged into one, cacophonous static of white noise, one sound indistinguishable from another like feedback inside her head. Broken by the staccato chatter of an assault rifle, just one Marine breaking discipline but one was all it took. The three round burst grouped perfectly, each bullet hole less than two centimeters apart when they exited through the boy's chest in a spray of arterial red.

He stumbled, gasped for air he couldn't get with his lungs deflated and now the screams were higher-pitched and the shouts of command died away. He toppled to his side, coughing fitfully, each spasm of his chest matched with a splatter of blood from his mouth. Laurent wanted to run to him, wanted to check on him, but something anchored her in place, a conviction it was too late.

Too much damage had been done. She wanted to scream, wanted to cry, but she didn't give into the urge because she also knew what was going to happen next, and she had to be ready for it.

When the old woman waddled out of the line, unable to run but shuffling as best she could in a long dress that nearly scraped the ground, Laurent moved. The woman was a lost soul, a banshee wailing in the morning haze with a wild mane of grey hair tossing one way and then another as she lurched across the gravel road toward him. The Marines were spooked and Grieg was doing nothing to stop them, watching as if he'd wagered on the outcome.

"Stop!" Laurent yelled at the nearest of them as he raised his rifle, ready to shoot the old woman down. She stepped between them, pointing an accusatory finger at the Marine. "Goddamn you, she's not trying to escape!"

The trooper hesitated, the muzzle of his rifle going downward as he looked back to Grieg. The Colonel shrugged, making a dismissive gesture with the barrel of his handgun.

"Fine. Get her inside."

The old woman was still wailing as two Marines dragged her back toward the temple, but she didn't really attempt to resist.

There's no strength left in her, Laurent judged. *Is there any left in me?*

"I'm going to help check the next street over for stragglers," she told Grieg.

He barely acknowledged her, talking on the radio with someone back in the city hall. She thought she made out something about satellite coverage and when the *Sleipner* would have a workable angle. Just another factor in his paranoia. He'd sent out surveillance drones over and over, and over and over they'd gone down without explanation. Remote sensors had been sabotaged. Live patrols had seen nothing out of the ordinary, but they couldn't afford to go too far off the roads because the Marines were needed to guard the citizens, and Grieg wouldn't let the mecha out of town unescorted for fear of booby traps. It was ridiculous, but she expected nothing less from someone who had been, as the late Colonel Kuryakin would have said, a career crunchie, a foot soldier.

She couldn't bear the sight of him anymore. How did men such as him climb so high so quickly in the Supremacy military when Colonel Kuryakin had remained at his rank and position for years? Kuryakin had shown poor judgement in the end, but he hadn't been mad, merely ambitious. Was Lord Starkad mad as well, surrounding himself with people like him, or was he simply poorly advised, told what he wanted to hear?

She'd endured so much pain, so much horror to get the intelligence back to him, knowing it was her duty. And somehow it had resulted in her serving under a madman, watching a child shot down in the street. Maybe the narcissistic assholes who worshipped Ahriman had it right, and Mithra hated them.

By the time she was able to pull herself out of her thoughts, she found she'd actually gone where she told Grieg she'd be, to the warehouse where he'd confined Salvaggio's troops. She wasn't sure what it had been built to hold, perhaps food, perhaps raw materials for the fabricators, but it held men and women now, soldiers, mercenaries. She'd seen their looks when they'd been forced into the locked storerooms of the warehouse, after Grieg had decided Salvaggio wasn't useful as an ally. They were resentful but also unsurprised, as if they'd expected nothing less from Starkad.

A fire team of Marines patrolled the street outside the warehouse and she knew another team was inside. Not many to guard the thirty-some mercenaries, but Salvaggio's Savages were unarmed and locked up. Grieg had talked of killing them after Salvaggio's escape and she wondered if he would do it. He had the authority, as Lord Starkad's personally appointed representative and he had shown no reticence using it. It seemed almost inconsequential now, executing a few mercenaries, beside everything else she'd seen happen.

Something exploded. She stumbled backwards, reflexes guided by the post-traumatic stress of Terminus, tripped and fell into a pile of scrap wood, an empty spool that had once held superconductive cable. She landed hard, but didn't look down to check if she was injured or determine whether the wetness beneath her hands was water or her own blood. Her eyes were locked on the end of the street, on the black cloud rising from the blast.

The harsh percussion had rumbled up the street, rattling windows, but it had faded nearly as fast and been replaced by the deep, thunderous drumbeat of automatic weapons fire. A heavy caliber machine gun, she thought, probably not from a mech. Her first thought had been that one of the mechs had found a holdout and tried to root them out, but this gunfire was low to the ground and undercut with the harsh, anachronistic growl of an internal combustion engine.

A technical, that's what Kuryakin had called them, a civilian cargo truck or off-road vehicle rigged with armor and mounting a crew-served weapon. It was her best guess and she thought her old commander would have approved of her reasoning.

The Marine guards didn't ask her opinion, didn't pause to check on her or offer to help her up. They simply took off running toward the sound of gunfire, which she supposed was commendable for Marines but a bit short-sighted. Hot on their heels were another fire team, this one careening down the street in an appropriated civilian flatbed truck, one in the cab and the other three hanging on for dear life in the back, weapons ready.

Two more of Grieg's troops wandered out through the open, sliding door of the warehouse, checking both ways down the street. One, then an eyeblink later the other, fell before the sound of the shots reached her ears. Snipers. On top of a nearby building. And if they were exposing themselves now, that meant…

Boots scraping over the pavement. She heard them and there was a subtle tone to their impact, something qualitatively different from the soles of the Starkad Marines. Boots made somewhere else, just a slight difference in manufacture. Black-clad, armored, moving with tightly-wrapped urgency in an arrowhead wedge as they crossed the street. They swept in through the front door of the warehouse, pausing to check the two downed Marines, quickly and efficiently stripping the magazines out of their weapons before they tossed them away. Two of them stayed at the door to stand watch and, for the first time, she noticed they weren't wearing helmets, just balaclavas and goggles.

No ordinary ground troopers, then. These were Spartan Rangers.

The hoarse stutter of a suppressed carbine sounded several long bursts reverberating out the front entrance. You could channel the expelled gas from a gunshot, change and reduce its sound signature, but you couldn't completely silence it, and there was nothing at all to be done about the bullets travelling at supersonic speeds. Suppressors merely turned what would have been something loud enough to deafen into a sound on the edge of the comfortable.

Silence now, though, uncomfortable in the absence of return fire. There was no one left alive inside to shoot back. When the Rangers emerged, it was at the lead of a ragged cluster of Salvaggio's mercenaries, running free with a gleam in their eyes promising revenge and profit. They'd no doubt seemed intimidating and suitably martial to the colonists here, but to her, they looked like a pack of vagrants playing soldier, and spending a few nights sleeping in a warehouse with no showers hadn't helped.

She made no move for her pistol, just stayed where she was, afraid to move lest she attract attention, lying in whatever wet, trash-strewn mess she'd stumbled into, watching them abandon the warehouse. They weren't running out of town, though…they were going up the street. Toward the stockyard.

The mecha, she realized.

She should get on her 'link, call Grieg and warn him, warn the Marines guarding the stockade. She should. It was her duty.

Slowly and painfully, she got to her feet and backed into the alley until she was sure none of them were still waiting, watching, ready to put a bullet through her. Then she turned and ran back toward the temple.

Lyta Randell hadn't fired her weapon yet, and she was good with that. It had taken getting beaten up, blown up and battered over the course of the last few weeks, but she finally thought she was ready to accept the business of delegating the whole walking point and soaking up damage thing to younger people.

And of course, there was the whole business of having to ride herd on "Captain" Salvaggio, which took up far too much of her attention.

Shit, if that woman was ever more than a Sub-Lieutenant in anyone's army, I'll buy her a new mech.

First platoon thundered across what she'd been informed was imaginatively named Main Street as Second laid down covering fire against the Starkad forces firing from the cover of the stock pen gates. 6mm slugs punched through wooden fence slats and smacked into metal posts, driving the Marines behind cover as First moved into positions behind a line of cargo trucks parked in the street outside. The platoon leader, Lt. Wayne, made a familiar hand signal and…

"Move, now!" she urged the mech commander, pushing her forward.

Salvaggio was still favoring her leg, even though the Ranger medics had rebandaged the wound and given her a good dose of painkillers. *Enough she probably shouldn't have been operating heavy machinery, but oh well.* She slowed down the command group, which was a fancy name for Lyta, one of the medics and another enlisted man who was officially her aid but in fact was tasked with making sure she didn't get herself killed. Which was harder when they were crossing a free-fire zone at a fast walking speed, but if they didn't get Salvaggio to the stockyard at the same time as her mech-jocks, the whole issue was moot.

"You could have given me a damned gun," Salvaggio complained, grunting as she fell to a crouch behind the wheel well of a flatbed truck.

"We're fighting the same enemy," Lyta told her, peaking around the edge of the cargo bed. "That doesn't mean I trust you."

"You're about to put me in the cockpit of a damned mech," Salvaggio reminded her, amusement rich in her tone, though Lyta wasn't bothering to look away from the enemy positions.

"Then stop bitching." Lyta tapped the button on the side of her ear bud and spoke into her 'link pickup. "Lee, you guys almost here?"

"One mike, ma'am."

One minute...which seemed like no time at all until someone was shooting at you.

"Don't take time to stop and sight-see," she advised him. "And don't let any of those idiots get themselves shot."

"Those are *my* idiots," Salvaggio told her, overhearing her end of the conversation.

"Lt. Grant," she yelled to the woman instead of transmitting because the First platoon leader was only three meters away. A burst of return fire from the stockade slammed into the rear end of the flatbed not far from Lyta's head and she ducked instinctively.

"Yes, ma'am?" Grant called back, not coming out from behind cover to answer. *Smart woman.*

"The package is less than a mike out. You are a go."

"First platoon!" Grant bellowed almost before the echo had died from Lyta's command. "Prep the target!"

Half a dozen grenade-launcher equipped carbines swung upward almost simultaneously, as if it were a rifle drill competition and then fired with nearly the same precision, the six thumping reports blending into one. They were firing frags, anti-personnel rounds, which weren't quite as loud as you'd figure they would be, just snare drum reports and then a handbell choir of ricochets as wire fragments bounced off metal too thick to penetrate. And the screams. The screams were almost louder than the explosions, and reached further into Lyta's mind.

She'd made peace with the necessity of killing the enemy well over a decade ago, and if she were being honest with herself, she'd enjoyed some of them, the ones who seemed to deserve it, the bandits and pirates who tortured and raped and enslaved. But the screams of the wounded and dying, those she'd never come to terms with, never managed become inured to.

"Move!" Grant yelled, standing and leading the way, the way Rangers had always done.

Lyta straightened up from cover and saw one of the squad leaders fire off a door-breacher round into the latch on the main gate, the blast smashing through the simple, mechanical lock with a flash of sparks, sending the swinging metal doors fluttering inward. Grant rushed in shoulder-to-shoulder with a junior NCO, carbines stuttering covering fire, and the rest of her platoon flowed through behind them.

Lyta kept a hand on Salvaggio's shoulder, ready to hold her back should the woman show any signs of being a big enough dumbass to charge on in before the Rangers cleared out the opposition, but it proved unnecessary. Josephine Salvaggio had shown herself to be quite adept at self-preservation, and she seemed quite content to wait out the infantry battle.

Quick bursts of suppressed fire marked the Rangers' contribution, answered by ragged chattering. Not necessarily an indictment of the Marines' training as much as their panic and surprise. More controlled bursts until the return fire ceased entirely.

"Clear." Grant's voice was tight and strained and Lyta knew something was wrong. "Get me a medic up here."

She hauled Salvaggio up and hauled her along through the gate past the perimeter Second platoon was setting up. There'd been an entire squad defending the Savage mecha. She could see six bodies sprawled out, some having taken cover behind the legs of the row of banged-up Hopper scout mecha with just their feet sticking out into the open now. Starkad Marines worked in fire teams of four, so there was at least a squad's worth of bodies here. She trusted Grant to have made sure of all of them; this wasn't the sort of mission where they could take care of wounded prisoners and Starkad Marines didn't surrender.

Grant was sitting against the tree-trunk leg of a Reaper assault mech, her balaclava pulled off to reveal an anguished grimace on her lean face, one hand pressed against the upper part of her right shoulder, near the joint with the neck, where the armor was the thinnest. She'd taken a round there and blood was seeping though her fingers while one of her NCOs was fishing in his thigh pocket for a field dressing. A medic shouldered the platoon sergeant aside and pried her fingers away from the wound, slapping a smart bandage over it, coated with a chemical to stop the bleeding as well as painkillers.

"Is she going to be okay?" Lyta asked the medic before addressing Grant directly. The Sub-Lieutenant would tell her what she wanted to believe and she needed the truth.

"Doesn't look like any major arteries hit," the young enlisted man judged. "She should be fine, but we should get her back to the drop-ship, use the full diagnostic scanner on her as soon as possible."

"I'm afraid that's going to be a while."

"I can still fight, ma'am," Grant insisted, trying to push herself to her feet. "I can lead First."

The medic shrugged, looking helplessly at Lyta.

"The smart bandage should keep it closed as long as she doesn't get into any hand-to-hand combat."

"No promises," Grant smiled tautly, pulling her enhanced vision goggles and balaclava back on.

"Captain Lee is here with the mercs, Colonel," Lt. Wayne, the Second platoon leader, called in her ear from outside the fence. "And I have reports of enemy mecha headed this way, ETA less than two minutes."

He'd barely said the words when the first of the mercenary mech-jocks stumbled in through the front gate, nearly tripping over his own feet as he slowed from all-out sprint to a walk to avoid running into a feed trough. He was an older man with streaks of grey through the wild, black mane of his hair, and there was a manic quality to the set of his eyes, particularly when he spotted Salvaggio.

"Momma!" he said, grinning. "I knew you'd get us out of this, especially since you're the one who got us into it."

"I love you, too, Yuri," she said, making a rude gesture. "Now get in your damned mech and get ready to get the hell out of here."

"All of you get in your machines," Lyta snapped, motioning impatiently as the rest of the pilots pushed through the gates. They weren't much to write home about by the sight of them, but all she needed was running bait, and she hoped they'd serve for that. "We have Starkad mecha incoming and you won't stand a chance against them if you get caught in here flat-footed."

"Hell, we don't stand a chance against them out on the street either," the man called Yuri opined, moving far too slowly to one of the Hoppers.

"Just trust me," Salvaggio told him, told all of them as she limped toward the side of her Reaper, grabbing onto the handhold on the left leg and pulling herself up. "When have I ever let you down?"

"Is that a fucking trick question?" Yuri called down from the torso of his Hopper, yanking the release for the canopy to climb inside.

"Rangers!" Lyta barked, feeling a load lifting off of her shoulders without the duty of babysitting Salvaggio. "Police up all traces of our being here and clear the area to Rally Point Alpha. We want those Starkad mecha focused on these…" She pointed up at Salvaggio's Reaper, already beginning to hum and vibrate as the reactor fired up and power began flowing to the servos. "…not on us. Don't be seen, don't give them a reason to stick around town."

"Ma'am!' Captain Lee shouted, jogging up through the main gate and pointing off to the west, toward the main street. "Here they come!"

She followed his gesture and saw the glint of the morning sun off of metal just above the rooftops.

"Get out!" she roared, waving up at Salvaggio's cockpit. "Go! Go! Go!" Then to Captain Lee and the others. "Everyone! Out of sight now!"

Everything was chaos and clamor and men and women were dodging the swinging pendulum legs of mecha as they headed out through the main gate. Salvaggio led with her humanoid Reaper, faded white and tarnished silver like a tired, battle-worn warrior striding off to some ancient war. The mech's massive legs smashed through the stockyard gate, crumpling the metal into twisted uselessness and stomping it beneath her footpads.

Lyta stayed on her feet until everyone else had found a hidey-hole, a shadow to crawl into, in back rooms and storage sheds and beneath feed troughs, until her aid actually grabbed her arm and yelled into her ear over the thunderous stomping of mech footpads on the hard-packed dirt.

"Ma'am, get to cover!" the junior NCO insisted urgently. "I promised Colonel Conner I wouldn't let you do anything else stupid!"

"Oh, you did, did you?" She laughed. She couldn't help it. The kid really *was* blossoming into a real commander. "Well, let's not make our fearless leader angry then."

She ducked behind a thin, metal feed trough. It probably wasn't as solid a cover as the boy sergeant would have liked, but it was the only one around with a view of the street, and she needed to see. The last of Salvaggio's mecha were bounding out through the ruined gates, each seeming to take the extra moment to stomp on the crushed metal doors as if making some sort of philosophical statement on their captivity. They were picking up speed, overworked and aging servos whining in protest as a trot turned into a full-tilt gallop, not heading for the center of town or towards the seaport, but instead straight out, taking the rough, gravel and packed-sand track out into the wilderness.

They were a pack of mangy, flea-bitten horses stampeding off with Lipizzaner stallions in pursuit. The Starkad mecha didn't quite glitter in the sun, their camouflage paint protected against reflection. But they had the air of the new, of having come off the assembly lines at Stavanger only months ago and marched right onto the *Sleipner*; their jaunty stride seemed to match the over-confidence of their pilots, of their commander.

It'll work, she prayed. *It'll work.*

Two of the Starkad mecha lumbered out into the center of the street, an Agamemnon and a Valiant, looking for all the world like two hesitant soldiers, debating whether to pursue the enemy or stay at their posts.

Go, she urged them silently. *You know you want to go. You're mech-jocks, all balls and no brains, even the women. You want to chase after the rabbit like the other doggies. Just go.*

As if she'd whispered the words into their ears, the two assault mecha headed off after the others, following the Salvaggio machines, leaving the town for the Marines to defend.

And Marines, we can handle. She smiled the smile of a stalking wolf. *Maybe Mithra's listening after all.*

21

Josephine Salvaggio had never been happier to be inside her Reaper. She'd nicknamed it Battle-axe after one of her former mothers-in-law both for its violent temperament and balky interface, but today, the easy chair and neural halo felt like the embrace of an old lover. They meant power over her own destiny, something she hadn't had since she'd been stupid enough to get involved in all this shit with Starkad.

Should have just minded my own business and let the Supremacy have those two kids.

That was the problem with always having an eye to the next big score: you wound up sticking your fingers into too many mousetraps trying to get the free cheese. Maybe this time, she'd learn her lesson, play it straight for a while.

Yeah, right.

Life decisions later. Trying not to get killed in the next few minutes had priority. She jinked the Reaper to the left, back to the right, curving off the dirt road and back onto it, knowing the enemy fire would be chasing them soon.

There was a way to run a mech when someone was chasing

you, a way she'd learned in the Clan Modi Military Academy from a scarred and grizzled old man with a prosthetic arm and a rasp in his voice from smoke damage to his throat. She'd asked him once why she should take advice on fire-avoidance from someone who'd obviously failed at it, and he'd showed her the official After-Action Review of the battle. He'd gone in with a full company of mecha and his was the only one to emerge not totally destroyed. He could have ejected, but he'd chosen to hold the line instead.

It hadn't had quite the effect on a young Sub-Lieutenant Salvaggio the teacher had hoped. She'd determined then and there she wasn't going to sacrifice her one and only Mithra-gifted ass for anyone's politics. The only thing she was going to fight for was Josephine Salvaggio…and Josephine Salvaggio's bank account.

And how's that working out for you?

"Missiles inbound!" That was Yuri. For all that he'd been the first one in his mech, he'd fallen back to the drag position to watch everyone else's back because that was Yuri. "Scatter!"

"Negative!" she snapped over the general channel. "Spread our ranks but keep moving west! Support is to the west and if we run off on our own, they'll gun us down one at a time!"

No response, but she could see on her IFF display they were obeying her orders, fifteen blue arrows still pointing in the same direction but some slowing as they went off-road into rougher ground. The missiles hit, most of them splashing into rock and sand, shooting up huge, impressive fireworks shows of molten silicates, some blasting craters into the surface of the road. Jump-jets flared briefly here and there as her scout mecha boosted over three-meter-wide holes.

Ahead, only a few kilometers away into the purple dimness on the other side of the sunrise, was the Run, the canyon. They were already tromping along the course of the dried-up riverbed, though it was piled up with so many centuries worth of sand and gravel. Salvation was there, in the Revelation Run, if they could get to it in time.

Behind the last of them, behind solid, dependable Yuri in the last Hopper at the rear of their formation, were the demons hunting their souls to deny them salvation. A full sixteen, a company's worth, what she should have had for truth in advertising, but she'd lost three machines fighting the bandits for possession of this place and only two of their mecha had been salvageable after the battle.

Unlike her collection of shop-built Hoppers and obsolete scout mecha, Starkad had a full selection of scout, assault and strike mecha, though she noted they hadn't brought down any Arbalest missile vehicles. Probably hadn't thought they'd need them down here, where the only opposition they had expected was her and the locals. You could only load so many machines on one drop-ship, and Grieg had struck her as a man who trusted his infantry more than his armor.

"They're getting close, Josephine," Yuri said, his tone clipped. He'd actually used her name, which happened once in a blue moon, when he was too stressed, or angry, or worried to call her "Momma." He was the one who'd started the nickname. "I don't think we're going to make it."

He was right. The flat terrain mocked her with its sameness, its endlessness, at the edge of the canyon still sitting there looking nearly as far away as it had when she'd first noticed it despite dozens of loping, three-meter steps. She couldn't see the faces of the others surrounding her, only their long, desperate strides, ostrich-like, the clouds of dust billowing up behind them. She could imagine them, though, could picture every one of them.

Milla had been with her since the beginning, along with Yuri, yet he was perpetually baby-faced and underestimated by everyone who met him. She'd seen his war face in a dozen bar fights over the years, his teeth bared, eyes slitted, nostrils flaring like some ancient death mask. He'd be making that face now, she knew, even if the enemy wouldn't be impressed by it.

He'd have been making it when he died. A flight of missiles slammed into his Hopper all at once, four of them striking within a half-meter of each other, ripping through the reactor, the turbines and the cockpit in a blinding spray of plasma fire. The ground shook with the explosions, and someone, somewhere was wailing forlornly. Maybe it was her.

It was as if someone else made the decision, someone far younger and more idealistic than she'd ever been. It certainly couldn't have been her who slowed her Reaper's stride down to a trot and began the wide turn. It didn't even sound like her voice in her own ears when she spoke.

"Yuri," she said, "get them to the Run. I'll buy you as much time as I can."

"Josephine…." There it was again. She'd seen him rattled twice in one day. That couldn't be good.

"Do it, Yuri. That's an order."

"Yes, ma'am."

The Reaper she called Battle-axe wasn't new, wasn't new when her grandmother had been a girl, and she'd entertained herself for endless hours cursing the mech's foibles. Not now. Now, it surged with an energy that could have come directly from her soul instead of the old, repurposed fusion reactor she'd stolen from a shipment five years ago. The arms swung in time with the lope of the long legs, a predator on the hunt, circling her prey.

She found the assault mech in the lead wedge of the Starkad formation first, painting it with a laser just a half-second before she fired off her missiles. Smoke wreathed her cockpit and she felt the torso rock back at the flight of four long-range missiles streaking away at once. She kept the machine balanced and kept to the arc she'd begun to describe, circling back around into the midst of the Starkad formation, ignoring her first target and moving to the next, to an Agamemnon at the edge of the center wedge. The big machine kicked up tumbleweeds and Joshua trees in its wake as it tried to turn to meet her, a giant child dragging his feet in defiance. Another tone from the Reaper's laser targeting lock and another volley.

Only two more in her magazine and she wasn't even sure they'd make it to their targets. The missiles were black market buys, slapped together in a workshop on Trinity from parts stolen from warehouses or pirated from shipments, then sold and re-sold and Mithra knew whether the guidance systems worked or the explosives would detonate. It wasn't pertinent to her equations— she just had to keep them busy long enough for her people to get a little separation.

They'd spotted her now. Alarms were sounding inside the cockpit, yellow lights flashing as targeting lasers found her, and missiles were flying, some crossing each other's paths and self-destructing with a fireworks show in mid-air. An ETC cannon shell passed only a meter behind her, leaving a glowing ionization trail in its wake, but no others followed it and no energy weapons were fired and she knew why. She was running across their formation, putting them in each other's firing arc. It wouldn't last long, like passing through the eye of a hurricane, but for just a few seconds, she could shoot at them and there wasn't a damned thing they could do about it.

Might as well enjoy it.

She leveled the Reaper's right arm at a Peregrine scout mech unlucky enough to be the closest thing to her, toggled her firing control to the large laser mounted along the side and pulled the trigger. The actual beam wasn't visible, not even in the particulate haze the mecha were kicking up along the dry riverbed, but the heat from the intensely powerful burst of laser pulses ionized the air between her and the Peregrine into a plasma, a crackling bolt of lightning. It was a light-show, nothing more, but someone watching from the ground could be forgiven for thinking the lightning strike was what blew the hole through the scout mech's cockpit in a glowing halo of sublimated metal. The Peregrine stumbled in its long-legged run and plowed into the sand at nearly fifty kilometers an hour, ripping the left arm off at the elbow.

"Eat that, you Starkad piece of shit!" she yelled at no one.

The victory came at a price. With the Peregrine down, there was a clear lane of fire for two of the enemy machines and it didn't take them more than a second to realize it. She tried to cut her turn even tighter, tried to close the gap between her and the next of the Starkad machines, a broad-shouldered Valiant, but the time it took was time she didn't have, and she knew it.

Another little trick retired Major Ambedkar had taught her was narrowing her cross-section. She twisted the torso of the Reaper around at a ninety-degree angle to her direction of travel, putting her right side in direct line with the Valiant just as it fired. The Electro-Thermal Chemical cannon round missed by centimeters, so close she could feel the heat of its passage even through the transparent aluminum of her cockpit canopy, could feel the static electricity raising the loose strands of hair sticking out of her helmet.

The next round didn't miss. She hadn't seen the other mech fire, couldn't have even named the model, couldn't have sworn as to what weapon he used, but the pilot was a better strategist than the one driving the Valiant: he went for her legs.

An actinic flare swallowed up the view from the lower half of her canopy and the footpads of her mech slid sideways by at least two meters. Warning lights flashed yellow and red and she knew by instinct more than any conscious reading of the damage indicators that her right leg was skragged. She wasn't one hundred percent sure it was even still there, but she knew it wouldn't hold the mech's weight, and collapsing here, in the middle of a Starkad firing squad would be the very last thing she ever did.

She slammed both feet down on the jump-jet pedals and the Reaper screamed upward on columns of superheated air, slamming her down into her seat hard enough for her to teeth to clack together. She was thirty meters up, fifty and arcing forward, leading her out of the center of the Starkad formation but *oh, so damned slow…*

The plasma arc of a laser weapon flashed by and another damage indicator began blinking yellow, this time on her Reaper's left leg.

That's okay, I wasn't planning on running any marathons in the damn thing.

An annoyingly persistent whine warbled through the cockpit, a warning the jets were overheating and her mech's turbines were about to turn into large and highly effective fragmentation bombs. She didn't let off. What would be the point? Go out from a blown turbine up here or get blown to shit down there. Six of one…

She saw the mouth of the canyon now. It was only a few hundred meters away, so close and yet she wouldn't reach it. Her people were already there, the last of them disappearing around the first curve, safe in the arms of the Spartans, but she wasn't going to make it. She remembered a story her grandmother had told her once, a tale of the Old Religion about a man named Moses who had led his people through the desert for forty years until they'd reached the Promised Land. They'd finally reached it, but he'd fucked up somehow and his God wouldn't let him enter. He'd been able to see it, though, one glimpse before he died.

At least I didn't take forty fucking years…

The turbines hadn't quite reached critical when the laser smacked her out of the air. The left-hand turbine took the hit, the blades vaporized as they soaked up megajoules of heat energy in a fraction of a second, which was the only reason she wasn't killed instantly by shrapnel. Instead, unbearable heat washed over her and she began to fall.

Not all at once, and not straight down; the right-hand thrusters were still going, miraculously since the mech was over a century old. It couldn't handle the weight and the attempt was just going to make it fail faster, so she feathered it on purpose, coming down too fast but not at terminal velocity.

I'm just delaying the inevitable, she thought dolorously as the ground rushed up to meet her. *But isn't that what living is all about?*

The Reaper hit hard and she was fairly certain she'd slammed her head into the side of the cockpit somehow, even though the restraints should have prevented it. By the time the fuzziness in her head had cleared to where she could think again, she was on her side and she felt something very wrong and very painful in her back.

She blinked something wet out of her eyes and tried to focus on the readouts in her HUD, but there were none. Everything was dead.

Me, too.

She was down facing back the way she'd come, able to look up the dirt track of the old riverbed, able to see them coming for her. The Valiant was in the lead and she thought she knew who was driving the fancy machine. Captain something-or-other, the Mobile Armor company commander under Grieg. He was a real prick and it was going to suck getting killed by him.

She closed her eyes and waited.

"This is taking too damned long," Logan Conner murmured to himself.

He felt like a bug on a plate even tucked into the curve of the canyon, bathed in dawn shadow by the thirty-meter walls. It was one thing to know in your head the satellites weren't overhead at the moment, it was another to feel it in your gut.

He checked the Sentinel's sensor readout for the twentieth time in the last five minutes and, for the twentieth time, saw lots of nothing. They hadn't risked a drone or even as much as a remote camera for fear Starkad would spot it and get spooked; and it was impossible to see a thing around the bend in the canyon.

He was in the front of the formation and he knew Lyta would have chewed him out if she'd been around—Katy already had, in private. But his Sentinel was one of the most heavily armed and armored mecha they'd brought down with them and the first volley would be the key. When Starkad charged around that curve, they had to blast them back on their heels and it made sense for him to be in the front lines with the rest of the strike mecha.

Paskowski's Scorpion stood beside him, as if they were ready to reenact the battle between Logan's father and Duncan Lambert on the steps of the Palace at Argos back during the Treason. He'd been inside the palace that night, deep in a sealed bunker with his mother and Terrin, where they all should have been safe, but the captain of the guard had betrayed them, had sold the entry codes to Lambert's troops. His mother had joined file clerks and janitors in a desperate attempt to save her children and the other families in the shelter.

He remembered when she'd left the bunker, telling him to take care of his brother. He'd known, even at not quite eight years old. He'd understood she wouldn't be coming back. Terrin hadn't understood, hadn't accepted it even when they'd been told by their father, and he didn't think it was just the years separating them. Terrin understood the universe, but people were so much harder for him to figure.

Logan checked the view in the rear camera display by instinct, as if he could see Terrin and Katy and the others back there. He couldn't, of course. The other two platoons of assault mecha were arrayed behind him and the strike mecha, stretching back over a hundred meters to the next curve in the canyon. Terrin, Katy, Acosta and Franny were at the lean-to with a few of the civilians who'd stayed behind to guard the noncombatants among them, children and those too old or infirm to fight.

Katy hadn't been very happy about it. She'd wanted to go with the civilians in their technicals to assist in the fight for the town, but he'd convinced her it wouldn't be prudent to put their only qualified pilot in a vicious ground battle. It had been a near thing, but he'd also reminded her and Acosta that they needed to protect Kane until she gave them back the data crystals.

It was easy to forget about the data. His primary mission had been to get Terrin back, keeping the data out of Starkad's hands was secondary, but the abstract promise of the technical records was lost on him. He'd thought Terminus would provide them the means to rid themselves of the bandits and pirates, but it seemed the quest for them had done more for that than the actual discovery. Wholesale Slaughter had killed off the Red Brotherhood and the Jeuta bandits of Hardrada. Wholesale Slaughter was helping the people of Revelation regain their freedom and self-determination.

He'd thought he was done with Jonathan Slaughter, and maybe he was, but he wasn't sure he was through with the work they'd been doing. It was something he'd have to think about back home, when this was all over.

He was pulled out of his reverie by the flashing of a sonic sensor in his tactical display. It was picking up vibrations through the ground, rhythmic, regular impacts that could only be caused by one thing.

"Mecha inbound!" he announced over the general commo net. "Weapons hot!"

"It's us! Don't fucking shoot, it's us!"

He didn't recognize the voice but he knew the frequency—it was the one Salvaggio had given them.

"Hold your fire," he ordered instantly, letting his own finger off the trigger of his control yoke just before the first Hopper rounded the bend.

It looked like it had been put together in some backwoods colony workshop from spare parts, beat up and patched up over and over, but it wore the Salvaggio's Savages logo proudly. He expected the pilot to take it on through their lines the way they'd been instructed, but instead, he stumbled to a halt in a spray of sand and dust.

"You've got to help her!" he insisted, sounding desperate over the scratchy, tinny connection of his mech's radio. "Momma… Captain Salvaggio! They were gonna catch us so she turned back to slow them down! You've gotta help her!"

He was about to tell the man to pass on through the lines and follow the plan, but the rest of the Savages were rounding the curve as well, and stalling into a cluster right there at the turn, hesitating, bunching up. Cross-chatter began tying up the frequency and a few of the mecha began to turn back the way they'd come with a general feeling on the line they were going to go back and help Salvaggio.

The whole plan was falling apart before his eyes and the weight of dozens of lives, hundreds, pressed down on his shoulders until only one decision made sense.

Depending on your definition of "sense."

"Follow me!" he roared.

He pushed through the mass of light Savage mecha and took

the Sentinel from a rest to a long-legged stride to a loping gallop in just seconds. He cleared the bend in the canyon and the scene ahead mapped itself across his mind in stark clarity. Out on the plains, the Starkad light company was spread in a ragged, curving line, their formation distorted by whatever battle had just concluded.

A billowing cloud of red dust hung over the downed humanoid form of a Reaper assault mech, laying on its side with smoke pouring out of one of its jump-jets, its left leg twisted into uselessness. A Valiant had stopped just in front of the Reaper, poised like a duelist ready to give his opponent the *coup-de-grace*.

Logan painted him with a laser designator and launched a spread of missiles from the box-like pod on the Sentinel's shoulder.

"Spread out and take them," he said. Part of him wondered why he wasn't giving more detailed orders, issuing angles of attack for each platoon, but his gut knew the answer.

No battle plan ever survives contact with the enemy, and this one was no exception. It was too late for a plan, too close for complicated formations. There was only one thing left to do; hit them hard, hit them fast and hit them again before they knew what was coming.

The missiles beat him to the Valiant by scant seconds, ripping off the assault mech's right arm in a cloud of burning metal and sending it stumbling to the left, off balance. Logan lined up his plasma gun and fired off a shot into the left side, stripped bare of armor by the missiles. The bundle of star-bright ionized gas burned through the weakened section of the Valiant's torso and into the cockpit, and the mech spun away and crashed into a smoking heap.

Somewhere inside, the mech pilot was roasting, maybe burning alive. It was a single data point, a kernel of knowledge in a battlefield full of them to be filed away with all the others, but he knew it would haunt him later, when he tried to sleep.

He pivoted his mech on its right foot, sensing the incoming rush without consciously registering the warnings flashing on his tactical display. It was a strike mech, a Nomad, carrying nearly the missile load of an Arbalest but twice the armor, and it launched at nearly point-blank range with a four-bird spread. The Sentinel's anti-missile system fired automatically, a hail of small-caliber, high-speed rounds from the pair of mini-guns at its hip guided by radar and lidar and one of the warheads detonated prematurely, throwing the other three off course just enough to pass meters from the Sentinel's left shoulder.

Logan made no conscious decision. Things were going too fast for thinking, too fast for anything but pure reaction. He'd fired the plasma gun last and had known when he did that the capacitors would need a few seconds to recharge, so he'd switched automatically to the missile pod. He squeezed the firing control less than half a second after the Nomad fired and his flight passed through the fiery cloud of the warhead his anti-missile systems had intercepted.

Life or death in combat was a matter of centimeters and microseconds and sometimes just plain luck. The Nomad's missiles hadn't hit. His did. The missile pod on the Nomad's right shoulder took the brunt of the hit, the whole right side of the mech swallowed up in white fire as it staggered back under the impact. What was left of the pod's magazine blew in a secondary explosion and plasma erupted through the machine's chest and back as the fusion reactor shielding failed. The Nomad stayed on its feet, legs planted wide, but the upper torso was a flaming torch, nothing remaining but glowing, jagged shards of BiPhase Carbide armor.

Not a bad way to go. Fast, painless.

Assault mecha were screaming over his head, Kurtz leading

his platoon and Prevatt's into the center of the enemy lines. Paskowski's Scorpion was right beside him again, as if the man had appointed himself Logan's bodyguard for the duration of the battle, with the rest of the strike platoon spread out to either side, taking long-range shots at the Starkad mecha and advancing steadily, slowly forward.

Too slow. We're giving them too much time, too much space.

Logan broke into a run, knowing the strike platoon would follow, racing to catch up with the assault platoons and their jet-powered bounds into the ranks of the enemy lines. The Starkad mecha were trying to form up their ranks, trying to set up mutually supportive fields of fire, and he had to give them credit for the attempt. Someone was attempting to take charge and he spotted them immediately, knowing where they would be positioned because it was where he would have been.

The Scorpion strike mech was in the center of gravity of the attempted formation, pulling other mecha toward it with a moral authority strong enough to bend fear. Some were falling along the way, taken down by Kurtz and Prevatt, and off to the east a Starkad scout mech was being pursued back towards town by a mob of Salvaggio Hoppers; but everyone else was forming on the Scorpion.

Leadership like that should be rewarded, he thought. The man should have been promoted, should have gone on to an illustrious career and a long life enjoying the acclaim and responsibility he'd earned. *Instead, I'm going to have to kill him.*

Logan trusted Paskowski and his platoon to guard him against a shot in the back. He ignored proximity warnings and laser designators painting him and missiles flashing by and focused on the Scorpion. The Sentinel swayed beneath him, a redwood in a storm, the full weight of its fifty tons pounding craters into the ground with each impact. The Scorpion pilot spotted him three hundred meters away and opened fire, finally forced to think of his own survival instead of his duty. Twin balls of sunfire passed by Logan's cockpit close enough to char a line of black along the right side of his canopy and the sudden rush of heat took his breath away.

His stomach clenched at the proximity of death and he wanted to tell the others to target the strike mech, but they had their own battles to fight. They were giving him the shot. He had two flights of missiles left and he blasted one after the other, eight missiles, ignoring the overheat warnings blaring in his ear, ignoring the broiler oven atmosphere of the cockpit and the hundred-meter-wide cloud of incandescent smoke rolling over the landscape, and running after them, not letting up a step.

The Scorpion pilot had bare seconds and he used them just right. His plasma guns were already aimed at Logan's Sentinel and the capacitors must have barely had time to recharge before he fired both of them again, not at Logan's mech but at his missiles. The actual plasmoid charges weren't spread wide enough to hit the flight, but they didn't have to. The massive amount of heat the ionized gas bundles radiated was enough to generate a violent pocket of turbulence in the air between them and throw the first four missiles wildly off course. They streaked past the Scorpion and slammed into the ground almost a kilometer away, sending up fountains of debris almost unnoticed in the general chaos of the battle.

The Scorpion driver had nothing left for the last four missiles except tons and tons of armor. The fire of the explosions covered the vaguely insectoid mech in clouds of roiling fire, concealing it from Logan's cameras and sensors for vital seconds, and he used the time to close the distance. A laser from somewhere out to his left flashed against his missile launch pod, turning it to slag and nearly blinding him with the flash, but still he kept running, leaving it to the rest of his company to deal with whoever had shot at him.

His Sentinel was less than fifty meters from the Scorpion when the cloud began to drift away and the enemy strike mech stepped through the remains of it, scorched and cracked, and battered, but still alive. Logan smiled, glad the man hadn't gone down that way. He didn't deserve something impersonal like a missile strike, whoever he was. The Sentinel's plasma gun was recharged and Logan triggered it at just under fifty meters, aiming the blast for the cockpit. The Scorpion moved just before he fired and blocked the shot with its own left-hand plasma cannon. The armor hadn't been thick over the cannon to begin with, and the missile strikes had splintered part of it away, so only the thermal shielding for the actual cannon was left to stop the plasmoid, and it wasn't enough.

The magnetic coils behind the thermal shielding exploded in a hail of shrapnel and a balefire halo of static electricity arcing into the metal of the Scorpion's chest plastron. More smoke, more charred armor, but not a death blow, and now Logan's primary weapon was drained for precious, eternal moments and the Starkad mech would be ready to fire.

But Logan was close, only thirty meters away. He ducked to his right, using the damaged left arm of the other strike mech as cover, knowing the Scorpion couldn't turn as fast standing back on its heels as he could with his forward momentum. He still missed the jump-jets and the maneuverability they'd afforded his old Vindicator assault mech, but there were advantages to the Sentinel beyond its command and control suite and anti-missile system. There was all that mass behind his charge, ready to deliver in one, crushing blow.

He bit down on the mouthpiece inside his helmet, lowered his left shoulder and plowed into the Scorpion at close to thirty-five kilometers an hour. One hundred tons of metal and BiPhase Carbide and fusion reactor and puny, fragile humans collided with the force of a bomb going off. The sound was beyond pain, beyond deafening, just a vibration down to the bone, the peal of a bell the size of a planet. Seat restraints bit into Logan's shoulders, and hips, and chest, and his helmet smacked against the padding around his easy chair. His teeth chomped deeply into the soft plastic of his mouthpiece, hard enough to have broken every one of them off without it.

The Sentinel rocked backward but stayed on its feet, all its momentum transferred into the Scorpion and the massive Starkad mech toppled, upending almost in slow motion as if gravity itself was reluctant to take a side in the battle. The impact when it fell seemed trivial compared to their collision.

Lights were flashing and warning tones were ringing from a dozen different systems inside the Sentinel's cockpit, damage indicators blinking first red then yellow, as hazy and uncertain as he was. He squeezed his eyes shut for a long second and tried again to make sense of what he was seeing. The Sentinel, he decided, was still operational, if only barely, as was he.

The Scorpion was down, its left arm ripped off at the shoulder, its chest armor cracked into splintered shards, and yet its legs were still kicking, a cockroach smacked with a shoe but not quite dead yet, trying to right itself and find the darkness.

Logan snarled and hit his external address speakers.

"Goddammit, surrender and I'll let you live."

He was going against what he knew to be wise and practical. They weren't set up to take prisoners. He'd just have to cut the guy loose without his mech, which wasn't procedure, but... *Damn it, he deserves to live.*

The Scorpion driver wouldn't give up. He kicked again with his right leg, bringing around his remaining plasma cannon, trying to get one last shot off. Logan cursed in frustration and raised his mech's left foot up, then slammed it down into the Scorpion's cockpit. Weakened and melted armor gave way and the canopy smashed through into the rear of the cockpit and took the pilot with it. The Scorpion stopped moving.

Logan looked up, not wanting to see what was left when he stepped off the strike mech. Around him, the battle was nearly over. Surprise was what his old instructors had termed a force multiplier, and they'd had more than their share of surprise on their side. Burning Starkad machines littered the plains between the Run and the city and, as he watched, the last two were brought down from behind in desperate attempts to hobble away to some imagined safety.

Of his own people, the IFF transponders told a story of what a colder man might have considered acceptable losses. Three mecha too badly damaged to fight again but not immobile. Only one off its feet, its reactor inactive and the automatic distress signal already coming from the slowly descending parachute of the ejection pod. Two down from Prevatt's platoon, one from Kurtz's, but the only one disabled had been from Paskowski's strike mecha. Two of the Salvaggio Hoppers were down as well, though he couldn't tell if the pilots had survived and didn't see any sign of a chute.

He tried to speak into the general commo net but wound up in a coughing fit and had to try again.

"Paskowski, have your people check for survivors," he instructed, "and see to your pilot. Kurtz, Prevatt, send your damaged mecha back to the Run, and…"

"Logan, we have a big problem."

He frowned, recognizing Katy's voice on the radio and giving into initial annoyance that she would break operation security by using his real name and break military protocol by not using his rank. Then he paled as he realized how worried she'd have to be to do that.

"What is it?" he asked.

"It's Kane," she said, groaning as if the words caused her

physical pain. "She slipped out sometime this morning, switched jackets with another woman so we wouldn't notice. She went with the civilians for the diversion attack…"

"Oh, shit." He switched frequencies without another word.

"Kurtz," he snapped, taking off at a lumbering run even as he gave the order. "Your platoon's with me. We're heading into town."

22

Josephine Salvaggio didn't like being helpless. She hadn't liked it when she was a little girl, watching her mother struggle to raise her and her brother by herself after her father had gotten himself killed fighting a Starkad incursion, or as a teenager when she'd been told either she could join the Clan Modi military or they would take her younger brother.

She certainly hadn't cared for sitting in that stinking jail cell, waiting for Colonel Grieg to get around to torturing and killing her. But she would almost rather have sat in the cell again instead of watching the biggest mech battle she'd ever seen while trapped inside her wrecked Reaper, her strap releases jammed and her back hurting way too much to try to pull out her knife and cut herself free.

At least it looks like we won, she thought with just a little satisfaction. It wasn't much, but at least it included the possibility of living through all this.

She was beginning to believe she'd have to wait there on the ground until the Spartan medics made their way out here from town, but then she noticed movement. Not more mecha, but dismounts. People. Two of them, skinny and young and unfamiliar at first as she tried to make them out at a ninety-degree angle to the world.

Closer, only a few dozen meters away, and she finally recognized them. It was the kids from Trinity, that Colonel Slaughter's brother and his girlfriend, Terrin and Franny. They were still dressed in local clothes, but they'd gotten their hands on the same top-of-the-line carbines the Wholesale Slaughter infantry carried and were holding them like they'd been taught how to use them. She wondered for just a beat if they were going to pull her out of the wreck or just put a bullet in her out of spite for what she'd done to them.

Couldn't blame them, she mused. *I've done some bad shit in my life, but this time I really fucked up.*

The boy, Terrin, peered through the scarred canopy and she waved a hand at them to show she was still alive. It took a few minutes, but between them, they managed to find the catch to open the canopy. It took both of them yanking it, feet digging into the dirt for them to pull it all the way open.

"Are you okay?" Franny asked her. She tried not to roll her eyes. It was a stupid-ass question, but the girl was young, still.

"There's a knife strapped to the side of my right leg just above my boot," she told them, forcing herself to be patient. "If you can reach it, you can cut through my seat harness. But be fucking *careful*," she cautioned them as Terrin quickly lunged in to try to grab the knife. "I'm fairly sure I have one or two cracked vertebrae and I'd rather not wind up with a severed spinal cord if it's all the same to you."

Terrin sobered, nodding before he leaned into the cockpit with a bit more care and hesitation.

"And by the way," she added as he slid the knife out of its leg sheath, "thanks for coming and getting me. I don't know if I deserve it."

"Something my dad always says, ma'am," Terrin said, carefully sliding the edge of the knife through the tough material of her chest restraints, "is if you think you've screwed up, the good news is, you're still alive."

She yelped as she started to fall forward, but both of them moved to catch her, lowering her gently out onto the hard-packed dirt. She sucked in a breath, trying to relax despite the dull, knotted ache in her back.

"You still have time," Terrin finished, resheathing her knife, "to make it right."

"Go!" Lyta snapped, tapping Lt. Wayne on the shoulder.

She heard him relay the order through the platoon sergeant, and somewhere a faint echo through the squad leaders and team leaders down to the individual Rangers and in less than two seconds, the lead squad was across the street. Second platoon opened up on signal, their carbines sending a hail of 6mm slugs into the wood and sandstone and plaster of the city hall. Craters opened up in material never meant to be bullet-resistant and dust rolled away from the impacts.

The Starkad Marines ducked away from the fusillade. They had no choice, and she didn't fault their bravery, though she still thought they were scum. The Marine company was scattered around the town, guarding this place and that, and they'd been defeated in detail by the Rangers, who'd kept their forces together and moved from one objective to another. The city hall/constabulary building was the next to last.

"Second platoon," Lyta ordered, trusting her 'link this time, since Lt. Grant was at the other side of the formation, stretched up and down the street, ducked into any available cover. "Cease fire, cease fire! First, you are go for entry."

As if a switch had been flipped, Second platoon's covering

fire cut off, the last hammering report echoing into the hollow silence. A line of black-clad figures filed across the front walk, carbines shouldered at low ready and the point man set up on the far side of the door while the next in line fired a breaching round from his grenade launcher. The door slammed inward with a gut-punch concussion and the Ranger ducked away at a burst of gunfire through the opening. The point man whipped a grenade through the doorway and crouched low, rifle at the ready.

There was a sharp crack and a wisp of smoke out the open door, and the point man spun into the entrance, firing off a long burst from his carbine, the rest of his squad rushing in behind him. Lyta stayed where she was and let them do their job, her trigger finger tapping the receiver just above the pistol grip, impatient, dissatisfied with her inaction.

Muffled reports made their way out of the entrance, out through the shattered windows, gunshots, another breaching round, more grenades. They were running entry on the constabulary. A long but distant exchange of fire, then something still further away but much easier to hear, at the back of the building.

"They ran into the squad we put out to guard the rear," Grant reported into her earpiece over the comms.

Yes, thank you for today's Incredibly Obvious Report, she thought with far too much snark to let herself say it.

She didn't bug the platoon leader for a status report because that was just the sort of thing micromanaging assholes did and she'd determined years ago she wasn't going to turn into one of those. Instead, she waited until the firing had stopped and there was time for reports to filter back. Grant jogged down the street to her position, the woman's left hand covering her ear reflexively to better hear the calls from her squad leaders.

"The building is clear, ma'am," she told Lyta. "No Marine prisoners."

"What a shame," she murmured. "Civilians?"

"None," Grant replied, shaking her head. "Apparently, the intelligence we got from the militia back in the canyon that Grieg was moving all the civilians to the temple was correct."

"Then that's our next stop," Lyta decided. "Pull everyone out and form them up."

"Colonel Randell, do you read?"

It was Captain Lee. She'd sent him out with the sniper team to occupy the rooftop of one of the warehouses and keep an eye on the rest of the city so no one snuck up and bit them in the ass while they were concentrating on their objectives.

"I got you, Lee," she replied. "We just cleared the city hall and the constabulary..."

"You need to get over to the temple, ma'am," he cut her off, a strain in his voice she'd never heard before. "There's something going down here and I don't like it."

Ruth Laurent could smell their fear. They were silent but for the quiet sobs of a few children, and she wondered if they would have been screaming and pleading if there had been more air available inside the temple, if dozens and dozens of people hadn't been jammed in so close. The children and elderly had been given the seats, at least at first, but in the end, there'd been so many stuffed into the temple's worship area that everyone was standing or leaning. And staring at the fire-team of Marines, and Grieg...and the molded, half-meter sheets of plastic explosives affixed to the front walls.

She turned her own glare towards him, not so different from the look of the terrified captives. He was standing in the entrance corridor, nearly taking up the whole, narrow space and still managing to pace back and forth, a caged lion. Sweat beaded on his forehead and he licked his lips periodically, a nervous tic she hadn't seen from him before Revelation. In his right hand was a service pistol, the barrel still smoking.

Outside, sprawled on the carpet of the entrance walk, was the temple priest. An ancient man, probably a hundred years old, his skin tanned and stretched taut over a skeletal face, what was left of his hair grey wisps down to his shoulders. His robe was stained crimson from the gunshot wound in the center of his chest. He'd made the mistake of protesting when Grieg's Marines had set the charges. The Colonel hadn't argued with him, hadn't yelled at him, hadn't said a word. The gunshot had been so loud, so abrupt she'd nearly cried out herself.

"We've lost contact with Captain Sibelius and the Mobile Armor company," she informed him with a cool detachment to her voice she wished matched the feeling inside her gut. "Captain Gerhardt has not reported in from the city hall in the last ten minutes. We need to get back to the drop-ship and get reinforcements from the *Sleipner*."

"No." He didn't even bother to meet her eyes, just kept pacing, the gun in one hand and the remote detonator in the other. It had a hinged guard over the ignition switch and he kept flipping it up and down with his thumb, an incessant clicking. "These Goddamned mercenaries and their civilian militia will *not* defeat me. I will *not* disappoint Lord Starkad."

She checked the Marines out of the corner of her eye. She couldn't see their faces beneath the tinted visors, but their stance was nervous, uncomfortable. They understood the situation as well as she did. They were a fire team, three men and a woman, and they were probably all that was left of a company.

"We have another light company of mecha on board the cruiser," she reminded him, an unfamiliar edge going into her voice. "How will Lord Starkad feel if he finds out you failed in your objectives on this mission with almost half your Mobile Armor sitting in the cargo bay? Along with a pair of assault shuttles we could use to escort them?"

"They'd cut us down before we could reach the drop-ship." It was a half-hearted objection and she wanted to scream at him. "And we can't communicate with orbit from here anyway. They're jamming local signals and the drop-ship has our orbital communicator."

All right, she'd give him that. She squeezed past him, careful not to step on the priest's body. His eyes were still open, blood slowly clotting on his lips. His death stare was accusatory, as if Mithra Himself peered at her through the hazy blackness. Down the street, she began to spot them, formless shades moving from one shadow to the next.

"They're coming," she told him.

"I'm going to make them come in here," Grieg said, nodding to himself as if she weren't there, eyes glancing upward, outward, at the captives. "I'm going to draw them in to save the hostages. Then I'm going to blow it. I won't let him down, I'll take them all out at once."

"And then what?" she demanded once she'd been able to pick her jaw up off the floor. "They still have a company of mecha out there."

"But you'll have a chance then," he said, eyes feverish with what he probably saw as inspiration. "You can get to the drop-ship, bring down our mecha and secure the data crystals." He nodded, a smile spreading across his face. He probably imagined it was beatific and beneficent, but to her, it seemed totally mad. "I'll accomplish the mission through you, Captain. Would you do that for me?"

"Of course, sir," she said automatically, because you didn't contradict a madman with a gun and a shit-ton of explosives.

The Rangers were surrounding them, tucked into every bit of cover on the street, cargo trucks, rovers, storage bins. Every shadow, every nook bristled with weapons. One of them didn't bother with cover, though, didn't attempt to hide or take shelter. She strode across in the middle of the street, carbine tucked under her arm, her balaclava off to reveal a spiky, brunette mane and a face Laurent recognized from just the day before.

"You're Lyta Randell," Laurent said.

"I am," the woman replied, her voice strong and unwavering despite the outraged, sidelong glance she gave the priest's body. "You people need to surrender before any more innocent civilians get killed."

"You'll have to come in and get us!" Grieg roared from behind Laurent, only half his face visible from behind the door. "We won't be surrendering and you won't open fire with the building full of civilians!"

Laurent closed her eyes, squeezed them shut as if this were all a nightmare she could force herself to wake up from. When she opened them again, life remained a nightmare. She sighed and turned, heading back inside, stepping past Grieg.

"Did you hear me?" Grieg bellowed, his voice painfully loud in the entrance hallway. "You'll have to come in and root us out, and we can shoot at you!" He cackled, speaking aside to her in low tones. "We'll fall back to the rear of the civilians and when they get inside and try to get to us…"

Laurent's hand seemed to be moving under the control of someone else, someone with more courage and decisiveness than her. She pulled her pistol from its holster and raised it without a word, without a thought. Grieg caught sight of the barrel out of the corner of his vision and his eyes went wide.

"Laurent, what…"

She pulled the trigger. As loud as the shot outside the front entrance had been, this one was a million times louder, the concussion a vibration through her sinuses, a ringing whine in her ears. She lowered her weapon, tucking it crisply back into its holster and blowing a long breath out through her nose before she turned to the four Marines. They stared at her, one with his rifle half-raised, their expressions indiscernible.

"Colonel Grieg was guilty of rank incompetence and dereliction of duty," she declared. "I'm in command now and we're getting out of here. If any of you has a problem with that, the time to say so is now."

Behind them, the civilians were murmuring, confusion and perhaps just a glimmer of hope warring on their dirty faces. They didn't move, didn't make the rush she'd been afraid they'd attempt, perhaps sensing the end was near.

She couldn't look them in the eye. She felt too much shame for that. Instead, she bent down and pulled the detonator out of Grieg's slack, lifeless hand and walked out the front entrance, motioning for the Marines to follow.

"We're coming out," she announced loudly. "Hold your fire."

Randell was still standing there, but her carbine was held at low ready now, her eyes sharpened and seeking a target.

"Where's Grieg?" the Ranger officer demanded.

"He's in there, if you want him," Laurent told her, jerking her head back toward the temple. She held up the detonator. "This controls about ten kilograms of plastic explosives planted inside. I could use it to blackmail our safe passage out of here, back to our drop-ship."

She spat aside and tossed the switch into the ground at Lyta Randell's feet.

"I think enough civilians have been hurt." She gestured between herself and the four Marines. "We're leaving. We won't be captured and we won't surrender, so you can either shoot us down in the street or we'll ride that ship back up to the *Sleipner* and leave you to this miserable shithole."

Lyta Randell seemed to chew on the words, grinding them to powder inside her head, but finally she nodded.

"Let them go," she ordered her people. She motioned to one of her officers. "Get in there and get those civilians out."

Laurent was already walking towards the port, to the landing zone where their drop-ship waited.

"What's your name?" Lyta called after her.

"Captain Ruth Laurent," she threw back over her shoulder. "You'll see me again, Lyta Randell. And when I beat you, I won't need to hide behind civilians to do it."

Logan squatted on the ground at the feet of his Sentinel, staring down at the cold and bloodless body of Lana Kane.

As near as he could piece together from the shape of the wreck, she'd been manning the heavy machine gun in the back of the technical when a rifle grenade had busted the front axle and flipped the damned top-heavy thing right over. She'd broken her neck.

"So fucking stupid," he hissed under his breath.

It was over. They'd won, done exactly what she wanted, but she just couldn't stay out of the fight. She'd died at the edge of town, before she'd had the chance to fire a shot. More of the gun trucks burned fiercely or already smoldered, the alcohol flames burned out. Not one had survived to breach the town, though some of the crews had made it out. One of Prevatt's pilots was tending to their wounded as best he could, cross-trained as a medic. He'd already called for the Ranger medics, but it would take them a while to make it out this far.

He wanted to be angry about the data crystals, about the short-sightedness of taking their location to the grave with her, but all he could think of was her little brother and what the boy was going to do without her. Still, she'd given her life for something she'd thought was worth dying for, and now he'd have to do his best to make sure it hadn't been for nothing.

"Hey Boss," Kurtz called over his earbud—his helmet was back up in the cockpit of the Sentinel. "We got a vehicle incoming."

He rose and scanned the road back toward the canyon, but it was still too far away.

"It's one of ours," the platoon leader added.

He'd already figured. If it had been the enemy, he'd hoped Kurtz would have warned him. It took another minute for the small passenger rover to make it through the hedge of twisted trees and into the midst of the platoon of assault mecha. Before it stopped, he could already see Acosta and Katy in the cab…and in-between them, Lana Kane's brother, Alec.

"Why the hell did you bring him here?" he asked Katy when she stepped out of the driver's door. He instantly regretted the edge of anger in his tone, but he hadn't been able to contain it. When he'd radioed back to Katy and Acosta that Kane had died, he hadn't expected them to bring her brother out to look at his sister's broken body on the battlefield. The kid was obviously already holding onto the trauma of his parents' deaths.

"We didn't want to," Katy assured him, not seeming to take offense. "He insisted."

"He what?" The kid had never said a word to him, or anyone else that he'd seen.

Alec scrambled out of the car, his mop of brown hair ratty and unwashed, dirt smeared across his left cheek. He didn't run, didn't scream, didn't seem surprised when he saw his older sister's body. He knelt down beside her, his face impassive, utterly neutral, as if this were just a normal day and he was coming to visit his sister at work. He stroked her hair gently.

"She said this might happen."

Logan blinked, unsure for a moment who had spoken until he

realized it was Alec. The boy's voice was soft and a bit scratchy and raspy, as if he wasn't used to talking.

"She said it when she first came back," Alec said, finally looking up from his sister. "She told me I had to do something for her if anything happened to her."

Acosta had slipped out of the passenger's side while they spoke, and he seemed oddly restrained, not at all his usual, snarky self. He reached back into the back seat of the vehicle and pulled something out, a heavy, lead-lined storage box, dirt and sand still spilling off the edges of it. Logan hesitated for only a moment before he rushed over to Acosta, running his fingers across the surface of the lid, cold and metallic.

"He took us to where it was hidden," Acosta explained, "but only after we promised to bring him here afterward."

"She said it was important," Alec told them, still kneeling at his sister's side. "It was important that she keep her word."

Finally, it came, the crack in the boy's mask of detachment, just a twitch beside his eye at first before it spread across his face. The tears came, single tracks of tan skin visible through the dirt, then a flood washing it clean, though he didn't give into it completely, didn't let himself sob, kept his shoulders firm.

Logan turned away from the storage case, from the accomplished objectives it represented, and went down on a knee beside the boy, putting a hand on his shoulder. Alec didn't acknowledge it, still sobbing

"I lost my mom when I was younger than you," he said, the words pouring out of him, unplanned. "To soldiers in a war. And I was the oldest, so I had to be strong for my little brother. But it hurt keeping all that inside. It made me wish there was someone who could have been there for me, who could have been the strong one. Your sister did that for you, and I think that's the way she'd want you to remember her."

The kid didn't respond, but some of the tightness went out of the boy's shoulder under his hand. Katy slowly moved between Alec and the body of his sister, absently wiping something out of her eyes.

"Why don't you let us take your sister into town, to the temple," she said. Logan thought he heard a slight break in her voice. "We can let them prepare her for the funeral…"

"No." Alec's words were so soft Logan could barely hear them. "She wanted to be buried with our parents. At the old house, where they died. We have to take her there."

"Then we will," Logan told him. He sat back, the sand grinding into the seat of his fatigue pants, and let the charnel-house carnage of the battle wash over him. The ordure of death wafted off the town and he thought of something General Constantine had quoted to him once: "nothing except a battle lost can be half so melancholy as a battle won."

"I have a feeling," he said, mostly to himself, "we'll be burying quite a few bodies today. I hope it was worth it."

23

"We gotta figure out a way to get gravity in here," Kammy said, his broad features screwed into a scowl as he regarded the zero-g ration packet turning small circles in front of him, floating above the superfluous galley table. "I mean, why the hell did we even build any of this shit," he waved around him at the chairs and booths of the *Shakak*'s galley, "oriented like this if we knew we were going to be in free-fall the whole time?"

"Because that's the way the Imperial researchers built it in the first place," Tara Gerard reminded him, drinking coffee from a squeeze bulb and not looking too happy about it.

Terrin grinned at the sight, and at the thought of the lifelong spacers being uncomfortable eating in free-fall, but then his mind drifted to the problem of providing some sort of artificial gravity to the ship and let his thoughts spiral into that hole. Most ships boosted at one gravity between jump-points, but the stardrive alleviated the need for physical acceleration. Maybe they could spin the ship along its axis? Would the stardrive even work if the ship were rotating while projecting it? Probably not.

"Damn," he murmured to himself.

"Terrin," Franny's voice cut through the musing, the warmth

of her fingers on his hand bringing him back to the present. He looked over and saw her smiling and his grin widened. "You were lost in some astrophysical problem, weren't you?"

"I was just thinking," he admitted, "the stardrive manipulates spacetime. There's got to be some way we could use it to generate artificial gravity."

"Oh, man," Kammy groaned, "you do that, I will buy you the biggest steak they got in Argos. And then we could eat steaks in the galley instead of this shit!" He waved the food packet demonstratively. "Hey Terry, I'm sorry you gotta come back to us and be stuck with this for a welcome-back dinner. We were worried about you, bro!"

There was a murmuring of agreement from the ship's crew gathered in the galley for lunch and a few squeeze bulbs of juice or coffee were raised in a toast. Heat rose in Terrin's ears.

"Maybe the secret's in the data you brought back with you," Lyta said, speaking for the first time since she'd entered the galley. She'd been quiet ever since she and her Rangers had marched onto the drop-ship to head back to the *Shakak* twelve hours ago. "I hope there's something vital in it," she added, staring at the bulkhead as if seeing something the rest of them weren't. "The price was pretty high."

Terrin felt the air go out of him and he stumbled for something to say.

"I...I wanted to tell you, Lyta," he finally stuttered, "your officer, Captain Cordova, he saved our lives. He was a real hero."

"He was a Ranger," Lyta said flatly, as if that explained everything. "Tell me though, Terrin," she prompted. "I think we've showed our hand here, put all our chips in on this one. So tell me, was the data that important?"

"Lyta, it could change everything," he said. "The interstellar economy, the military, the whole balance of power in the Dominion. Eventually, everything's going to be different."

Lyta glared balefully at her food packet, then tossed it overhand toward the recycler mounted on the far bulkhead. It spiraled tightly and sank home inside the dark opening.

"Different isn't always good," she declared, then pushed herself out of the galley.

An awkward silence fell over the cluster of tables as Kammy and Tara stared after the woman. Kammy headed after her with the grace of an acrobat, frowning in concern, while Tara went back to her dinner with a philosophical shrug

"Damn, what's gotten into her?" Terrin wondered after the buzz of general conversation had picked up enough to cover his words.

"I don't know," Franny said, "but there was something I wanted to ask you about. Back in the canyon, we were talking about something and I just…"

Terrin sucked in a breath, screwed up his courage and kissed her. Franny stiffened slightly, but then she returned it, a hand going to his neck to pull him closer. Someone in the galley noticed and hooted their appreciation, but he didn't care.

Life was just too short.

"I feel like we've been here before, Captain Laurent," Lord Aaron Starkad said, his tone light and airy but the chill of his ice-blue eyes showing the real story.

Two Marine guards had escorted him into the holding cell, but he waved them back to the door, approaching the fold-down cot where Laurent had been sitting when he entered. She had leapt to attention and was still locked up, eyes staring straight ahead at the sterile blankness of the white walls, trying to keep an eye on his motions with her peripheral vision. Starkad dropped onto the cot casually, propping one polished, calf-high riding boot up on the edge of it and draping an elbow over his knee.

"Sit down, Ruth," he urged her, patting the mattress of the cot. "Talk to me."

She eyed him warily but did as she was told, sitting at the edge of the cot, feet planted on the floor, hands flat beside her.

"I want you to tell me why you think this mission failed so spectacularly, Ruth," he whispered in her ear, his voice soothing, as if he were her closest confidante. "Tell me how Grieg managed to fuck things up so bad you had to shoot him in the face."

She restrained the bitter laugh trying to force its way out. She should have known those Marines would talk, eventually.

May as well go all in.

"Colonel Grieg was an idiot," she told him frankly. "He alienated the mercenaries when they were willing to work with us, alienated the civilian population and tried to use brute force when bribery would have worked more effectively, and then he failed to recognize the fact our enemies had beat us to the punch and were already on the planet. Once that became clear, he totally lost his composure and instead of adjusting his battle plan and adapting to the situation, he gave up and decided on pointless suicide."

Aaron Starkad peered at her far too closely for far too long before he finally nodded.

"That matches what the Marines told me. They were…disappointed in their commander."

She let the breath she'd been holding out very slowly and gradually through her nose, not wanting to sound guilty or nervous.

"What are we to do with you, Captain?" Starkad wondered. "Every time you go on a mission with a superior in command, he winds up dead and you end up one of few survivors."

"May I be allowed to make a suggestion, Lord Starkad?" she asked very, very carefully.

"But of course, my dear," he said warmly. "That's why you're still alive."

A shudder ran up her spine but she refused to give into it.

"I think you should make me your Chief of Intelligence, sir."

"Oh-ho! Do you really?" He laughed, not with mockery she thought, but with actual delight. "Oh, my newly-lovely woman, what a marvelous suggestion and one with enough nerve that I am quite willing to give it a go." He pressed his fingers together and eyed her over his clasped hands. "If you're given this responsibility, *Colonel* Laurent, what would your advised course of action be for your Lord Supreme?"

"The Guardianship of Sparta can't be allowed to have this sort of power unchecked," she said, firmer now, stronger, more confident.

"You advise open war, then?" He cocked an eyebrow curiously.

"Not open, my lord," she corrected him. "We were nearly able to stage a coup in Sparta once, with Duncan Lambert. We were minutes away from having our man on the throne, doing our bidding, the first step towards uniting the Dominions under the Supremacy."

She smiled, baring her teeth.

"This time," she said, "we'll do it right."

This concludes Wholesale Slaughter, but *MAELSTROM STRAND*, the fourth book in the Wholesale Slaughter Series picks up the story, and the mystery continues!

- Now that Terminus is gone, will Starkad be satisfied,

or will they still be seeking vengeance against Sparta… and Logan?

- Is the data Terrin saved enough to change the balance of power, or is it simply the tipping point toward interstellar war?
- How long can Logan Conner ride the razor's edge between heir to the throne and mercenary mech-jock?
- Has Lyta Randell finally made an enemy in Starkad Intelligence officer Ruth Laurent who she won't be able to overcome?

Find out what happens next!
Grab *MAELSTROM STRAND* now!

WHAT'S NEXT IN THE SERIES?

WHOLESALE SLAUGHTER
TERMINUS CUT
YOU JUST READ: REVELATION RUN
MAELSTROM STRAND

FROM THE PUBLISHER

Thank you for reading *Revelation Run*, book three in Wholesale Slaughter.

We hope you enjoyed it as much as we enjoyed bringing it to you. We just wanted to take a moment to encourage you to review the book on Amazon and Goodreads. Every review helps further the author's reach and, ultimately, helps them continue writing fantastic books for us all to enjoy.

If you liked *Revelation Run*, check out the rest of our catalogue at www.aethonbooks.com. To sign up to receive a FREE collection from some of our best authors (including one from Rick Partlow) as well updates regarding all new releases, visit www.aethonbooks.com/sign-up

SPECIAL THANKS TO:

ADAWIA E. ASAD
JENNY AVERY
BARDE PRESS
CALUM BEAULIEU
BEN
BECKY BEWERSDORF
BHAM
TANNER BLOTTER
ALFRED JOSEPH BOHNE IV
CHAD BOWDEN
ERREL BRAUDE
DAMIEN BROUSSARD
CATHERINE BULLINER
JUSTIN BURGESS
MATT BURNS
BERNIE CINKOSKE
MARTIN COOK
ALISTAIR DILWORTH
JAN DRAKE
BRET DULEY
RAY DUNN
ROB EDWARDS
RICHARD EYRES
MARK FERNANDEZ
CHARLES T FINCHER
SYLVIA FOIL
GAZELLE OF CAERBANNOG
DAVID GEARY
MICHEAL GREEN
BRIAN GRIFFIN

EDDIE HALLAHAN
JOSH HAYES
PAT HAYES
BILL HENDERSON
JEFF HOFFMAN
GODFREY HUEN
JOAN QUERALTÓ IBÁÑEZ
JONATHAN JOHNSON
MARCEL DE JONG
KABRINA
PETRI KANERVA
ROBERT KARALASH
VIKTOR KASPERSSON
TESLAN KIERINHAWK
ALEXANDER KIMBALL
JIM KOSMICKI
FRANKLIN KUZENSKI
MEENAZ LODHI
DAVID MACFARLANE
JAMIE MCFARLANE
HENRY MARIN
CRAIG MARTELLE
THOMAS MARTIN
ALAN D. MCDONALD
JAMES MCGLINCHEY
MICHAEL MCMURRAY
CHRISTIAN MEYER
SEBASTIAN MÜLLER
MARK NEWMAN
JULIAN NORTH

KYLE OATHOUT
LILY OMIDI
TROY OSGOOD
GEOFF PARKER
NICHOLAS (BUZ) PENNEY
JASON PENNOCK
THOMAS PETSCHAUER
JENNIFER PRIESTER
RHEL
JODY ROBERTS
JOHN BEAR ROSS
DONNA SANDERS
FABIAN SARAVIA
TERRY SCHOTT
SCOTT
ALLEN SIMMONS
KEVIN MICHAEL STEPHENS
MICHAEL J. SULLIVAN
PAUL SUMMERHAYES
JOHN TREADWELL
CHRISTOPHER J. VALIN
PHILIP VAN ITALLIE
JAAP VAN POELGEEST
FRANCK VAQUIER
VORTEX
DAVID WALTERS JR
MIKE A. WEBER
PAMELA WICKERT
JON WOODALL
BRUCE YOUNG